THE
HUNTING GROUND

THE
HUNTING GROUND

J. ROBERT JANES

MYSTERIOUSPRESS.COM

OPEN ROAD
INTEGRATED MEDIA
NEW YORK

To the past there is but the present.

Author's Note

The Hunting Ground is a work of fiction based on fact. Though I have used actual places and times, I have treated these as seen fit, changing some as appropriate. Occasionally, the name of a real person is used for historical authenticity, but all are deceased, and I have made of them what the story demands. As with the St-Cyr and Kohler mysteries, I do not condone what happened in German-Occupied France during the Second World War. I abhor it, but feel the times must never be forgotten.

Acknowledgments

The Hunting Ground incorporates a few words and brief passages in French or German. Dr. Dennis Essar, of Brock University, very kindly assisted with the French, as did the artist Pierrette Laroche, while Professor Schutz, of Germanic and Slavic Studies at Brock, helped with the German. Should there be any errors, however, they are my own, and for these I apologize.

1

It was quiet now, no more fighting, no more tears. Through the tall French windows of the kitchen, I could see the children outside and I wondered, as I have so often of late, whether I ought to take them to England.

The Nazis were threatening war. First it was the Saarland, then Austria, then Czechoslovakia, and now Poland. Hitler wouldn't stop. France and Britain would have to go to Poland's aid, but if they did, and I took the children to England, Jules and I would part company—he'd never let me have the children, not if he could stop it. And anyway, who was to say France wouldn't keep the Germans out, but if she weakened and couldn't, what then?

The faded orange-red brick of the courtyard always trapped the sun, and I remember those bricks as if it were yesterday and I were still there: the warmth that emanated from them, the smell, the roughness. Jean-Guy was only seven when it all started, and I remember a day in late August 1939, remember the sight of him playing in the sandbox. He had mountains and valleys, roads and tunnels—bridges, railways, houses, farms, so many things, and I could understand, of course, why he had wanted it all to himself. Marie-Christine would have destroyed things—not intentionally, ah, no, she would want only to help or to build a little something herself. To dig perhaps.

Jean-Guy was so like Jules. You saw it in the pinched, aristo-cratic face, the hawkish nose, thin upper lip, tight smile, dark brown eyes that hid so much and tried so hard to analyse, some-times with great success, sometimes with utter cruelty, believing as he had, that he'd said and done the right thing.

Totally committed to his play, he brought the train up to the station. I can still hear the lineman shouting in the near distance and see that one waving his lantern.

Then the train started up. Yes, yes, that train . . . I can't ride one of those things, but I hear the sound of the wheels and remember. Marie-Christine was only three when it all started. Three!

She had placed herself safely under one of the pear trees. Not too close, yet close enough so as to be a constant reminder of the fight and to trouble the conscience of a brother whom she could both hate and love with equal passion.

Normally cheerful and industrious, Marie always painted boldly with the strength and flourish of her grandmother, whom she loved without question. Torn sheeting covered the dress, forming an enormous smock that trailed to her ankles. Sweat dampened the silky ash-blonde curls that would, in time, turn to an auburn through which the sun would shine copper-gold.

Now and then, the watercolours I no longer had time to use wouldn't mix with the water. At these times, she would scold the brush and talk sternly to the glass of water that was perched half on and half off the edge of the chair. She'd get thirsty, too, and drink the water. 'Red wine—yes, it was wine, *maman.*' *Ah, mon Dieu*, they had been so little, so innocent, and I . . . why I had thought we might just get away with it.

The château—increasingly I had found myself wanting to call it that, to tell people I lived in this great big beautiful house in the woods on the edge of the Forest of Fontainebleau, but it was really just a manor house, *une maison de maître.* Built in 1794, owned always by the de St-Germains, its pink stucco, grey trim, shutters, slate roof, and faded brickwork had the air of ruin about them as if, in just being there, they had stayed too long.

There were seventeen rooms, countless family heirlooms and priceless pieces of art, long corridors, a grand entrance, and a staircase, the huge and cluttered attic, the kitchen—our refuge—with its courtyard at the back. Nice . . . Oh, for sure, it was nice, but it was also lonely and that, too, was a part of things.

There were no other houses around us, no neighbours, just Tante Marie and Georges who lived down the road in the cottage, housekeeper and gardener when it suited them or their loyalty to Jules.

In Fontainebleau, the shopkeepers tended to think Jules had money because he lived in such a big house and his family had once been well-off. Pah! How crazy it was. Far better to have lived on the farm near Barbizon with mother. There the people had earth and manure under their fingernails, and that was always good for building character if nothing else. Barbizon wasn't that far from the château—just six or seven kilometres through the forest, more by road, of course, but all the closer to Paris. *Bien sûr*, there were plenty of tourists, both in Barbizon, for the artists' colony that had once been there, and in Fontainebleau for the *palais*, the hunting lodge of kings. But who could be friends with tourists and the hordes from Paris when they took over everything, crowded the cafés and shops, and pushed you out of the way even though you lived nearby and had done so nearly all your life?

Yes, we should have stored the furniture and things and leased the château. Living off the income would have made life easier. Mother wouldn't have minded. She adored the children. After she had become used to having us, things would have been all right.

But I mustn't lie—not to myself. Paris . . . I was only thinking of escaping to my lover, my husband, Jules.

I remember taking a handful of flour from the bin at my knees. Sprinkling it over the dough I'd been kneading, I blew stray strands of hair from my brow and cursed the heat from the wood-fired stove. Deftly, I shaped a loaf for Marie. It would be in the shape of a fish that day, with great big eyes and scales all down its back and sides. I would baste the loaves with beaten egg yolk and a little sugar to make the crust a golden brown and give the fish a bit of a glaze. Surely, a little sugar wouldn't hurt her teeth? Just a little.

Jean-Guy had started the fight by demanding the whole of the sandbox and his sister's brand-new shovel. He really ought to have been punished. I should make his loaf into the shape of an ugly toad. Yes, a toad.

This I couldn't do. He had asked for a tiger. Every day, he reminded me of his father.

Covering the loaves with a damp cloth, I set them to rise some more on the shelf above the old iron range. Wiping my hands on my apron, I tried to tidy my hair but knew it would only be a mess. Jules was then forty, a professor of art history at the Sorbonne. I had met him there and we had fallen in love, he eight years older than I. We had been married for seven years before it all started. Well almost. Well, six-and-a-half. Jean-Guy had decided things.

Jules had liked younger women but . . . why, I'd been the younger one, just twenty-five and full of happiness, eager, so eager for life. Jean-Guy had been born that spring, a short two months after the wedding. Thank God for the château then, for the loneliness it provided.

Like so many of the French intelligentsia, Jules expected me to be housewife and mother, to cook his meals, do his laundry, look after his family's house, and never question why he was staying overnight in Paris, the weekends, too.

Lots of the girls had worshipped him. I'd been a fool to ignore things. Janine, my little sister, had been almost at the same age as I had. Twenty-six and ripe for mischief. A dangerous situation. Something had had to be done. We had to have money, too. Jules had expected it to grow on trees, I suppose. I only know he wanted to go on living as his father had.

Yes, money. That had been a part of it. Money and my sister.

The children played in the warmth of the sun and quiet of the garden. I took off my apron and washed my hands and face at the pump by the sink. Then I ran a comb through my hair and went outside to study their handiwork.

'C'est une chatte, maman. Une grosse chatte!'

Marie-Christine stood back too. Paint-covered fingers gripped one chubby cheek and pulled the lower eyelid down as she looked up at me and then at the painting. 'Babette,' she said. 'The cat, it is named Babette.'

I adopted a wise and thoughtful air. 'But it's such a frightening cat. Am I to think it must be chasing a mouse?'

'It has already caught one,' she confessed shyly.

The eye was a little inflamed. A speck of sand from the fight? I wondered anxiously. 'Darling, don't look at me like that,' I said, betraying my very English side, my irritability.

She blinked. Tears rushed into her great big eyes. I crouched and, heedless of the paint, took her into my arms. Lifting her up, saying, 'Oh, my, you're getting heavy!' I stood there studying the painting.

Droplets, blotches, bold strokes, and swaths of colour had been blended harmoniously and that was the remarkable thing. At three years of age, the child had an artist's eye. There was even a faint suggestion of a tail. As for the rest of the cat, I was certain she could see it.

'*Ah, bon*, you're a painter, *chérie*. Another Millet or Rousseau, one of the Barbizon school. No, wait a moment. Cézanne, I think. Yes, you have that boldness. Some day you will be a great artist, or maybe even a potter like your grandmother.'

Taking a corner of the smock, I dried her eyes and dabbed at the paint on her cheek. Her nose was cool, the lips warm and wet. I tidied her hair and ran a smoothing hand over her brow.

Not for a moment did those hazel eyes leave mine. They were so innocent and full of love. Just like mine had once been before it all began.

'Paris, please. The Sorbonne. Department of Art History. Yes, Operator, I know the lines are still bad. Yes, of course, I'll wait. Look, I want to speak to Jules de St-Germain.'

Zurich is a lovely city and they've let me out of the clinic for the afternoon. The nurse who accompanies me has asked to do a bit of shopping.

J. ROBERT JANES

I return to the table and wait for my call. Out over the lake, the water shimmers under the alpine sun. The air, it is so pure and good, but I can't breathe in deeply, not yet. They say it may take years.

Even coffee is too much. I have to drink it well watered, and preferably made from roasted barley and acorns. The ersatz stuff. Caffeine is still too much even though it's the autumn of 1945, and I've been out of Bergen-Belsen for nearly six months, the last two of which have been spent in this place.

Rare in this city, and beautiful, sunlight glints from the coffee-pot. It may take an hour for that call to get through. Everything's in such a shambles except for here. Almost the whole of Europe's been torn to pieces. It's crazy being able to sit on a terrace like this among everyday people who enjoy a smoke, cuddle tiny dogs, read a newspaper, eat cake, or stir coffee.

They can't know why I listen all the time for the sound of hob-nailed boots or for the shrieks, or wait for the beating that must come before the bullet or the axe.

'Madame, your call to Paris.'

It's such a civilized thing, the telephone, so everyday the touch of it makes my hands tremble as I hear the operator saying, 'Paris, you must wait. *Allô . . . allô,* is that Zurich?'

'*Ici,* Zurich.'

'Your party's on the line.'

'Is that Jules de St-Germain?' I ask.

There's silence at the other end, the crackling of a bad connection. '*Oui, c'est moi, c'est Jules de St-Germain.*'

'*Le mari de Lily?*'

Again, there's silence. 'Yes . . . yes, I was once her husband.'

'*Ah, bon, monsieur.*' That's all I say. I hold the receiver from me and I hear him cursing:

'Are you the one who sent that thing to me?'

I put the receiver down. The man behind the counter looks questioningly, but I walk out to my table to sit in the sun, to shut my eyes, and to remember.

My name is Lily Hollis—Lily de St-Germain, though I'd love to

6

delete that upper class de. I didn't choose to do what I did. Me, I'm ashamed to have survived.

You see, the death sentence had been passed long ago and the order had finally come down. We went out behind the hut. I remember that it was raining and that there was a wooden chopping block standing in a sea of mud. There were boot prints all around it. We could hear the guns of the approaching British. It was only a matter of hours until our liberation and yet these bastards were going to kill us.

Seven . . . there were seven of us women. Some fell to their knees to pray. Some stood erect and tried to sing the "Marseillaise." I reached for Michèle's hand and was struck hard across the face.

The rain . . . April's a wretched month in the lowlands to the north of Hanover. There was always water everywhere. It dripped constantly through the roof and from the fir trees.

The axe came down. Michèle turned swiftly towards me. 'Lily . . . Lily . . .'

I held her. I felt her frail body trembling. I couldn't stop her tears; she was far too young.

Another of us was grabbed and flung to her knees before that thing. A boot pressed the head down as if it were a log. The axe went up . . .

In the confusion of those last hours at Bergen-Belsen, all but one of us died. Stricken by what had just tumbled in front of me, I was conscious only of a burst of orders, all in German. The sounds of gunfire.

Guards and executioner fled. The axe was left lying on the ground. Michèle Chevalier's lovely brown eyes stared up at me.

I knelt. I remember reaching out to her, but I couldn't stop shaking. Her hair had always been so like my daughter's but, of course, they'd cut it off and shaved our heads again.

All dead . . . all of them. Both the men and the women, my comrades-in-arms. Tommy Carrington and Nicki. My sister, Janine. Even my two children—I'm certain they're dead. Certain! Me, I was the only one to live. Can you imagine what a burden that's been?

I think it was a British corporal who discovered me some hours later. I know someone took me to a senior officer who said, 'My God, get her out of here.'

The number on the inside of my lower left forearm is blue, and when I press a finger against the skin, its seven digits open out a little and their edges are blurred.

Lily Hollis—Lily de St-Germain. No matter how hard I rub, this number will never go away, and I know that somewhere there's a record of my name against it. There were so many of us in the camps— millions, I suppose. Such confusion at the end. Still, it's only a matter of time until the doctors and nurses discover who I am.

But for now everyone thinks Lily de St-Germain is dead, that she died by execution in Bergen-Belsen.

You see, *mes amis,* I've sent them all their little black pasteboard coffins just like we did with the *collabos* during the Occupation, each with their name in white chalk on the lid, a large cross at the top, and at the foot, between the two V's-for-Victory, the cross of Lorraine, and I've come back to remind them of what they did.

The children were having their rest or private time. Hopefully, Marie-Christine would be sleeping, for Tante Marie and Georges had come. Freed for an hour, I left the house but, at the road, paused to look back as if I couldn't leave them yet.

The château was partially screened by beeches and cedars of Lebanon. Framed by tall, spiked iron gates, it was seen across a lawn that needed cutting and was bleached by the sun. Smoke trailed above the grey slate roof, thinning as it merged with the cloudless sky.

Tante Marie would look after the rest of the baking. Though she'd complain about the quality of the bread, she and Georges would eat it well enough.

I remember that I smiled then and gave a gentle laugh, for I liked the two of them and thought they must like me, though it was often hard to tell.

Brick-red flowerpots full of crimson geraniums flanked the low stone steps to the front entrance. The doors were almost French windows, for the panes of glass didn't quite extend to the floor but stopped at a quarter panelling of wood. In the storey above, the windows were French but there were no fanlights, they were simply tall and rectangular, their balconies being an expense that was never added. Shadows made the glass appear dark and rippled.

There were five of these windows upstairs, and together with their open shutters, they occupied very nearly the whole of the wall. Above them, there were two gabled windows in the attic. Four chimneys marked the ends of the main part of the house. On the west side, however, the wing was a storey-and-a-half. Recessed, too, from the main wall, it had its own door and a window upstairs but with curved lintels of cut stone, not fanlights. Here, too, there was a chimney on the outer wall.

It was an imposing house. Stolidly French and looking of wealth, but smelling of mould and decay.

There was no question that it would soon need a new coat of paint, and I decided then that I had better do it myself. The lane led through the grass off to my left, only to swing round in front of the house. Roses grew beneath the windows, some white, some pink, masses of daisies, too . . .

I remembered that house as I'd first seen it. A château—*ah, oui, oui*. Even in the heat and stillness of that afternoon, I had to admit that it was very beautiful.

Crossing the road and the small pasture beyond, I entered the woods and began to climb, but at a place where some trees had been felled, I again looked back.

The Château de St-Germain sat in a clearing, nestled in a cup of land and surrounded by woods. To my right, to the east, the road continued towards Fontainebleau some seven kilometres away. From there, one of the main roads ran northwest to Barbizon and Chailly-en-Bière. It was deliciously wild, yet not wild at all. In fact, if one thought about it, Fontainebleau was only about sixty-five kilometres to the south-southeast of Paris, not far from the junction of the Loing and the Seine. The trains were good, so it wasn't that much of a journey. The trains . . . there I go again. Yet it could be isolated, too. Listening to the whistles, the engines, and the rumbling of the wheels made me lie awake at night thinking of the city and wondering about my husband.

The slope ahead of me grew increasingly steep. The warm scent of beeches and oaks, of rotting leaves and humus gone dry with the summer's heat, came from all about me. Soon, however, the forest closed around me, and I could no longer see the château.

Now I was on my own and, shutting my eyes for a moment, pausing to lean against a tree and remember my first visit here, but all I can hear now is the sound of their footsteps in the leaves, that awful crisp, dry crackling and then . . . why then, the ragged sound of gunfire.

Rising straight above me, a grey stone tower broke through the edge of the trees. It was Norman perhaps, though no one knew of its origins. Built so long ago, its circular walls and tumbled blocks remained a local mystery.

Patiently, I picked my way over the stones, always climbing. From time to time, I would reach a ledge and stand there breathing hard and listening to the silence, remembering again until suddenly I was running to the tower. Then, suddenly, I was at the edge of the cliff. While the tower rose behind me, the land fell abruptly to stunted scrub, bracken, patches of barren sandy soil and copses of mature trees.

Hunted over by kings, a private preserve of the wealthy from the Middle Ages right through to the Revolution and to Napoléon himself, the Forêt de Fontainebleau was very wild in places like this. Oak, beech, ash, birch, and poplar spread into the distance with scattered clusters of pine and clearings where they had all been felled.

There were deer, wild boar, rabbits in plenty, and foxes to be sure. There were birds, too, partridges, pheasants, and doves—the pigeons. And nearly always when I went there in the autumn and winter, I would hear the hunting horns and think of the days when hounds were fed the still warm stag and the king and his retinue dined on other things.

There was always the chance a person might find something. Perhaps a louis d'or, perhaps the jewelled handle of a dirk or buckle of a shoe. When a place has been hunted over by kings, all sorts of things can be left behind, even trip wires and grenades.

There might be brigands, too, of course. Far to the north, much nearer to Barbizon and the farm of my mother, there were gullies and caverns in which fortunes might once have been hidden. Who knows? It was just a thought, had been so then.

I gave a shrug. I filled my lungs and sighed. Every time I came here, I remembered that first time. Jules had brought me to the tower when I had come from Paris to meet his father. The tall stone walls had kept the sun out and drawn their shade. Scattered about the floor were large blocks of stone that had fallen from the battlements, but in the centre of the floor he had levered several into place as an altar, a boyhood thing. He hadn't chosen one of the rooms in which to make love.

We had made love there, though, but that had been a long, long time ago, and Tommy . . . why Tommy had used the tower, too, but for purposes of his own.

That night, I listened to the wireless in the library, and they told me that at five a.m. that morning, 1 September 1939, Germany had invaded Poland. What I had feared had come to pass, and I felt alone as never before.

In the morning, I took the children to the farm to stay with mother and went on to Paris, unannounced. On the eve of war, so many had fled the city, the inbound trains had been empty. One could walk down the rue Mouffetard, as I just had, and see so few people the experience was frightening. Nothing, though, like the Exodus that came in June 1940 and a day or two ahead of the blitzkrieg. Through the morning's haze, opalescent and diffuse, the cupola of the Panthéon rose ethereally, lifting itself up from the narrow, walled-in street to touch the sky. The Fifth Arrondissement, the Latin Quarter, was the habitat of students. Tenements; small, cheap hotels; bistros; cafés; bars; street hawkers; taxi drivers; *maisons de tolérance, maisons de passe*, and *putains* who often challenged passing men in hopes of a little cash.

My sister was a sewer rat. Janine knew the worst of places. Water dripped constantly from the faucet. The gunk-plugged sink in the washroom at the far end of the corridor trapped its puddle before slowly drinking it in. Chipped enamel gave rust stains. Crinkly hairs were everywhere, some brown, some peroxide-blonde, others black. All transient.

The stench of a clogged bidet was overpowering, that from the toilet in its own little closet next door, revolting. There wasn't a bathtub anywhere—*merde,* no! Such things weren't necessary.

Transfixed, I listened to the water, the building, the courtyard, and the street. Why did I feel so threatened? Not by Jules and Janine, but by something else. The city. Whistles in the night. The rushing tramp of hobnailed boots. Shouts in German, cries in French.

There is no other sound like that of boots. Compressed, shut in, the windows crowd. Shutters are closed or open. Shades are drawn, but there are no balconies, and I'm running and cry out once, for I've stumbled and fallen. Scrambling up, I race along the street. I've torn my stockings—my only pair! My knees are bleeding. I've scraped my hand . . .

But I'm here, well before all that, in the washroom on the sixth floor of that ramshackle tenement. Can you imagine what it must have been like to run up those stairs, to hear their boots on the stones, their shouts, their whistles, and the dogs?

I was pregnant, damn it. Pregnant!

Forgive me—that came much later. The tenement had a narrow courtyard that opened on to the rue Mouffetard. The door to that courtyard was set in a high, wooden wall. Bolts held it shut. Garbage tins and refuse were everywhere on that second day. Cats, dogs, children with runny noses—the poor, they didn't leave the city like others, but why had they to look at me like that? Their expressions revealed not just suspicion, but also a wariness that was tempered with fear. Yes, fear.

If only I'd known then what I know now.

The entrance to the house was from a narrow, cockeyed wooden shanty of a structure, a slot that jutted out and didn't face directly down the length of the courtyard but sideways as if ashamed. Electrical cables, fuse boxes, and broken meters lined both walls, but there was no outer door, so it was open to all weathers and all defecators. One went up a short flight of steps then, suddenly, there was a door.

From behind the armour of a bent, wrought-iron grille, the concierge took one look at my outfit, huffed, raised her bushy black eyebrows, and snorted contemptuously.

The rush of garlic and bad teeth overwhelmed. There were clouds of cigarette smoke in her tiny cubicle. To sit all day in such a place . . . 'That one,' she shouted, when I asked for Janine. 'Hah! She should charge for it. Then maybe she could pay her rent.'

The Himalayas of those stairs began. I thought to count them but soon gave up. The boards were old and dished, and when I reached the top floor and found the room, a note had been left for Jules. *À dix-sept heures, chéri. L'Académie Julian.* At five and one of the city's long-standing schools for artists. *Chéri . . . la salope!* An art class at a time like this!

Jules, of course, hadn't been in his office or anywhere near it. I had left a note for him, the suggestion of dinner together, but had they ever made love in that room of Nini's? Had she cried out in ecstasy to paper-thin walls and flung her head from side to side as he'd pushed her to orgasm, eh? Hairs to hairs?

Above the sink, there was a mirror. Ages old and cracked, of course, but I remember looking at myself in that thing and watching the door behind, fearing it would open in a rush and they'd . . .

No thoughts of Jules, none at all but . . .

Later . . . that came later. Please, you must forgive me.

The silver backing had peeled. Smoke had damaged one quarter of it, and the half-moon of that burn had spread from the lower left out under the glass, brown against the peeling silver and the stains, so that my face appeared as if . . . I can't say it, but I must! Tortured. There, at last, I've said it.

I had a lovely linen dress then, something very special. *Très chic*, you understand. Off-white, superbly tailored with an open collar that plunged to matching cloth-covered buttons, buckle, and belt. My waist was slim—how could it have been otherwise with all that slugging to do at the house and in the garden, the children, too, and an unfaithful husband?

I looked smashing in the dress. Half-sleeves, with cuffs, extended to just below the elbows so that the soft tan of summer was exposed. The band of my wristwatch matched the alligator leather of the handbag whose strap was slung over my right shoulder. The hat was fedoralike and in a soft beige. I had added a band of linen to match the dress. Like a lot of women then, I wore the hat tilted to one side with the brim pulled down a little so as to give that sense of mystery. No lipstick. Hey, listen, *mes amis,* I had good lips, nothing but the best; wore high heels, too, and a coat in case it might rain or get a little chilly.

My hair had been newly washed and brushed—held at the back with a barrette so that it fell to shoulder length but gave some fullness beneath the hat and was very fine, would take the sunlight and become a lovely soft amber, but there was no sunlight in this place. None. Small, pear-shaped earrings, encrusted diamonds, a gift from Jules's father, were worn. Now why had that old man given them to me? Had I reminded him of someone or had he had a taste for me?

The earrings had been quite old. In my innocence, I had thought they'd been his dead wife's.

Ten thousand francs? I wondered. Fifteen thousand . . . How much could I get for them with this war upon us? Let me leave before it became too late. Let me take the children to safety.

The shop was on the rue du Faubourg Saint-Honoré, not far from its intersection with the avenue Matignon. I remember thinking that I had to be by myself for a while, but when I came to the shop, those feelings left me. The window was magnificent. *Ah, mon Dieu,* such things. An Aubusson tapestry was draped over one corner of a Louis XIV lacquered commode. Fabergé and Lalique were cast among the silver and gold, the antique jewellery as if rained from the heavens. A bronze of Rodin's was draped with pearls. Another bronze—much, much earlier, was by Orazio Mochi who had died in Florence in 1625. Chinese watercolours on rice paper were also there, with blue-white porcelain and jade figurines dating from thousands of years ago, while leaning against one of a pair of late Regency carved beech-wood armchairs, a splendid oil on canvas by Henri Fantin-Latour showed gladioli and roses. Another canvas occupied the opposite side of the window—Renoir's *Vase des Fleurs*. Then at the back, raised on an inlaid lime-wood button box and framed by everything, there was a sumptuous nude by Luis Ricardo Falero. *La Toilette*. A dark-haired, dark-eyed beauty.

The man who had come to stand beside me took no notice of the nude but concentrated on a pair of Dutch parcel-gilt tazza made by Abraham van der Hecken in 1600. Amsterdam . . . Lovely things. Christ dividing the loaves and fishes. The one tazza was filled with a sultan's spill of rings, necklaces, and brooches; the other lay on its side as if rolled about in the act of robbery, but why did he concentrate so hard? Why did he give that fleetingly triumphant grin, as if he'd been searching for something endlessly and had suddenly come upon it?

But then he took to looking at me in the glass, and I had to quickly avert my eyes. I confess I found him attractive. It was exciting to have him look secretly at me. It made me momentarily forget the war, the worry, made me feel . . . Ah, how should I say it? Proud . . . yes, proud of myself for a change.

He was about . . . *mm*, thirty-four, maybe thirty-six? It was hard to tell. Tall and rugged of build, he had a carefree nature about him. The suit jacket was slung over the left shoulder, the shirt collar was undone, the tie askew. In many ways, I have to confess he looked somewhat English, not French, you understand. Italian? I wondered, but from the north, not the south. American . . . Was he one of those?

The wavy light brown hair was thick and curled about his ears. The brow was high and sloping back from eyes that squinted with mirth, slanting away and slightly downward from a strong and prominent nose. The jaw was square, the chin also jutting out so that when he smiled, ripples folded and creased burnished cheeks to join the furrows that had burst from the corners of the eyes.

That smile . . . Tommy often gave it in the worst of situations. It was disarming, engaging—so many things, and one couldn't always tell what was meant.

The lips were as wide as the chin and turned up at the corners a little. Manly lips, kissing lips, even then I noticed this. Most women do, isn't that so?

We talked a little, neither of us facing the other directly, but he watching me in the glass—the war, what it must mean, Poland, that sort of thing.

I glanced at him several times, gaining confidence. Feeling better, more at ease, I thought, You devil, you've been undressing me, but had he really?

He mentioned my accent, and I told him I was half-French, half-English, caught in the middle of the Channel, so to speak. 'My mother is from Provence, but I grew up outside of Paris, near Barbizon. In the summers, that is. In the winters, we lived in England. My father's English.'

'Care to tell me your name?'

His French accent was horrible. 'Lily. Lily de St-Germain. My husband has a château in the woods to the west of Fontainebleau and just on the edge of the forest.'

'How lovely.'

Until I die, I will remember those two words and how Tommy said them. Like a schoolboy, tickled pink that fate had brought us together.

Fate . . . Dear God, forgive us all.

We looked at each other steadily in the glass of that window. How can I ever express that moment? I *knew*—that's all I can say.

'I must sell my earrings,' I said to break the impasse.

Quickly, I took them off, and he looked at them in the palm of my hand, was serious now and puzzled.

'Why? They suit you. They go with the outfit. This guy will only cheat you at a time like this. He's got buckets of that stuff.'

Tommy indicated the window. I shrugged and said, 'I have to take my children to see my father in England before it's too late.'

16

Though he nodded solicitously, he had to say, 'Surely you're not that broke?'

It was my turn to smile, and I did a little sadly. 'Just because I live in a château doesn't mean I'm wealthy.'

The husband then . . . You could see it in his eyes, though he had no wish to hurt me. 'But your interest in this window? All these things. You appreciate them, Madame de St-Germain. You must be accustomed to such things.'

Had he been so wrong about me? he wondered. Had I misjudged him?

The shop was full of lovely things. Tommy circulated while I asked about the earrings. At a point in the discussions, he even leaned into the front window to explore something. This set the shopkeeper off and the man grabbed my earrings and went to speak to him.

They had a quiet talk. That smile, that grin broke over Tommy's face as the shopkeeper's voice began to rise and then to lift even further in, '*Jésus, merde alors,* I would not even *bother* to cheat the *salope*! Out, I tell you. Out! Tell the slut I've no interest in them. Thirty thousand francs? You're crazy. Crazy like a horse that has had turpentine shoved up its ass!'

Red in the face, the shopkeeper roared back to me and shouted, 'Stolen, madame? Not for anything would I buy these!'

He slammed the earrings down on the display case. Behind him the eyebrows arched as Tommy heaved a shrug and said, 'Sorry.'

In anger, I snatched them up and fled. How could he have been so cruel to me, a perfect stranger, a mother of two children, a desperate woman?

Not until the avenue Matignon did he catch up with me to put ten thousand francs into my hand and say, 'The rest will come later, but let me buy them from you.'

I turned away, he touched my shoulder, gave a gentle chuckle— I can still hear it. 'Relax,' he said. 'It was all just a game. I'm sorry I had to use you like that.'

What does one do in such a situation? I threw the money into his face, swung hard and fled.

*　　*　　*

Dust filtered through the warm, still air, caught in the slanting rays of the sun as the patient scraping of charcoal on drawing paper came into the silence and the leftover taint of fixative mingled with that of gum arabic.

I eased the door shut behind me but didn't move away from it for fear of being noticed. There were perhaps thirty students at their easels, arranged in a semicircle about the model. This at a time of war.

Folds of white sheeting had been draped over a high stool and, on this, my sister sat with her toes touching the floor. Her slender legs were slackly parted, the arms stiffly at her sides so that the hands could grip the edges of the stool and hold the pose.

Janine's shoulders were flung back, etching the sharpness of the collarbones. Her breasts were lovely—even now I must force myself to admit how envious I was. A suckling's midnight snack, a lover's feast! Plump but firm and round. Uptilted, the nipples flushed even in repose, no signs of a child yet. None of that swollen look, or of the aureoles enlarging. The waist was slender, the tummy flat, the hips but slightly flared. That gorgeous *cul*, that ass of hers, was all but hidden.

Every time I looked at Nini, I thought of Renoir's painting of Jeanne Samary. Young and vivacious, those same dark, warm eyes, that same mop of dark black hair that was feathered over the brow and fluffed out in carefully contrived carelessness to emphasize the eyes.

Jeanne Samary's expression was the look Nini would get when a young man who was foolish would dare to tell her she was beautiful. Nini would compress her lovely lips and stare openly at him. Silently, her eyes would ask, Well, *mon ami,* what are going to do about it?

The tangled nest of her *préfet*'s goatee seemed trapped, the mons pouting a little and wanting to be scratched, for Jules was standing at the back of the room, in the other corner. He hadn't even noticed that I was there.

'Lily, wait!'

'No! It's true. You *are* in love with her!'

He caught me on the stairs, gripped me tightly and as I wrenched away, I spat at him and raced for the street. Down, down the stairs . . . down . . .

Halfway across the Pont des Arts he caught up with me. My Jules. Handsome, arrogant, tall, and thin.

A barge passed beneath us, chugging slowly up the Seine, sending waves off its bow as his hand moved from my back up to my neck and into my hair. '*Chérie,* relax.' Twice that afternoon I'd been told to do that! How could I?

'Lily, listen to me. Nothing's wrong. So I was looking at your sister. Would you want me to lose interest in such things?'

As if his *bitte* was in danger of falling off!

'How are the children?' he asked.

'Fine.'

The last of the waves smashed themselves against the quays. Old men fished in the sun, one person sketched, and I couldn't help but ask myself again, How could they do such things at a time like this?

'What do you say we go to the hotel and settle this?' he said.

'So that you can pull me on like an old boot?'

'Look at me,' he said, and I knew that if I did, I would weaken. How can I describe it? Every time he smiled at me like that, a fire rushed through me.

He was tired and worried—I could see that at a glance. There were touches of grey in the tousled black hair that had receded a little but was feathered thickly and brushed well back. He had good, strong teeth, my husband. Very white and perfect. Jean-Guy had them, too.

Not for a moment did those dark eyes leave mine. 'You're not an old boot. Besides, those are usually far too loose.'

'Unless they've dried out.'

'Lily, Janine means nothing to me. How could she? Things have been hectic these past few months. I've had to take on two more classes and some of the administration. People keep leaving as they're called up. I'm to do a national inventory of all the paintings and sculptures in private collections. Everything of importance must be listed with its value.'

'The *Boche* won't come here, will they?'

He didn't shrug or even gesture with both hands but looked at me sternly and said, 'The times are going to change because they must. Poland will be crushed.'

I hardly noticed how he had said it, but wish I had. Instead, I said, 'I listened to the wireless last night. I think I should take the children to England until we see what happens.'

'How long will you be here today?'

No argument about the children because there could be none, not in so far as he was concerned. 'Until the last train. I . . . I didn't bring anything with me.' No diaphragm, no pessary. Nothing.

That train rushes on. That night closes in and I'm sitting here all alone, listening to the sound of the wheels. Now a gap between the rails, now the briefest of pauses, then another gap. Racing . . . always racing. Cows and farms, lights winking in the night, the barriers down at a crossing. No lights. None. The blackout . . .

Jules . . . and I'm remembering that hotel room of his, us standing naked beside the bed. My right arm rested over his shoulder, that hand not touching the hair at back of his neck, not yet. In uncertainty, I placed the palm of my left hand on his chest and felt the skin and its curly hairs, was a little sideways to him, for it was always best like this at first, and I constantly reminded myself that English women just jumped into bed and went at it hard, but I didn't. I tried not to.

Hesitantly, we kissed. Lightly, timidly, I explored his lips as he did mine, he with his left hand on my seat and caressing it, smooth, so smooth and soft that skin.

Another kiss followed, still timidly, still exploratory, like first-time lovers—it must be that way, but then my other hand slid up into his hair, and I pulled him towards me, all passion, everything else forgotten.

We fell back on to that bed. I cried out to him, kissed him again and again, felt his kisses on my throat, my breasts.

Came like a rocket. Ah, how can I ever forgive myself? The tension of the day, the fear—that awful fear of knowing you might lose someone you love.

Jules thrust himself into me one last time, and I felt the throbbing, jerking, hammering of his lovely cock, and wrapped my arms and legs about him. Kissed him, hugged him, didn't want to ever let go of him—ah, all those crazy things one thinks of at such a time.

Only then, as he raised himself up a little to look down at me, did I reach back under the pillow to lie languidly beneath him with love in my eyes.

There was an earring under the pillow, and I hid it in my fist because it wasn't mine and I was too upset to confront him. A faceted citrine droplet that dangled from the end of a tiny length of silver chain, the links so delicate, the weave of them the work of great patience and skill.

Old but not that old. Edwardian perhaps. Victorian? The Moulin Rouge, the Alcazar, the Cirque Medrano? The 1920s? I wondered.

Winking in the half-light of that train, it stared up at me.

'Madame . . . madame, forgive me for waking you, but there's a call from Paris. An inspector from the Sûreté Nationale, a Gaétan Dupuis. They must have asked to have your call traced.'

I nod. I shake my head to clear it of its memories. 'Has my nurse come back yet from her shopping?'

'Only to leave a few parcels, to check on you and go out again.'

'Good. Did this inspector ask for me by name?'

'Ah, no, madame. He has simply asked if the caller was still here and if he could speak with you.'

'You gave him no details?'

'Of course not, madame.'

What is it about the sight of a telephone that terrifies? The instrument stands in judgement, the receiver lies as if wounded, and you know that the Gestapo will be listening.

Dupuis . . . the thinning hair, those mouse-brown eyes whose look could be so intense, the front tooth that was capped with gold, the nicotine stains.

'*Allô? Oui, oui, c'est moi. Qu'est-ce que vous désirez, monsieur?*'

That voice comes back to me. It's like yesterday. I want to scream, to cry out and turn away from the blows. I want to vomit, but they've shoved me under again, and I can't breathe in anything but water and must have air! They yanked me out but only at the last moment . . .

'Madame, what is it?' asks the manager.

'Nothing! Nothing. Forgive me, please.'

I hear Dupuis breathing at the other end of the line. Paris, 11 rue des Saussaies, the offices of the Sûreté, those also of the Gestapo. The caller asks, 'Madame, which camps were you in?'

I say it like a confession. I can't stop myself. 'Auschwitz and Bergen-Belsen.'

Dupuis sucks in a breath, and I see him holding it as they've thrown me to the floor and lifted me up to face him yet again. 'What's your name, please?' he asks.

Please? *Ah, nom de Jésus-Christ,* what is this? 'That I can't tell you. I'm not the one you'll be dealing with. I've only been asked to contact you people.'

'Then there's something you ought to know, madame. Our consciences are clean. We've been cleared by the Résistance. The matter's been settled.'

'*Ah, bon*, Inspector, then you have nothing to worry about.'

'Madame, I must tell you . . .'

'Inspector, there's nothing you or any of the others can tell me that I don't already know. You've received your little black coffin. The post was good, *n'est-ce pas*? You'll get my instructions soon enough.'

I hang up. I stand there shaking so hard I can't control myself and am afraid I'm going to piss, but then a hand gently touches my shoulder. Startled, I defiantly turn, but it's only my nurse who says, 'Madame, what have you done?'

'Nothing! Can't you see that I've done nothing!'

It's exactly the answer I first gave them.

2

My refusal to discuss what happened today has put them all on edge. Even though there are grey spots on my lungs and the x-rays aren't good, Dr. Zimmermann has asked that I think about leaving the clinic if I can't put my total trust in them.

Dr. Morganfeld is more cautious. After all, he's Jewish—the juice and diet man—one of the lucky ones who got out of Austria in 1937, so he has, understandably, a monstrous feeling of guilt to overcome.

Dr. Laurier is a woman whose grandparents lived in a little place called Oradure-sur-Glane until the Das Reich, the Second Panzer Division of the Waffen SS, came and destroyed everything. She's been home to see it, is a specialist in such matters, the only psychiatrist at the clinic, but is still suffering to cope. It's Dr. Laurier who has asked the others to allow me to decide what's best for me and who has said, in the privacy of the corridor, 'I'll get you across the frontier if you wish.'

You see, I have no papers, and if you have no name, only a number, you haven't got a chance.

'Will you really do that for me?'

'Yes, of course. I'll ask to accompany you tomorrow on your trip into the mountains. I'll simply say we talked it over and you decided not to come back.'

I think she knows whomever I telephoned will start to look for me, and that it would be best if I went into hiding.

'I can let you have some money,' she says. 'Swiss francs. Good hard cash.'

'You should have been with us, Doctor. We could have used you.'

'It's not going to be easy. Things have changed in France. There's a terrible bitterness. Brother is now after brother.'

She's so sensitive, she would never have made it through the camps. 'Would you send this telegram to Dr. André de Verville, Apartment 7, 34 boulevard de Beauséjour, Paris? If you could do that after I've left the clinic, so much the better.'

I hand her the slip of paper on which is written, *André, Michèle has asked that you remember how it was*.

'And the sender?'

She still hopes I'll confide in her.

'Put something down,' she says. 'It'll be easier that way.'

More information. 'Just sign it "Simone." He'll know who it's from.'

'Why won't you tell us your real name?'

'I can't. Not yet. Not until I've remembered it.'

Everything I own is packed into one small brown cardboard suit-case. The shoes they gave me after the camps, the skirt, blouse, coat—all such things have been neatly placed in readiness. I won't sleep tonight. The pills they've given me have been flushed down the toilet. In the privacy of my room, even in its darkness, I will remember while there's still time.

One spiralling leaf fell from a golden beech, and then another and another. In the silence of the forest, the sound of leaves break-ing away and coming to rest was all around me. Poland had been utterly smashed in less than fifteen days. Now, virtually the whole of the German army sat on our border and those of Belgium and Holland. When would it come, the invasion? When would the pos-turing stop?

I remember that I had a feeling I must do something, but there was also a lethargy. I'd been betrayed by my husband's infidelity with my sister, was mixed up and still trying to sort things out. Then, too, there was a latent danger, a frustration at the butchery, the arrogance, the whole attitude of the Nazis, a hatred, yes, but buried then—hidden just beneath the leaves like the ground.

I had come home from Paris. We'd had a treasure hunt, me and the children. Most successful. The source of the earrings my sister had been given. The faceted citrine droplets.

Jean-Guy had found the jewel box in the attic—pewter-bound, with a lock and, fortunately, its key. The box had been buried beneath some things, wrapped in an old shirt. The treasures of my father-in-law's mistress, recovered at her death, I supposed, by some lawyer—ah, the French, you have to know them to believe such things.

Had she killed herself? I wondered. Had that been it? There were cameos, bracelets—one of black opals, another of rubies, sapphires, ivory, and jet . . .

Another and another of rhinestones, the cheap and the gaudy intermingled with the good as if the giver had known the difference, but the recipient hadn't.

Russian silver. An emerald-and-diamond tiara, a priceless thing. Far too much for even the best of the other contents of that box. Something for a princess or an empress, something especially made by a court jeweller. One hundred or 150 years old, perhaps a little more.

The central emerald was almost round—a broad and stunningly deep green oval larger than the last joint of my thumb. Perfectly matching faceted emeralds, some square, others round or rectangular were all held by finely beaded, very thin wire gold, while scrolls, and swirls of diamonds in silver ran between the emeralds—1,031 diamond brilliants, 46 emeralds.

Now you know why I was worried.

Hidden in the forest, I took that thing out of my canvas shoulder bag. I'd wrapped it in a chamois and, for a moment, I simply stood there gazing down at it.

The sound of the leaves came to me again. Everything in me said to put it back and run—take the children to England and claim no knowledge of it. But, *ah, mon Dieu,* I didn't know what to do. It was Jean-Guy's buried treasure, and he was very angry with me for having confiscated it. Oh, for sure, he wouldn't tell his father, not for a while. The attic had always been off-limits for the children. Jean-Guy knew this. On pain of death he wouldn't confess, and if death didn't suffice, the shame of being ostracized would, but for how long? Soon the whispers would begin. Soon Marie would pry the secret from him and . . . Would he give the secret away at school?

I ran my thumb over the encrusting stones. I tried to think of where it might have come from. Marcel? I wondered. Jules himself? Had my husband found it in some forgotten drawer at the Louvre and simply brought it home?

Marcel was a pal of his, an artist of sorts, a freeloader. I could never understand why Jules and he got on. Always smoking, always gassing about, that one—both the mouth and the other. Posturing. Of all of my husband's friends, I had liked him the least.

Jules would miss the tiara if I were to take it from him and go to England, but I couldn't do that, not yet. First, I had to find out the truth.

'Madame, my apologies. It's the weather, the times. Perhaps if I might come in? A cup of coffee, a glass of wine?'

The weather . . . the times . . . The local people always blamed one or the other. The war. *'Monsieur le maire,* what is it you want with me?'

Self-consciously, the portly mayor of Fontainebleau took off his fedora and ducked his shoulders as if to launch himself through the door. When I didn't step aside, he let me have it. The English . . . they had no respect. I could see this in his expression. 'It is not *you* I wish, madame. It is your husband.'

'Jules . . .'

'*Oui.*' Picard mopped his florid brow and tugged uncomfortably at the knot in his tie. I would not be easy to deal with. 'The taxes, madame. They haven't been paid in some time.'

The taxes. Anxiously wiping my hands on my apron, I stepped aside. 'I was in the kitchen, you understand. We're canning pears. Please, you must forgive me.'

Preserving pears in a place like this! The mayor went to put his fedora on the Louis XIV side table then thought better of it. A pair of small, alabaster *baigneuses* caught his eye. He couldn't help but look at them. The naked bathers were magnificent. Such breasts, such hips . . . 'Madame,' he managed, hurrying after me until those shoes that had taken him everywhere, to the farm of his brother, the slaughterhouse of his cousin, even to the council chambers, scuffed a carpet of exquisite design. There were tapestries, too, and paintings. His wife would badger him for details.

We entered the kitchen, he to exclaim, '*Ah, merde alors,* what is this?'

Having blurted it out of shock, he quickly retracted the exclamation. 'Pears,' he laughed. 'But, of course, it's that time of year.'

The kitchen was a shambles. On the tiled floor to one side of the cluttered table, a freshly shattered jar of preserves had spread shards, juice, and halves of fruit nearly everywhere, while on a stool in front of the big cast-iron range my son, wearing a giant bib and worried frown of an alchemist, stirred an all but overflowing cauldron.

On her hands and knees a blonde-haired, weeping child of three made futile attempts at mopping up the mess but had miraculously not yet cut herself. Chocolate sauce, half-eaten, sampled bowls of stewed pears, mounds of peelings . . . his eyes settled on the neat rows of jars. There was an army of them.

Pears . . . the sweet aroma of them was everywhere, and outside in the courtyard, there were bushels still to come.

I shrugged and gave him a sheepish grin. I thought to say 'provisions for a siege,' but didn't dare. 'It's their first time at canning, you understand, but they're doing such a good job I'm going to have to reward them.'

Surprisingly, the pears were tasty—he had realized I'd put cinnamon sticks in with them—and when the chocolate sauce had been added by the little girl . . . 'Do you like cooking, Marie-Christine?' he hazarded.

The spoon dribbled sauce on the floor. Shyly, hesitantly, she looked up at him and then mysteriously away and all around the room. After a moment, she whispered, *'Je préfère les chats, monsieur.'*

Jean-Guy was more direct. 'It's fun,' he said seriously, 'but not so much as picking them.'

I sent them out to gather windfalls. Nothing was to be wasted. Responsibility had to be delegated to give them a sense of self-worth.

Over a glass of wine, a Château Coutet, a Barsac and not inexpensive, Alphonse Picard apologized profusely and wiped his handlebar moustache. 'Between us, madame, it's those people in Paris. They're always after money. A little here, a little there. They never stop. Now more than ever, of course. If there's some reason . . .'

'Please. How long have the taxes not been paid?'

'Two years, madame. I'm sorry.'

Ah, Sainte-Mère! 'How much does my husband owe on them?'

Picard cleared his throat and drained his glass. 'Seventy-five thousand francs.'

Three hundred and seventy-five pounds sterling at the official rate! I stared at my glass. The wine was golden, a little sweet for that time of day, but so nice with the pears I had gone down into the wine cellar and had opened a bottle just for spite.

Now I was to pay for it.

'Madame, please don't distress yourself. You mustn't think the authorities will throw you out of your lovely house.' He clenched a fist. 'I, Alphonse Picard, mayor of Fontainebleau, have some say in such matters. Leave it with me. Another month, two, perhaps even three, then a little payment, you understand. Just enough to sweeten the syrup and keep those jackals at bay.'

Never mind the war, the threat of the Germans.

I blinked and forced myself to smile. 'You're very kind, *Monsieur le maire*. It's not every day one meets with such compassion.'

'Ah, think nothing of it.'

The English were not so bad—the English, what had he been thinking? Madame de St-Germain's mother was French!

We talked of the war, of the district, of the forest, and of Fontainebleau. When next in town, I promised to come to see him.

I gave him two jars of pears and pressed on him a third, and even now as I remember it, I wonder if that wasn't what helped to save my life.

'Dr. Laurier, could I ask you to send another telegram for me?'

It's late. She looks up from her desk. She removes her glasses and asks me to sit down. 'A cognac? It'll help you to sleep.'

'No . . . no, nothing for me, thanks.'

There's a notepad beside the clinical paper she's been working on. This she drags in front of her. 'Well, who's it to be to this time?'

More information. 'A firm of insurance agents in London.'

She gives a nod and waits. I hear myself saying, 'Fairfax, Gordon, and Scharpe, 83-A Lime Street. They were an old, established firm of underwriters before the war. They had a reputation for persistence.'

'Anyone in particular?'

'A senior partner—Gordon, perhaps. Look, it really doesn't matter. Just do as I . . .'

'There's no need to get upset. I haven't telephoned De Verville. I'm trusting you to handle this yourself.'

'Then please send only this: *Tommy was killed*. That's all.'

'The sender?'

Does she think she's being clever? '*Lily*. Just say it's from Lily.'

The car was huge, a dark, shiny forest green with sparkling chrome and a bonnet that must have been a kilometre long. It sat behind my tiny Renault on the drive before the house, and the hiss of my whisper was urgent. 'Jean-Guy, come back! Marie, you, too. *Vite, vite*.' I caught them by the hand and held them fiercely.

Together we watched him from the safety of the woods. He took off his jacket, loosened his tie, then used one arm of the jacket to polish the headlamps, even to spit on the chrome. The rims of that thing were wire-spoked, the tyres white-walled and huge. A man of means, then. The man from in front of that shop on the rue du Faubourg Saint-Honoré. Suspenders held his trousers up, as before.

He played with us. He let us think he hadn't seen Jean-Guy run out like that, sat on the front steps and opened a cake box. With a pocketknife, he cut himself a large slice only to decide that wine was needed and an apple, one of ours.

The cake sat there in the afternoon sun. The wine came from a well-stocked hamper in the car. '*Maman*, he will eat it all!' whispered Marie urgently.

'Let him choke on it,' I replied.

'You're a *vase de nuit, maman*! A real stinker.'

'Jean-Guy, he . . . he isn't a friend, not this one. Behave yourselves. Let me deal with him.'

Each step we took brought us closer, and when at last we'd come round the car, he grinned at me and I realized then that he'd chosen to sit on the steps so as to be at eye level with the children. '*Salut, mes amis*. Want some cake?' he asked. 'A glass of wine, Lily? A peace offering. Sorry I didn't get here sooner, but things . . .'

He gave a distinctively personal shrug I was to see so many times, but left the war unsaid. It was too nice a day, and Tommy was always like that. The day came first, and he liked nothing better than to be outside, buggering about in an old pair of boots, cords, and a knitted turtleneck sweater, preferably dark blue or black. *Ah, oui, oui, avec un* Schmeisser in the crook of one arm and a satchel of ammunition in his other hand.

Not looking up, he cut the cake. 'Lily, I wish you'd stop hating me. I want to help.'

'Why? What the hell am I to you? If I'd had the chance to sell those earrings, you wouldn't have found us here.'

'And we wouldn't be talking. I'd miss that, I think.'

He held out a slab of cake to Jean-Guy. A travelling salesman, an estate agent—what was he, some sort of magician? A *gâteau Saint-Honoré*—he'd known I'd see the significance of that with its *pâte sucrée* circle, golden brown at the edges. Droplets of *pâte à choux* had been baked and split in half to be filled with *crème chantilly*, the whole given a caramel glaze and a garnish of fresh fruit.

He had had the *pâtisserie* in Fontainebleau bake it specially, and that, of course, meant that he had waited at least a couple of hours and had paid dearly for the privilege—Henri-Jacques Rouleau would have seen to it.

'Then it's peace, at last, and we'll drink to that,' he said.

So we sat in the sun on the steps, the four of us, and we had our little feast. Very soon, Tommy was showing off the car, a Packard he'd had shipped all the way from America, from some little place in Montana where his 'old man' was a 'car dealer.'

Jean-Guy was the first to sit in his lap and steer that thing, then Marie. We went for a drive. I threw caution away. How can I explain it? He made me feel good, made me laugh, but it wasn't only that.

The children quickly came to love him, and when children do, it's very hard to say no.

'*Maman*, can he stay with us tonight? Please . . . ah, please,' said my son, no thoughts of Tante Marie and Georges, or what they would say to Jules. No thoughts of anything but that he should stay.

Defeated, I smiled and gave a futile shrug. 'But, of course, *chéri*, if he'd like to. There's plenty of room.' How could I have known what he really wanted?

The Aubusson carpet was soft, of a swirled beige with shades of yellow, blue, and red to complement the linen of the walls whose flowered pattern, on a pale yellow background, offered muted tones of green, rust, soft pink, and faded Prussian blue. At one end of the room, there was a fireplace with wrought-iron firedogs and square blue tiles. The furniture—the big double bed—was Majorelle, bought at the turn of the century and cherished ever since. The carpenters had matched the burled walnut with panelling about the fireplace and wide mouldings against the ceiling. Under the mantelpiece, the wood was gently arched to match the curved top of the mirror above.

Meissonier-patterned candlesticks of tall, spun gold with white candles were reflected in that mirror. The blue porcelain vases were full of late asters, beech leaves on their branches, goldenrod, stalks of straw, some barley heads, too. Tommy stood there looking at that room, and I remember thinking how like the window of that shop it was. That same quickness came to him, that same sense of intense interest. He let me see this in the mirror as he said in English, 'My God, this place is a treasure.'

A 'treasure'—did you get that, eh? I did. It frightened me. It made me think Jean-Guy had spilled the beans.

There were two sketches by Toulouse-Lautrec, one on either side of that fireplace, gorgeous things purchased by Jules's father years ago. Tommy stood back to look at them—all interest now in the female form, a boldness, too. The sketch on the right, nearest the first of the windows, showed a young woman pulling on her stockings. She was naked except for these and a towel that had been carelessly draped about her neck, and her breasts were full and squeezed between her upper arms, she leaning over, bending an upraised knee . . .

Tommy gave a gentle chuckle—one I was to mistake for appreciation, but one I was to hear him give so many times. As if bemused, as if discovering something for the first time, as if a student of man's weaknesses: the flesh.

The other sketch was of a dancer at the Jardin de Paris and I wondered, as he looked at it, if the two women hadn't been one and the same and my father-in-law's mistress. The earrings . . . that citrine, of course.

Tommy had that quality about him. He could make you see something that had eluded you. He could open your mind and make you see the truth, even about yourself.

There was a chaise lounge by the fireplace, covered in the same painted velvet as the bedspread, then at the far end of the room—

reflected, too, in the fireplace mirror—there was a gorgeous Majorelle armoire of burled, inlaid walnut whose tall, floor-to-ceiling mirror was flanked by subordinate closets and topped by a curve of bevelled glass and walnut.

Tommy inspected everything with the enthusiastic eye of a connoisseur while I watched him with feelings of embarrassment. How many times had I stood naked, reaching out to open that thing? How many times had Jules seen my reflection in both of those mirrors, the front, the back, from the two ends of that room?

There was humour in the look Tommy gave me, mischief too, the devil. 'I like it,' he said in that horribly accented French of his. We were to nearly always speak *en français,* and I still can't believe that he got away with it for so long.

'Let's have a cognac in the library,' I said. We'd lighted a fire there.

He stood grinning at me, and I knew then that if he wanted me, I would betray my husband. But we had the cognac, and the betrayal came later. Much later. Please don't be disappointed.

Millet's *Goose Girl Bathing* hung on the wall above an armchair. Millet had sketched her in the forest, of course, for there everything is elemental—either this or that, life or death, and the shadows, the shadings that were draped about her and in among the trees and blades of grass told you this.

An absolutely gorgeous painting, one of my favourites.

Tommy warmed his cognac by the fire. He hadn't wanted to sit in one of the stiff-backed Louis XIV armchairs, not him. He had kicked off his shoes and had plunked himself down on the floor, knees up, elbows resting on them. No tie now, the shirt collar open.

I remember thinking then how much he must like to be by a fire. Again, it was something elemental. He didn't just want to look at those flames, he needed to. They were a part of him and he of them.

I sat some distance from him in one of the chairs. 'Lily, why did you choose that particular shop? I'm just curious. Nothing else.'

'Me? I had overheard Jules and Marcel talking about it. Marcel is an artist. Jules has always been interested in rare and beautiful things. I thought . . . Ah, how should I know? A place to start, I suppose.'

'Auguste Langlois, Maison des Antiquaires. *La plus belle vitrine d'art et d'antiquité.*'

This had been written on the window above. 'Was there something wrong with that shop, other than what I encountered?'

He caught the note of anxiety but shook his head. 'I just wondered. Langlois would have cheated you and I couldn't have that. Jules has sold things there, has he?'

'I . . . Ah, I don't know. I shouldn't think. No, my husband wouldn't have. Not him. He's a collector just like his father was.'

Tommy swirled the cognac in his glass. Dipping a fingertip into it, he flicked it at the fire. 'This is good stuff,' he said, tossing off the last of his.

'One shouldn't waste it,' I countered.

'I didn't. The bluer the flame, the better the cognac.'

I thought I knew what he was thinking and said, 'Apart from a very small amount, my husband doesn't give me any money. Everything is done on the account, as it was in the days of his father.'

'Then you'll accept the thirty thousand francs I'm still prepared to give you for those earrings?'

'I don't think I can leave just yet.'

'But you know you're going to have to. Sooner or later, the Germans will be here. France won't stop them, Lily. For the present, they're unbeatable.'

'How is it that you can be so sure?'

Silent for a moment, he withdrew into himself, then said, 'I can't. It's just a feeling I think the two of us share in private. Like myself, you're afraid they really can't be stopped and that it's going to be a very long and unpleasant war. The Nazis . . .'

Again, he left things unsaid, making me wonder what he did. 'Has your husband been called up?' he asked.

'In the general mobilization of last August? Ah, no. He's essential where he is.'

'The Louvre. They're crating everything they can and shipping it to repositories in châteaux along the Loire. I can't imagine that place with its doors closed and locked.'

'He's at the Sorbonne, a professor.'

'But is also attached to the Louvre.'

'Yes. Yes, he's there also.'

'What have they got him doing?'

At times, Tommy demanded answers, and this was one of them. It wasn't simply the determined look in those deep brown eyes with their touches of green, or the set of his chin. It was everything about him. 'He's making an inventory of all the holdings in private collections.'

Again, I heard him say, 'How lovely,' like a schoolboy—tickled pink but with the salt of larceny. 'It'll be done in time then,' he added. 'He'll see to it. You can bet your bottom dollar.'

I had to wonder how much he actually knew about Jules. 'In time for what?' I hazarded.

'For when the Nazis arrive, as they will.'

He asked if Marcel could have sold things to that shop, and I realized then what he'd been after all along, and I knew I couldn't lie to him, even though the items would have to have been stolen. 'Marcel, he's not above such things.'

And the husband must know this, but all Tommy did was to nod curtly. For him, for me the matter was closed, or so I thought. But, of course, it wasn't. It could never have been, not with someone like Tommy.

You mustn't think that I paid no attention to the day-to-day events of the war or that I was self-centred and uncaring of the tragedy that was happening to others. At the time of Tommy's visit, and from then on, that whole business was constantly with me, but just like everyone else, there were things I had to do. The children, school for Jean-Guy in Fontainebleau, sometimes the car, sometimes the walk, mostly our bicycles, but if I'd known then what I know now, I'd have driven to and from everyday. There was also the firewood to get and split, the house to clean, the garden, et cetera. Jules and all that mess with my sister.

Having joined hands with Hitler and eaten the eastern half of Poland, the Russians now threatened war with Finland. A German submarine had penetrated the British naval base at Scapa Flow and had sunk the *Royal Oak*, a battleship, with the loss of 833 men, most of whom had been asleep. Mines were being sown at sea by aeroplanes. The RAF was dropping leaflets on Berlin. Leaflets! Can you imagine? Sides were being chosen. Nearly one hundred sixty thousand men of the British Expeditionary Force were stationed in northern France along the Belgian border, but the British were not doing their fair share, according to the French who had, by then, mobilized something like two-and-a-half million men. To be British was to be . . . ah, what can I say? Suspect? Unwanted? This feeling was to grow strongly later, after the defeat, the old animosities surfacing. Jeanne d'Arc, Napoléon, and all that rubbish.

Tommy's warning kept coming back to me and I thought again and again about taking the children to England while there was still a chance. My father wasn't well, so I could use that excuse. I wanted so much to see him but Jules wouldn't have let me take the children, not at a time like that or any other. No, if I went, I'd have to kidnap them. So I waited. I thought a lot about it. I tried to lay in enough things to help us over the worst of times. Petrol, food, clothing, medicines—all those sorts of things, even pears. Everyone else was hoarding, so why shouldn't I?

Tommy's thirty thousand francs was my escape money, and I thanked God each night for such generosity in a fellow human being—he had let me keep the earrings and had said we should simply consider it a loan—and sometimes as I lay there in my loneliness, I made love to him in my mind.

But more of Jules, more of my husband. In that last weekend of October 1939, the train had brought them from Paris in the early morning. We'd been to the *palais*, the Château de Fontainebleau so deserted our steps had echoed. Jules knew the owners of Vaux—the Château de Vaux-le-Vicomte—so we had gone there, too. Such beautiful things, so many of them.

Now our guests sat about two picnic tables that had been placed end to end among the pear trees so as to catch the sun. Jules was at the far end, with Janine on his left, everyone eating, drinking, endlessly discussing politics and the war. Oh, for sure, it was good to see Simone and André de Verville again, nice of Jules to have included them, Simone, in particular, for she was special to me, but the others . . . Apart from Marcel Clairmont, whom you know I didn't trust and would rather not have had as a more-or-less permanent house guest, I simply didn't know them.

In secret, from behind the parted curtains of Jean-Guy's room, I looked down at those tables. Louis and Dominique Vuitton were thin, stiff, greying, black-haired, and from the Ministry of Culture and the Louvre, respectively, and wasn't it nice how some couples could have their fingers in so many pies?

As is often the case with a married couple, it's either the one or the other who is dominant. A strand of ancient Egyptian beads was held out from that long, skinny neck, those little bits of history fiddled with as if nothing. Worn in a tight ponytail, that woman's hair had been stabbed by an antique silver barrette, which flashed in the afternoon sun. Carnelian and agate signets of spice traders had been made into bracelets, others into rings. A bitch draped in antiquity. Nefertiti? I remember thinking. The hawklike nose, pinched face, hard dark narrow eyes, pencilled-in eyebrows, mascara, rouge, and lipstick, made me wonder what she was after. Little boys or little girls, for her eyes kept returning to my children. Am I being too harsh? A Royalist if ever there was one, a Fascist anyway, and bitter enemy of the Third Republic.

Those two were friends and associates of my husband, and mustn't business always be combined with pleasure, especially at a time of war? They were very influential, and paid servants of that same Republic.

The rest were young—friends of Janine's. Michèle Chevalier was the baby and absolutely exquisite. Twenty years of age? Ah, no, eighteen I think. Deep brown eyes that were so serious at times, shoulder-length wavy light brown hair in which there were reddish tints. A manner of delicately tracing the tip of a forefinger under the soft, warm curve of her chin when in thought. This I found touching. Superb breasts, lovely kissing lips, an absolutely unbelievable figure—I was to see it later. Naked, you understand.

A musician, a violinist and a good one, too, or so Janine had told me. A student, of course, but when would my Jules try to seduce her? Nini's dark flashing eyes kept flicking to Michèle who sat some distance from her on the opposite side of the tables. Had overtures already been made?

Vuitton also had an interest in Michèle, that wife of his encouraging this. She would touch the girl's hand and say something while looking to her husband for agreement. He would then study Michèle and gravely nod or delicately knuckle his thin grey moustache then give a tight little smile or say something profound to which his wife would respond. From the room up here, he looked to be about sixty-five, she on the tired side of fifty and trying hard to hide it, and I became afraid for Michèle, something that would only increase as time went on.

Henri-Philippe Beauclair was a tall, thin, and bespectacled Socialist. He had asked me to show him the house and when confronted by the embarrassment of a marriage bed he had known was being betrayed, had confessed that though he liked restoring paintings at the Louvre, and was worried about his job, as a chemist he was probably of far more use making explosives.

Michèle had a passing interest in him; he would die for her.

And Dmitry Alexandrov, what of him? A White Russian from that *quartier*, he had about him the air of a closet Communist. Nini had picked him up in a bar and had felt sorry for him, but shouldn't have. Not with that one. Dmitry probably knew every Russian waiter, chef, and *plongeur* in Paris, and what they didn't steal for themselves from the kitchens, some of them would have stolen for him.

He was twenty-six, short, with the broad shoulders, strong arms, and hands typical of the Russian peasant. A stocky ox with slicked down, flaxen hair, he had invested in a barber for the weekend, had made certain the haircut would last, but was it butter he had used, or the brilliantine of someone he'd met on the street?

The faded, grey-blue eyes were seldom still, he taking in every-thing and giving little away. As a student of electrical engineering, the French army should have had him by now, for Paris and all the major centres had been systematically drained of tradesmen by the military. Had he ignored his call-up papers?

He looked as if eating a last meal, as if searching for a way out, the eyes widely spaced about a cart driver's nose and hooded beneath the strong, bland forehead with its thick, fair eyebrows.

Marcel wasn't particularly fond of him—overripe cheese on a plate of meringues—and was still in that faded blue smock he al-ways wore, the red handkerchief knotted about that swarthy neck, the black beret looking like the drooping pancake of an angry al-batross.

Yes, Marcel Clairmont was being his usual self, smoking his filthy cigarettes, coughing, hawking up wads of phlegm to be chewed, swallowed, or spat to one side, gesticulating like a fisher-man, regaling any who would listen with his stories, his lies, his laughter and politics, the paintings he hadn't sold but was going to. *Merde!* Some men . . .

Janine looked so lovely, fresh and gay. No housework, no meals to get. No children to care for or to keep you awake at night when they're sick or there's thunder and lightning or the distant sound of approaching guns.

'Lily, what is it? What's wrong?'

Simone had been watching me from the doorway for some time and I, in my bitterness, hadn't even realized she'd left the table. Jean-Guy and Marie-Christine were with her, haunted eyes surveying their mother.

'Nothing. I'm just worried about this war. I'll be down in a minute.'

'It's Jules, isn't it? Jules and Janine.'

I nodded. I couldn't look at her. Even then I wasn't worried about Jules and the Vuittons. I should have been!

'Jean-Guy, take Marie and go downstairs to your father,' said Simone. 'Let me talk to your mother, just for a little.'

She kissed them both and watched as they walked to the head of the stairs until I felt myself being taken and firmly held. Simone was taller than me, with thick, wiry, dark black hair that fell to her shoulders and was worn back off her brow and teased out at the sides. Her eyes were strikingly grey, the face a smooth, if delicate oval, the slender nose turned up a little and always shiny.

'So what can I do to help?' she asked. 'Smack Jules's face or Nini's?'

We kissed on the cheeks. She dried my eyes and somehow got me calmed down, but for a long, long time she simply held me, then we talked, just the two of us as we always did, and finally I told her what I'd done.

The wine cellar was dank, low-ceilinged, and filled with rows of dusty bottles whose sleep had been left undisturbed except for the spiders. Simone knew of the *cave*, of course, but even so, was aghast at the bottles of Château Lafite, Château Latour, Château Mouton . . . '*Bon Dieu, de bon Dieu de merde,* don't you two ever touch these?' she asked.

'Not since Jules's father died. Now the bottles just wait, and we spend our money drinking other stuff.'

'But why?'

I shrugged. 'He has a thing about his father—the family name. The old man was a collector, a connoisseur in the true sense of the word, even if I didn't think much him or he of me. Jules knows he can't afford to follow in his footsteps, so at least he has preserved the collection.'

Our shadows moved over the rows of bottles to the walls beyond. At the very back of the cellar, there was a room where some empty barrels, pipettes, a press, and other wine-making things were stored. From there, a door and a stone staircase led outside to the garden, and when I opened this, shaded sunlight entered.

Gingerly, I lifted the cloth. My friend caught her breath. 'Lily . . . *Ah, mon Dieu,* it's so beautiful.'

It was. 'In my anger, in my jealousy, yet have I done this. Sometimes fate brings out the best in us.'

I'd made a sculpture in wax, in the style of Rodin, a perfect likeness of Janine posing nude before that drawing class. Even her expression was there.

Slowly, I turned the wheel on which I'd sculpted the piece. It was as if Nini's soul had been bared: the trace of mockery on her lips, the hint of debauchery in her eyes, the taunt. My little sister.

The depths of the wax had suggestions of blue, and at first Simone thought this had been accidental, but then she realized with a start, that it wasn't so. Like the organs of the dead, the blue showed through the translucency of the wax.

'What will you do with it?' she asked.

'Show it to him, of course, but only after I've escaped to England with the children.'

'And for now?'

I knew she would hate to see me go, but upstairs in Jean-Guy's room, I'd realized that I absolutely had to leave. 'For now, I'll do nothing. I'll let them have their weekend, for it will be good, will it not, to see my husband playing with his mistress and thinking he's putting one over on me?'

At Dr. Laurier's earnest knock, I open the door to hear her saying, 'Lily . . . your name is Lily de St-Germain. That firm in London has said they'll reply in the morning. I think we should wait until they do.'

'I can't. I have to go back. My sister . . .'

'Was she also killed?'

'In a hail of bullets. I saw her smashed to pieces. She died, and they wouldn't let me go to her.'

'Is that why you were crying? I could hear you from down the corridor.'

'Yes . . . yes, that's why. For her, for Simone, for all of us.'

'The night's too long to be alone, Lily, the room too dark. Let me stay with you. Talk to me. Please try. You'll feel so much better. Someone has to listen. That's what you really want. Pick up the story wherever you left off. Let the memories come.'

*   *   *

The memories . . . that weekend . . . I was sitting in front of the fire when my sister came up behind me. 'You're being too quiet tonight. Don't you want to join us?' she asked.

I shook my head. 'I'm tired. It's the children, Nini. They take the stuffing out of me sometimes.' I forced a smile, then drew the shawl more closely about my shoulders.

'Want another vermouth?'

'I think I need it. Has Simone taken Jean-Guy up to bed? Check for me, will you? He'll procrastinate, and you know how she is with him.'

Janine gave my cheek an affectionate touch. 'You do look tired. Has André spoken to you yet?'

'Of what?' I asked, sitting up in alarm.

'About the tonic he wants you to take. He says you look as though you need iron.'

'*Ah, merde!* Am I to be dissected like one of his patients? I'm quite all right. André does not have children.'

'You're angry with me.'

I turned away. 'Of course not. Why should I be?'

Neither of us said a thing. Janine didn't move but kept her hand on the back of my chair. I wished we could have a little tête-à-tête like old times, but that could never be. Not now. 'Nini, what will we do with them tomorrow? Sit around all day worrying about the war? Let's take them to Pincevent, to the sand pits, and then, why then to the millpond.'

I had said it like a person pleading for her life. Somehow Janine found the courage to look at me and touch my cheek again. 'You really are worried. What is it? Why don't you tell me?'

Did she really want the truth? 'It's nothing. It's just a feeling I have about this war. Me, I want the weekend to be like it used to be for the two of us.'

'Then I would like that, too. Yes, I would.'

The breath of her perfume lingered with the lightness of her touch, and as I turned to watch her leave the room, Janine caught sight of me in one of the mirrors that flanked the doorway, and for an instant saw the depth of my desperation.

Then she was gone from the room, her bright skirt swaying in such a businesslike way, and I returned to my gazing into the fire. Pincevent, why had I suggested we go there? It was down in the valley of the Seine, on the river flats just at the bend above where the Seine and the Loing were joined. Thousands and thousands of years ago, it had been a ford in the ancestral Seine, the migratory route of reindeer herds at the close of the last Ice Age. Nomads had hunted them and worked the nearby cliffs of chalk for flint. Now dredges mined the sands creating craters and mountains as if the place had been a battleground, which it had, after a fashion, for the river would have run red with blood and the slaughter would have been terrible.

I could hear the shrillness of our childhood shouts as we had hunted imaginary reindeer much to the delight of our father. I could hear the quiet exclamations as we found, in some discarded ball of clay, the imprint of a long dead leaf, the hard spear point or scraper of Magdalenian man. How beautifully those people had made their stone tools, how clever of them to have done such things. The relics of later ages had been there, too, all churned up by the dredges, and our father, showing as much delight as ourselves, had introduced us to each period of history. Bronze daggers, bits of iron or tile, some coins from late Gallic times, others from the Romans who had conquered them. So much, and in the warmth of a summer's sun, my sister, having eluded us, sitting proudly atop the highest mountain of sand with delight in her lovely eyes and a great big grin.

There's a time for tears and a time when one has shed far too many. Dmitry Alexandrov found me all alone by the fireplace and, for a moment, I think he was struck by the way I must have looked like someone out of the past. The suit I wore was of light beige velvet, the needlepoint of a darker shade of brown. Very Russian, very tsarist, worn that evening, but not because of him.

The lace blouse was ruffled, and at the throat, pinning a silk kerchief, was a bit of antique silver. How in keeping I was with that drawing room, with the sumptuousness of it. The furnishings were nearly all from the mid-eighteenth century, some still covered with the original Beauvais tapestry.

Before the soot-blackened grey marble of the fireplace there was a pair of superb gilded bronzes, one of a running stag, the chase, the other of a griffin. Above the mantelpiece, there was an ornate antique clock he couldn't quite place. Meissen . . . it might be. If so, a small fortune at any one of several dealers in Paris.

Even at a time of war, such things would have had value.

'Madame, your apéritif. Janine has asked me to tell you that Jean-Guy has successfully been put to bed. She's now up there with him.'

'And Simone?' I asked, anxiously drying my eyes.

Alexandrov drew in a breath, for the poignant look I'd given must have reminded him of Katerina or of Alyosha, someone out of Dostoevsky at any rate. 'Madame de Verville's in the kitchen. Your husband's with her.' You need have no fears on that score.

I took the vermouth and swallowed a sip to steady my nerves. As it went down, my eyes began to water again, and I realized that he had deliberately added cognac. What was it with him? He looked not at me but into me, stripping away everything but the truth.

'What is it you do in electrical engineering?' I asked.

He let the hardness of my voice pass. 'The generation and transmission of electrical power. The electrification of the railways, which will surely come on a much more extensive scale once this war is over and won.'

But won by whom? I wondered. 'The wireless?' I asked. 'Have you knowledge of that?'

His eyes gave nothing away. 'Of course, but it's more a hobby than anything else.'

Was it? 'Could you fix one? Mine has too much interference, too much of the . . .'

'Static?'

'Yes.'

'Please.' He indicated that I should show him the way. As I got up, I handed him the glass and he tossed off the rest. 'That's only to make sure it won't be spilt on your lovely carpets.'

How thoughtful of him. The price . . . The weekend would cost us a fortune we didn't have. Still, there was the wireless.

'Does the aerial run up to the roof?' he asked. 'The forest, the hills . . .'

Had he looked the place over even then? 'No. I've strung ten metres around the outside of one of the windows in the library. Until recently, I was getting London very clearly. It's a loose connection. A wire, I think, that runs between the tubes. When I tap the console, the static increases.'

'Have you any solder—a bit of scrap silver perhaps? Something with which to fix it more securely?'

Dmitry mended the set using an edge of the brooch I was wearing and the heat from the poker of the kitchen stove. The brooch had been one of those from the jewel box, and Jules hadn't even noticed my wearing it.

An uncomfortable silence settled over the dining room table, a pause, and then the muted sounds of hesitant cutlery, the accidental ringing of crystal on china as a wineglass was hurriedly set down.

I waited for Jules to answer. When he didn't, when he gave Janine, who was sitting on his right, a little more wine, I said, 'The taxes, my husband. Why haven't they been paid?'

The wine bottle paused. Michèle Chevalier blanched and swallowed with difficulty. Dmitry Alexandrov, who was sitting opposite her beside Marcel, went on eating as if nothing untoward had happened. Henri-Philippe Beauclair, alarmed for sure, hesitantly fingered the tablecloth.

The Vuittons waited with bated breath. This was news, scandal, embarrassment, the hour of decision too, no doubt.

'Well?' I demanded harshly.

'Well *what*?' Jules lowered the wine bottle and set it carefully on the table among the tall-stemmed, air-twist glasses and the golden Meissonier candlesticks.

'You know very well.'

'This is neither the time nor the place to discuss such matters.'

I put my knife and fork down. 'When else is there time? We're never alone for a moment. Pardon, please, Simone, André, Henri-Philippe, Michèle . . . I didn't mean to imply that you are not welcome and gladly, but the taxes haven't been paid and something must be done about them.'

'They'll be paid next week.'

'How? You've nothing in the bank but a few thousand francs. They've written about a loan you took out some time ago. I know, my husband. I opened the letter.'

For a wife to have done such a thing in France at that time or any other was to commit a sin far worse than adultery, but Jules simply looked at me and, for the first time that weekend, a sadness came into his eyes, and I realized he understood the matter only too well.

The candlelight flickered and threw shadows on the walls where bluebirds and doves—all sorts of birds—sang silently from the exquisite prison of their flowering cherry trees. From the belle-époque chandeliers came the sparkle of diamonds among their many-faceted crystals.

'I'll have to sell something, I suppose,' he said at last.

He looked so handsome. Even then I had to confess that given but the slightest opportunity I would have forgiven him.

'Such as?' I asked sharply.

'*Merde,* how should I know? A painting. Can't you understand what a place like this costs? Can't you understand that the price of everything we might sell is down?'

'Either of the Lautrecs in your bedroom would fetch two hundred forty thousand francs at least,' commented Marcel dryly.

Vuitton glanced at his wife. Henri-Philippe looked as if he had swallowed something he shouldn't have but didn't want the hostess to know.

'The dancers?' exclaimed Jules, the argument bound to flare into absolute outrage now. 'How could I possibly sell those?'

'Quite easily,' said Marcel, 'but they would leave shadows on the walls to remind you of the loss.'

He knew—oh, how he knew my husband, almost as well as I, if not better. The sweaty red silk kerchief was still knotted about his swarthy throat. The bristles were still there under the chin and on the cheeks.

Subdued, Marcel had hardly spoken a word at the table. He had been short of money and had tried to borrow without success. Now I understood his outburst perfectly, or so I thought at the time.

'Of course,' he shrugged, 'there's another matter. Perhaps you should ask your charming wife about it.'

The smile from Jules was swift and unkind, the looks from the Vuittons of broken glass. 'What did you do with it, Lily?' he asked.

'With what?' I managed.

'The jewel box.'

Jean-Guy, that brooch . . . 'I don't know what you mean. What jewel box? Your mother's? It's locked up in the bedroom, in the bottom drawer of that armoire your father bought.'

There was only the two of us now, one at either end of that table, the faces of the others but a blur to me. 'You know very well what I mean,' he said. 'Where is it?'

I shrugged, gestured with my hands, and tried to lie my way out of it, then foolishly said, 'What box? What jewellery? Is this something you've hidden away and tried to keep from me?'

He smiled again, triumphantly now, but then let it fade, and I knew, as he glanced at the Vuittons, exactly how much he resented my intrusion into his affairs and theirs.

'It was in the attic, Lily. Some bits and pieces my father gave to Angélique Morin.'

'His mistress!' I said, wondering what the hell the Vuittons had to do with it?

Jules ran an agitated hand through his hair and then let me have it, 'Yes! The woman who meant more to him than my mother ever could.'

'So?'

'So I want it back. All of it, Lily. If there's to be any selling to pay the taxes or whatever, I'll be the one to make that decision.'

'And myself? Don't I have some say?'

'It's not your concern. What I do with my family's home and finances is my affair and mine alone. To put it bluntly, it's none of you business. Jean-Guy will inherit everything.'

I was shocked. 'And Marie? Does she get nothing? Would you give everything to your son and nothing to your daughter for fear she would marry and someday inherit it all should Jean-Guy die? God forbid such cruelty. In a father who should care, it's shameful.'

'Lily, I want the jewellery. What did you do with it?'

'Me? Pah! I know nothing. Ask them—ask your friends. Ask Marcel here. Perhaps he knows. Perhaps he was short of money.'

At an urgent knock, one of the nurses entered, saying, 'Dr. Laurier, excuse me, please, but . . .'

'Well, what is it?' asked Dr. Laurier. 'I told you not to bother us.'

'I'm sorry, but there's an urgent call from Paris, form an Inspector Gaétan Dupuis. He's asking if we have a patient by the name of Lily de St-Germain.'

'What time is it?'

'Two thirty-seven.'

'Tell him to call back at a decent hour. There's no one available to talk to him at present.'

'He won't take no for an answer.'

'Then tell him we don't have any patients by that name.'

The nurse leaves us and Dr. Laurier says, 'Would you like me to make us some coffee? I'd offer a cigarette, but Zimmermann has said they're out of the question.'

'No, I'm fine. Thanks for listening.' She's so polite, so calm, has such a soft voice, but are we to avoid Dupuis like the plague?

'We're they all killed?' she asks.

'Not all of them, no.'

'Jules—your husband?'

'Jules wasn't killed.'

'Marcel?'

'That I can't tell you. I simply don't know.'

'But not your husband and not the Vuittons? Lily, exactly what have you in mind?'

'Nothing. I simply want to go home so that I can remember how it was.'

'But you're burdened with guilt?'

'Because I survived when others who were far more worthy didn't. Because there are things I did for which I'm ashamed.'

'You desperately need help. You know this, don't you?'

'What I need most is to remember. You see, they robbed us of everything else in the camps. They even tried to steal our memories, to ridicule them, to debase them, to grind us into the ground. I can't lose my memories, not until . . .'

'Until what?'

'Never mind. Look, the least you can do is leave me alone. I don't *want* to talk to you. I never did! It's far too hard for me. So hard, I feel like I'm breaking to pieces!'

It's an outburst I regret, but she reaches for my hand anyway and says she's sorry. 'Now that we know your name, there's no need for us to slip you across the frontier. The French Embassy will provide you with a temporary identity card and passport.'

'I never had a French passport. I wasn't considered a citizen. Besides, I'd sooner slip across. No one else is to know exactly where I am. Not for a bit.'

'This Dupuis?' she asks.

Sacré nom de nom, she's so innocent! 'Yes, him, especially.'

'And the Vuittons?'

'Them also, and my husband.'

'And Tommy? What about him? How certain are you that he was killed?'

'Very. There's no question of it, nor that it was my fault. Me, I'm the only one who's left.'

'And Marcel—he's a possibility, isn't he?'

She wants so much to offer hope, but hope is delusional. 'Marcel might be alive. I really don't know. We never could tell with him. There was always doubt in my mind. I'll have to settle things about him later. As yet I've been unable to trace him.'

I know she's thinking I've made other phone calls and sent other little packages in the post—that black pasteboard I insisted on having, that piece of white chalk, but she doesn't say this. 'Is there more to that weekend you were telling me about?' she asks.

'A little.'

She fidgets. She craves a cigarette almost as much as I do. 'Dupuis will be here in the morning,' she says. 'He can catch a flight from Paris. Even with all the difficulties of travel, Zurich's easy for such a one. He'll have the authority.'

'My things are packed. I need only to get dressed.'

'You could tell me about it in the car. There's a place I know of, a hut in the mountains. I could take you there until . . .'

'They'd only kill you, Doctor. Just get me across the frontier. Please don't try to alert the Swiss police. Dupuis will be watching for just such a thing and will only think you know more than you're saying. Just let me deal with it myself.'

'Strasbourg . . . We'd better cross over into Germany and head for there. At least, that way your transit papers will be of some use. I can simply say I'm returning you to the hospital in Bremen.'

She's so green it hurts. 'Katyana crossed the frontier at a little place called *Au-Dessus-de-la-Fin*—Above the End. There are some fields and woods, rough farms, pastures. Tommy said she used a farmer named Marius Cadieux and his son. They're good, reliable people. They never charged a sou for the service, and we used it several times. Not myself, you understand. Only some of the others and those they were taking with them. Packages, we used to call them. Downed British aircrew, escaped prisoners of war. Spain, too, of course.'

It doesn't take us long. The car is warm, the night still dark, and I know she's debating whether to come with me and still thinks I'm suicidal.

'Katyana . . . that's Polish or Russian. Look, I really wish you'd confide in me, Lily. I'm certain we could help each other.'

I stare emptily out the window towards the lake. There are houses in the darkness, moonlight shimmering on the water, trees, and more trees—sometimes I used to count them as the railway cattle trucks rumbled eastward with their cargoes of humanity. 'Katyana was Nicki's wife, but they came into things a little later on.'

'And the rest of that weekend?'

'Please slow down. Let's open the windows and have a cigarette. Me, I'll inhale the secondhand.'

Rebuked, she begins to relax, and as I light a cigarette for her, she says, 'Thanks. I needed this. So, okay, that weekend.'

I begin it again. I remember it as it all was, my sister, the memory of her and of Pincevent. Barges plied the river. The Bugatti touring coupé Jules loved to drive was parked beside the economical two-door Renault I had forced him to buy in 1937. The night before, he hadn't even come to bed.

Janine was sitting on the sand, holding Marie between her knees. In the palm of her hand, there was a scraper, a small flint tool that had once been used to clean and prepare reindeer hide.

'Where's Jules?' I demanded.

'With Marcel.'

'But I thought . . .'

'Lily, what you thought wasn't correct. Marie-Christine and I've been breaking open the clay balls, haven't we, darling?'

'Stone tools, Mommy. Hunters.' She scrunched up her nose so seriously, we both had to laugh.

We began to hunt in earnest, two sisters, two childhood friends, and the children. In spite of everything, I had come prepared. When nothing further was found, I let Nini see me take a Roman coin from my pocket and secret it in the sand. 'Jean-Guy, try here. Here's a good place, isn't it?'

With him digging between us, and Marie crawling into my lap, I looked steadily into my sister's eyes but couldn't say what I'd wanted so much to say.

Later, with the children happily playing at our feet, I told Janine that I would try to go to England to see our father and perhaps stay for the duration of the war. Jules wasn't to know. This she understood. 'You ought to come with us,' I said, only to see her shake her head and hear her say: 'Ah, no, not me. I belong here. I'm far more French than you.'

There wasn't any sense in arguing. There never had been. 'I'll tell Papa we've been here. He'll like that, and he'll understand why I wanted us to be together. May I take the scraper to show him that we can still find things here?'

'Yes, certainly. Please do.' I knew she was thinking we might never see each other again. I felt the same myself, and couldn't be angry with her.

The knife was razor sharp. From the windows came the sound of driving rain, from the skies above, that of thunder. Lightning filled the kitchen, momentarily startling me so that the yelp I gave caught in my throat as the sound of thunder rolled away.

Blood ran over Marcel's fingers and thumb. He gripped the throat more tightly to still the jerking body. Then he laughed as the eyes glazed over, and he slit the skin, first around the neck, then down the stomach and around each of the legs.

Yanking off the pelt, he gutted the thing into a basin. 'A rabbit slips its skin like a whore sheds her clothes, Lily.'

I had never seen Marcel kill anything before. 'You took pleasure in that. Why couldn't you have hit it on the head first?'

The dirty stub of a dead *Gauloise bleue* clung to his lower lip. He gave a ragged cough, brought up quantities of phlegm, and spat into the sink. Swiftly lopping off the head and feet, he said, 'Would it have mattered?'

'If you had been the rabbit, yes.'

'And the whore?'

'I . . . I don't know what you mean?'

Jules, the Vuittons, and the others were upstairs in the library listening to the wireless. 'That your sister's being one and that because of what she's done with Jules, you've accused me of stealing from him.'

'And didn't you?'

Marcel washed the carcass and laid it with two others in the cast-iron casserole. Adding chopped garlic, some butter, thyme, and oregano, a liberal wash of the rough wine he preferred, he said, 'I didn't, and you know it. Lily, why must you hate me? Jules is my friend.'

'Your benefactor. Hah! He couldn't lend you any more money, could he? Are your things in hock? Has the concierge confiscated them in lieu of back rent?'

He dried his hands on one of the tea towels, left streaks of blood, struck a match on the stove, and lit that filthy stub. Again, he coughed. 'You're jealous of me, of the attention Jules pays to my paintings. Aren't you curious to find out what I would do with that piece you made in wax?'

'You?'

He tossed his head to one side, threw up his bushy black eyebrows, and became the Marseillais fisherman he ought to have remained. Short, swarthy, and with brawny arms, he had the gut that perpetual sponging brings.

'Me, for sure,' he said. 'That piece, Lily. That gorgeous piece of ass. Janine.'

He had had no business finding it, but he and Jules must have been searching for the treasure. 'You would melt it down.'

Sadly, he shook his head and began to cut leeks into the casserole. Some carrots, handfuls of quartered potatoes, the whole of a cauliflower followed, after which he laid strips of fatty bacon over everything.

Then he stuffed the casserole into the oven, burned a thumb, and swore as he slammed its door.

'I would do no such thing. I may be a pig, I may even be a poor artist in your eyes, but I know good work when I see it.'

Apprehensive now, I asked, 'What would you do with it?'

'Me? Remember, madame, that it was me who suggested this. Me, I would take it to a foundry and have it cast in bronze. Even at a time of war, I would do this, paying a little extra, of course.'

'You couldn't pay a sou for anything.'

'Then let's leave it, eh? Let's give it time. Then go to the Gallery Pascal on the rue la Boétie and see for yourself.'

That was a street of old mansions, many of them cut up into little hotels, galleries, and other things, and I couldn't believe him. I never could anyway.

'Why don't you talk to your sister?' he asked. 'Perhaps if you told her how you felt, she would leave Jules alone.'

'I can't. It's not her fault. She's not a whore. It's Jules.'

'Men can want a lot of women, but women can't want a lot of men, eh? You're a purist, Lily.'

'I didn't take that jewellery.'

'And neither did I.'

'So?'

'So now Jules trusts neither of us and we two hate each other a little more.'

'Lily, I want it back.'

'You're afraid, my husband. Is it that you're worried someone else might discover what's in that box?'

'Just what's that supposed to mean?'

'A certain tiara, I think. One that the Vuittons must know of. One with emeralds and diamonds.'

I thought he would hit me, but he held back, flashed a cruel smile, and said, 'It's a fake. Worthless paste!'

Had I been so wrong about it? 'The box is in the cellar, under the barrel my sculpture's on.'

He didn't sigh or smile with relief. He simply looked through to the other room to where that bitch Nefertiti was sitting. 'I'll tell them it's safe, and you'll put it back in the attic where you found it, but after we're gone. Even though they were worried about it, your little outburst last night had the desired effect. Vuitton and that wife of his have agreed to use us as a repository for some of the extra pieces from the Louvre. They'll be arriving in a few days. Give the men a glass or two of wine. Nothing from the cellar, but make a big fuss over them. Everything depends on our being designated.'

Everything, even if they *were* worried about a fake.

3

At midweek, in the late afternoon, I took the children and walked down the road to see Georges and Tante Marie. The Morissettes had been retainers of the de St-Germains for years. Tante Marie had had a good deal to do with the raising of Jules. Childless, Georges looked up to him as he would to a son who had gone off to university and become a success.

The news I was bringing wouldn't sit well, but what else could I have done? Someone had to tell them their services could no longer be afforded. Not that Jules ever paid them much. Five hundred francs every quarter, sometimes seven hundred. What they didn't get in cash, they more than made up for in bread, cheese, apples, pears, vegetables, a few old boards, some wire and nails, tools now and then, an old coat, whatever they could manage to scrounge or borrow. I'd have done the same, of course. Still it wasn't fair of Jules to have forgotten to pay them this past quarter nor to have asked me to let them know. It could only bring trouble for me.

Leaves blew about on the road or piled up in the ditches where Jean-Guy went to kick them. Marie-Christine kept stopping to examine something, an ant, a bug, a last butterfly that warmed itself. All about us the air was cool and full of the scent of autumn. The road went up and down over gentle rises and for a moment, one precious moment, there was nothing else but the three of us and the open road.

Then the cottage came in sight, laid against the woods, basking in the last of the sun. Georges was splitting firewood in the yard. Tante Marie was taking in some laundry. Stuccoed years and years ago, the cottage was in need of repair. One old horse, a gaggle of geese, a few scruffy chickens, and a pig kept them busy. They had little else to do now but live from day to day and gossip.

I knew that's what they'd do once I'd told them the news. Straight off they'd hitch the horse to the wagon and go into Fontainebleau to see Tante Marie's sister. Had they told her already of Tommy's visit? Had Jules been informed of it and said nothing?

As Jean-Guy called out to them from the top of the last hill, they both stood still, rooted to their little plot of earth. Suspicion, a wariness of strangers, the sharp divide between the classes—all these and more ran through my mind.

Georges Morissette was seventy-two; Tante Marie, who knows? Some said sixty-five; she said sixty-one, but that couldn't be. Some said eighty, and it was those who had felt the acid of her tongue.

Georges lowered the axe and ruffled Jean-Guy's hair. Marie-Christine clung to me, intuitively understanding that her brother was the favoured even though she bore Tante Marie's name.

'Madame, is something the matter?' he asked.

'Ah, no. We're just out for a walk. It's so beautiful, isn't it? All this?'

I indicated the last of the autumnal colours. He was mystified. Giving a shrug, Georges lifted a hand to scratch the grey stubble of a cheek, then got under the double chin and did the throat. 'Beautiful . . . perhaps, but the winter, eh? That'll be something with all this talk of war. You should be splitting wood like me and not strolling about.'

'We've already done the wood. Today, we took up the last of the onions, didn't we, Marie? Jean-Guy, he has come home from school at noon to tie them in perfect bunches. Together we have hung them from the beams in the storeroom.'

Georges clucked his tongue and slid his thumbs under the broad straps that held up the baggy, faded *bleu de travail* yet let his stomach move with ease. Squinting into the sun, he pushed back his black beret and rubbed his forehead until a glint of opportunity came into his dark brown eyes. 'You mind the mice like I told you. That old place, it needs work, madame. My cousin's boy, young Louis, the one who lost his foot in the train accident, he's good with the hammer and saw, you understand. If Monsieur Jules would like the eaves fixed, Louis and me, we could . . .'

Grâce à Dieu, Tante Marie had gone indoors with Jean-Guy. I hoisted Marie into my arms. 'There's no money, Georges. Jules has asked me to tell you this.'

Again, the old man clucked his tongue, but this time he ground the back of his false teeth. 'No money.' Sadly, he shook his head. 'And what are you going to do about it?'

'Me? What can I do?'

'Stop squandering it in Fontainebleau.'

Muttering to himself, he led me into the house. 'You'll take a glass of marc, I suppose?' Wine would not be strong enough.

'Of course. Please . . . Georges, if there's some way, I'll repay you for all you've done.'

'Why? What are we to you? It's the times, madame.'

By some sort of osmosis, Tante Marie sensed not only that there was no more money but that they wouldn't be paid what they were owed and that the land their cottage was on and the cottage, too, could well be in jeopardy.

She was taller than her husband and thinner, her plain, flowered housedress clinging to an angular sparseness. Once blonde and blue-eyed, and quite pretty some said, she was now iron-grey, hard-eyed, and tired most of the time, or so she would complain if given the least opportunity. 'Jules hasn't said this. It's you who have done it.'

I shook my head but clung to Marie. 'It's simply that he doesn't make enough money.'

Tante Marie was swift. 'The taxes?'

They had already heard, of course, but I told them anyway. One couldn't keep secrets, not from these people, not for long. They'd have factored in the income taxes, too, that Jules had probably not yet paid. *Merde,* even I hadn't thought of those until now. What were we to do?

'Your sister?' asked the woman, pinning me down so that the marc, that rough wash of the barrel, dribbled over the chipped crystal Jules's mother had thrown out ages ago. 'Any fool could have seen that coming. Why didn't you?'

I shrugged and clung to Marie.

'Has he been gambling?' accused the woman. 'Have the two of them run off to Monte Carlo again?'

Again! I pleaded with them to tell me what they knew, though of course they wouldn't, but Monte Carlo, the casino this past summer, that loan Jules had taken out at the bank, the taxes, too? 'I'll see that you're paid your back wages. That's the least I can do, but if you should care to come for a glass of wine or bowl of soup, you're most welcome.'

The open road beckoned, and I tried to tell myself that the day was still beautiful, the air still clear and cool.

'*Maman*, look!'

That dark forest-green Packard was parked in front of the house again, but of its owner there was no sign.

There's a damp handkerchief crumpled in my fist. Dr. Laurier has stopped the car at the side of the road, but I've no recollection of her having done so. The dawn has broken. 'Forgive me. It's stupid of me to cry. Tommy . . .'

'He was your lover, Lily. You have every right.'

'He was my comrade-in-arms, damn you. I could have stopped it all, don't you see? Me, I was to blame for everything.'

After a moment, I hear her say, 'We can get something to eat in a little while. You've a phenomenal memory. Your ability to live in the past is truly remarkable. You make me feel as if I'm right there with you.'

'I've had to use my memory. It's fed me since the autumn of 1943, since when I was taken.'

'By Dupuis.'

'By him and some others, but mostly by the Obersturmführer Schiller of the SS, the lieutenant.'

'Tell me about Tommy. I'd like to know more about him.'

I hear the car start up. I let my mind drift. I try to tell myself that Schiller's no longer a problem, that he's bound to have been killed or put in prison, that I'm finally going home and soon the nightmare will be over.

The last of the embers glowed in the fireplace. Tommy gave a contented sigh and eased a sleeping Marie-Christine off his lap and into my arms. I knew I was at a very dangerous point. I still couldn't get over his dropping in. He'd been to Switzerland, was on his way to England. As we left the library, I let my mind drift back over the late afternoon. The bulky cable-knit sweater, baggy brown cords, and boots were still fixed in memory. He had been down at the end of the garden, eating an apple and examining the lay of the land with the curiosity and delight of a prospective buyer. In that broken, atrocious accent, he had said he hoped the intrusion wouldn't inconvenience me, but my delight had all but overwhelmed me, and I had begun to wonder about him.

'Marie, sleep well, my little one.' Bending over her, I tucked the covers up, added another blanket, and left the door ajar in case she should waken in the night.

Tommy was in Jean-Guy's room, standing by the bed, examining the model fighter aeroplane that hung by a length of string from the ceiling. In the half-light from the corridor, we were very close. He had raised two partridges just before we had found him that day. 'Will you really take him hunting tomorrow?' I softly asked. 'He's so excited, he'll dream of it all night.'

'He should. I did when my dad first promised to take me with him.'

'And the permit? Will you break the law and cause me to lose my husband's boyhood rifle?'

A single-shot Browning, a lovely gun and just the thing because it was so light and one couldn't miss with only one shot.

Tommy grinned. I could see that he was just as excited by the prospect as Jean-Guy. 'If we shoot at all, we'll do it quietly.'

Softly closing the door, I led him back to the library. 'Would you like another cognac?' I asked, my voice uncertain. The embers had all but lost their glow. The need to be held by someone was so very strong in me. The need to feel the warmth of a lover's arms if only for a night, made me silent and ashamed.

'Another cognac,' he said throwing more wood on the fire, and took the bottle from me and replenished our glasses. 'Tell me about your husband?'

'There's nothing to tell.' I shook my head and took a quick sip, but had it shown, my wanting to go to bed with him?

'Is your passport French?' he asked.

I was startled. 'My passport . . . ? Ah, no. I've never changed it. Being married to Jules, I've simply taken things for granted. No one here has asked. Why should they? I'm as French as any of them.'

This time, he sat in one of the chairs but leaned over to rest his elbows on his knees so as to be closer to the fire. 'I assume you know, of course, why you haven't been issued gas masks. Only those with French parents are getting them as of now. Surely, Jean-Guy has told you this. The school . . .'

A scraped knee, a torn shirt. Nothing said by my son, but his pride hurt by something I hadn't even understood: a British mother.

I told him then that I'd wanted to take the children to England, but that Jules had said they were sending some things from the Louvre to be stored here.

Tommy nodded. 'That was wise of him. I'm glad to hear of it.'

But would it help? I could see that he was thinking this over but was too conscious of my feelings to have said.

'What did you do with the earrings?' he asked.

'Me? I put them back in the box where they'd come from.'

That led to a discussion of my father-in-law's mistress, to reminders of the Lautrecs, and finally to my showing him the contents of that box.

For the longest time, he simply sat looking down at that jewellery, the firelight catching the intense interest over which I could
have known nothing then.

At last, he fished out the tiara. 'It's paste,' I heard myself saying. 'A fake but obviously a very good one.'

Tommy set the box aside and ran a thumb over the emeralds—
I'd have given anything to have known then what he did for a
living, his reason for being here, for showing up at the oddest of
times.

He chuckled and said, half in wonder, half in surprise, 'A fake.
Who would have guessed? Well, even if it is one, I'd still like to
see it on you.'

What can I say about that gown I went to put on? I had three
of them and chose the one I thought would suit best. It was sleeve-
less, with a V-neck, and of a dark brown, incredibly soft velvet. I
parted my hair in the middle at the front and pinned it tightly
back, wore those earrings, too, and sandals. *Dieu merci*, that gown
still fit, for I'd not worn it in such a long, long time.

Tommy had switched on the wireless to listen to the news
but when he saw me in the doorway, he turned it off and said,
'It suits. Do you know, I think I like it. Yeah, I really do. It's fabu-
lous.'

He gave a low whistle, and only then did I realize he'd spoken
in English.

The tiara was somewhat heavy, a tight fit, and I wondered, as
I self-consciously took it off, why it should weigh so much. The
lead, I supposed. All those rhinestones.

Tommy put that thing back on my head. He indicated that
I should turn around slowly several times, then took me by the
hand. 'Would you care to dance?' he asked. 'You're incredibly
beautiful, but you don't even know it, do you, and that's something else I really like.'

It was a silent waltz, and it took us from one end of the library to the other, light as a feather. A superb dancer. Flashing diamonds and emeralds in gilt-framed mirrors, laughter in his eyes.

Again, he held me by the hand and looked steadily at me. Breathless, I smiled back at him, the excitement all too clear in my eyes and as I felt him come closer, he said, 'I think I'd like to kiss you. May I?'

Hesitantly, lightly, oh, so tenderly. '*Mm,* a little more, monsieur.' And it was wicked of me. I blame my French half entirely, you understand, for at that moment I wanted him more than anything. How was I to have known he'd lied to me about that tiara? How was I to have known why he had done a thing like that?

There were greenish tints in his warm brown eyes, no laughter now. 'What is it with you, *mon ami?*' I asked. 'You come, you go, you come back again. Is it that I remind you of someone you lost?'

He didn't answer. He leaned closer, and closer still, and putting a finger under my chin, lifted it up to give me the sweetest kiss ever, and when I heard my breath escape, I said, 'Come to bed with me. Let's have this moment together.'

'Are you sure?'

Ah, mon Dieu, he was even asking! *'Oui, mais bien sûr.'*

How was either of us to know what the future would hold? Even now, when I think of Tommy, I have to think back to that night, to the start of it all. We danced some more. He held me in front of the mirror that was above the fireplace, stood behind with his arms about my waist. 'Fix it in memory, Lily. Remember what we look like together. Treasure the moment no matter what.'

'Always?'

He nodded, looked as if he had just made a commitment himself. 'We hardly know each other,' he said.

'It doesn't matter, not with us.' I was so certain then.

I remember that the gown had fallen to lie on the carpet, crushed velvet with crumpled lingerie carelessly dropped on top of it, the tiara among the folds, the earrings that had been removed one by one. Naked like a fine piece of sculpture, he had such a handsome body—tall, lithe, muscular, the cheeks of his buttocks tight, the cords across the waist taut, the shoulders fantastic, the back straight. Every feature I memorized, even that he had been circumcised, the testicles full and the one hanging a little higher than the other, and I can't think of him like that for what they must have done to him. Schiller . . . The Obersturmführer Schiller, the lieutenant. My sister, Jean-Guy, and Marie . . .

Forgive me. Let me dry my eyes and blow my nose. Let me bow my head in shame because it was all my fault.

While I lay on my stomach in that bed, so warm beneath his hand, the candles glowed on either side of us. Twists of gold, shafts of white with dribbles down them. Tiny, bright flames of softer gold.

Caressing the warm contours of my seat, he ran his hands up from the base of my spine to the nape of my neck, let his fingers slide into my hair which he kissed, then he kissed behind the ears, first the one and then the other lightly. 'You're lovely, Lily. You're absolutely gorgeous.'

I must have murmured something, or was that later on? I simply don't know. I do remember turning over and spreading my legs a little more and that I felt him holding my breasts, not touching me down there yet. Just kissing my shoulders, again the ears, the lips, the tip of my nose and forehead, those kisses lingering as if he, too, had to fix the memory of them forever.

Ripples of pleasure spread to my middle. I had good breasts, not too big, you understand. Not bruised or burned by cigarettes, not then. I was secretly proud of them even though I knew my sister's were far more beautiful. He lifted one to his lips, and I felt him kiss it tenderly. As he wrapped his arms around me, a gossamer of candlelight gave shadows to the ceiling where fleurs-de-lis looked down on us. He had such nice shoulders. Lovely kissing lips. The muscles in his back . . . It's all mixed up now, for I had begun to explore his body as he explored mine. The tiny, curly hairs at the nape of his neck—I remember caressing them as he kissed the flat of my tummy and began to explore the rest.

Pushing my hips up, I found an ear and breathed, '*Ah, mon Dieu*, that's lovely. Please don't stop.'

Later . . . was it later that I lay on top of him? I do remember pushing myself away so that my middle was pressed more firmly against him and I could feel the base of his erection, the hairs above it, and could rub myself up and down a little and move from side to side, something he encouraged, for he held my breasts again and lifted me up a little to suckle them and trace out the aureoles with his tongue.

Later . . . was it later that we lay there again facing each other, him saying seriously, 'Always be straight with me, Lily. If you want out, you must say so. There's no one else, and there won't be.'

I remember thinking then that if he and Janine should meet, which they might, Nini would take a fancy to him. *Merde*, but I knew I couldn't ever let it happen. 'Come in me. Let me feel you inside me.'

Had he understood my worry? Had he known then about my little sister, that she'd do it with a man just to please herself and not care about the consequences?

Holding off, he began again to caress my middle and to rub his fingers gently up and down, exploring, finding, stroking, pushing lightly down, then tracing the tip of a finger around and up, and over and along, the muscles contracting in me, tightening: contact, tighten, release, and again and again, his lips on mine, his cock stiff against my leg, me reaching down to take it in hand, me wanting it and wanting it. *Ah, mon Dieu, mon Dieu.*

I began to toss my head from side to side. Ripples of pleasure, waves of it. Contract, tighten, release, and tighten more as I cried out and let myself go, took him in and wasn't conscious of what I said or did, only wanted him and wanted him.

Tommy drove himself into me. Now out. Now in again and deeper, the muscles contracting fiercely at the last, the pleasure of coming taking over completely as I arched up, found his lips again, and clung to them, kissing him and kissing him as I came and came, each wave of the orgasm topping the one before until he, too, came at last and let me see the ecstasy that had filled his eyes. 'Lily . . . Lily . . .' How could I ever forget the sound of his voice as he gave a cry and I felt him throbbing within me, felt the hot stickiness of his semen and wanted it so much, I can still remember hoping for a child.

For a long, long time afterwards, I remember lying there, wrapped in his arms, kissing him, telling him how good he had made me feel.

'Do you think you're still capable of loving someone like that?' asked Dr. Laurier.

The windows of the restaurant look out over the valley of the Aure. Mountains are all around us. We're on the outskirts of Solothurn, heading for Bienne and the turn-off. Everything is so very clean.

'In what way?' I ask, not looking at her.

'Sexually, of course. Lily, have you lost the ability, the desire?'

'Me? Are you kidding? Hey, listen, my friend, they beat all that sort of thing out of me long ago. I'm so shrivelled up inside, I'm dead.'

'But . . . but you can remember it so vividly?'

'*Une sacrée bonne baise,* eh? Is that what you mean?'

'You know it is. You needn't be embarrassed.'

'*Ah, bon*, Mademoiselle la Doctoresse Laurier, what I remember most is his smile, the look in his eyes, their happy, mischievous glint, their warmth for me and my children. These I must never lose. All the rest pales by comparison, though I enjoyed it, of course.'

'What will you do when you get to the house?'

Have I told them to meet me there? This is written all over her. 'The house might not even be there anymore. It might have been bombed to pieces or burned to the ground. Me, I don't know or care. I only know that the forest will be waiting.'

In the morning, after that night of illicit love, two partridges were hanging by their feet against the redbrick wall of the courtyard. My breakfast had been laid out on the kitchen table: coffee with milk, porridge, two eggs, toast, jam, sliced pears, and apples. Enough for ten. Jean-Guy was to be waiter.

I had to laugh, had to kiss and hug them both. Jean-Guy was so excited. '*Maman,* I have hit one! Monsieur Tommy, he has held the gun, but I have pulled the trigger.'

Nothing would suffice but that I be shown the bullet holes. Both partridges had been killed by a single shot to the head. Marie-Christine, still in her nightie and one slipper, looked at me in such a way I had to wonder if she had seen the love in my eyes for Tommy, but will I ever know? This, too, has haunted me day by day for it carries its measure of guilt.

We decided to go for a drive, and I took him first to the Caves of the Brigands. There the hills of the Fontainebleau Forest break into tangled, scrub-clad rocky gorges that slope down to interfinger with the flat farmlands to the northwest. Stubbled grain fields, haycocks, and newly plowed fields are pastoral under a bright autumnal sky across which white clouds lazily drift. A few people were about on the land. Some were harvesting root crops, others onions and cabbages. In one distant field, three women gleaned stubble as women have for hundreds of years.

I lifted my arm and pointed, heard myself saying, 'Barbizon, as Millet and Sisley would have painted it. The dappled colours, the froth of gold the autumn brings, the touches of green and brown from the branches. Ancient roofs and broken fences. Look how the light plays on them, Tommy. It's incredibly beautiful, *n'est-ce pas?*'

My mother's farm was at a crossroads out on that plain. It's about two kilometres from the caves. The low, tiled roof of the house is set in the midst of an isolated copse and half-hidden by the hanging branches of a giant willow, now golden. Before the farm, the fields are flat; beyond it, the same, but to the southwest are the first scatterings of the village and the road we took that day.

Barbizon had only one major street, a line of dusty shops, the bakery and *pâtisserie,* a milliner's, wine merchant's, two hotels and restaurants for the tourists and people from Paris, lace curtains in the windows of the houses, sunning cats, and one dog that almost missed us.

We were through the village in an instant and all too soon at the farm. Unbidden, the children noisily got out of that great big car to run and shout to their grandmother . . . But I can't go on. Please, it isn't necessary now. Suffice it to say that mother only confirmed what I wanted to hear her say. That we should go to England with Tommy. Never mind the things that Jules was having sent from the Louvre. Never mind the house. Just go. Leave while you can! Live while you're in love.

I never questioned anything else. I closed and locked the château, threw the key away. Finished, or so I had thought, but life is not so simple, nor is it so kind.

The wind was raw. It was another morning—later by a fortnight, and all the guilt and agony of that crossing are behind me. The refusal of the military at Le Havre to let us leave the country. The threat of submarines, the endless hours of seasickness cooped up belowdecks with the children, bundled in our life jackets all the time, the stench of stale tobacco smoke and vomit everywhere.

Tommy never took no for an answer, not if he thought the objective necessary. We had driven to Cherbourg. He had paid handsomely, under the table you understand, and we had crossed over from there.

This wind was from off the Bristol Channel, from over the highest peaks of the Quantock Hills, and I was standing beneath the spreading, empty branches of a massive beech in the graveyard that was beside the little stone church at Aisholt, in Somerset. I shut my eyes and ran fingertips over one of the ancient headstones. I felt the damp withdrawing into the pits and hollows of letters that were all but gone.

From Taunton, the road runs east to Curry Rivel, Langport, Somerton, Lyndford-on-Fosse, and Camelot, its castles, knights, and kings, if one believed.

With eyes still shut, I remembered it all, the days, the drives, the man, my father leading Nini and I on a chase through time. How very different he was from Jules, how so like Tommy.

I had come home to a death, to a first hard casualty in what was soon to become my private war, my own little bit of hell. Me, I had thought myself so lucky. Suicide is an unpleasant thing, so hard to accept in one you've loved.

Now, of course, I can understand the need for such a thing. But in those days . . . ah, what can I say? I was simply too naive.

The church, the rectory, the stained-glass windows I had so often viewed from within and without, all drew my attention to a God no different than the one to whom I prayed at Mass in France.

That little church had been built in the fourteenth century. The bell tower had tolled its call to the faithful ever since, its warnings of war as well.

A figure emerged from the manse, bareheaded as usual and wearing the threadbare tweeds and gumboots I will always remember. The hair was wispy-silver and a little too long, the man short, swarthy, and ruddy faced with sincere and honest grey-blue eyes and wire-rimmed spectacles whose lenses were bifocal and octagonal.

He addressed the day with the vigour he always had. He was nearly eighty, or was it eighty-two? George Arthur Martin, our padre, my father's greatest friend and caretaker.

Would the talk today be of infidelity, the need to forgive, that of a husband for his wife, the children for their father, or of common sense and the war? So far he had said so little of any of these things it made me wonder about him.

'Lily, you mustn't dwell on things. Now, you really mustn't. He's gone to his Maker and the sound of the guns has been silenced at last.'

No more screams in the night, no more terror. The legacy of that other war that ended such a short time ago. The reason my mother could no longer live with my father. Well, one of them. Perhaps you have noticed that my little sister was typically French, whereas me, I was . . .

'Is it time for coffee, do you think?' he asked.

A wisp of hair fell over the Saxon's brow. I gave him a smile that pleased him immensely. I said quite gaily, 'Let's walk a bit. I want to see the hills once more.'

They were to the west, north, and south of us. By making a circuit of the garden, we could compass some of the finest scenery in England. Arthur let me take him by the arm and gave a contented sigh. 'You've no idea how good that feels to a man of my age. Just because I wear the cloth, doesn't mean I can't enjoy the company of a beautiful woman. I've seen you blossom again, in just these past two weeks. You've got rosy cheeks, my girl. You're beginning to think you can cope with life—no, I don't want to hear about it unless you want to tell me. It'll take time for the place to get inside you. It has a way of its own. Do you know, when I first saw you I thought, dear Lord, that girl's been ill, but now . . . why now, you're one of us again. It's a right proper feed, isn't it, this place of ours?'

I squeezed his arm, drawing myself closer to him. Together we looked to the east, towards Avalon, then north across the Quantock Forest to Longstone and Beacon Hills. Heather and gorse lay on the crowns of the highest hills, while on the slopes below, there were oaks and beeches.

Neither of us spoke, for to do so would interfere with the moment. To the west, the Quantocks rose to their highest, while beyond them lay the Brendon Hills of Exmoor. To the south lay Aisholt Common, Cothelstone Hill, the Vale of Taunton Deane and the Blackdown Hills beyond.

'It's a land of poets and kings, Lily. Of writers, too.'

'Father was very ill, wasn't he?'

'No more, no less than when he first came home from the Great War, and your mother saw the difference it had wrought in him. Time and the peace of our countryside did a lot for him. It was good for him to come back here.'

For the sake of us girls, our family had spent the war years here. My father had wanted to become a writer, but had ended up being a schoolmaster and then going off to that war. Trapped, that's what he'd been. Trapped by the need for money a growing family presented, trapped by the love he had borne the woman of his dreams, the girl he'd met as a student while travelling in France.

'Come now, let's have that coffee. There are some things that we must discuss.'

He had put the kettle on the hob. Coffee wasn't his usual. First thing he liked a good cup of tea, but ever since I'd been coming to the hill of a morning, Arthur had thought the change would do him good, and I had made it for him. The book-lined study of dark oak contained not only a fireplace, ample desk, and leather-bound chairs, but also a big bay window whose leaded glass over-looked the garden.

There was a bench before that window, its plush wine-red mo-rocco just as worn as when I first remembered it. Leaning against the backrest, I stretched out my legs and cradled the cup and sau-cer in my lap.

Arthur indicated the garden with its wealth of hidden paths and rose arbours. Of a spring or summer, there would be banks and banks of colour in wild profusion with phlox, lavender, ni-cotiana, and so many others piled against sky-blue asters, white daisies, and goldenrod.

The apple trees, the Damson plums. 'God is out there, Lily. Do you know, I've a confession to make. I'm afraid I've made a very poor clergyman. I feel Him most when working in my garden. Some Sundays, I can hardly wait to get out of that pulpit.'

'It's always so lovely, even at this time of year. Nini and I still speak of it.' He would tell me now, in his own good time. I knew he was hunting for words.

'This young man of yours. I like the cut of him, but Aisholt's a little place. People talk—my good godfathers don't I know it. He's not involved in the war—that's a strike against him, even if he is an American and they're not in it yet. The point is, my dear, if Jules were to . . .'

'He'll never give me a divorce. The Church wouldn't allow it. In any case, he must know by now that I've run off. This will hurt his precious vanity. I love Tommy, Arthur. Heart, soul, and mind—every particle of me. I've never felt this way before.'

'But you hardly know him?'

Again, I heard myself saying, 'It doesn't matter. Not with us.'

'What's he do for starters?'

'He's in insurance.'

'Fairfax, Gordon, and Scharpe, the underwriters. Number 83-A Lime Street. Back to back with Lloyd's and very thick with them, I should think. Rates within rates. The point is, what's it all mean?'

I heard my cup rattle against its saucer. 'Has something come up that I don't know?'

Arthur didn't avoid it. 'You have your doubts. I knew you had. This "treasure," Lily.'

'What "treasure"? Please, what is this? Has Jean-Guy . . .'

'My dear, your young man has a secret compartment in the boot of that motor of his. Ideally suited to smuggling, I should think. Apparently, he took this "treasure" when you left your husband's house.'

'Arthur, that's simply not true.'

'I take it then that you've no knowledge of his having done. Perhaps he did it to help you financially? I gather there's some jewellery, a tiara . . . Jean-Guy called it a crown.'

'It's paste, Arthur. A fake, for heaven's sake!'

He set his cup and saucer aside. 'Have a look around. I'm sure you'll find it then. But wait. Half a minute now. This firm of his doesn't just underwrite insurance policies. They underwrite the underwriters.'

'We are the select, *la crème de la crème*, Madame de St-Germain. A pool of very wealthy, influential families are behind us. Need I say more, *hmm*? We cover colleagues who have taken positions on objects of great value and when we get burned, we employ men like Tom Carrington to apply the salve. He's in East Anglia at the moment, commiserating with the Count Alexis Nikolai Ivanovich Lutoslawski.'

'A Polish count?'

'That is correct. A refugee.'

'Who's been robbed?'

The man behind the antique desk nodded. 'Robberies like this seldom get into the press. One doesn't want the world to know, *hmm*? They were very good, very select. German or Russian agents must have tipped them off. Paintings, Old Masters, tapestries, a quantity of Russian silver, small pieces of sculpture—very early things those. A matched pair of duelling pistols . . .'

'A tiara.'

'Yes, a fake unfortunately, as you've admitted to our Tom. The questions we must ask ourselves, my dear woman, are how on earth did your husband come by it, and where, please, is the real one?'

I sat there in that office, cold tea before me in a fine china cup. The muted sounds of London's traffic filtered through the oak-panelled walls and the leaded windows across which great *x*'s of tape had been pasted.

Charles Edward Gordon was the son of one of the original founders. He had a high, domed forehead, a thin tonsure of brown hair, the stooped shoulders of a big, tall man whose frame had long ago resigned itself to overwork, overweight, and the years.

The face was fleshy, the jowls drooping like those of an old bulldog.

The eyes . . . I can still remember how he looked at me with suspicion, curiosity—amusement, too, because he obviously must have known something about Tommy and me—and what else? A sense of wanting to go deeper, a gamble, too, perhaps? Ah, it was hard to define.

He reached for his pipe and began to pack it, the motions a ritual he had no need to concern himself with. 'At least one hundred thousand pounds, Madame de St-Germain, probably a good deal more. The tiara of the Empress Eugénie, sold at auction with the rest of her jewels after the flight to England in September 1870 and the collapse of the Second Empire.'

'France would love to have the real one back, I suppose.'

'The Royalists at any rate,' he said, as if sucking it from his pipe. 'Your husband, madame, is he a member of the Action française?'

Those were not quite Royalists but close enough. 'Jules? Ah, no. Jules wouldn't wish for the end of the Third Republic and a return to the days of the royalty.'

Or would he have? The Action française were notoriously Fascist and very far to the right, the Vuittons too, no doubt. But Nini . . . Nini was to the left of centre and would have warned me. She wouldn't have put up with him for a moment.

Intently, Gordon watched me, but all I saw of him behind that cloud of tobacco smoke was the smile he momentarily gave as he asked, 'Think about it, will you? Let Carrington know. Our Tom's a good chap, very thorough. Been with us for . . . now let me see.' He fished about for a notebook he'd no need of. 'Five years. Has it really been five? Seems like forever. War heating up in France, is it?'

The British were already calling it the Bore War; the French, *La Drôle de Guerre*, the Phony War. 'This business seems so far from it,' I said weakly.

'Oh, my goodness, no. We reinsured the policies on the Lutoslawski collections back in '38. They were shipped here from his estates in eastern Poland last summer, as per the conditions of our agreement. Out in the nick of time only to be stolen, madame. Stolen. A good bit of them at any rate.'

'How much of a bit since that tiara was a fake?'

I think then that he suddenly realized I might not be so easy. 'Four-and-a-half million pounds. Priceless objects of *virtù*. A terrible shame, what with this war and all. Still in their crates and only just off-loaded. Whisked away, shipped back to the continent, no doubt, and quickly sold off to be quietly hidden. God only knows. Need I say, the war has put us in a very difficult position? The firm has always backed its colleagues. There are no risks in this business, only bad rates. Still, it's not going to be easy. It certainly isn't. Carrington is one of our fast-dwindling links with the Continent. Most of our chaps have already been called up. Tom has an American passport, the eye and mind of a hunter. Go and see Lutoslawski for yourself. Let me ring Tom and tell him you're coming. Yes, I think that would be best under the circumstances. We'd like to have you on our side.'

*　　*　　*

Lowestoft is on the Suffolk coast. Tommy stood at the far end of that platform in the greying light of a grey day in that third week of November 1939. I remember that his overcoat was of a flecked beige tweed, that the collar was up, the fedora pulled well down against the wind, and that his hands were in the pockets. I think then that he thought he had lost me. I knew I feared I'd lost him.

'Lily, it's good of you to have come. Did the kids mind it very much? They're okay, by the way. I've only just spoken on the phone to Arthur Martin and his housekeeper.'

'Why didn't you tell me you'd taken that box? Oh, for sure, I can understand why you took that tiara, Tommy, but Jules . . . Did you not ask yourself what he would do to me when he found out, even though he must have stupidly bought it on the sly?'

'I'll take it back to him. We'll let him keep it because it's not the one we want.'

He took the shopping bag from me—I'd managed to buy a few things in London. Still distant from each other, we walked into town. Lowestoft was a seaside town, though not so popular as Blackpool or Brighton, but the war was everywhere in signs, warnings, places one could no longer go, shore batteries, too, the Royal Navy. We finally found a small restaurant. Over chowder, bread, and tea, I still couldn't face him.

'Lily, please. If I could have told you, I would have.'

'When did you first know I might be connected to that thing?'

The breath went out of him. 'At that shop on the rue du Faubourg Saint-Honoré. There was a ring from the Lutoslawski collection in that grab bag of stuff Langlois had placed in the window.'

The things in that silver tazza. Breaking bread into my soup, I nodded curtly. 'So you used me, is that it?'

'I didn't know you then, or even if we'd ever meet again. It was business, Lily. What else was I to have done?'

Business . . . How many times is that excuse given? 'Then after having said we must always be straight with each other, you admit you lied to me?'

He set his spoon down. 'Can you ever forgive me?'

'Arthur mentioned a secret compartment in that car of yours, a smuggler's hideaway. I've not yet had a chance to ask my son where it is.'

Tommy caught up with me. I had even left my purse behind. 'The compartment's under the rubber mat in the trunk. You have to take the mat out first. There's a spring release at the side of one of the rear lights. The left one. You push it in and the lid pops open. It's an old rum runner's trick, but lots of custom's clerks search like crazy, so I always have a wad of cash handy.'

'And the available space?' I asked angrily.

'Enough to hold several paintings in their frames. Lily, they didn't just steal the tiara. The firm stands to go into bankruptcy unless we can recover the goods.'

'Use a thief to catch a thief, eh, is that it? And what am I supposed to do if Jules tells the Sûreté I ran off with his fake and all those other bits and pieces of his father's mistress?'

'He won't for that very reason. Come and meet Nicki. He's not just anybody. He wants to tell you his side of it. At least do that before you make up your mind.'

It was sad to see a proud man in defeat, too old to fight a modern war, too young to die without caring. Even at the age of sixty-two, Alexis Nikolai Ivanovich was still extremely handsome. One automatically thought of kings at court and of men in uniform. My first sight of him, however, was through the mizzle down a forest lane that was flanked by fir trees. There were two greyhounds with him, and these had lifted their heads to stand sculpted at our approach.

Caught in that moment, Nicki was totally unaware that he was no longer alone. He wore the high black boots of a cavalry officer, the tucked-in, rough brown corduroy trousers, coarse linen shirt, and open leather jerkin of a peasant. No hat, no cape—I don't think he ever cared much about the weather, certainly not in the years I was to know him.

His fist closed about a branch. He broke off a bit, crushed the needles, and brought them up to his nose, a man remembering. A pea cast out of its jar to roll uneasily on the floor of England.

The fens, the bogs, and the forests of Suffolk did little to ease the isolation but only served to give poignant reminders of home, of a place I'd never heard of—lands halfway between Biala Podlaska and Pinsk, to the east of the Bug. A place of forests and marshes, of mud, horses, and few if any roads. One of sleighs and sleigh bells in the frozen night of a river's meandering.

Of wolf hunts that were terrifying.

Nicki had the warm grey eyes of a man who had lived and suffered much. They were widely spaced beneath a strong, wide brow and dark, wide eyebrows. The curly black hair was touched with iron grey and beaded by the rain. The beard and moustache had been carefully trimmed.

He wasn't tall, nor short—of about my height. Yes, exactly it. Eye to eye, with slightly pinched cheeks, high cheekbones, a full, broad nose and half-hidden lips. A hand whose grasp, like the rest of him, betrayed an iron will.

I remember that he held my hand for what seemed an eternity. He had a lovely wife, not much younger than myself, and his third, I think. Six children, two sons who had been killed in the war, one who was in the RAF, two who were now at boarding school in England, and one who was still at home with them, a girl of five.

He didn't speak English, only Russian, German, and French, in addition to his native Polish. Though I didn't know it then, this was to be the first of several such meetings, but in the forest, in the rain as he gripped my hand, he looked right into me.

In silence, Tommy watched the two of us.

'Now I know why he's so taken with you, Madame de St-Germain. Please, a welcome to my humble estate. Was your journey tiring?'

I remember thinking then that his French was very good, very Parisian. Hands in the pockets of my overcoat, I shook my head. 'Only strange. In France, there are so few signs of the war. In London, and in every little station I passed through, there were posters, regulations, arrows pointing to the air-raid shelters, men in helmets, people carrying their gas masks, antiaircraft guns in the parks.'

'Yet in London, the restaurants and theatres have reopened, and some of the evacuees have begun to trickle back to their homes in the city. This is a war that has only just begun, madame. The worst is yet to come. You're very lucky to be out of France. If I were you, I'd let Tom get you and the children to Montana. That would be by far the wisest choice. Distant from the madness that has yet to come.'

Even though Poland had been savaged.

We began to walk back towards the house, which was perhaps a half-mile from us. The dogs ran on ahead. Tommy moved so as to put me between him and Nicki and make me feel at one with them. This gesture he was to repeat so many times, yet each time I always felt as if I, too, was special, a bond between them.

It was then, I think, that I first realized that what must have begun as a business relationship had somehow changed. Oh, for sure, Nicki would insist that the insurance he had paid for should cover his losses. There would be no question of this, no matter what, yet for all their differences, the two of them had drawn a lot closer.

Tommy genuinely liked him, and he wanted me to like Nicki, too.

'You mustn't be angry with Thomas, madame. What he did may seem inexcusable. The tiara of the Empress Eugénie is only a small part of the tremendous traffic in great works of art this war has already caused. The Nazis are systematically plundering my country. Day by day, trainloads of priceless pieces come into the depot they've set up in Kraków. Some lie out in the rain, there are so many.'

Can a brave man stand and cry before a woman he has only just met? That one did, nor would he turn away. 'Schiller,' he said, as we started out again. 'The Obersturmführer Johann Schiller of the SS, the Schutzstaffel. In 1938, the Nazis sent art experts to my country. We thought not to trust them, and we didn't, but . . .'

Nicki paused to pluck a last wild aster that was half-hidden among the dense grasses at the side of the lane. Droplets of rain clung too it. 'For you,' he said, and shaking them off, fixed it through the buttonhole of my collar.

'But I, like others, Lily, had to greet these strangers. Two art historians travelled with this Schiller, one a Polish higher-up in the government and supposedly working on a book. My family had many beautiful things. Perhaps I was vain, perhaps a little naive, but I showed them through our house and tried to learn from them what I could so as to warn the others.'

'That's when Nicki got in touch with his insurance agents, a London firm, so we came into it as we had in the past when backing that agency,' said Tommy.

'The Nazis have their spies, Lily. Here in England, as well as in France. Often they work through a fifth column. Poles who would do their bidding, though there weren't so many of them; Frenchmen and Englishmen who are still too willing to sell out their countries. They tracked the treasures I had had shipped to London and had them stolen.'

'Nicki's certain this Schiller was behind it, Lily. Apparently, the Reichsmarschall Göring has an eye for Raphael, Rubens, Leonardo da Vinci, and a lot of others.'

'Icons also, and of great value, madame. Those from the Byzantines of the early twelfth and thirteenth centuries. *The Holy Mother with Child, Our Lady of Light*. Icons by Theophanes the Greek, others by Rublyov, my paintings by Jan Polack, and other great Polish artists. The Hellenistic terra-cottas from the third century B.C., the Roman and Etruscan glasses. Schiller, madame.'

A hardness crept in to Nicki's voice that I was to hear again and again. 'Not in uniform, so of course he claimed he wasn't of the SS but of an insurance firm my family had once used. Thirty-two years old, blond, arrogant, tall, and extremely handsome. The blue-eyed Teuton with a scar down the left cheek that he wears with pride.'

'A *Schmiss*, a duelling scar,' said Tommy. 'Apparently, Schiller fences with some of the Prussian nobility, but he's solidly of the Sicherheitsdienst.'

'The Security Service of the Nazi Party, their SS and their Gestapo,' said Nicki. 'Has your husband ever had contact with this man?'

'Schiller?' I managed. What did I know of the SS and the Gestapo? I shrugged. I think I said something lame like, 'Jules, he doesn't tell me everything. I'm just a wife.'

'But has the lieutenant ever visited your house?'

'The château?' I shook my head. 'Jules is very jealous of his family's estate and very protective of the works of art and other things his father left him. Please, you must remember that, in France before the Great War, there was no income tax, so his father, he could buy lots of lovely things and did.'

'Then you've no idea how your husband came by that fake?'

Nicki had done the asking; Tommy the waiting. Me, I was caught between the two of them as I shook my head, so it was then that I mentioned that last weekend with Jules and of how my husband and my sister had brought their friends: the Vuittons, Louis and Dominique, my Nefertiti; Dmitry Alexandrov, the Russian student of electrical engineering; Marcel Clairmont, also.

Nicki glanced shrewdly at Tommy as we reached the house, a half-timbered, canted, ramshackle place dating from the mid-seventeenth century. Standing in the rain, they detained me a moment more.

'Was your husband completely fooled, Lily? Tricked by the Vuittons?' asked Tommy. 'I don't know of them and neither does Nicki, so anything you can tell us would be useful.'

'Or was it this young Russian?' asked Nicki. 'Someone must have sold it to your husband, who couldn't have looked too closely and was far too anxious to lay his hands on it.'

A fake he had then discovered and hidden away with the rest of that stuff. 'If I knew I would gladly tell you, but I simply don't.'

We went indoors to shake off the wetness and hang our things in the great hall beside a roaring fire. There were several of Nicki's compatriots—the place was a refuge for them. Nicki's wife was circulating, now a touch here, now a word there.

The tiara sat on a little table all by itself. I remember that they both stood back a little as I looked at the thing. 'It's so beautiful,' I said, 'even if it is a fake.'

Neat vodka, ice-cold and in small, clear glasses, was offered, and

I took one and quickly downed it as the others did. 'Why not try it on?' asked Nicki's wife. She had such a lovely, all-encompassing smile, warm yet shrewd, a toughness, too, I was to learn much later. The thick mass of red hair was worn loose, yet stunning, the sea green eyes the most beautiful I had ever seen.

Katyana Lutoslawski handed that thing to me and I turned it this way and that, felt the emeralds, knew that all eyes were on me as she said softly in the most beautiful French, 'Please put it on for us. Don't be ashamed to wear it even if it is a fake.'

How could I have known then what I know now? I put the tiara on. They all oohed and aahed. The men bowed. Someone proposed a toast and the partying began.

I don't remember when it was that Nicki and Tommy told us of the last wolf hunt they'd been on. I do remember reliving it as if I'd been there.

They have a way of hunting wolves in eastern Poland that must be unique. In the depths of winter, the snows lie deep. The frost is so cruel, it snaps the branches and makes them creak as the moon gives shadows of silver to the ribbons of ice that are the rivers.

A freshly killed pig is drawn behind the sleigh, and the wolves come to this if not to the scent of the terrified horses. They snap at the pig, dash ahead to nip at the forelegs and tendons of the horses. One man controls the reins, the other shoots. Both are bundled in furs, and they race through the forest, laughing, shouting, drunk on vodka and excitement, the sleigh bells jangling.

'It's a way of taking wolves,' said Nicki, the nostalgia all too clear. 'We share with them the thrill of the hunt.'

I remember touching the base of my throat. Somehow the top buttons of my blouse had come undone. I was thirsty. I was hot. 'Does the sleigh never turn over?' I asked.

Nicki held me with a look. 'What if it did? Would it not be better to die like that than to live like this?'

We telephoned the children at their suppertime. I was most conscious of the need to reassure them. Marie-Christine gave wet kisses and tears to the telephone. Jean-Guy was very brave and told me not to worry, that he had been given a puppy to look after and that he was being allowed to take it for walks.

'On my own, *maman*. I don't get lost anymore.'

I let Tommy speak to them. It was he who told Jean-Guy to be careful and not to wander far from the house. He was to keep an eye on his little sister and to tell Arthur if anything was not as it should be. 'Your mother will be home tomorrow.'

Two days—that's all the time I was away.

Nicki's friends and associates were mostly fellow cavalry officers. I remember that there was a major with a snow-white moustache, a ready laugh and an eye for the ladies. The hands, too.

I remember that the talk was of the war, of a savagery I couldn't have imagined.

We went up to bed early. We excused ourselves—they'd talk and drink all night. They'd scheme and do so all over again, just itching to get back at the Nazis and the Russians.

Tommy built up the fire. There was no furniture in that timber-ceilinged room, other than a single chair and a heap of fox furs and wolf skins. Wrapped in my lover's arms, glowing with the warmth of alcohol, animal skins, and that fire, we experienced sex at its most pleasurable, and in the morning my children were gone.

'You're going home just like you did back then,' said Dr. Laurier. 'Your children had been taken from you.'

'Yes, but because of me, they're now gone forever.'

'Lily, let me come with you. I want to. I think I need to.'

It's Oradour-sur-Glane all over again for her. 'You wouldn't last a minute.'

'Must you be so harsh? It's not in your heart to be unkind.'

'Oh? Hey, *écoute-moi, ma chère doctoresse*, I've a Luger and some other things stashed in that house. Me, I'm heading for it and when I have that gun, I'm going to make them feel how it really was for us.'

'I still think I should come with you.'

'It's impossible. I'm sorry. You haven't an inkling of what's involved.'

The land before us is grey with snow. Fir-clad hills flank the mountain to spill down into a valley through which a stream flows. On the other side, the valley wall rises through a turf-covered, rocky slope to a low stone wall. Marius Cadieux is the typical Jura peasant. Proud, lean, wiry, wizened, weather-beaten, and suspicious, but able to grin about it. A man of about sixty-five or seventy—it's hard to tell—but just being with him makes the past seem all that much closer.

'I can breathe the air of France,' I tell him.

'Ice fog more likely,' he quips. 'If we're to go over, madame, we had better leave now.'

'How far is it?'

'Only a few kilometres. There's a road on the other side at *Derrière-le-Mont*—Behind-the-Mountain. My son has the sawmill. He'll help us. I'll get him to take you to the train.'

'So, it's good-bye, Doctor.'

I reach out to shake her hand. The wind is from the north and it stings my eyes. 'Please contact me,' she says. 'Telephone the clinic and let me know the moment you get there.'

She's so innocent really, a lot like Michèle but much older, and again I have to tell her, 'Don't go back. Not for at least a fortnight. Ring up Zimmermann if you must, but don't, for any reason, let him know where you're staying.'

'I have my other patients, Lily. If I'm not going with you, then I have to go back.'

How many times was I to hear people say to me that they had to go back, how many times was I never to see them again?

'Please don't. Please just listen carefully. Dupuis wouldn't be so anxious were it not for the crimes he committed. He and the Ober-sturmführer Schiller always worked together, and what the one didn't know, the other did. Both would kill you without hesitation.'

'Then why go after them?'

'Because Schiller can't possibly be there and the others never worked that way with Dupuis, so I'll have him all to myself.'

'Telephone the clinic. Let us know how you get on. Promise me you'll keep in touch. The war's over, Lily. It's time to let things lie. It's time for the healing to take place.'

She's so earnest, I know she's grown very fond of me—a mistake one must never make if one is to survive.

'Send that cable to Dr. André de Verville as I've asked you to.'

'What about that firm in London? They were going to get back to us today.'

She can't bring herself to let go. Another mistake one must never make. I look back at her. 'Forget about them. *Ah, mon Dieu,* Doctor, don't be such an idiot. Go into hiding for a little like I've asked you to. Give me a chance to settle everything.'

We reach the stone wall. I'm all out of breath from such a climb. Cadieux says, 'Are you ill or something?'

I shake my head. 'Just tired.'

She's still standing there watching us. Not a wave, not a last gesture of farewell. Just a lonely woman on a hillside with the mountains all around her.

4

'The Louvre, please. The office of Middle Eastern Art and Antiquities, Egyptian desk. A Madame Dominique Vuitton. Yes . . . Yes, of course I'll wait.'

Those dusty back corridors will ring with her steps. The confusion at the Gare de Lyon is the usual—streams of hurrying, indifferent people, trains coming, others leaving. Paris again—I can't believe I'm really here.

From Besançon I caught the train to Dijon, and from there to here. *Ah, mon Dieu,* the destruction along the way. Locomotives on their sides, tracks ripped up—delays and delays while the work crews repaired things. Whole villages in ruins, parts of towns but shattered shells. A country awakening from the ravages of war, but I must confess, the sight of locomotive boilers ripped apart still continues to excite me. A fistful of properly placed plastic can do a lot. You mould it against a bearing housing out of sight. It's just like bread dough. You make a rope and tuck it up against a rail . . .

'Madame . . . madame, this is Lily. I thought you'd like to hear from me personally.'

As with Dupuis and Jules, there is a momentary silence as she wonders if the sound of my voice is correct, but finally says, 'You can't be Lily de St-Germain. She died in a concentration camp.'

'Oh? Which one, please?'

'Bergen-Belsen.'

The acid's there, and I let her hear the traffic in the station. 'Madame, you and the others are to meet me at the house. That's where things began, and that's where they'll end.'

'Dupuis has gone to Zurich.'

'Good!'

'You're crazy. We'll never agree to meet you.'

'Madame, the Résistance and its tribunals may have cleared you for lack of evidence, but I've come back to put the icing on the cake. You've a choice, *n'est-ce pas*? Either we meet at the house, or I go directly to them now.'

'Where are you?'

'Which station do you think?'

I leave the receiver dangling. I pick up my little cardboard suitcase and walk away from the counter of this bar, on which I found the telephone and purchased the still necessary *jeton* for the call. There are no SS hanging about, no plainclothes Gestapo, either, or *gestapistes français*, and this I can't understand at first. Just Parisian *flics* with their hem-leaded capes and white, leather-covered, lead-weighted truncheons, and those boys, they're the same as ever. Not dampened at all by what happened and what they did to help it happen. You'd think they'd all been in the Résistance, just like everyone else.

The taxi driver sucks on a dead fag and gives me a disdainful look as if I didn't have a sou. This hasn't changed much, either, but he's had to put up with operating a *vélo-taxi* for four years, so there's a hint of humbleness when he realizes I might have suffered and actually been in the Résistance.

We negotiate. Me, I don't want to waste money, but time is essential and the request a little unusual. 'I'll pay you in Swiss francs, which you can readily exchange on the black bourse for American dollars.'

'Get in.'

I've hit the right nerve. He won't say another thing. In silence, I'll close my eyes and talk to Michèle and Simone, to Tommy especially and to the others. I'll say, Hey, *mes amis*, I'm finally going home.

From Milly-la-Fôret, the road runs east into the forest, winding a little past some hills and valleys where the aqueducts are quite clearly seen below and to the left. We climb a little more, reach the hill called the "mountain," *la montagne,* and finally turn towards Arbonne. Then it's east again and on to Fontainebleau. Every tree and hill and rock and valley bears a name, for the French pride themselves in calling each part of their wilderness something apt and lovingly descriptive. It was the winter of 1940 when I made this same journey with Tommy, dusk already, just as now, but then there was snow, and among the trees I knew there would be no other sound but its soft falling. A hush that was and still is so beautiful.

Tommy was at the wheel. Two months it had taken us to leave England. The British—my God, they could be stubborn. The Winter War in Finland was the excuse. The Russians and the Finns, the Nazis waiting.

Through the long tunnel of the forest, the road ran beneath branches to which the snow clung, and that, too, was beautiful, but there were ruts in the road, those of the woodcutters' wagons. I searched, I hunted for something more to still the aching in my heart, for we'd hardly spoken.

'Stop! Stop here.'

'*Jésus merde alors,* madame, are you crazy,' exclaims the taxi driver. 'There's nothing here.'

'There *is*! Please just do as I've asked.'

He swings the taxi round and leaves me at the side of the road with a flute of the lips and a kiss of three upraised fingers.

I wait until he's out of sight, then let the forest come back to me, the scent of it, the autumn feel that is now almost winter—in late November 1945 not January 1940, though, as it was when Tommy said, 'Lily, please don't do this. Let me come with you.'

I had shook my head. Snowflakes melted as they hit the windscreen. 'For us, it's over. I have to be with my children.'

'Your husband mightn't let you stay.'

'Even though it's a fake, he wants the tiara back, and the rest of that box of his father's mistress. This he has agreed to in exchange for my returning it.'

Tommy knew that to say he was sorry was senseless, but he did try to say something and I should have let him finish. 'Lily, that tiara . . . Jules might . . .'

'Hurt me? Why should he, please, if it's worthless and I'm bringing it back?'

'Anger. Pride. Talk—I can give you lots of reasons. Fear for one. Fear of what I might now do.'

'The police, the Sûreté?' I said, reaching for the door handle. 'He doesn't know what you do, so why should he think you'd be interested in that thing or that you even know of it? He never once blamed you for having stolen it from him, only me.'

As I walked away, I knew he was watching. At first, I refused to turn to look back at him, but then I did, to see him raise an open hand, a last gesture, a final farewell.

The tall iron gates have ice-cold spikes like bars! I clutch them. I stand here looking off towards the house I once called a château. The lawns are all overgrown, the grasses tangled. Some of the shutters have been closed but are splintered—smashed! One swings and bangs in the wind. What glass there is reflects the autumn shadows of the late afternoon.

The pockmarks of bullets are sprayed across the coral pink of those stuccoed walls. Grenades have exploded.

I bow my head, cling to those bars, and try to shut out all that has happened since, try not to think of anything but that day, but it's impossible, for over and over again the belt falls on my naked back as, through bruised and battered lips, I yell, 'I know nothing!' Choking, vomiting, I cry out again and am knocked to the floor.

They have shaved my head and all the rest, but finally some sense returns and I hear myself saying, 'Lily . . . Lily, what is this?' and angrily wipe the tears away. '*Idiote,* try to get a hold of yourself. Ignore the DANGER: DÉFENCE D'ENTRER PAR ORDRE of that signboard. Get back to the 22 January 1940 at four on that afternoon: sixteen hundred hours, damn you!'

Smoke curled from the chimneys then, but mostly it was from that of my kitchen. My suitcase was of leather, not cardboard as now. My steps were uncertain, just as now, the wrought-iron gate stiff with the frost, though, not rust. It wouldn't close behind me then and it doesn't want to now.

I didn't go to the front door. I went round the back to my courtyard with its orange-red walls of brick and stood looking out through the orchard, already deep in its winter. Each tree was so beautiful, I felt I could reach out to touch the bark and be as one with it. I desperately needed friends.

Marcel was waiting for me. A line of his washing hung above the stove. Some woollen socks, two shirts, a smock, a pair of trousers, and one of underpants. A dishcloth was grey.

'Well, Lily, so you're back at last.'

'What the hell are *you* doing here?'

'Me?' He dug three fingers under the dirty red neckerchief and tugged. 'I'm simply looking after this place in your absence.'

'Where are the children?'

'Must you bristle like a wounded sow? They're with Georges and that wife of his, at least they will be when Jean-Guy gets home from school. Jules has made his peace with those two, but since he's told them you'll be back, they've been keeping to themselves.'

And in a huff, no doubt. 'Is he very angry?'

Marcel coughed—wheezed in terribly and hawked up such a wad he had to chew it before spitting into the firebox. 'Jules,' he muttered, savouring the moment. 'If you mean about that bit of paste you lifted and the rest of those things, then *ah, oui, oui, bien sûr.*'

Yet he had let me come back. I pulled off my gloves and dropped them into a chair. 'And the rest?' I asked. 'That other business?'

'Your ass.' Marcel savoured that, too, and went on, 'Me, I wouldn't know since that little sister of yours still wraps the warmth of her lovely *chatte* about his *bitte* whenever she feels the need or he does. They dine out most nights, of course, and yes, I think she might be putting on a bit of weight.'

Was there cruelty now? 'What, exactly, do you mean?'

The buttons of his flies were undone. He looked at them, then up at me before pulling in his stomach and going to work.

'Is she pregnant, damn it?' I stamped a foot.

No one could shrug like Marcel. The gesture said so many things like, *Merde*, why should I care?

'I think so. Yes . . . yes, she has that look about her. Like a croissant that has been stuffed with almond paste but before it's been shoved into the oven.'

Two months . . . three. Jules wouldn't have cared about Nini. To have fathered children by us both would have been a tale to tell all others, if only to save face, knowing, of course, what they'd all be saying about him behind his back.

'I'd better go and get the children.'

Marcel tossed his head, arching those bushy black eyebrows of his as he gestured expansively and said, 'Why tempt the fates? Why not give them a little surprise and save yourself a lot of grief? Let's have some coffee. Let's try not to hate each other. I think you need a friend, and as for myself, I'm perfectly willing to let bygones be bygones.'

'What the hell is it that you really want?'

'In return for my friendship and loyalty?' He wiped that swarthy nose with a knuckle. 'A look, I think, at that thing you've brought back.'

The tiara. 'It's in my suitcase with the box. It's all there, even the earrings that his father gave me.'

Marcel found us two cups and filled them, adding a liberal dash of cognac to both and a little more to his own. Pawing through my lingerie, he took out that box, for I'd wrapped it in a slip and Tommy had, of course, smuggled it back into the country.

Greed has a way of lying just beneath the skin. Marcel's pores were craters whose hollows were filled with black, but there were also bumps that seem to breathe, red swellings that the years and the drink had only encouraged. 'So, it's really back,' he said, and heaved a grateful sigh, still couldn't believe what was in his hands.

'Now maybe, *mon ami,* you'd be good enough to tell me how

you two came by such a thing in the first place? That's exactly as the tiara of the Empress Eugénie would be if it was real.'

He was startled. 'Me? But I had nothing to do with this. I only learned of it from your son.'

Timidly, I touch one half of the kitchen door. I rub one of the windowpanes and peer inside. Cobwebs are everywhere. Everywhere there's rubbish. No furniture—not even my kitchen table, on which I used to knead the bread dough and cut or shape it into sculptures.

A litter of broken plaster lies where I used to stand. The bare ribs of the lathing are exposed in the ceiling above. There are old rags, glass, bits of china—Marie's Peter Pan bowl, her coveralls . . .

Some pots. Splintered boards. Clots of dust. They even took the stove. Soot marks the place where the chimney pipe was torn away. The door to my storeroom is gone, but a corner of splintered shelving reveals that it is empty, and I can't move, can't breathe. It's all rushing back to me. 'Jean-Guy,' I cried out. 'Marie . . . darlings, look who's here.'

'*Maman!*' They flung themselves into my arms. Wet kisses, hugs, and caresses. They were all over me like puppies, and I was all over them.

I throw a shoulder against the door. In anger, I kick and shove, but it's useless. I haven't the strength. What have they done to me in the camps?

The coach house is empty—more debris, more litter. No packing cases. None, only broken bales of mouldy straw and brass shell casings—9 mms, some 7.92's, a blood-soaked German tunic, and forage cap. These guys were from the Waffen SS.

A rusty crowbar. I bring it down at that kitchen door of mine and hear the glass shatter, hear the sound of a Messerschmitt's guns, the explosions of its cannon shells as they hit the road, the car, the kids, and myself. God help us, everything! *Jésus . . . cher Jésus . . .*

Dust settles on the road as a stunned silence enters and the door swings open. There is a last tinkle of falling glass, a silence that reminds me of that road during the great Exodus from Paris immediately before the fall of France, but then I'm back here in time again, back to that January 1940.

We sat before the stove, the three of us. Marcel had taken himself off, and I didn't care where. I had an arm around each of them. It was very cosy and all the rest, and we watched the flames through the little gaps of the draught plate in the firebox door. The aroma of baking bread warmed us and to this was added the scent of the split pine, which crackled as it burned.

Marie tugged at my sleeve and lifted her big hazel eyes to mine. *'Maman, qu'est-ce qu'une salope?'*

For a moment, I couldn't answer. Georges and Tante Marie were behind this, but what else had they said?

'A woman who has been unfaithful to her husband.'

'Unfaithful . . .' Marie puzzled over this. She scrunched up her nose and twisted her mouth from side to side. 'Is it like animals?' she asked.

Jean-Guy said nothing but, from his stillness, I knew he was alarmed and I wondered what was being said at school.

He was not long in confessing. 'You ran away with Monsieur Tommy. Everyone says you did.'

'And what did you tell them?'

'That he was good and kind, and that he's going to come back if Papa doesn't look after you better!'

Wisdom in a child? Note this, too. Note also that my son had been placed in a most delicate position. On the one hand, there was his father, whom he still adored. On the other, was Tommy, whom he missed with a small boy's longing. It wasn't fair.

In the morning, we went for a hike. I had to see the stone tower again, had to look over the forest. Tea from the thermos in hand, and the children nestled against me, I tried to forget things, tried just to let us be ourselves as it was before, but when three biplane fighters drifted lazily over the woods from the little airfield near mother's farm, Jean-Guy insisted they were Morane-Saulniers. 'Four-zero-sixes, *maman*, just like the model that hangs above my bed.'

The one I had patiently helped him to build, that father of his having seldom been home and of far too little patience.

The fighters began to climb. Like graceful birds above the tapestry of winter, they soared. Each of them rolled over and over as they fell away and the sound of their engines gradually dwindled on the frosty air.

'*Flut . . . plut! Flut . . . plut! Prr . . .*' Marie giggled. Pursing her lips, she gave the engine noise again then frowned fiercely and said, 'Dive . . . Dive . . . *Mm-rmm! Blum, blum . . . T-te! T-te! Mm-rmm!* Look, Jean-Guy, they're coming around for another pass. They'll machine-gun all those dirty Poles. Kill! Kill them! *T-t-te! T-t-t-t-te!*'

We had had some visitors, fresh from the war in Poland, and I hadn't known of it until then, but they hadn't been Polish refugees, you understand. Marie had only picked up what Tante Marie and Georges must have repeated in the kitchen.

There's the broken head of a china doll in my hand. I've obviously retrieved it from the rubbish at my feet, but have no memory of having done. It was one of Marie's favourites, and I set it carefully on an overturned packing case to remind Jules of our little daughter. Then I'm right back there again, living in the past.

'Marcel, another cognac? Me, I think I need it.'

'You were never much of a drinker, Lily. Why not tell me the reason.'

I gave the usual gesture. 'This place, I guess. Coming back to it feels strange. Has something happened in my absence?'

'The shipments from the Louvre. The crates that are stored in the attic and in the coach house.'

'A few parties perhaps? Some new friends? That sort of thing?'

He snorted, laid his eyes on me and grinned. 'I wouldn't wish to say.'

'Then tell me of that husband of mine. What's he been up to, besides my sister?'

'The tiara? How should I know?'

'The friends, the new ones, who were they?'

'Wise men from Berlin via Poland and then Switzerland, I think, and following their star.'

'What's that supposed to mean?'

'That I shouldn't tell you but will.'

'The price, please?'

He threw more wood on the fire. 'Your trust. Your friendship. I'm not all bad. Oh, for sure, I like to fiddle a bit and borrow when I can't possibly repay, but soon one will have to decide, eh? You, me, that old whore down the road with her shrew eyes and that husband of hers with his sticky fingers. All of us will need friends we can absolutely trust. Take me on credit so that when the time comes, the bank will repay you.'

'Trust? You? *Merde alors,* why should I?'

He tossed off the cognac and reached for the bottle to pour himself another large one. 'Because, *ma chère,* your husband is digging his own grave and ours.'

'Action française?' I asked and saw him nod.

'A splinter group, perhaps. The Vuittons have this little scheme of theirs to not only return that tiara to France as a rallying talisman, but to store things here, there, everywhere, so that no one will really know what else is being stored. I may be a shit, Lily, but I'm not political. I've no feelings that way except for the safety of my ass.'

And what better way to hide things. 'Well, at least you're being honest.'

'Then I'd better tell you that Jules has remortgaged the house to the tune now of twelve-and-a-half million francs.'

'He *what*? But why?'

'Why, indeed?'

'Have the taxes not been paid?'

'Your husband doesn't think it will be necessary, since the house has been designated a repository.'

Even though mortgaged for such a sum. Charles Edward Gordon had told me that the Empress Eugénie's tiara had been bought at auction for one hundred thousand pounds sterling in 1870.

Had Jules borrowed roughly two-thirds of that to buy it, only to discover it had been a fake?

The cognac in my glass, the tiles of the hearth, the flames that ran along the logs . . . I saw all of these as I tried to figure out what it must mean. 'The Action française . . .'

'Its Comité Secret d'Action Révolutionaire.'

The armed faction. 'But . . . but that was broken up by the Sûreté in 1937?'

'Only to go underground, Lily. Just like in 1937, Vuitton and that wife of his can hardly wait until the Third Republic and all it stands for are gone.'

'And Jules?'

'Like I've just said, doesn't think he will ever have to pay the taxes.'

'Or that mortgage?'

Marcel didn't smile. I think it was then that I realized how much he had valued the friendship and encouragement of my husband. 'They wanted him to put up the money for that thing and he did, which sealed—if I may say so—the house being designated a repository.'

Even though they must then have found out it was a fake. 'And the visitors?' I asked. 'Who were they?'

At other times, that shrug of his would have infuriated me, but now I simply didn't know what to think.

'Three Germans, this much I do know, but your husband, madame, insisted that I leave by the back door like a dog of which he was ashamed.'

Poor Marcel, his feelings had been hurt, but unwittingly he had given me the key with which to unlock his secrets. I couldn't sleep that night. At two a.m.—or was it three?—I pulled on my things, took torch in hand, and plodded out through the icy mizzle.

It was strange to see all those crates from the Louvre lined up in rows and often stacked several high in the coach house. Good and dry, locked up, and protected by sheaves and twists of straw, each crate bore a number and letter boldly on one side and at the top. There was no other identification. I could only think I was in some Aladdin's cave. Rodin, Bourdelle . . . Carpeaux's *The Three Graces*, Michelangelo's *The Slaves*.

Only sculptures, you understand, because of the lack of climatic control. But there were other crates, flat ones—paintings—in the attic of the house, and wasn't that a good place to store such things? Out of sight and out of mind?

I walked among the centuries of those crates, passing the beam of light over them. Shadows fell or were thrown upon the walls and the timbers above. My breath billowed with hesitation, and I knew I was afraid, for I remember touching the rough boards and thinking that if they'd emptied the Louvre and scattered its treasures, had they not done the same with all the other museums in Paris and other cities and towns? And why, please, had they done this if the government and all those concerned believed so firmly in the invincibility of the armed forces?

Paris alone had so many beautiful museums, so many treasures—the private collections of the rich as well. Jules had his lists of those. It would be so easy to hide things among the others. Nicki's treasures—some of them perhaps? The paintings . . . Botticelli, Raphael, da Vinci, Gauguin, Matisse, Degas, and Van Gogh, Cézanne, *aussi*. Tapestries, small pieces of sculpture, the icons? I asked myself. The Roman and Etruscan glass. Collections of rare coins.

Jean-Guy was the one to tell me of the duelling scar, Marie . . . ? Well, Marie told me that the lady with the funny eyebrows and the curious beads had asked her about Monsieur Tommy.

'Is he with the police?' she had asked.

Marie had shaken her head and had no doubt rolled her eyes as she had said, 'Ah, no, madame. He is a hunter of wolves especially.'

The front hall is littered with debris. The walls are full of bullet holes. Everything of consequence is gone, even the newel posts and the railing down which the children would slide.

Suddenly, I can't take it anymore and have to have a cigarette. Shaking, my hands can hardly keep still, and I fumble with the matches, stare at them and at all the trash. The black and shrivelled gauntlet of a dispatch rider lies beside a hobnailed jackboot. Bloodstains are on the stairs, and in the litter of papers at the foot of them are the beginnings of a last letter home, dated 20 August 1944, as well as the maps and things that soldier was carrying.

Finally, the cigarette is lit, and I'm coughing and holding my chest, for I mustn't inhale. Looking up the stairwell to where the crystal chandelier once hung, I catch the head of another match under my thumbnail—I still have my nails, you understand. They've not been yanked, though why or how this could be, I can't imagine, given all the other things those *salauds* did to me.

There's now quite a heap of papers at my feet—unconsciously, I must have been gathering them—and to the sulphurous odour of the match, comes the stench of cordite, mould, blood, puss, and urine.

Agitated, I stub out the cigarette and grind it under the toe of one of those shoes they've given me. God only knows where they got them, but am I thankful for them? This I really don't know. There's a dark side to those shoes, something I don't want to think about. Not yet.

I step gingerly over that heap of papers—I can come back to it. Yes, that's what I'll do. I'll wait until they're all upstairs looking for me and then I'll light the place on fire and wait to shoot them as they try to escape.

Going into the main dining room, I even close the doors, though this is difficult. Again, there's nothing. Wine stains, food stains, pus stains, urine stains seem everywhere. Excrement has been smeared on the patterned silk of the walls where Chinese birds once sang amid cherry orchards that blossomed by green-latticed houses and pagodas.

But even so, I'm back here then, in that January of 1940. Jules had wasted no time in paying us a visit. He had brought the Vuittons, that woman bundled in grey furs with tiny silver bells dangling from the chains about her scrawny neck. The husband was in severe mink to which a broad collar, thick gloves, and a freshly blocked fedora gave a glacially added touch. Marcel was still with us, so it must have been Georges and Tante Marie who informed Jules that I was back.

They crowded into the dining room. They shoved everything aside and dumped that treasure chest of Jean-Guy's on to the middle of the table. That sea of polished mahogany had waves and scatterings of antique jewellery: diamonds, opals, rhinestones, and all the rest.

The tiara. *Ah, mon Dieu*, how anxious they were. They passed it from hand to hand without a word to me, but was there doubt in madame's eyes? There was nothing but a heartless appraisal in the dark blue eyes of the husband.

Jules left the tiara with them and strode towards me, and as I backed away, I told him, 'If you think you're going to get rough with me, forget it. That thing really is a fake, just as you told me. Royal families always had such duplicates made to fool would-be thieves. Is it that you paid far too much for something you thought was still a bargain, my husband? Is that why you mortgaged the house of your father to the tune of twelve-and-a-half million francs?'

The blow when it came caught me by surprise and knocked me against one of the sideboards. A decanter fell. I really hadn't thought he would do such a thing. 'So you got taken, eh?' I shouted. 'Well, I'm glad, my husband. Glad, do you understand?'

'Smuggled out of France and then smuggled back in, was that it?' challenged Madame Vuitton.

Jules demanded to know who Tommy worked for and were we still in love, and I told him that business was finished the day he himself took the children from me, but that I would tell him nothing else.

He gave me a little smile that was not only swift but also vengeful, but was there a hint of sadness beneath it as well? Oh, for sure, we'd fought before. Lots of times, but nothing like this.

I think he knew it, too, for he said, 'You may think you're tough, Lily, but I'll tell you right now, you're not. And as far as you and I are concerned, we're finished. I'll let you stay here with the children, but only if there's no more trouble. One more attempt to leave with them, and the police will be notified.'

'Even though you're guilty of having purchased stolen property, something I'd be sure to tell them?'

'She will, Jules!' hissed that woman. 'She's already done us enough harm!'

'The children are mine, Lily. Under French law, and that of the Church, you can do nothing.'

'What about that thing?' I asked. 'Just what is it that you three intend to do with it? Give it to the Comité Secret d'Action Révolutionnaire of the Action française, eh?'

Struck by this accusation, my husband backed off. 'Marcel should say less and think more about it before he does.'

I was left alone with Vuitton and that thing; they even closed the doors on the two of us.

'Well, Lily, I must say I'm surprised you came back.'

I held my throbbing cheek. 'Since you don't have children, you couldn't possibly understand.'

This reference to the couple's infertility was ignored. 'Is it that you and that lover of yours are wondering what happened to all the other things from the robbery in which this was taken, and who helped us to get it?'

I didn't answer. He fixed a loupe to one eye and picked up the tiara. 'You know far more than you should and that is very foolish of you. To be British at a time like this . . .'

'To be trapped without French citizenship—is this what you're implying?'

The loupe was lowered. 'I'm merely suggesting that, in view of what could well happen to France and very soon, it would be wise of you to be careful. My wife has many powerful friends. She can help Jules a great deal. You'll be safe here. Nothing will happen to you and the children. Why not be sensible? Tell us everything you know. Is that too much to ask? This lover of yours . . . he's not here to protect you, is he?'

Returning to the tiara, his scrutiny with the lens lasted several minutes during which he said nothing. Of medium height, but bulking large because of the fur coat, he had the pallor of the senior civil servant, the blotches too much childhood exposure to the sun can bring in later life, and a habit of hunching his shoulders forward while concentrating on something.

As he set the tiara aside, he said, 'Perhaps we should take a little ride in the morning. Yes, that would be best, I think. I'll suggest it to your husband.'

Marie's bedroom is the first, and the hardest, for me to enter. There's no glass in her window, only the splintered sash. An empty satchel lies discarded in front of it, a toss of spent cartridge casings amid the strewn plaster where once a man laid with his gun.

I step a little closer, come finally to rest my hand on the side of that window. Always, I will remember the softness of Marie's hair against my cheek, the way she turned to look questioningly at me. They weren't going to use one of the cars. Instead, they'd found a glossy black open sleigh, the relic of some family fifty years ago, and that could only mean we wouldn't likely be taking the well-travelled roads.

The horses were frisky and weren't from any nearby farm, either. Marcel held one of them by the bridle, and as he fed it a dried apple, he looked up at me past Madame Vuitton, who ignored him completely, as did the husband.

Since Jules knew how to use the reins, he got up front but sent Jean-Guy to tell us it was time to go. Even in the depth of winter, Dominique Vuitton wore mascara, rouge, and lipstick. Eyeshadow— the kohl of the Egyptians? I asked myself. The lips were tight, and I was made to feel shabby in my overcoat and mittens, having forgotten to bring my scarf and toque.

It was Marcel who handed me his own. 'Remember what I said,' he said, and we two looked at each other while she wondered about us, as did that husband of hers and my own.

But all too soon we were out of sight of the château, and I found myself asking had Marcel tried to warn me of something? Only once more did Dominique Vuitton bother to look at me. The painted eyebrows arched; the prominent cheekbones, high and slanting away, gave ridges to the narrowness of her face, the knife of hardness to her expression. She was like the madame of a brothel who was surveying an object that must please a wealthy client but who had her doubts.

There were many side roads. Most were deeply rutted by the logging wagons of winter, but just before Arbonne, there was one that cut through the forest to the *buttes,* to flat-topped hillocks with steep sides. Jules took us there. It was very private, very quiet except for the snorting of the horses.

We all got down. Snow overwhelmed my shoes, and I worried about the children losing theirs, for it was deep and more had begun to fall, but even then I couldn't have suspected what was about to happen.

Firmly, Vuitton took the children by the hand. Vapour billowed from the nostrils of the horses. Jules gave me a look I was never to forget.

'We have to have the truth, Lily. Exactly who was this man you ran off with, who does he work for, and how much did you tell him about what's being stored at the house?'

'He's a salesman of sheet music from Chicago.'

'What are he and his friends planning?'

'I'm not telling you or the Vuittons anything. We're finished and you've said it yourself.'

Curtly, he nodded. 'You're to wait here with the sleigh.'

'Me?' I looked around. I remember saying, *'Ah, non . . .'* remember thinking I'd better run, but they came out of the woods, all with double-bladed axes. Some were older than the others, but all wore the blue denim jackets and dungarees of woodcutters. Some had not shaved in days, others not in years, and the snowflakes clung to them.

Vuitton waited at the edge of the clearing with my children. That wife of his looked back. My husband said, 'Lily, I'll ask you once again.'

Then he, too, walked away, and I felt myself come up against the sleigh.

*   *   *

Frost ringed the glass of the big French windows of my kitchen. Beyond the courtyard shadows, moonlight bathed the orchard. It made the snow crystalline, and as I touched the glass, I stood there in my robe and pajamas. There were no slippers on my feet. The tiles were freezing, but I didn't care.

The deer had come again to forage. Timidly, they moved among the trees, and I knew I should scare them off. Each nibble was at least a pear or two or more in season, an apple, or a plum, but I couldn't do that because for me it was a ritual of healing. The robe fell open, the cold washed in, but I couldn't move.

There were five does and a buck whose winter could be his last. The tip of my nose touched the glass, fogging it with my breath. I took a chance and carefully rubbed the fog away. The deer were so graceful. One even stood on its hind legs. February 1940 had been bitter—harsh in the forest. Cruel!

My love went out to them and they, in turn, sent theirs back to me. No hurting of another, not with them. No ganging up to beat and punch and kick and rape. Just life and living and getting by from day to day. No sleep at night, of course. How could there be? Tears were of no use. They were all gone anyway. There were the children to care for, and nothing could be said of it. Perhaps that was what hurt the most. That and what they did to me while my children were taken for a little walk in the forest, and had to have heard me.

The deer stopped. Suddenly, they froze all motion. In an instant, they were gone, bounding effortlessly through the orchard and into the nearby woods.

I watched. I held my breath, and out into the moonlight came a man. He paused among the trees to survey the house, but the cold drove him on. He was dog-tired, had come a long way on foot, and when he reached my courtyard, he passed into shadow only to find me looking through the glass at him. He was startled—stunned to find me there. 'Go away, damn you,' I told him.

'Lily, let me in. The police are looking for me.'

He rattled the flimsy lock. I weakened. 'The police . . . ? What is this, please?'

I opened the door, and he shoved past me to drag off his shoes and things.

'Why did you do that to me?' I asked.

'Because I had to. Because it was stolen, and your husband had no right to have it.'

'You could have told me the truth.'

He asked for some light so that we can see each other better. I refused. He opened the door of the firebox, and I moved away to stand behind the table, then to back up against the wall, which became the sleigh, so that I gripped my head and dug my fingers into my scalp and wanted to scream!

The children would hear me. The children . . .

'Lily, what happened?'

How often was I to see men stand like that? Broken, stricken, cursing God and the enemy and themselves. A father with his son still bound to the execution post, a husband huddled over a bloodstained figure that lay sprawled in the street.

'Lily, what did they do to you?'

My face was crushed into the snow. Their hands were on me. One pinned my arms and had a knee against my head. Others held my legs. I tried to move, tried to crawl forward, to scream, to get away, but they were laughing at me, and my trousers were down around my ankles, my seat was up. I had told them the little I really knew, yet they still did that to me, and their laughter broke in waves that drowned as another of them rutted at me to the hoots of the others.

Again, Tommy asked what happened, but my head was bowed, and I couldn't find the words to tell him that most of all there was rage against him and rage against them.

That to tell is to fear. That I mustn't say a thing because I'd been warned not to.

Putting his fingers under my chin, he gently lifted it, gasped, drew in a breath, and held it, then stepped aside to let the light shine better on me.

Flickering shadows couldn't hide the angry scabs of a scraped cheek where the ice and snow had torn the skin, nor the blackened eye whose purplish bruise had turned to yellow.

My lips were still split and painful.

'*Ah, bon*, monsieur, now you see what my husband had them do to me. Are you pleased? That tiara we took to England was never a fake. You knew it was the real one, Tommy, but you let me think otherwise because my husband had told me it was. I should have guessed. I should have had more sense. I was just too stupid.'

'Only an expert could have seen the difference.'

'Vuitton was such a one.'

'We didn't know how closely your husband was involved. We had to find out.'

'So, having recovered the real one from me, you substituted the fake, and let me hang out the bait for the wolves.'

'Can you ever forgive me?'

'How could I after what we've shared?'

'I still love you.'

'Ah, no, monsieur, you love only your job. You're a hunter, just like Marie has said.'

He left me then. As I watched, Tommy put on his shoes and coat, closed the firebox door, and turned to face me one last time. 'We honestly didn't think your husband would hurt you like that, Lily, but then I found that his friends tried to kill me in Paris. Two nights ago, I came back to my hotel room, and they were waiting. I don't carry a gun. That's not my sort of thing. I ran down the corridor and made it to the stairs and the street, heard three or four shots well behind me, but now the Sûreté are claiming I shot and killed a man. It may have been an accident; it might have been intentional. I've never trusted some of the Sûreté's rank and file. But they've got a body—some poor bastard who was staying two rooms down from mine. The newspapers are full of it. My mug's been plastered all over the place, and that can only mean they don't want me finding out who stole Nicki's things and where they ended up.'

'Where will you go?'

'Antwerp, if I can, and over to London as quickly as possible. If not, Lyons, Marseille, North Africa, and London. I don't relish spending time in a French jail where they can get at me. Not with the connections those friends of that husband of yours must have.'

The Action française. 'The frontiers will be watched. The Nazis will help them find you—the one called Schiller, the lieutenant who's in the SS. Jules had them to the house while we were in England. Marcel thinks they must have slipped into France from Switzerland after first having been in Poland.'

He was in the orchard when I called out, 'Tommy, wait! I'm sorry I had to tell them your last name and who you worked for and what you did. I tried not to, but they . . .'

The bricks of the courtyard were like ice against my bare feet. 'Please come back. Let me hide you for a little, and we'll work something out. I'll drive you south. I don't know but . . .'

I fed him as I was to feed so many in the years to come. Full of soup, bread, and cheese, he sat there with his feet ankle deep in a basin of hot water, he to tell me that two of Nicki's paintings had turned up at an auction house in Brussels, me to tell him what I knew of the Vuittons, the things from the Louvre, and the Comité Secret d'Action Révolutionnaire. 'Their "Action" gangs. They'll destroy the Third Republic if they can.'

The Royalists and the Action française didn't agree on everything, but Tommy knew France had a fairly strong fifth column that was just itching for the Germans to invade, the old order being replaced by the new, which was really somewhat older: kings and queens and all that rubbish, or dictators who could tell everyone what to do.

Reaching out to me, he said, 'Somehow we've got to get you and the children out of France. The States would be best, Lily, a visit that's at least long enough for the worst here to have happened. No one would send you back, not then. You'd like Montana. Jean-Guy and Marie certainly would. Promise me you'll come if I can find a way.'

For me, the healing had begun, but it was much more than this—though I wasn't to have known it at the time—it was a change in our relationship from that of lovers to comrades-in-arms.

*   *   *

'Madame de St-Germain, je m'appelle l'Inspecteur Gaétan Dupuis, Paris Sûreté. Vous permettez?'

May I. 'What?' I asked as if I didn't already know.

'Come in.'

Wet snowflakes had settled on the olive brown fedora and shabby overcoat whose top button had come undone and was hanging by a thread.

'Please, madame, much valuable heat is being lost through this open door of your husband's.' Digging a hand into a pocket, he hunched his shoulders forward as if to butt me out of the way. 'My card and badge will confirm what I've stated. One can, of course, appreciate your nervousness, since the house it is quite isolated.'

Patently ignoring the obvious threat, I stood my ground. 'A policeman . . . but why?'

His was the shrug of a *flic*. 'Merely a few questions. You have a friend, an American.'

There was a black Citroën parked out front, but he had chosen to come to the kitchen door, hoping perhaps that I had not seen that he hadn't come alone. Short, rotund, seemingly looking diffident but far from it, the warm brown eyes flicked over everything, noted the children still behind me, grinned and ducked his head, the happy father figure in an instant.

About forty-five, he had bags under the eyes, warts on the left side of the rather fleshy nose that had been broken at least twice, I felt, and a small brown mole to the left of a chin, which had caused him trouble shaving that morning.

With a sinking feeling in the pit of my stomach, I took the fedora from him and waited for the overcoat, which was heavier in one pocket than in the other, an observation of mine he quickly noted, for he said, 'Put it over a chair. That one will do well enough.'

Kicking off his rubbers, he ran a hand over his thinning hair before patting the pockets of a suit jacket that must have been with him for years, taking out his pipe and tobacco pouch. He smelled of wet, coarse wool, garlic, onions, and peppermint-flavoured anise bonbons, which, I assumed, he took for his ulcers—he had that look about him.

An upper front tooth, to the left, was capped with gold, the crowns of the others stained with nicotine and too much coffee.

No tribunal would ever doubt my word. He wasn't as tall as myself, so when he looked at me, he had a way of slowly lifting his eyes as if they, too, were heavy and he perpetually tired.

Packing the tobacco down and lighting the pipe, he looked at me and said, '*Ah, bon,* madame. This friend of yours . . . Apparently, your neighbours . . .'

'Georges and Tante Marie.'

Dupuis nodded. I turned to tell the children to go up to their rooms, but he stopped me. 'Children are often overlooked in matters such as this. Please allow them to remain.'

I remember that he liked my kitchen, its spaciousness and warmth. He made a great thing of the view out over the vegetable gardens and into the orchard. He even asked for coffee, when I'd offered wine.

There were biscuits for the children, and I remember that Marie lifted an extra one for her dolls and that Dupuis noticed this as he did everything else. 'You've seen the newspapers?' he asked me.

In the wood box there were several ready for lighting the fire. One, however, was much thinner than the others, and I knew I shouldn't have saved that scrap.

Unraveling it, he said, 'All but two pages from yesterday's *Le Matin*. Children, have a look at what remains of this torn photograph.'

'It's Monsieur Tommy,' said my son.

'Wanted for murder,' whispered Marie, before asking if she might be excused.

'She wants to play with her dolls,' I blurted.

'Yes, yes, of course. So, Jean-Guy, is Monsieur Carrington here in the house?'

There wasn't a waver. 'No, monsieur. Bad people hurt my

mother, but it wasn't him, and he isn't here. We haven't seen him since our visit to England.'

I was shocked. I hadn't known my son could lie with such a straight face. Dupuis tussled the boy's hair and laughed as he gestured with his pipe. 'Of course. Now go and keep an eye on your sister so that your mother won't be worried about her.'

He listened as Jean-Guy fled. Mapping out the very room, he retrieved his gun from that overcoat pocket and said, 'Madame, where is he?'

Though I couldn't have told you then, that weapon was a Lebel Modèle d'ordonnance, one of the old 1873s with the 11-mm black-powder cartridges that would often misfire due to dampness after having been stored for so long. Since the French never throw anything out, the police, the military and Sûreté were accustomed to saying 'two shots are always better than one.'

'There's no need for that revolver,' I heard myself saying. 'He's not here.'

'Then where?'

I shrugged. Even then I waited for the blow, but it did not come, only later in Paris, in the Prison du Cherche-Midi, where I hit the wall and felt blood rushing from my nose. 'Look, how should I know where he is? He wouldn't risk coming here, knowing he was wanted for murder. He's not like that. He'd have been far too worried about us.'

'And a repeat of your accident in the woods—is that what you're implying? Ah, yes, an unpleasantness, madame. I was sorry to hear that such a thing had happened.'

'Then you'll do something about it?'

'But, of course.'

Like Vuitton, there was only that unfeelingness in his gaze. I took the coffeepot from the stove and refilled his cup. 'He's not a murderer, Inspector. Those people tried to frame him so as to stop him from getting too close.'

'Perhaps you'd tell me, then, exactly what he was involved in but first, madame, how is it that he even knew of your accident in the woods?'

'I never said he did, Inspector. You assumed I had told him.'

I added milk to his coffee, then one, two, and three little spoons of sugar, he shaking his head at a fourth.

He took a biscuit and dunked it. I sat down and told him what little I could, but he had the habit of always wanting more and of fleshing out the details for himself so much so that in the end, I realized that he knew far more about it than myself.

'So, madame, a word of caution. Don't harbour this man a moment longer. Give him up, and I will personally see that no further harm comes to you.'

He still hadn't put the gun away. Big, ugly, scarred, and looking as if accustomed to banging criminal heads, he left that six-shot revolver on the table close to his right hand so that I would be tempted to repeatedly glance at it.

'He really isn't here, Inspector.' But was there something of Tommy's behind me? I wondered.

Dupuis read my thoughts. 'Those woollen socks,' he said.

'Which?' I asked, not turning to look towards the stove where they had been hung last night. Instead, I reached for my cup, hoping my nerves wouldn't betray me.

'You'd better look,' he said.

There were no socks or anything else of Tommy's, but my response was still not good enough. 'I can have this place searched,' he said. 'Your husband has already given the authorization.'

'And has the district magistrate, Inspector?' I snapped my fingers for the piece of paper he would have to produce. In those days, one could still demand such a thing. Later, of course, the police didn't even bother with permission.

It didn't ruffle him in the slightest. Instead, he cocked that revolver and said, 'Such a reaction in one who was once so attractive, only suggests that you're hiding him.'

'Then search and find out for yourself. He left here three days ago.'

'*Ah, bon,* and this newspaper, madame? Where was he heading, if he really has left? Provence, was it?'

Even then he *knew* of my mother's having always spent her winters there. 'Spain, I think.'

'And not near Barbizon at her farm, eh? He could have walked there easily from here.'

'He said he had clients in Barcelona who would help him.'

It was then that his associate rapped on one of the French windows. Dupuis got up and went to open it, they to talk of tracks in the snow that had fortunately all but been covered. 'Those of a man, Inspector, leading here.'

'And none leaving?'

'Two sets to her car. The man's and the woman's. Hers return from where the car's now parked.'

'Then it's as she says, and he's gone from here.'

'Shall we leave you and go to Avon to check out the trains?'

That 'we' meant there must be two subordinates, the other still tramping about or already upstairs and waiting.

But Dupuis answered, 'No. It's perhaps just as well to leave him on the run. Yes . . . yes, that would be best. A man in such a position can only look back and wonder if we're following, and he might well be stopped at the frontier in any case.'

Even now, I have to wonder what Dupuis must have wanted from me, but I knew that he wasn't going to push things. Maybe they would watch the house from a distance, maybe simply depend on Georges and Tante Marie to inform.

Tommy had got into that car of mine, and I had driven him out to the main road and back, he to walk on his hands into the house and me to then walk in those tracks and obliterate them.

'Madame, I should arrest you, but as that would leave your children without their mother's love and care, we'll leave the matter for now. Just don't ever cross me again.'

A bargain, was that it? 'I repeat, Inspector, that he murdered no one. The others did, and I would urge you to have them identified, charged, and arrested. I'm sure that you will find that among them were some, if not all, of those who violated me.'

Long after they had driven away, I remained staring out at the road until at last I felt it safe enough to check if all the locks were on before going slowly up the stairs while still listening for Dupuis.

Tommy was quietly playing cards with my children.

Swallows have lived in the attic. Plastered to the roof timbers, their nests form shallow cups that are drenched with long-dried, spattered grey. Rubbish is everywhere. Not a thing of value has been left. There are cobwebs, great nets of them, and they blow about in the draught that comes in through the broken windows. Again, there are scattered shell casings. Even so, I try to remember because it was here that so much happened.

The crates were stacked or leaning against one another among the relics of my husband's family, who must have believed their secrets should remain hidden and that one never threw anything out lest those same secrets be exposed.

But Tommy was standing beside me. We were looking at the crates, and I knew we were both wondering if some of Nicki's treasures were among them. The children were asleep in their rooms, the lantern was on a chest, and light from it was reflected in the bevelled glass of an antique cheval whose spindly stand was broken years ago.

'Since Dupuis wasn't interested in these,' said Tommy, 'we can only surmise that he's not in on the whole picture.'

The Action gangs and the robbery, Schiller and the Nazi connection. 'Hence Jules and the Vuittons will soon arrive to see if you've broken into any of them, all of which means that you will have to leave.'

There was a warmth and sincerity to his eyes that I desperately needed, but he said, 'I have to, for your sake.'

'Why not open a few of them?'

He shook his head. 'They're safe enough for now. That way, we can come back. I'll talk to the firm and to Nicki, and we'll see what can be done. There must be something. Those people can't go unpunished for what they did to you.'

The attic was huge and cluttered with old and still very fine things. The light was soft as we threaded our way among wicker chairs, a baby carriage, a bureau, a washtub, a pile of carpets. There were boxes of china, lamps, and lanterns . . . The images come at me: a hat stand, a dressmaker's dummy, spinning wheel, even a sheathed sword, but did an ancestor of my husband's really go to war under Napoléon? Was he killed in Russia?

It was dark, for the lantern was now far behind us, giving a horizon that was irregular but glowed as if the sun were going down, and as Tommy reached for me, I was terrified and pulled away, but the kiss was so tender, he so hesitant and conscious of what had happened to me, I let it continue. Hands were soon placed on my hips, and though I flinched, I let them stay until the spasm passed and I felt myself pressing against him.

Dragging him back a little, I sat down on something. It was an end table. There was just room for me to wrap my legs about him, and I couldn't think of anything else. I had to have him in me, had to forget the laughter and the shouting.

In a rush, my legs tightened, for he had lifted me up and was softly saying my name over and over as I felt his tears mingle with my own. Perhaps Georges was out there watching us—spying— and I hoped he was because then he'd see me doing this among the relics of my husband's family.

Throwing back my head, I pushed myself against my lover, had to get closer and closer, had to have him in me deeper and deeper, and as I felt him coming inside me, I wanted to cry out but was silent.

The throbbing ended, the kisses lingered, and finally I murmured, 'Now please take me to bed downstairs.'

Two nights later, the children and I saw him enter the forest. He wouldn't be taking the train from the station at Avon, which was just on the other side of Fontainebleau. This much we knew for sure, and in the morning of that third day, I took the children to Paris. There were things I had to do, questions I had to ask.

Wind tugs at a torn photograph among the litter of others that have been dumped from drawers that are no longer present. It's one of the first of my children—Jules obviously having taken the photo, happier days back then—Jean-Guy at his birth, love in my eyes as I lift a nipple to his anxious little lips and feel the tug of them. Did I once possess such a gentleness?

Another of Marie at the age of two is in the bath, splashing. Always, she loved to do that! *Ah, mon Dieu*, you should have seen her.

Another shows the dog we once had before Jules got tired of it and Georges hit the poor creature with the axe. Yes, the axe!

There are others of my father and mother, from the days before the 1914–1918 war. The candlelight makes the photographs a deeper shade of amber, but the wind comes back and a sudden gust sweeps through the house stirring the dust and the ghosts, banging things and creaking others as it drags the candle flame out and I let go of the photos to remember Paris in that winter of 1940, my sister near to death. André de Verville had come at my summons. He was a very good doctor, but even he was doubtful and furious with good cause, for the concierge hovered about the door to Nini's room, and at his, 'For God's sake, Lily, do something!' I gave her five thousand francs in exchange for her silence and promise to keep my sister's room. Abortion was illegal, you understand.

'We'll take her to the hospital now,' I told the woman. 'Nothing will be said of where she lived.' It's a reassurance she questioned, as she should, but André, he went downstairs to bring his car closer while I sat in the chair he had vacated and I reached for Nini's hand.

'Why?' I asked. 'To do such a thing, Nini?'

Her eyes were closed. She was so pale. 'Marcel told me what that husband of yours had let them do to you on the orders of the Vuittons. Me, I couldn't keep the child a moment longer.'

'So you went out and got some butcher?'

The nod she gave was very slight. There were tears and these flow freely. 'I didn't want it to live, Lily. I wanted us both to die.'

'Did you love him?'

There was a brief smile, a shake of the head. 'I only went with Jules to show you what that bastard was really like.'

She'd have done it too. '*Imbécile*, you could simply have told me!'

Again, there was that brief smile, gone too soon. 'You wouldn't have believed me.'

'So he's left you, just like this, that pig. I'll kill him!'

Nini didn't respond. Anxiously, I pressed my fingers to her wrist. The pulse, it was too faint.

She had a sepsis in her womb.

At a noise, the present comes back, and I know I must get that Luger before it's too late, but am afraid to go down into the cellar, afraid of what it will tell me about myself, and can't yet leave the memories of that visit to Paris.

The Fourteenth Arrondissement was the home of Breton immigrants, of impoverished writers, poets, and artists. Most of the prostitutes there were *Bretonnes*, chunky, blonde- or brown-haired farm girls who'd come in hopes of finding work of a different sort. Montparnasse was full of them. Cow-eyed, docile until beaten by their pimps, they eyed me as I walked along the streets, searching always until at last, I found the address.

Number 7 rue de l'Ouest—how I remember it still. There was a very long courtyard with a ramshackle, two-storey house at the far end, behind which there was a solid stone wall that rose out of question.

The house had arched French windows, all but one of whose shutters were closed. There were two round windows to the left of these, and at the base of that wall, there was a heap of broken boards. Iron grilles guarded the cellar windows while a broken down-spout hung precariously from the eaves, and children played in the ever-damp and freezing cold as an old woman rinsed pots at the courtyard tap, behind which thin frozen dishcloths hung, and there were cats, cats and a dog that was afraid.

There was a carpenter's shop for the picture framing, so that was handy unless the credit had all run out. Practically all of the other windows were tall and narrow, some with curtains, their shutters open. Others were with their shutters closed, those, too, of the concierge's *loge*. Marcel's window faced straight down the length of the courtyard, and I gave it a last glance before pulling the rusty chain that would, I hoped, ring a bell.

Of course, nothing happened, and when I stood back to look up again at that window behind which some shreds of gauze hung, I noticed that half the louvres were missing from the shutters. Frost was on the glass. Icicles lined the sill.

'Marcel, it's me. *Oo-oo.* Hey, up there, Marcel!' My breath steamed. The children stopped their games as I yelled again.

Finally, a small boy with a runny nose and hair down over his eyes, handed me a small stone. 'Not too hard, madame. He's painting the lady again, and you mustn't break the window.'

The stone hit the glass. Several seconds passed until there's a bellow, '*Nom de Jésus-Christ*, can't a man work in peace?'

It was the first time I'd ever heard Marcel talk like a real artist. Even in my troubled state of mind, I was humbled.

'Lily . . . ?'

'Marcel, I need to talk to you.'

He had a paintbrush in hand, and I heard him saying, '*Merde!*' just under his breath but not under it enough. 'A moment then.'

The woman was the mother of the boy who handed me the stone. Shyly, she smiled at me and reached for her clothes. She was chunky, big-breasted, had hips and a seat that flared, was all woman. We waited while she got dressed. Marcel asked me if I'd any money. 'Just a little, Lily, for the boy.'

I wanted to say, I'm sorry I spoiled your fun, for I know he and the woman would have gone to bed later, but I gave him a hundred francs of Tommy's money. 'For the boy. Ask her to buy him a hat and a scarf.'

The woman disappeared, and for a few moments silence reigned as we sat among the clutter of paints, brushes, and canvases, the two of us staring into our glasses at the cheap *vin rouge* he had offered.

'Nini's in the hospital now. I'll ring them later.'

He tossed off the wine and wiped his lips on the back of a hand. 'For what it's worth, I tried to get Jules to help her and when he wouldn't, I tried to get her to go to a doctor.'

'I know. I wanted to thank you. Marcel . . . ?'

'Oui.'

'How deeply is Jules involved with those people?'

'Don't question things, Lily.'

'I have to! They tried to kill my . . .'

'Lover? The American . . .' Marcel nodded and set his glass aside. Again, I heard him say, 'I shouldn't tell you, but I will. The robbery was to gain them money with which to buy guns and explosives since they are no lovers of the Third Republic. Half the loot came here to Paris in a van, the other half . . .' He gave a shrug. 'Those paintings and things could be anywhere.'

'Brussels, I think.'

'Perhaps. Who knows? Vuitton and that wife of his are in very deeply. It was she who convinced Jules to put the money up for the tiara so that they could hold it out to the new France as a reminder of a heroic, regal past, once the country has been defeated.'

'Hence the mortgages on the house.'

'And his anger, Lily. They're afraid of what you and Thomas Carrington might do. If I were you, I'd take the children and try to get back to England. The *Boche* are coming, and when they do, the Channel will be closed and the door shut so tightly no one will get out.'

'Have you been to any of the Action's secret meetings?'

'Me? That bitch would never allow such a thing.'

Then Jules had tried to get him in, and Marcel had been turned away. 'Where do they hold such meetings?'

'Never in the same place, so it shouldn't matter to you, and I wouldn't ask if I were you.'

'Have you seen this man with the scar?'

'Schiller? *Ah, merde,* I'm such a fool, aren't I? Yes . . . Yes, of course, I've seen him. He was here with Jules not long after you had your little "accident." '

'Is the Swiss frontier such a sieve to the Nazis?'

'His French is very good, very Parisian. He's a real organizer, too. Probably a different passport every time.'

'Was he with them when they tried to kill Tommy?'

Marcel shrugged and asked, 'How should I know?'

'Because I'm asking, *mon ami*, not accusing you of having been aware of it beforehand. I simply need to know.'

'Then yes. Yes, I think he was, but he would have let the Action gang do the dirty work. Who was he, the one they claimed your lover had killed?'

'I don't know. Just somebody who stuck his head out of a room. They needed a body and they got one.'

'And the American?'

'Gone back to England, I think, but may never know if he got safely away.'

'Then don't wish for letters that can be opened and read. They'll kill you, too, if you're not careful. They won't even ask Jules. They'll just do it, the children or not, even them if they have to.'

'Are some of the things they took hidden away among those crates from the Louvre?'

Marcel dragged out his cigarettes and offered them, but I shook my head, for I didn't use tobacco back then.

He struck a match and let the flame burn down a little as he thought things over. 'Those crates . . .' he said. 'Yes, yes, I think they could well have done that, now that you mention it.'

I asked him about Dupuis and he said there was a good chance someone from the Sûreté could be working with this Nazi and the Vuittons. 'The Action française have lots of such connections, even within the Church.'

'And this war the *Boche* have started?'

'Here very soon, I think, but not soon enough for them.'

'And Jules, my husband?'

'Every bit as anxious as they are. He has to be, doesn't he, with a mortgage like that?'

Number 104 rue des Amandiers is in Belleville, the Twentieth Arrondissement, a place of hills, narrow streets, and hastily thrown-up houses of long ago. Originally, there were three villages—peasants, small landholders, truck gardeners, a few pigs, vines, some fruit trees, that sort of thing. Paris overtook the place. Peasants from the Auvergne came, then Russian and Polish Jews, Ionian Greeks, Armenian Communists and, more recently, German Jews.

It was a melting pot with the largest cemetery, and I was struck by the thought that Marcel also lived near a cemetery. The room of Michèle Chevalier was above the clothing shop of a Russian Jew who had taken a French wife, his third or fourth, I think, for the place looked as if he's given to drink and still wished he was home in Mother Russia.

The shop was not far from the gully through which the *ceinture* ran day and night, so that Michèle and all others there had the sounds of whistles in the night and the shunting of freight trucks.

She would also hear them on her way to Germany but later, you understand.

The Russian looked like Tolstoy but was all gush when it came to his beautiful princess. 'The virgin,' he said, fingering the cloth of my coat. 'You're in luck, madame. She'll be sitting up there all alone, wringing her hands instead of practising for the concert. She'll have counted her sou for the tenth time and realized that all things must have their price, even her little capital.'

How very French of him, but I didn't say another thing. I simply went up that narrow staircase, which seemed to reach for the sky if it could, and sure enough, that's exactly how I found her. The deep brown eyes were wide and full of anguish, her light brown hair brushed across splendid shoulders to catch the sunlight.

'Michèle, I must talk to you.'

'Nini's going to die, Lily!' The girl burst into tears and I had to comfort her—how many times was I to do just such a thing? She was only eighteen. A genius with the violin. 'Jules . . . Jules wants me to dine with him after the concert,' she blurted. 'I can't, Lily. I'll throw up all over the place.'

So he'd already made approaches! 'He has the organ of a cockroach, Michèle.' I was very firm with her, very strict. I stood in front of her bowed head and told her about Nini and my husband, told her all about the whores he must have had and their diseases, how the itch of the vagina scratches the inside of the scalp, though, of course, I had positively *no* experience of such.

She sobbed, tried to blow her nose. Somehow I got her calmed down. The offer of a thousand francs was gratefully accepted, but we both had to wait for another rush of tears to pass. I told her I wanted her to keep an eye on Janine. She was to let me know the moment there were suicidal signs. 'If she survives.'

'Nini wouldn't do that, Lily.'

'I think she might. Now tell me, please, did she ever confide in you about my husband? Not their sex life. With that I can use my imagination. His relationship to the Vuittons. Nini's to the left, Michèle. Not a Communist yet, but someday who knows?'

She smiled wanly. 'You're the older sister with whom she has always tried to compete but looked up to.'

We shared an apple, she eating it slowly as she said, 'Jules is very far to the right, Lily, but still careful of what he says to others, so I don't know what he's really after. More and more, though, he's become involved with important people in the government. Tonight, we were to dine with the minister of finance.'

'Let him give coins to some whore. You'll do the concert then spend the night at the bedside of my sister. Tomorrow, you'll take the train to Avon, and I'll meet you there.'

I gave her another five hundred francs and this, too, she took without a word. 'Jules is involved in something dangerous, Michèle. No matter how broke you become, you are always to come to me for help, not him, is that understood?'

She nodded and I placed my hands on her shoulders and tried to ease the tension. Her hair was so soft, her skin like the surface of a pearl. She was really still a child, and I wondered what would happen to her if the Germans should come.

'He has a diamond bracelet, he plans to give me tonight, Lily. It's very old—Russian, he said—but from Poland. Madame Vuitton insisted that he give it to me with her compliments.'

'The concert's cancelled for you. Get your coat and hat. Pack a few things. We'll go to the hospital and just have time to catch the five thirty. I must call Simone and ask her to take the children to the station. Yes, that would be best.'

Those eyes looked up at me. She took me by the hands and

shook her head. 'I have two solos. If I don't show up, I'll never get another chance.'

Could I trust her not to weaken? I was to ask myself that question time and again, but I nodded. 'All right then, it's fate, but don't go to dinner. If you do, the Vuittons will be there to watch what happens when you receive the bracelet.'

Michèle walked with me to the door. We embraced as dear friends should. 'Have you seen Marcel?' she asked. 'The casting of your sculpture of Nini is superb, Lily. So beautiful. It was bought right away from the Gallery Pascal on the rue la Boétie. By an American, I think. A man with a great big car.'

'And the money?' I hazarded.

'Eighty thousand francs. But . . . but I have thought that this . . . ?' She clenched the bills I'd given her. 'Didn't Marcel tell you it had been sold?'

Seventy percent of eighty thousand francs was fifty-six thousand, not a sou of which had I seen! 'Marcel, forgot to tell me.'

'Then that is shameful of him.'

Once again, I listened to the wheels of a train. The children were nestled against me. I hadn't had time to visit with Simone. If Nini pulled through the next few days, she'd live but be sterile. André had asked to give me a checkup, but I'd told him I'm okay. To miss one period is not much. The trauma of the rape, that sort of thing should make a woman stop for a while.

But how things rush in to haunt me. Tommy would have lost the car, that bit of sculpture and all the other things he'd had with him in Paris. So who, then, had my sculpture? And what about Dmitry Alexandrov, that other Russian, that student of electrical engineering and friend of Nini's?

Just give me a little time. We are almost to the war and its subsequent Occupation, and of all of us, Dmitry was the most prepared.

5

The walls are close, the house silent. As I run a hand along the plaster, I step over rubbish, picking my way through, must make no sound.

My son's room is a shambles—no furniture. That's all been broken up for firewood or carted off. Books, papers, smashed toys, and his clothing are scattered, bringing instant grief that must be suppressed. On one wall, there's the tattered picture of a fighter aeroplane that was cut with great diligence from a magazine and glued, against all the rules of his father first and then of the Germans, for the fighter is French.

The model we worked so diligently on has been crushed. Animals of some sort have been in, for their droppings are dried, grey, ash-white, crinkled, and with little hairs sticking out of the pellets. Was it an owl? I wonder.

I know I absolutely have to have the Luger that's in the cellar yet still can't force myself to go down there, for the horror of what I did is too much. Instead, I rub the glass of the only windowpane that's left, using a sleeve of this coat they've given me. Like the shoes and all the rest, I don't know where they got it. Some poor corpse, I suppose. Some poor soul who didn't make it.

I hold the candle away. The orchard is out there. My potting shed . . . I remember that it was raining heavily the day Dmitry came to see me. I think it was towards the middle of March. The exact dates are blurred, you understand, but the war in Finland had ended, so it must have been just after 12 March 1940.

Tensions had begun to climb. The army had sent two men from the barracks at Fontainebleau to stand guard at the gates. There was a notice on it, also on the entrance to the house and doors to the coach house—REPOSITORY OF THE LOUVRE. TRESPASS FORBIDDEN. TRANSGRESSORS WILL BE PROSECUTED. BY ORDER OF THE MINISTRY OF CULTURE.

The guard was changed regularly and kept up twenty-four hours a day. Me, I had nothing to do with them except perhaps to exchange an occasional greeting or offer coffee, that sort of thing. Nice boys. Shy and not knowing when or if the war would come. Lebel rifles, the old 1914–1918 Model 1886 with the small, round magazine for the 8 mm cartridges, and useless if all you had were captured German 9 mms, or the .303 leftover British stuff from Dunkerque, but I only came to know of this later on, you understand.

Dmitry had obviously watched the house for some time from the cover of the woods and had taken a wide circuit to avoid the guards and come in through the orchard.

I remember that he was in uniform, that he was drenched to the skin, and that he carried a small brown suitcase. I knew he must have gone AWOL, but I went downstairs to the kitchen and let him in, the children crowding round. Were they frightened by his appearance? Subdued . . . yes, that's the word I want.

'So what brings you here?' I asked.

The flaxen hair was plastered to the stocky peasant's brow. The faded, grey-blue eyes tried to smile, but he knew it was useless to lie. 'A little "unofficial" leave, madame. The shit that stayed frozen all winter in the latrines of the Maginot bunkers has now begun to thaw. We were forced to stand ankle-deep in it and to lie in our bunks just above it, so the whole of my gun crew simply voted on a holiday. Now maybe the higher-ups will start shovelling.'

'Or shoot you.'

'May I?' he asked. He didn't bother with the children or propriety. He took down my washtub for his laundry and began to pull off his things. The boots came first.

'Jean-Guy, some papers,' I said. 'Drain the boots and set them near the fire. Marie . . . *chérie*, go upstairs and find the monsieur two towels. Two, you understand?'

She was learning her numbers, so this had to be emphasized and every opportunity taken. 'You haven't got lice or bedbugs, have you?' I asked, only to see him shake his head.

The forage cap and tunic fell into the tub, Dmitry pulling off the thick woollen shirt until naked, he stood warming himself at the stove, the marble of his flesh hard with muscles, but chapped on the inner thighs and on the knees by the coarse heavy wool of the trousers. His *bitte* was uncircumcised and drooping, but loosely extended and long enough, oh, for sure, the curly flaxen hairs damp even there. 'I'll get the towels,' I said.

'Some cognac, too, madame.' There were goose pimples all over him. The broad back, strong arms, and buttocks were those of Michelangelo. Jean-Guy was mesmerized by the sight of him. Me, I was embarrassed because Dmitry felt he could do this in front of me, and must have heard something of what had happened.

Wrapped in towels, he wolfed the soup, bread, and cheese I set before him, and gradually the children regained their normal shyness. It was always nice to have a little company.

'Would you like more soup?'

'It's so good, madame, I can only say yes. A thick potage of vegetables, leftover rabbit stew, and chicken stock, the very essence of the marrow. You don't waste anything, do you?'

Even this opportunity to talk? I wondered but didn't reply. I filled his bowl, then decided to feed the children and myself a little early. Was I hungry? Was I eating for two? I guess I was.

Together we shared our meal. Food always helps at times like that. He asked about Janine, and were Jules and she getting on? From these and other things he said, I gathered that he'd been in the army for some time. 'Janine will pull through, thank God. Jules . . . he hardly ever comes here.'

'And the Vuittons?' he asked, looking hungrily at the bread. I made such good bread in those days.

'He's with them, I guess.'

He gave a nod, me telling myself that he knew all about what had happened to me and asking how could this possibly be: by letter from Janine, or by unofficial visit to Paris? I decided that he'd come through Paris but had chosen not to tell me.

'How are Michèle and Henri-Philippe?' he asked.

'Good, I think, but I didn't see him.'

'But you and Michèle spoke of him?'

'Not really. No . . . no, as a matter of fact, we didn't.' But was he interested in Michèle, I wondered, or worried for Henri-Philippe's sake? I simply couldn't tell.

Dmitry had a way of buttering his bread that was foreign to me. He would cut a thick slice and lay it on the outstretched map of his left hand. He'd scoop lots of butter, half-melted by the heat of the kitchen, and make three or four passes over this map before probing for pockets of resistance around the crust.

Then he would pause to examine the slice as if not just grateful for the privilege of devouring it, but satisfied he'd covered every bit of the terrain before doing so.

He had strong teeth, good and straight, not chipped or stained, and absolutely white. 'Michèle, madame. Your sister's very worried about her and unable, as yet, to do anything about it.'

'Did Nini send you here?'

'Am I not allowed to stay?'

'For how long?' I asked.

'Two days. When the uniform's dry, I'll leave.'

'And go back to the front?'

'If the invasion hasn't started by then.'

He did a strange thing then—unexpected at least. Jean-Guy was sent to fetch a jar of plum jam from the storeroom. That, too, was spread over the map as if to hide the butter before he sprinkled a few droplets of cognac over everything and cut the map into four sectors.

Presenting each of us with one of them, he said, 'Your sister is getting much better, madame, and sends her love. For myself, I was sorry to hear what had happened to you.'

We ate in silence. Marie got jam and butter all over her chin and tried her best to lick it off.

Wiping her face with the dishcloth, I nervously said, 'Have your coffee while I see if I can find some things for you to wear.'

The washroom of the de St-Germains—my God, you had to have seen it in those days to have believed it. The room was just along the corridor on the other side of the staircase and facing on to the orchard. Gargantuan, it had slabbed grey marble on the floor, white brick tiles on the walls, and the bathtub of white alabaster that was nearly twelve centimetres thick. How had they carried it into the house?

Gold taps gave water, with a brass rack standing nearby for the towels. There were mirrors on the armoire doors, glass and stained glass, the life-size statue of a standing nude on a little pillar, the girl with one arm upraised, her right knee a little forward, the left breast thrown up. A peacock was clasped like a pillow in the right arm, against which the cheek was pressed, her eyes closed. A delightful thing in white marble. Art Nouveau, of course. How many times had the old man passed his hands across her bottom, the bidet waiting?

Now it is all gone. The tub smashed to pieces like the broken shell of a strangely shaped coconut whose meat, now dried, still clings.

There are little heaps of mirror glass beneath each of the splintered doors to what's left of the armoire, and I'm seeing so many images in this room. Tommy in that tub, ripples on the surface and steam rising. Me kneeling over him, laughing, kissing . . .

Dmitry wafted bubbles. The suitcase was with him even there. He had asked for the loan of a razor; if possible, a toothbrush and a bar of soap. So what, exactly, was he carrying in that little suitcase, and why had he never let it out of his sight?

He spoke of the boredom of the troops, of their drunkenness, their depressing searches for female flesh in the bistros and cafés near the front, their absences without leave. Many times, he had heard the propaganda broadcasts of the Germans from across the no-man's land that led to the fortifications of the Siegfried Line and fifty Panzer divisions. 'Frenchmen, lay down your arms. This is a British war. We have no quarrel with you.'

I sat on the little stool we kept for such things, but there was no way I could avoid looking at him. The mirrors took care of that. We drank wine now. Red or white, what did it matter? He was a little drunk; me more than that because there was something about him I simply didn't like. 'Which side are you really on?' I asked. It was stupid of me, I confess.

Dmitry filled the sponge and squeezed it over his head. 'No one's but my own.'

'You know lots about wireless sets.'

'Merely enough to get by.'

'And the Action française, how much do you really know about them?'

'Enough to keep my nose clean, madame, but if you're thinking I'm interested in that little bauble of your husband's and the Vuittons, forget it. I only want to survive what's coming.'

'So why the interest in the contents of my attic and the coach house?'

I had found him in both places.

The shoulders lifted, the sponge came up again. 'Janine told me to take a look.'

Did she keep that suitcase for him in her room? I wondered, but told him not to leave a lot of water on the floor.

'Don't you want to use the bath?' he asked.

I hesitated—it took a lot of wood to heat that boiler. He looked at the statue but didn't smile. Me, I thought I knew what he wanted and said no.

Later . . . how much later was it? One, two, maybe three o'clock in the morning. Just like now. There was a noise in the cellar, a scraping that drew me because it was so furtive. Rats? I wondered.

I had a candle then, too. In the wine cellar, there are broken bottles all over the place, but those were not broken then. But now I set the candle down and begin to pry at the wall. It took me five days of periodic searching to find this block of stone he'd removed. A space had been hollowed out behind it.

There were two French army service revolvers wrapped in oil-cloths—Lebels, the Modèle d'ordonnance 1873—several boxes of the old black-powder, 11 mm cartridges, and a German Luger pistol, the 1908, 9 mm semiautomatic—yes, that's the one that's finally in my hands—but I couldn't understand back then how he had come by it and the others. Stolen, the Lebels, yes, of course, but had he crossed the lines and killed a German officer to get this Luger? He could have, I was certain, but had he bought it perhaps?

There was a black leather wallet with snapshots of a blonde-haired girl of twenty. Papers and a passport gave the name of Daniel Albrecht, an electrician of German descent from Strasbourg in Alsace. The membership card for the SS had a number, and I didn't quite know what to do. First, because of the SS, of course. Second, because he had thought it safe to hide such things in the house. And third, because he obviously intended to come back for them.

The weapon was, of course, covered with Vaseline, and still is, and it is in its holster. I used it many times and always was able to hide it here. The Vaseline comes away with each wipe of the rag I've brought, the metal blue and untarnished, and there's a crosshatching on the butt that improves the grip immensely. It's my gun, it was my gun. The clip isn't quite full, but just the way I left it, though the spring is stiff, and I thumb this, pushing the bullets down and letting them come back. Several times I shuck shells into and out of the breech until I'm satisfied.

Then I reach into the hole in the wall to feel for the extra cartridges only to remember that I'd almost run out. *Sacré nom de nom!*

The knife is still where I left it wrapped in its oilcloth. I run a thumb over the nickel insignia of the SS, the lightning barb and the death's-head we dreaded. Once, twice, I release the blade. It leaps. It's fast. A shock hits your hand every time. Fifteen centimetres of cold, hard, double-edged, razor-sharp stainless steel.

Now I have what I need, and as the cellar holds me, I listen to the house, to the continual racket the wind produces before I snuff out the candle and sink down to the floor to lean back against the wall and remember.

Never good, the news grew steadily worse. On 9 April 1940, the Germans invaded Denmark and Norway, the Danes capitulating in four hours.

I took to fretting. There had been no word from Tommy. Day by day, I felt I might have to leave France in a hurry. I packed two suitcases for the children, a third for myself, and kept these ready by the door. When I could, I bought extra petrol for the car, storing it in old wine bottles down in the cellar.

Food became precious. The roads south would be clogged by the fleeing. I would have to force my way northward through them to reach one of the Channel crossings. Would it be possible?

I was pregnant, and it was beginning to show. I want to stress this because it wasn't Tommy's child.

June . . . it was then June of 1940 at last.

'But I *am* British! I have a British passport!'

'I know, madam. I can see that, but you're married to a Frenchman. Only those French women who are married to Englishmen can be granted visas.'

'Visas? I have a passport. I have a house in Aisholt. My father was British and a veteran of the Great War, damn it!'

'Madam, there's no need for blasphemy. I assure you everything that can be done is being done.'

'And you won't let us leave the country?'

To him, I had cast my lot with the French who had broken and run from the Germans, so now I could bloody well put up with them! 'I'm afraid that's impossible.'

'Listen, you, I have two children. I'm nearly four-and-a-half months pregnant.'

The assistant secretary at the British Consulate in Paris twisted the ends of his moustache. 'Look, even if I were to do as you wish, I very much doubt you'd reach the Channel. The roads are clogged with refugees from Belgium and the north of France. They're being bombed and machine-gunned—strafed, damn it—just as is everything else.'

'I must go south, back to Fontainebleau and the house?'

'It would be best. Find your husband. He really ought to be with you. Now there's a good girl, eh? Next? Who's next?'

'*Salaud!* You have condemned me and my children to death!'

The City of Light was silent. Not a soul walked the streets, not a car passed by. All along the avenue Victor-Hugo and then down the Champs-Élysées there was no one. The cafés were all closed. Even the police seemed to have left, the pigeons, too. In Place de la Concorde, wind stirred the dust as I stopped to check for traffic. There was none.

Everyone had fled—nearly two million. Not the poor, of course, but everyone else who could. André de Verville and a Jewish colleague were the only ones left in a hospital with twelve hundred patients. Simone had gone to help them.

I drove through the empty streets. South of the city, the main roads were all blocked with every imaginable kind of vehicle. The wealthy and the middle class carried their birds in cages, their dogs, their goldfish. Some had mattresses on top of the cars to protect them from flying shrapnel and cannon shells. They honked, swore, cursed, and the line of traffic crept ahead. Others came from behind, and soon our little car was swallowed up.

Jean-Guy and Marie lay on the floor in the backseat, covered by blankets. They complained of the heat, the darkness, and of thirst while I shouted at them to be quiet and concentrated on the traffic.

Fresnes came up. We had made it to the prison, but even the guards had left, and though I couldn't hear the prisoners crying out from their cells, I imagined it. The car began to overheat. Anxiously, I watched the gauge and gripped the steering wheel. When the sound of aeroplanes came, everyone else ran screaming from their cars, but the planes flew overhead, dark shapes against the sky. Me, I was simply far too petrified. Late that night, having been in the driver's seat for more than nine hours, I managed to draw to the side of the road. Out of fear of losing our place, out of necessity, I had wet myself several times. The children had done the same and worse, but were now so exhausted and overcome by fumes that I had to drag them from the car and make them lie on the grass. As I went to get water, the child within me gave a wrench. I cried out and gripped my back, hung on to the pail, and shut my eyes.

The spasm passed.

We were near Grigny late in the afternoon of the following day. I would try for the farmhouse of my mother, would never make it even to Fontainebleau, but again people ran from their cars or tossed their bicycles aside and raced for the fields. This time, the furious *tac-k-tac-k-tac* of the machine guns ripped along the road, and I yelled at the children to hide themselves, but from all around me came the sounds of shattering glass and ripping metal. Rag dolls fell in the adjacent fields or were tossed to the road. People screamed hysterically, cried, wept, and huddled.

When the Messerschmitt Bf 109s had passed, those that could picked themselves up but hesitated uncertainly. By a stroke of luck, the little Renault hadn't been touched. I was near to the edge of the road. The ditch was shallow and wide, the field beyond it flat. In the distance, a side road ran parallel to us.

'Hang on!'

The car wouldn't start. Again and again, I tried it. Petrol, were we out of petrol?

The engine caught at last and I drove into the ditch and across the field. Racing along the side road, we passed the traffic. I took a left, another and another, went east towards the Seine only to be forced to the right, the right!

Back at the *route nationale*, I nudged our way into the traffic again as the day began to cool and the sun to set, and when the German fighters returned, I pulled the children out of the car and ran like everyone else, but the scream from the Stuka was petrifying. Nailed to the earth, I gripped the children and fought to shut out the sound of that siren. Jean-Guy was huddled beside me. Marie . . . Where was Marie?

The *tac-k-tac-k-tac* of the machine guns faded, but by then the sound of the bomb had come rushing back to engulf me. 'MARIE! MARIE!' I cried.

Knees . . . I must bend my knees. I must push hard. 'Jean-Guy . . . Jean-Guy . . .' I gave a scream, the first of many.

It's morning now, and Dupuis, my husband, and the others haven't come for me yet, but I know they will. The last leaves are falling from the pear, plum, and apple trees in the orchard behind the house. Dark red to brown or yellow, each leaf is different, unique, yet all are the same. They lie on top of the rabbit hutches, have been swept into corners here and there. Against the grey-white, sun-bleached wood, they look so beautiful but, of course, the rabbits are no longer here and the cage doors have been left wide open.

I used to feed those leaves to my rabbits. In an apron, old skirt, socks, boots, beige cardigan, and faded blouse, I didn't play favourites. One couldn't afford to.

There were five rabbits, and when I came to the buck, which had all the pleasures of mating and none of the responsibilities, I withheld the leaf but only for a moment. His dark blue eyes gazed dumbly at me. He was white and black and rusty brown, with big, floppy pink ears, and I wanted so much to call him Hitler.

Instead, I would summon a tired disinterest and tell him, 'Someday we're going to eat you.'

I had bought him in the market at Fontainebleau, had paid far too much, but even then, in those first few weeks, I had known how essential he would be. That part of me had remained practical—the no-nonsense Lily, sharpened, yes, by the years of practice Jules had given me.

The other part was already dead. Jean-Guy and I would feed the rabbits and kill them one by one. If a doe didn't produce, she'd be the first to see the pot. One quickly shaved life down to its essentials.

France . . . What had happened? The château was in the Occupied Zone, nearly three-fifths of the country and the whole of its northern part. One needed a permit to do almost anything. One couldn't go near the English Channel or Atlantic Coast, nor Belgium, Switzerland, or Italy, or into the Pyrenees to Spain, et cetera. All of these frontier areas were in what was known of as the Forbidden Zones, the *zones interdites*.

There were regions within regions, and each of them in the *zone occupée* was under German military control. Those people had needed offices, and they had had to be billeted. I could understand this, but why had God insisted I look after three of them?

There were windfalls lying about, the last of the pears. Each of the rabbits got one—sliced with my Opinel, the peasant's standby, which never seemed to leave me then. Sliced so as to be pushed through the gaps in the wire.

The buck saved nothing for a hungry moment. Neither did any of the does. They ate constantly as if there would never be a tomorrow, just like prisoners would, something I came to know only too well.

'*Maman?*'

'*Oui?*'

'I've made something for Marie. It's a doll's house.'

'Jean-Guy, you're sister's dead.'

'NO, SHE ISN'T! SHE RAN AWAY!'

I grabbed him by the arm and shook him violently. '*Dead!* Did you hear me? We saw the cross. They buried her in that field along with the baby.'

The rabbits watched, chewing all the time while Jean-Guy's dark eyes blazed in tearful rebellion. 'Marie wasn't wearing a dress!' he blurted. 'She was wearing her brown overalls! I saw her!'

I wanted to slap his face. As always, my eyes rapidly misted at the mention of Marie, and I turned quickly from him. 'Don't you dare give me hope!'

There were thousands missing—displaced people all over the country. Advertisements in every newspaper, but I was always like this to Jean-Guy. I wouldn't go in search of Marie. I *wanted* to believe his little sister was dead.

'Forgive me, please. I'm so tired today, I wish I could just go to sleep.'

'You're always tired. You're not any fun. Make us some loaves of bread. Make Marie an elephant. Use the Germans' flour!'

Believe, hope, pray. Let him have his little dream even if it hurts.

He was growing tall, was thin, was all I had. I smothered his jet-black hair with kisses, caressed his cheek, and let my hand linger on a shoulder. 'All right, but first, could you look after the house? I need to be by myself. Let me go for a walk in the forest, to that old stone tower like we used to. If anyone asks, tell them I've gone to gather acorns. That, at least, is permitted for the present.'

'Rudi helped me with the doll's house. He made me measure things exactly. We first made a sketch, *maman*, and then a detailed plan.'

'That was kind of him. Now go and paint it. Yes, that would be best. Tell Gefrieter Swartz that there's some old paint in the storeroom.'

'You don't need to call him a private first class corporal, not when Herr Oberst is away. Rudi says that Rudi is good enough.'

'And Obersturmführer Schiller, what does he say about it?'

'He's in the forest again, making sure there's enough timber to make the charcoal and lumber the Reich needs. Rudi says they're going to cut down all the trees. He says the lieutenant means business and that we must be very careful with him.'

Never had there been such a beautiful autumn as in that year of 1940. For weeks on end, the skies, as if in punishment, had been clear. Perhaps God had granted the French a time of healing. Perhaps it was only the pause before another harsh winter. Oh, for sure, Paris had been declared an open city during the blitzkrieg, and I was aware that all the theatres and restaurants had reopened almost on the day of the Occupation and that there were already the beginnings of a black market. But this was all hearsay to me. Travel permits to visit the city were still very hard to obtain. Already there were rumours of food shortages and worse, and there was not enough fuel for cooking. In some suburbs of Paris, where there was no producer gas, communal kitchens had been set up in apartment blocks. Coal that used to come by barge no longer did because the Germans had seized all the barges for the invasion of England. Nearly one-third of all trains and other rolling stock had been sent to the Reich. Virtually all petrol-driven vehicles, including two-thirds of the buses, had been requisitioned solely for the use of the military or the French police. Then, too, there was the curfew, ending at five, which was four in the old time, Hitler having put us on Central European time. In consequence, the central market, Les Halles, the belly of Paris, was open for a few hours late in the day, and what was offered was pitiful. Farmers fed their milk to the pigs, and the children of Paris went without since the milk trains had also been stopped. France was being bled not yet of its people, except for the one-and-a-half million who were prisoners of war, but of its economy. The need for forced labour would come later.

Having not even noticed the beauty of the trees, I reached the stone tower, and for a moment, that old familiar excitement came, but I deliberately shut it out and sat down to lean back and warm myself in the sun. I had to think about how I was going to cope. I was a British subject and by rights should have been sent to the internment camp at Besançon in the Franche-Comté, but so far the Germans hadn't demanded this. Jules now had a very important job in Paris, and it must have been because of him that I'd been left alone.

Rudi Swartz wasn't so bad. Left to guard crates of statues and paintings that he couldn't have cared less about simply because he didn't know or care about such things, he had quickly made himself useful. He was forty-two years old, watery-eyed, a dumpling of a man with a wife, two sons, and a daughter back home on the family farm near Rendsburg in Schleswig-Holstein. Jean-Guy and he communicated by gestures and occasional words in broken German or French. I knew that Rudi liked it at the château. If he had to be stationed anywhere, it was by far the best of postings.

After Poland, it was paradise. He had seen things done there that he hadn't liked.

And the others? I asked myself. The Oberst Gerhard Neumann, the colonel?

Neumann made me nervous. It wasn't sexual, wasn't life-threatening in any sort of way, it was just that he believed he belonged and that everything in the house, apart from the children and myself, would eventually be his.

The Lieutenant Johann Schiller was another matter. The scar down the left side of his face was one thing, his association with the Vuittons another, and his knowledge of myself, never admitted, yet another. I knew that he was in the SS because Nicki had told me this when I'd met him with Tommy, but because the army—the Wehrmacht—was in control of Occupied France and frowned on Himmler due to the excesses of the SS and the Gestapo in Poland and at home, Schiller had to be careful. As a result, he didn't wear his SS uniform. Instead, he wore a Wehrmacht uniform and was ostensibly here as a forester. I think Oberst Neumann knew Schiller was SS, but he didn't let on, just kept his distance and left well enough alone.

So Schiller came and went and drove my little car, and I had to, of course, provide him with his meals and do his laundry, just as for the colonel. Rudi I fed, but to his great credit, he did his own laundry, and often that of the other two.

I must have spent about twenty minutes at the tower. I didn't want to leave. I found a pear in the pocket of my apron. Savouring each bite, I shut my eyes and let the tears come. Marie had loved pears. More than once, she had made herself sick on them. If only I hadn't run from the car. If only . . .

Something made me stiffen. Not knowing whether to cry out or not, I waited.

'Lily, don't turn. There's a man hiding among the rocks and pines below you. He's about five hundred metres from the face of the cliff and the same to your left. Just finish your pear and pretend to go to sleep. We'll meet you late tonight at the potting shed. If you can, let us have the key to your mother's farmhouse, a few matches, a scarf, and an old blue denim jacket, money, too, and a gun, a pistol or revolver, if possible.'

I didn't even think when Tommy asked for this last. Dmitry Alexandrov hadn't come back to collect his little cache. For all I knew, he could have been killed. The Lebels would be safest for them if caught, the Luger I would keep, and though it's now in my hand, though I'm standing in the courtyard behind the kitchen, leaning against the bricks, looking out through the orchard towards that shed, I can still hear Schiller saying to me, 'You were out walking today, madame?' as if it had only just happened.

As usual when the Oberst Neumann was away, the lieutenant ate alone in the main dining room, always by candlelight and always in Neumann's chair. 'Well?' he demanded.

'Is that a crime?' I asked.

He waited for me to place his dinner before him. A chicken casserole, buttered squash, creamed leeks, and potatoes, nothing fancy.

'Why should it be a crime?' he asked. 'The woods were particularly beautiful today. You went for acorns, the Gefreiter said?'

'The squirrels must have taken them all.'

He gave a half-smile as he reached for the salt—always the salt first, even before tasting what was before him. 'You could have had sacks of them.'

'Can't I just go for a walk?'

He tried the casserole, but I could seldom tell if it was to taste with him. The long fingers wrapped themselves around one of our air-twist glasses. He was drinking a Château Mouton, the 1923, had access to the cellar and helped himself, always writing the bottle down on the list so as to compensate my husband in Occupation marks or the new francs the Germans had insisted on, at twenty of the one to the other. And since the cash couldn't be taken out of France or sent home anyway, the soldiers emptied the shops and sent those things instead. Neat, wasn't it? The shortages at home were solved, and everyone kept happy since the French love to sell things.

'A walk?' he said, to remind me of it. 'Of course, yet you don't tell me the truth?'

The candlelight flickered on the scar that ran from the corner of the left eye to the chin, a glazed, long lens that accentuated the bluish shadow of well-shaven cheeks and the close-set deep blue eyes. 'There was no attempt to lie, Herr Obersturmführer. I did intend to gather acorns to roast and grind for our coffee, but when I reached the tower, it was so lovely, and I was so very tired, I forgot about them.'

Of a deeper shade than Dmitry's, his hair was the colour of ripened flax, cut short, parted on the left and brushed back to the right. 'Admit it, madame, you were there to meet someone. A lover?' he asked without a smirk or smile.

'No one, Herr Obersturmführer.'

'You must get lonely.'

'I simply don't think about such things.'

'All women do, especially the attractive ones.'

'Is everything to your satisfaction? If so, I'll see that Herr Swartz is fed.'

'*Ach,* our Gefreiter Swartz, yes, yes . . .'

I waited for him to finish what he'd been about to say, but he only shook his head. 'It was nothing. You may go. Some coffee later, in the living room. You will join me then, Frau de St-Germain. I insist.'

Merde, but the *salaud* had put the needle in anyway! And, of course, he wouldn't let go of the *Frau* business, not him. Exceedingly handsome, he was arrogant beyond words, ambitious, and totally without conscience, though I was only to discover this last with time.

A car passes by on the road near the house. I stand and wait. I hope, I pray it's my husband and the rest of them, but the sound of it disappears in the direction of Arbonne. Dupuis will, of course, be back in Paris this morning. They'll have a conference right away. Vuitton will tell him I've telephoned. That wife of his will insist that something be done. Jules . . . Jules will want to talk to me first and will refuse to understand that the past is everything for me.

None of them will think of André de Verville until the last possible moment. They'll leave him to fret and think seriously about killing himself. Of all of them, he's their weakest link, so there is a little more time.

I step back into the kitchen, try to remember how it was that night when Tommy and Nicki first came to me in the autumn of 1940.

The kitchen was all but in darkness. Firelight flickered from the draught in the firebox to touch the scar. Schiller's grey-green Wehrmacht tunic was unbuttoned, the jackboots newly greased and polished. It was 2:03 a.m., and I had thought the house asleep, had forgotten entirely that I was to have had coffee with him earlier.

He was sitting there waiting for me with a tulip glass in hand. The Walther P38 he always carried lay on the floor beside the bottle: dark green and mould-encrusted glass against gun-metal blue and the warm brick red of the floor tiles. I couldn't have known then, but now do, that the P38 9 mm is a very rugged and reliable weapon.

'Where do you think you're going?' he demanded, taking in my corduroy trousers, hastily tucked-in nightgown of heavy, coarse flannel, the cardigan, the torch.

'I thought I heard something at the rabbit hutches.' I was still in the doorway.

'What's that in your other hand?' he asked.

'Nothing, Herr Obersturmführer.' I had quickly dropped the woollen socks and heavy sweater behind a chair.

'Give me the flashlight, and I'll check the rabbits for you. It's not safe for a woman to go out at night. There are still too many transients.'

'As you wish, Lieutenant.'

'Johann . . . Please, Frau de St-Germain, it's not always necessary to address me by rank.'

'It helps to keep things in their proper perspective.'

'So, the rabbits, yes. What was it you heard? A fox perhaps?'

It had been a lie, and he knew it. 'I couldn't sleep. I *thought* I heard something.'

'Brandy . . . do you like it, Lily?'

Is he a little drunk? I wonder, and shake my head.

'Then sit down anyway. This war will soon be over. Perhaps you had better get used to things.'

'In what way?'

Again, there is that smile. 'In lots of ways. By telling me the truth, by no more late night walks without permission. After all, there is the curfew to consider.'

And it's against the law to be out there after it, even here.

'We've heard reports,' he says. 'News travels fast. I just thought I should let you know.'

'Reports of *what*, Herr Obersturmführer?'

The drawstring of my nightgown is still undone, and as his eyes fall to it and my chest, he says, 'The Wehrmacht and Oberst Neumann won't always have the upper hand. Things will soon change. Security is bound to be tightened. The Gestapo . . .'

'And the SS?'

'Of course.'

'But aren't you in the Wehrmacht, too?'

Setting the brandy aside, he takes the torch from me but lets his hand linger on mine, then leaves the pistol lying on the floor as he says, 'I'll check the rabbits for you.'

The firelight flickers. Sparks erupt from a knot of pine, and these awaken me to the smell of drying herbs, yeast, soup, so many things as I glance again at what he's deliberately left, my knowing Tommy and Nicki are waiting for me.

Had he seen the rucksack I had packed for them and left ready in the storeroom? Had he already found the food, the wine, and the letter I had written, telling Tommy about Marie and where she was buried and that Jean-Guy still insisted she was alive?

Had he found the two Lebel revolvers that were still wrapped in their oilcloths?

Touching my throat, I waited. Staring at the stove and not at that gun was difficult, but had he left it loaded? I wondered. It was a question I couldn't answer, though I knew that it was what he would have done.

'Nothing,' he said with a toss of his head and a grin. 'All present and accounted for.'

My back was to the stove, and he'd boxed me in, and I knew what he wanted of me, but he said, 'Your flashlight, Frau de St-Germain.'

Again, there was that grin. I pressed my knees together and held on tightly for I feared I was going to flood the place and he knew it, too. 'Think it over,' he says. 'Don't keep me waiting.'

Leaves cling to what is left of the whitewashed glass of my little potting shed. I nudge the door open and step hesitantly inside. There are two trestle tables, one on either side of the heavy planks that form a narrow walkway between. Shards and pots, bulbs that have shrivelled up long ago, remind me of memories I want, so many of them.

'Tommy . . .' I managed and was in his arms and fighting for his lips. As I cried, he held me tightly.

'Lily . . . *Ah, mon Dieu*, how I've missed you. Are the kids okay?'

'There's no time. I've brought you some things. Go now. Go quickly.'

'Are there Germans staying in the house?'

'Three.'

'Schiller?' asked Nicki.

I told them it wasn't safe. 'I'll try to arrange something. The stream . . . the tower.'

For a moment, we stood under the stars. 'Did he see us this afternoon?' asked Tommy, still holding on to me.

'I really don't know, but I left him not twenty minutes ago, and at supper he asked if I'd been meeting someone at the tower.'

'In that case, is your mother's house safe?' asked Nicki.

'With him, with them, it's too hard to tell.'

It's Tommy who asks, 'Can you get us into Paris?'

Very quickly, I let them know I'd need travel permits from the Feldkommandantur in Fontainebleau, and that these are very hard to get. Every second I'm with them is too many.

'What about your sister?' asked Nicki. 'Could she help us?'

I told them I could only try. 'For now, check out the farmhouse carefully, and if you stay there, light the stove only late at night. Draw all the curtains. Don't shine a light, even a glimmer, or it'll be seen from a distance and they may be watching the place. I just don't know.'

Each of them embraced me. Tommy slipped into the straps of the rucksack as I handed Nicki the duffel bag, and he said, 'Don't worry. We'll be all right.'

Tommy kissed me, and I whispered, 'Please be careful. Something isn't right. Schiller knows more than he's letting on.'

Five minutes . . . was it even that long we were together?

I had several good gardens out here, dug by hand, no horse and plow for me. Rabbit and chicken manure were budgeted plant by plant, old leaves and humus worked in, horse manure, too, when I could manage it, well rotted, of course.

Walking down the long tunnel of my orchard, picking my way through the fallen branches, things come at me hard. Tommy and Nicki, the children, always them, their shouts, their laughter, the little squabbles that were so important to them. Michèle and my sister, even Jules.

Stepping into the house, I make my way upstairs to find the bedroom in ruins. Rubbish is everywhere, no furniture, no paintings on the walls. Someone has tried to light the fire, but the act of doing must have been interrupted and a litter of cartridge casings for a Schmeisser lies not far from the darkness of the bloodstain he must have left. The sheath of his knife has been cast aside and is empty, and as I stare at it I'm right back in time. There was no sound. The room was in total darkness as I came to stand beside that bed in which Schiller was waiting. Could I do such a thing? Must I? It was seven or eight kilometres through the forest and across the fields to the farmhouse, probably a lot more for Tommy and Nicki since they wouldn't know the terrain as well as myself.

My belt came undone. I lowered my trousers, stepped out of them, and dropped the nightgown at my feet. Tommy would understand, but the thought of Schiller was almost too much for me. It was freezing. A hesitant step was taken. He had given me an ultimatum, but would he let the matter go if I climbed into bed with him?

He stirred. I waited. I clutched the covers I had lifted and listened hard.

The bastard was asleep.

Two or three days passed. I can't remember exactly, but the war of nerves continued, then Schiller was called away and I took a chance.

The Feldkommandantur was in the *hôtel de ville* along with all the other civic departments. Guards flanked the entrance, over the top of which a swastika flew. Though it wasn't yet dawn, everyone was at work since being on Berlin time in the autumn and winter meant getting up an hour earlier in the dead of night. Still, I hadn't got used to it. They would ask me questions. I would have to have a very good reason for going to Paris.

Jean-Guy had said good-bye. Lost in thought, I watched as he rode his bicycle down the street and turned the corner towards the school. Rudi would look after him and if not Rudi, then Georges and Tante Marie. I only knew that I had to get to Paris. Tommy and Nicki couldn't chance waiting long at the farmhouse. My mother would return, and that would only complicate matters further.

There were no civilian cars. Bicycles lined the avenue in front of the town hall, and I wondered what we'd all do when winter came. Walk, I supposed. *Ma foi*, I'll say this of the Occupation, it sure toned up the legs. But contrary to popular opinion, some women grew fat because whenever possible, they ate like bears awaiting hibernation. The cinemas brought this out. Always the most popular films were those in which there was a meal—a banquet preferably, and I thought, I'll wager the war will set a new style in French films. From now on, they will always show people eating and enjoying their food. Whole stories will be centred around the dining table or out in the garden over coffee and cakes. Some people used to dream about those scenes in the camps. People went crazy dreaming like that.

An army lorry passed by me, then a black Citroën with two men in the back. What might have been a busy street had the look of desolation. Still it wasn't so bad there, not yet. There was plenty of food, if not the variety one wanted, and not too much interference, not really.

I chained my bicycle to a tree and crossed the road. To apply for a travel permit, it was necessary to fill out a form and submit one's papers. These were then checked by the mayor and, if acceptable, given the forwarding stamp of approval.

Since most applications were unacceptable, you would have thought the process would have been fast. Long before I got there, the benches had all been filled and a line had formed down one side of the corridor. People coughed, wheezed, blew their noses, or puffed on their fags. Everywhere there was the odour of bad tobacco, stale sweat, garlic, onions, anise, and cheap perfume. Wine, too.

They shuffled, grumbled, talked of the weather, the harvest, of anything but the war and its Occupation. While some acknowledged me with a nod, others viewed me with suspicion—after all, hadn't the British run away at Dunkerque to protect their little island and self-interest?

Most knew of my husband and his mistress, of my rebellious infidelity, so there was this to contend with as well. Others who had been jealous of the house gloated smugly because now I was just like everyone else.

It was almost noon when I finally sat down in front of the mayor. Alphonse Picard was brusque. Shoving some papers aside, he looked across the cluttered desk. I'd be difficult, he knew. 'Madame, the Germans, they do not want you to go to Paris.'

'Am I under some sort of house arrest?'

'Ah, no. It's just that they would prefer . . .'

'But I must see a doctor.'

'Why not Dr. Rivard?'

I shook my head. 'I need to see Dr. André de Verville.'

He raised his bushy eyebrows, tugged at his moustache, gave a massive shrug at the futility of trying to deal with unreasonable women who should count themselves lucky, then said, complainingly, 'But why? Rivard is very good, *n'est-ce pas*? You take your children . . . excuse me, madame, your son to him.'

'I have a problem. For this, I need a specialist.'

'But . . . but what sort of problem? *Ah, mon Dieu*, madame, the Germans . . .' He cast anxious eyes towards the door and leaned a little forward. 'The Germans have said you're to be discouraged from attempting to leave the district.'

'Then I must go to see them.'

'No! Ah, no, madame.' He ducked his head to one side and dragged out his handkerchief. 'Please, what sort of problem?'

He blew his nose.

'Must I discuss it with you?'

'*Oui*, in confidence, of course.' Again, he lowered his voice. 'Madame de St-Germain, I'm responsible for the conduct of everyone in the district. Please, you must understand, your sister . . .'

'Janine? What's she done?'

Picard shrugged. 'Nothing, I think. They simply can't find her. She has "disappeared" like so many and that is reason enough to cause suspicion.' He cleared his throat, stuffed the handkerchief away, reached for his anise-flavoured lozenges, and got right back to business. 'Your problem, madame?'

Nini missing . . . Dmitry not showing up . . . I would have to bluff my way through and get into Paris to find out what had happened to her and if she was mixed up in anything. 'I'm still bleeding. As you know, I lost a child during the Exodus. André de Verville is a specialist in such things.'

Picard expressed sympathy but remained adamant. 'Well, why not see Dr. Bilodeau in Nemours? It's much closer.'

'His fingers wander.'

'His *what*? Ah, I see.' *Pour l'amour de Dieu*, was I making it up? he wondered. Bilodeau . . . Danielle Anjou, Josianne le Belle . . . other young girls, his own daughters perhaps? Fingers . . . Paris . . . Why did

I have to choose Paris? 'Very well, but I must warn you, madame. You are English. One false step and . . .' He clenched a fist.

As he signed the permit, I hesitated, then asked, 'Are our friends watching my house for someone?'

Picard's mouse-brown eyes were filled with sadness. It would have been much better had I not asked. 'I didn't hear you, madame. Please, you are to take this along to the Feldkommandant's office. The colonel will have gone to lunch, but his assistant will stamp and sign it for you. Two days, that's all I can give you. Please don't try to smuggle food into Paris. It's against the rationing. They'll only think you intend to sell it on the black market.'

He walked me to the door, but kept me a moment. 'My regards to your husband, madame. Perhaps if . . . if you were to ask him to explain how things are, Monsieur Jules could make you understand. Please don't give the Germans any reason to arrest you. They would only blame me and then . . . Ah, what could I do for all the others?'

I knew that what he had said was perfectly true and happening throughout the Occupied Zone, yet it still angered me, and I said, 'Besides, there's the loss of your pension. We wouldn't wish the family Picard to go without.'

The threat of losing their pensions is what encouraged so many civil servants to cooperate with the Nazis.

'Talk tough, if you like, madame, but face reality. For the moment, the Germans have chosen to be kind.'

'But not to the Poles, the Czechs, or anyone else?'

'I'm sorry you lost your little girl, but please don't let that tragedy make you foolish. Talk to your husband. Don't do anything in Paris until you have first spoken to him.'

Paris, through the hush of what was the busiest time of day, was somewhat surreal. Bicycles—*vélos*—were everywhere, their crazy *vélo-taxis,* too. So few cars and lorries were about, to see one was to experience a moment profound. That one sat lost and alone, far along the Champs-Élysées beneath the chestnut trees like a bank robber's car with the streams of bicycles passing by or parked side by side in endless rows.

Here and there, a *vélo-taxi* nudged out into the silent stream. There were Germans everywhere around Place de la Concorde—all types of uniforms. 'Tourists' mostly, for the High Command must have been using Paris for rest and recuperation, but businessmen, too. Lots of French girls fraternizing. Lots of laughter, lipstick, makeup, short skirts even in the cold, silk stockings . . . Could they still buy those? Later, the girls painted on a beige wash, drew lines up the backs of their legs, or went without. The shoes hadn't yet become difficult. Later, those things, with their hinged wooden soles, would make them sound like frisky, two-legged fillies if they didn't fall apart or jam. All the barges had disappeared from the Seine, most of the statues from the streets. The circular cast-iron sheeting of a *vespasienne,* however, still revealed the boots, shoes, and trouser legs of men standing shoulder to shoulder as they urinated. Some things never changed, but the signboard of its posters exhorted the public to be wary of strangers, to report suspicious things, to save, conserve, and be grateful for the protection of the German soldier. England is the enemy. There were ordinances about the blackout. The curfew now began at midnight, the last trains of the métro were at eleven. Most of the theatres and restaurants closed at ten thirty, otherwise people must stay the night until five a.m. when the curfew ended.[*]

I stopped to read a copy of the proclamation of 20 June 1940, badly tattered and weathered. Acts of violence and sabotage were to be severely punished, but none have happened that I knew of. Everyone was having too good a time, or so it appeared. Firearms were, of course, forbidden, but I was willing to bet that a few had been kept. No one was to assist non-German military personnel or civilians who were attempting to escape—were we to help only the German ones, and not those of the RAF and others still on the run from Dunkerque?

---

[*] Curfew times were often changed at will, though generally settled down to the above.

Though this was soon to be forbidden, you could still listen to your wireless, but God help you if you spread news that was contrary to the good of the Third Reich, i.e., the results of British bombing raids as reported over the BBC French broadcast from London.

No insults would be tolerated. All gatherings were subject to approval. The administration of the state—the police and schools, the banks, too—was to continue under the French as before the Occupation. Failure to report to work or to reopen your shop or place of business was punishable by fines, and imprisonment in the first instance and confiscation in others. Hoarding was to be considered an act of sabotage and subject as such, I guess, to the death penalty. Prison, anyway. The pears I had preserved, the apples, vegetables, even though I had three boarders. The .22 calibre rifle that Tommy and Jean-Guy had used—now hidden in the cellar, in an old piece of pipe; that Luger of Dmitry Alexandrov's that I had kept, but did the Occupier really need an excuse? Ah, no, of course not.

Beneath the notice was another. It was signed by General Studnitz, the first, if temporary military commander of Greater Paris, but it applied to the whole of Occupied France. Art treasures were not to be removed from their present places—that was fair, wasn't it? Transfers of them needed his approval—fair again?

Those whose value exceeds one hundred thousand of the new francs had to be reported *in writing* by their owners or custodians—ah, now, what about that? What about that nice diamond necklace you had kept for years in a safe-deposit box since your grandmother left it to you? Things that had been in the family for years? Gold coins that had been stashed away for your old age? Art treasures and valuables . . .

The auction was in the Jeu de Paume and, at first, I couldn't understand how such a thing could happen, for this had been the place of places to see special exhibitions. Then it was crowded with crated and uncrated paintings, exquisite pieces of sculpture, tapestries, and other *objets d'art*. There were several large collections of Venetian glass, of coins both Roman and more recent. Each crate, each piece, bore a stamp or tag with the name of its former owner and the letters ERR, the Einsatzstab Reichsleiter Rosenberg, the agency for the confiscation of works of art that had once belonged to Jews, Freemasons, and other enemies of the Reich.

The ERR was my husband's employer. Those lists Jules had made were being put to use. In loneliness and despair, I walked through several fortunes worth of art. No one stopped me. No one questioned my being there. Perhaps they knew who I was. Perhaps they had been warned to expect me.

Jules was waiting. Blue-washed, sticking-paper–X'd glass was above and all around us in the greenhouselike walls and ceiling of this former tennis court of royalty. Crowded . . . *Ah, mon Dieu*, German officers and senior officials were everywhere, but scattered among them were the art dealers and not just those from Paris and France, but from Switzerland, the Reich, Belgium, Holland, lots of other places—experts who had already sold themselves to the new order or were simply there to take advantage of the situation.

There were also members of the police, the Sûreté, and the Gestapo, though there were few of the latter at this time, and they kept to themselves.

'Seven hundred thousand francs.'

'Eight hundred thousand!'

'One million!'

'One million, two hundred thousand!'

'Two million.'

'Two million francs, *mesdames et messieurs*. I have two million going once . . . going twice . . . going three times . . . and sold to the Reichsmarschall.'

A Teniers oil on canvas, an absolutely gorgeous painting. Sold to the commander-in-chief of the Luftwaffe. At two hundred francs to the British pound, that was only ten thousand pounds sterling, or at twenty francs to the Occupation mark, one hundred thousand of those and a fantastic bargain, especially as the Occupier sanctioned the money and it was worthless almost everywhere but in France.

Jules accepted the bid from Göring's chief buyer. It was all so nice, so friendly. Handshakes all round but no sign of the cash. Perhaps that would come later, perhaps never.

My husband, how could he do this? Göring was the man whose brave pilots had murdered our little girl.

Barging through the crowd, I knocked champagne glasses aside as I headed for that monster. There was no mistaking Göring even though he'd come in mufti: that bulk, that ham-slabbed face with its pig-blue eyes and skin that was flushed. *Maudit salaud . . .*

Jules grabbed me by an arm. 'Herr Reichsmarschall, permit me to introduce my wife, the sculptress of that little piece I presented to you.'

Presented . . . What was this?

The cigar was raised but paused as he surveyed me, and what he said or did not say was completely lost, for my courage left and I stared bleakly at his shoes, knowing everyone was watching me now and that I'd betrayed myself. '*Enchantée,* Herr Reichsmarschall. That is a lovely Teniers you have just acquired.'

How could I have done this? As I watched, the lips began to move, and I saw the dampened end of that cigar as it paused before them, his smile now flaccid, his nod of dismissal curt as he turned away to confer with his art experts.

As Jules and I hurried from the auction, we passed the Vuittons, and I caught a look of utter hatred from that woman. Outside, Jules was far from pleased. '*Idiote,* just what the hell did you think you were going to do? Spit at him?'

He hurried me to a cellar office in the Louvre, which was cluttered with priceless things, threw me up against its door, and hit me three times. Blood trickled from my broken lips, but somehow I managed to say, 'Don't ever do that again, or I'll kill you. I swear it!'

That shook him a little, but he still couldn't keep anger from him. 'Lily, these people mean business! Don't you ever cross them.'

Finding a handkerchief, he offered it, but I used my own. 'How can you do this?'

At least we'd talk now, he thought, and tried to smile. 'Göring's really not so bad. He's got an eye for what's exceptional and is still fond of the Impressionists, though the others aren't. You of all people should appreciate him for that.'

A common bond. 'What I understand, my husband, is that you're engaged in a monstrous theft. You're building yourself on the sorrows of others.'

'No more than most. I've repaid the mortgages on the house. I've money in the bank.'

'And the taxes?'

I was still the same, would always be that way. 'There's no need. You know as well as I that the house has been declared a repository. It's under the protection of the Wehrmacht and not subject to taxes.'

'And is that glorious Army of the Occupation protecting the Einsatzstab Reichsleiter Rosenberg? Has the German Army legalized the looting of works of art?'

'Of course not. The military governor of France has expressly forbidden it but . . .' He gave a sheepish grin, a shrug. 'But there are those who wish it to continue.'

'Who?'

'The Führer, for his museum in Linz; the Reichsmarschall, for Karinhall, the villa he has on his estate in East Prussia; the Nazis, Lily. Even Himmler buys.'

'And you, my husband? What about you?'

He turned away to sit down behind that desk of his. 'I've made my choice. Now you must make yours, but remember, please, that one more outburst like that and I may not be able to protect you. A word, that's all they'll need. Why not be sensible? The house is far more comfortable than the internment camp at Besançon. Jean-Guy still needs his mother. You can keep an eye on things for me. Schiller . . .'

I waited, but he left it unsaid and irritably asked, 'Why have you come to Paris? How did you convince them and that mayor of ours to give you an *Ausweis*?'

A *laissez-passer*. 'When you had expressly asked them not to?'

'Why, Lily?'

'Because I must see André.'

'What's the matter with you?'

He was worried now—alarmed. *Ah, bon,* he *needed* me to watch that house of his. 'Ask André.'

'Lily, wait.'

Out on Place de la Concorde, Jules told me exactly how things stood. 'Why do you think you've been allowed to stay in the house, you with your English passport, your friends, and that sister of yours? It's only because I'm useful, Lily. If you want to thank somebody, thank Göring. He's the one who gave the order allowing you to stay.'

Göring . . . *My wife, the sculptress of that little piece I presented to you.* My sculpture of Nini, the one that Tommy had bought and that was stolen from him by the Action française thugs and Schiller.

'Make the best of things. Buy some new clothes, some shoes, a lipstick—whatever you want. Here, let me give you some money.'

There were one-hundred- and one-thousand-franc notes, several five-thousands, and all of them brand-new. If I had thrown them up in the air, they would have floated slowly to the ground and neither of us would have stooped to pick them up.

Like a whore accepting her 'little gift,' I took the money. It was far too needed to refuse. We found a café. I let him order something, but what it was, or if I drank it, I have no memory.

He asked about Janine. I said I hadn't heard.

'She's still missing,' he said. 'Dupuis thinks she must have gone underground.'

'Dupuis is an inspector with the Sûreté.'

'The criminal investigation branch. They're hand in glove with the Gestapo because they have to be. Someone's been plastering Résistance notices up all over the place and also printing a newspaper.'

Nini would do this—a start. 'She must have gone south with all the others. She'll still be in the *zone libre.* It's crazy to think she'd be messed up in anything like that.'

'Just don't try to find her. They would only have you followed, Lily. You wouldn't want to lead them to her, would you?'

'And Michèle?' I asked. 'Have you managed to break into the safe and plunder her little capital? Was it exquisite, my husband? Another virgin?'

'Your sister wasn't.'

'I wasn't thinking of her. I was thinking of myself.'

'Michèle is also missing, as are Dmitry Alexandrov and Henri-Philippe Beauclair.'

My sister's friends. But Dmitry . . .

I know I asked Jules about the Vuittons, and was he still involved with them. 'I can never forgive you for what they did to me.'

Immediately, he withdrew, was almost brutal about it. 'We had to know. Too much was at stake. Besides, those guys were only to have threatened you. It . . . it got out of hand.'

'Did it? On your orders or those of the Vuittons?'

I started to get up but heard him saying, 'Just keep the house in readiness. When the time comes, we'll be there with Göring. Then you'll see how things really are.'

'And Schiller?' I demanded.

'Do everything you can to keep him happy since he probably won't be staying with you much longer. There's far too much else for him to do.'

What can I say? It's to my everlasting shame that later I didn't have the courage to have Jules killed when I could so easily have done so. The others had left the matter entirely to me, yet I always hesitated. There would be no little black pasteboard coffin for him then, only recently, and from Zurich.

Bedrooms are such intimate places. One makes love to one's husband while dreaming of another. One dwells on the fantasies afterwards, asking of their necessity. One tries to understand, to forgive, but the doubts crowd in, the hopes, the aspirations, and the secrets.

Could I kill him today or tomorrow? This I really don't know, even after all I've been through.

The plaster's been ripped from the ceiling above me. The flowered linen of the walls is spattered with bloodstains. Heaps of rags become heaps of my clothes, a negligee, a torn stocking—I pull it out and hold it up. I remember saving it, can you imagine that? One silk stocking, the last of them. Such vanity. Ruined at the knee when I fell in the rue Mouffetard as I ran to warn my sister. What was I going to do with it? One never threw anything out in those days.

The wind stirs and I let go of it, ask myself, Why did I fall in love with Jules? Why? Over and over again, I must tell myself, as Tommy insisted once, Jules couldn't have been that bad or I wouldn't have married him.

Perhaps that's so. Perhaps it's just that in this life some of us are lucky and others aren't, but like Georges and Tante Marie, like all the local people, I'm inclined to blame the weather and the times. Of course, at that particular time I was also pregnant with Jean-Guy, though not desperate, not destitute, you understand. I could have gone to live with my father in England. Me, I thought I was really in love, and for a time I was.

The gate squeaks. I flatten my back to the wall. An avalanche of broken plaster pours over my shoulder. My heart's racing. Have they finally come?

A man of about forty is out there—it's too hard to tell from up here, but I don't think I've ever seen him before.

Shade from the broken louvres of a shutter falls on my fingers. He wears a grey fedora and grey tweed overcoat, grey scarf, and black leather gloves. There's no sign of a car on the road. He must have left it some distance away so as not to let me hear it. Then why make that noise at the gate? To let me know, eh?

He's read the no trespassing notice. In spite of this, he starts up the drive. From time to time he looks up here but can't possibly have seen me.

He's not heavy, not overly tall—medium in many ways. Nondescript—that's what counts. Plainclothes Gestapo? I wonder, even though I know they've all gone from here.

His cheeks are fair and closely shaven, the face a smooth oval that is neither too narrow nor too wide, and betrays few if any of the war's ravages. Is he British? I wonder, but discard the notion as he comes closer and closer before finally passing out of sight below me.

The front door is nudged open. Slowly, cautiously, he steps inside, and I thumb the safety off the Luger. It would be just like Dupuis to send someone from Paris.

Stealthily, he picks his way over the rubbish, is selective, and doesn't seem to mind the papers. It's the glass that bothers him, and he avoids it, sending a signal to me. Now only the wind is heard as it slips under the eaves or finds the shattered windows, and I know he's been sent to kill me.

A cigarette butt has been left to smoulder in the safety of the fireplace of the main dining room, but it's a classic Gestapo ploy, that gesture. He doesn't cry out, hardly ever makes a sound. Each step he takes is calculated to bring him closer.

A fleeting shadow leaves me wondering where the hell he is, but now he's even closer and steps quickly into the kitchen, my kitchen, but there's more glass, and I hear his shoes scrunch on it as he gives a muted '*Sacré nom de nom,*' and I know he's really from Paris, a former *gestapiste français.*

His back is to me. The toe of a brown Oxford nudges the rusty crowbar I used to break in, and he can't understand why anyone would do such a thing when entry has been so easy for him.

Puzzled, he fingers the broken sash of the door as he looks out through the orchard, only to then pick his way over the glass. Soon, he's looking at the remains of the potting shed where I used to meet Tommy and other members of our *réseau.* Is he putting it all together? Has he been told to look for this shed?

He must have some familiarity with the orchard, for he makes a careful circuit of my vegetable plots that are now so overgrown they almost look as if they've never been used. Is he looking for unmarked graves or my recent footprints?

Waiting, I hear the guns, the cries of my friends and comrades, the bursts of a Schmeisser, the single shots from a Walther P38 as I see them kneeling on that very ground, those that are left. They have dug their own graves, and as Schiller, tall and arrogant in his SS uniform, stands behind each, he raises his pistol for the *Genickschuss*.

Only that's all gone now, and soon this man stands beneath one of my apple trees looking up curiously at the frayed end of the rope that hangs from a sturdy branch.

He's tall enough to touch the end of it and does. Hunching his shoulders against the cold and damp, he again heads for the house only to walk round the side and out to the road. Me, I could so easily have killed him.

6

They'll come for me now. Probably, like him, they'll leave their car some distance, will split up, for he'll have told them I'm here. One will nudge that front door open, another the back with one in reserve. I had better do the unexpected.

In the kitchen, there's a German ordnance map. I fish it out, tear off a strip, search for the stub of a pencil and in big, black letters print: *ATTENDEZ! JE VAIS REVENIR.* (Wait! I'll return.)

This I nail to the front door with the tines of a carving fork. Then I sign it, *Lily Hollis*, and disappear back into the house to wait for them.

Always there's that night in my thoughts, and I'm walking the streets of Paris knowing there's no price like that of my innocence. Jules had warned me not to try to contact my sister. Me, I was so green I had let them follow me.

Like fireflies in the darkness, the bicycles passed by. Occasionally, at the corners of the streets, there were faint blue-washed lights. Otherwise, there was only the night above and the shapes, the silhouettes, the sounds of hesitant steps.

Hurrying across the boulevard Edgar Quinet, I frantically tried the main gate to the Cimetière du Montparnasse. It was the best of places to disappear into during the day, the final home of so many, of statues, angels, griffins, and hobgoblins, too. A city in itself, its crowded stones rose constantly upon one another in a jumble of darkened crosses to the length of the wall that would shut me off from the avenue de l'Ouest if I could but get over it, but it was impossible of course! At six p.m., they locked up the dead, and that was it. I barked my shins but made no more noise as he lit a cigarette. It was Dupuis and he was standing nearby, but did he *want* me to see him? Each time he took a drag, the cigarette glowed, and all I had of him was this and the dumpy silhouette.

Something fluttered past, terrifying me—a bat, who knows— and Dupuis moved calmly away to search elsewhere, leaving that cigarette for me to find burning on the edge of the kerb.

Dupuis . . . He was so clever, that one.

Later . . . but a few moments later, I was at Marcel's. The woman was naked and clutching the bedclothes to hide herself, the boy asleep on the floor beside the bed, curled up like a little dog. There were black, curly hairs on the barrel of Marcel's chest, and it was easy for me to see that he had the hanging fruit of the well endowed as he rasped, '*Jésus, merde alors*, Lily, what is this?'

I switched off my torch. 'I have to talk to you about Janine and the others.'

'*Idiote*, it's well after curfew! In any case, what are you doing in Paris?'

The woman sank down and pulled the covers up over her head. 'Don't wake the boy.' That's all she said. Marcel reached for his shirt and trousers, and together we moved away to look out at the night, down the length of that courtyard towards the rue de l'Ouest. 'Listen,' he said, 'I don't know where your sister and the others are. I think Dmitry stole a van and picked them up just before the invasion, but I've told no one of it until now.'

That only made me suspicious of him. The flat reeked of oil paints, turpentine, and other things, like a *vase de nuit* that needed emptying. 'Jules could give you lots of money now. Why don't you go to him?'

'Never. It's not pride, if that's what you're thinking.'

'Then what is it?'

'Look, it doesn't matter, eh? Some things are best left alone.'

'The Vuittons?'

'They'll be after you, too. They want Jules to be completely free of past associations.'

'Could Nini have made it to the *zone libre*? She'd go to Provence, to mother's. They could have holed up there. Damn it, Marcel, she's not mixed up in anything is she?'

'Résistance leaflets, newspapers? Me, I simply don't know.'

'If not the Free Zone, then where?'

His shoulders lifted. 'The farm perhaps, but they'll be watching it. Jules will have told them to.'

Tommy and Nicki would have made very careful circuits of it. 'Can you get someone into Paris for me?'

Assessing me through the darkness, he hazarded, *'Peut-être.* I still have a few contacts.'

'In the black market?'

'In that and other things. When would you want this person to be moved?'

He now knew that someone could well be at the farmhouse so there was no sense in my hiding it. 'Three days from now. He'll be there, but well hidden.'

'Is he a British airman? Janine could be in that business, Lily. For myself, I've thought it entirely possible but, again, I've said this to no one but yourself.'

How kind of him! 'So why not keep it from me, too?'

'Because I choose not to in spite of the risk.'

'How much will it cost me to have someone moved?'

'Five thousand francs—half in advance, but make it some place deep in the forest. Near the buttes perhaps.'

Why had he suggested such a place? 'Must it be there?'

'Certainly, because Schiller and the others will think you would never go there again. Now push off before that concierge of mine calls in those neither of us want.'

Again, the city awaited, and I didn't really know if I'd ever make it because Simone and André de Verville lived in a posh block of flats on the boulevard de Beauséjour not a stone's throw from the Bois de Boulogne and me, I arrived in the dead of night. They were frantic, of course.

'You *what?*' snapped André.

'I've ridden here. I stole a bicycle. It's outside, so you'd better bring it in and hide it. I'll take it home with me tomorrow.'

He tore his hair and gestured at the idiocy. 'Lily, you *can't* be doing things like this. You promised.'

He had warned me earlier, at his consulting room. 'But I didn't realize they would have me followed. Dupuis and the others slowed me up.'

'That Sûreté? Well now you know what it's like. I just hope no one saw you coming here except for Laforge, our concierge, who will be lecturing me first thing in the morning!'

Which was true, of course, but . . . 'It's pretty dark out there, eh?' It was no mean feat to cross the city and the Seine after curfew. I had avoided two street patrols and managed to walk right by the control on the Pont d'Iéna, both of whom had been laughing and seeing how far they could piss into the river, but . . . I'd better not tell them this.

Simone was sitting on the arm of a chair in her dressing gown and slippers. 'He's right, Lily. It's no time to be fooling around. But Marcel, *chérie*? Why go to a man no one should trust?'

André had pulled on his coat. 'Yes, why? Just what are you involved in?'

Me, I needed to quickly learn how to lie and wisely decided to use a half-truth. 'A small investment. I've some potatoes and things. I was hoping to find a way to get them to you.'

He glanced at Simone then said, 'Potatoes,' and lifted his eyebrows. André was typical of the French intelligentsia, thin, greying, sharp-featured, tidy always—even in pajamas and silk dressing gown—dark-eyed, fifty-two, and twenty years senior to his wife. A very good and successful doctor, but with a practice that I knew was falling to pieces: wealthy Jewesses mainly, so he wore a certain stripe the Nazis wouldn't like, though neither he nor Simone were Jewish and I knew they would not have backed off, not then.

'I'll go and get the bicycle,' he said, 'and apologize to Monsieur Laforge, not that it will ever do any good. Some coffee, Simone. Maybe something stronger. Lily, really, you've scared the life out of us and put us in the soup as well!'

As he left the room, he muttered, 'Potatoes might help.'

'Marcel's not to be trusted, Lily.' said Simone. 'You know this far better than we do, so why, please?'

The shoulder-length black hair was wiry and thick and desperately needing its brush and comb, the grey eyes betraying an uneasiness I didn't realize I was to see time and again in the years to come.

'Tommy's at the farmhouse with Nicki.'

'*Ah, merde,* you can't get mixed up in anything like that, not with Jules and the Vuittons! Even we have seen how close they are to the Nazis.'

Sitting at her feet, I folded my arms about her knees. 'For us, we have to decide.'

'But . . . but why now? Why not give us a chance to learn the ropes? Every day there are changes. New ration cards, new ordinances, more and more papers to fill out. This place . . . They've already been here to question André about some of his patients.'

'The missing ones?' Those who had gone south during the Exodus and had stayed away, fearing the worst if they came back.

She nodded. 'Their valuables, their houses . . . Lily, what are we going to do?'

'Decide. Tommy and Nicki will be here in the city in three days.'

'*If* Marcel keeps his word! How can he? He never has.'

'I'll look the ground over first. They'll both be armed.'

'You'll *what*? Hey, listen, you, I'm not hearing this! What's got into you? Marcel . . .'

'Will you hide them for me?'

Me, I let her cry her heart out, this friend of mine, and tell her, 'They have to link up with someone. I don't know who he is, but it must be important.'

Somehow a presence of mind was summoned. 'Has this any-thing to do with the auctions at the Jeu de Paume?'

'Perhaps.'

*   *   *

Darkness does something to a person after you've been in prison for a while. You never know when they'll come for you. They may give you a cigarette, your last; they may beat the shit out of you, so you try to sleep, but are always wary. Your mind goes round and round asking, Have I told them this; had I better say something else?

Huddling in a corner—shaking—it's never pleasant, so I've walked the six or seven kilometres through the forest, have left the 'Château' de St-Germain for a little. The wind is from the northeast out of the Baltic it seems, and I'm standing amid the ruins of my mother's farmhouse near Barbizon. The ashes lift with the wind when I stir them, and the smell comes to me: old, damp, musty, so many things.

They put it to the torch after having *dragged* that poor woman out and shot her.

Forgive me. If only I'd known, but let me remember the time before it happened, because I must. A time of warmth, a tender-ness I could never have believed possible.

We sit there, just the three of us, and I couldn't believe what's happened. I couldn't! 'Marie . . . Nini . . . How I love you both for this.'

Marie *was* alive. Nini *had* gone south to Provence. She had found my little girl safely with her grandmother. Some people had picked Marie up in the confusion and had taken her with them on the Exodus. Marie *had* run away just as Jean-Guy had said. She hadn't been killed.

I was a mother again—whole, complete, with two hearts to protect and all the fears that go with such a thing, and I couldn't keep my hands off Marie. I touched her hair, her back, looked at her, said how much she's grown. My sister watched me, and finally the daughter she had adopted took a hesitant step towards the mother she'd thought lost. Then it was Nini who couldn't keep her hands from touching us. It was, of all the moments in a war that was filled with so many, the most profound for me.

Only later did we talk of Marcel, and only later did I tell Tommy and Nicki about the lift I'd arranged. Smoke rose from the lantern on the kitchen table. Marie slept in my arms. Nicki cleaned and loaded the Lebels, checking them over yet another time.

Janine had just made us some sandwiches, big, crusty things of meat and cheese, the last of the food she'd managed to bring from Provence. There were olives, too, and a bottle of wine. 'Marcel can be trusted this time,' she said, 'but maybe not the next. He's an odd one, Lily. He runs deeper than you'd think.'

Me, I had to tell her how it really was. 'But he will wait to see what we're up to. If he must sell information, he'll make certain of what he has to offer.'

Tommy wasn't pleased with this analysis. 'Perhaps we should forget about it and try some other way.'

Nini reached for the olives. 'Then there would only be trouble because Marcel would feel he had to strike while he could. No, it's best you go, but give me a couple of days. After I've taken Marie to Lily at the house and made a big show of it, I'll go into Fontaine-bleau and turn myself in. Those *gros légumes* will have to send me to Paris where I can then be of much use to you.'

The big vegetables, the brass, the *Oberbonzen und Bonzen*. 'And is that wise for yourself?' asked Nicki.

My sister had a way of smiling at a man she liked. It was very delicate, very subtle, you understand. A slight twist of the lips. Very seductive.

'It's the only thing I can do. Oh, for sure, Marie and I crossed the demarcation line from the Free Zone without a permit, but lots of people are doing it. I had to return my sister's daughter. The *Boche* can't all be without heart. Besides, they might not even check. They might be so anxious to see me, they'll forget all about it.'

'Which leads us to Michèle and the others. What has happened to them?' I asked.

She indicated that I should hurry up and eat something, that the time for me being there was running short. 'Michèle and Henri-Philippe split up with Dmitry and me in Lyons when the van finally packed it in.'

'And Dmitry?'

Nini could shrug like no other woman. 'We slept in the fields. One morning, I awoke to find him gone.'

I grabbed her hands. 'Is he a Nazi, of the SS?'

She shook her head. 'He's a Communist. He didn't tell me this. *Ah, mon Dieu*, how the hell could he? I found out in other ways— friends, associates of his, a little by following him, too.'

There was the sharp click of a hammer, but when we looked at Nicki, he only shrugged, though he had one of the Lebels in hand and we knew he hated Communists, but all he said was, 'War makes strange bedfellows. I wonder who he killed for that Luger you've still got hidden?'

When I told them of the rest of the cache, Nicki said, 'Burn the papers. Don't keep them around. Bury the wallet where they'll never find it. Don't trust the stove with leather. He can always get himself another set of papers after we've checked him out. *After*, Lily.'

It made me wonder what Dmitry would have to say about things.

Tommy walked me across the fields and into the woods until we came to the road I was to take. We had said so little to each other, we still seemed at a loss for words. I knew I dreaded their linking up with Marcel's contacts. Tommy also knew how I'd be feeling about meeting them where I'd been attacked. 'Be careful,' he said. 'I'd hate to lose you.'

'Hey, listen, I'll be seeing you in two nights. Marie's safe!'

'And I'm glad for all of us. Your sister's quite a girl, Lily, but is she too impulsive?'

He'd seen this, hence his silence. 'Nini will be okay. That one will grow up fast because she has to.'

I didn't ask what he and Nicki were planning. Very quickly, we dropped into this way of working. What one didn't know the Nazis couldn't pry out. Later, of course, I absolutely had to know.

'What will you do if Schiller's there in the house?' he asked.

'I'll stay right there and keep him busy.'

Tommy's kiss was hesitant. I think some snowflakes were falling, the first light dusting of the 1940–1941 winter that was to be so harsh.

The dawn hasn't broken yet. It's still pitch-dark, but how many times was I to drag myself home like this, dead beat only to appear as if refreshed by a night's sleep? The note is still nailed up there by that fork. I run my fingers over it, feel the jamb of the door, a touch . . . just a touch. Have they come as requested?

The door is no longer the way I left it. There *is* something—a feeling, a sixth sense, call it what you will, but you either have it or you don't. They've come.

Cautiously my fingers move down the jamb and across the stone sill until I find the length of thin wire. So it's to be this way, is it? No confrontation. No, 'Lily, let's talk things over.'

Just as I've suspected, there's a car parked down the road. I give it a careful circuit, run my fingers lightly over its dented wings. A Citroën—prewar, real vintage, a 1937, I think. Black, with lovely flowing lines. One of the Sûreté's, *ah, oui.* Dupuis at last.

With my SS knife, I let the air out of every one of the tyres and fade fast into the trees, for that hunting ground of kings is to be hunted over again, and I must remember everything I will need, only this time it's me who's the hunter.

Tommy waited beside me in the forest, just near the turn-off to Arbonne. Nicki had gone to watch the road. It was two days since I met them at the farmhouse, and Marcel's contacts hadn't shown up. It was almost dawn.

We didn't know what to think. For them, for me, the waiting had become an agony. Should they return to the farmhouse?

Should they hide out in the forest and try to make a run for the *zone libre*?

There had been no opportunity for love, none in which to lie in his arms. Again, I asked him, 'Are you sure of the address? Simone will hide you, but you must get a message to her first. She'll know what to do about their concierge.'

Faintly on the cold night air the sound of a *gazogène* lorry finally came. Since it had a firebox that produced wood gas to power its engine, there was a certain misfiring of the engine, the grinding of ancient gears, a hunkering down before each gentle rise. Those things, they didn't have any more than sixty percent of the power of a gasoline engine.

Soon there were voices, the pungent aroma of wood smoke, and the squeal of ancient brakes. '*Sacré nom de nom,* is this the fucking place? Hey, *mais amis,* are you the ones we're suppose to collect?'

There were pigs in the back of the lorry, which the smoke and the banging of the engine had frightened. The poor things squealed, making a racket of their own. Thirty or so were haunch-to-haunch and terrified as light from a torch briefly passed over them before coming to rest on the money in my hands.

'Ten thousand francs, madame.'

'Ten? But . . .'

Nicki says, 'Give it to him.'

There were no names and I didn't see their faces, but knew Marcel had done me in again.

'*Vite, vite,*' said someone. 'Get in the back.'

They were gone and I had to return to the house alone.

The axe fell once, the axe fell twice. Blood splashed over the chopping block. A head rolled away, but it was not a human head. No young girl vents her bowels at the moment of her death. The eyes of Michèle Chevalier didn't stare up at me, not yet.

I was down the road from the house. Georges was butchering

rabbits. I held the children by the hand. There was snow, and all around the woodpile it had been trampled.

Another rabbit was seized by the hind legs and ears. It jerked as it was taken from the cage, tried desperately to get away, but he swung it up high in the air. Marie's eyes follow it. She was very silent, very intent. Her lips were parted in a gasp as the rabbit came down hard in a rush of brown fur, Jean-Guy watching it hit the block as its eyes burst.

Up came the axe. The black beret, stained by the grey of snotty forefingers and thumbs, was pulled down, for we'd come at his summons. 'Madame, your husband wishes me to tell you that your friends are not wanted.'

Georges had been to Fontainebleau again to talk to his wife's relatives. 'Which friends?'

'The two who came three nights ago, late and well after curfew. I saw them, madame. There's no sense in your lying.'

Fortunately, I had an answer for him. 'That was Michèle Chevalier and her boyfriend, Henri-Philippe Beauclair. They're on their way back to Paris from the south, and the colonel has said they might stay for a few days.'

The stained butt of his Gauloise bleue was pinched out and budgeted in a small, flat tin as he clucked his tongue, ground his false teeth, and began to skin the rabbits. 'It's not the colonel's house, madame. Monsieur Jules has asked that they leave.'

The skin was pulled off as he continued. 'We have only the interests of our employer at heart. If there are goings on at the house, they must be reported to Monsieur Jules.'

'Who is paying you again, but how much, please?'

Bundled in an old coat, boots, scarf, and crocheted hat, Tante Marie appeared with the iron casserole. 'That is no business of yours. Be thankful you've been left alone.'

One by one, the little corpses were laid side by side and the skins collected. 'They'll be gone in two days,' I told them. 'The Lieutenant Schiller wishes to interrogate the two here, so there's nothing you or I can do about it.'

They didn't look at one another, only at the rabbits, Georges wiping his hands on the skins. 'You'll be the death of us all, madame.'

'Then you'll only get what you deserve!'

I dragged the children after me, those two watching, one on either side of that chopping block with the wood piled up under the roof of their shed—oak, beech, and pine. New wood. Seasoned wood. Lovely stuff!

'There was a third visitor, madame,' he called out 'This is the one who must definitely leave.'

The pilot Michèle and Henri-Philippe have brought me. 'There is no third person!'

It's Tante Marie who says, 'Would you like the Germans to look for him? Be sensible. Don't bring trouble down on all of us. Just let him leave. It's not your affair. It certainly isn't ours.'

He was badly burned about the hands, but would they have me turn him out in this weather, 22 January 1941? I remember the date because, late the previous night, we had listened to the BBC London and had learned of the British and Australian breakthrough at Tobruk.

Of Tommy's and Nicki's getting safely into Paris, there had, as yet, been no word.

The dawn has come. The house is still. There's no sign of Dupuis or any of the others. They're afraid to show themselves, but from where I'm sitting in the forest, I can watch the place and remember.

I never once questioned what I should do about that pilot. For me, his life was precious. I remember, though, that his hands were black, that the encrusting scabs leaked pus and the fingers couldn't move as he lay in the spare bedroom next to Marie's. I'd locked the door and had brought him some soup. 'Can you sit up a little?' I asked.

He was only nineteen, just a boy, had been flying aeroplanes since the age of sixteen. 'In the bush,' he had said, and I had seen the dream of it in his eyes and known he wanted only to go home to Canada.

His name was Collin Parker. He was tall, big, and once strong; more than filled the length of the bed. I set the soup down and took hold of him under the arms. Collin pushed himself up with his feet.

He gave a sigh, didn't complain. 'How are things?' he asked in a whisper.

'Okay. Schiller's interrogating Henri-Philippe first, in the library.'

The soup—a broth of chicken stock, finely chopped vegetables, and a little wine—was just what he needed, but he couldn't eat much. He was too weak. 'You're going to have to turn me in,' he said.

We both knew this, but I told him to hang on. 'Once Michèle and Henri-Philippe get to Paris, André de Verville will come. He's a very good doctor.'

'Can't you trust anyone local?'

'They give me no reason. Fontainebleau is replete with collaborators and *Boche*. Now eat, please. At least a little more.'

His Bristol Beaufort had been on coastal patrol out of West Malling in Kent when the weather had socked in. They'd drifted off course and had been shot down over Rouen. Collin had crash-landed in a field. Of the others in the crew, he remembers only the flames and the screams, which are with him all the time. His hands had been welded to the stick, but somehow he'd been thrown clear or had gotten free of the wreckage, though with no knowledge of this.

Luck played such a part in things. Luck found him with a farmer who passed him on to another and another so that he made a wide detour around Paris only to find himself alone at our railway station in Avon.

Luck caused Henri-Philippe and Michèle to get off the Paris-bound train and pause to stand beside him. He'd been trying to make sense of the timetable, had thought he might head for Spain. Henri-Philippe noticed that his hands were leaking through the shabby woollen mittens he'd been given; Michèle asked if he might, perhaps, need a little help in reading the timetable.

I'm the one who cut the mittens off. 'Now try to sleep.' I left the soup—I could get that later. I closed and locked the door, wiped my hands on my apron, and tried to tidy my hair.

That house . . . How it all comes back to me. The corridor was long and filled with such lovely things, but it passed by the open door to the library. Their voices were muted, for they were sitting at the far end of the room, facing each other across the small oval of a Louis XV gilt-wood table. The Louis XIV chairs were really very uncomfortable, and Schiller had chosen the setting, even the furniture they'd use.

Henri-Philippe would be able to look out the French window to see Rudi standing guard at the gate, and if Schiller wanted it, knees would touch 'accidentally' to generate increased fear, and we would't know what he'd asked Henri-Philippe or what answers had been given.

Pale and afraid, Michèle was waiting for me in the kitchen. She'd brushed her lovely light brown hair and tied it behind with a dark brown ribbon. The blouse and heavy cardigan suited her, but she couldn't panic, couldn't weaken. 'Just answer readily,' I told her. 'Repeat if necessary, but don't offer information. Let him do the digging.'

Henri-Philippe was not allowed to talk to her or to me. That bastard sent him outside so that he could watch the house and wonder what was going on. Michèle was in there a long, long time, and when he'd finished with her, she went straight to her room in tears.

Then he sat by the window, at that table with his answers, and finally in the uniform of the SS at last. 'Is your daughter glad to be home?' he asked me.

'Of course.'

'Perhaps now you'll be a little more friendly, Frau de St-Germain. Perhaps you'll find us Germans not so bad.'

I stood and waited but didn't look out the window, for I knew Rudi would be blowing on his fingers and that Henri-Philippe would have tried to share a cigarette with him. Rudi would have had to refuse such a kindness simply because Obersturmführer Schiller was with us and Oberst Neumann had warned Rudi to behave as one of the Occupation's troops should.

'Tell me about Michèle,' said the lieutenant.

'There's nothing to tell. They're just a couple of young people who ran away like everyone else when the blitzkrieg came. Now they've finally obtained permission to return home to Paris.'

'Yet they don't do so immediately. They stop off to see you.'

'Is there something the matter with that? They were worried about my sister and anxious for news.'

'Your sister, yes.' He turned the pencil in the fingertips of both hands as if it was the shaft of a millwheel and he the miller of us. The flaxen hair was precisely parted, the jackboots gleamed. 'The girl's a violinist, I gather. Is she good?'

'Certainly.'

He smiled that tight little smile that buckled the scar as he said, as if doubting me, 'Friends of your sister. Associates?'

I shoved my hands into the pockets of my apron. 'Associates in what, please?' Marie, where is she? I wondered. Jean-Guy, he was at school.

The pencil was set aside. The fingers tidied the papers before a smoothing hand passed over the back of his head. 'Let's leave that matter for the moment. Please . . . please have a seat. You must be tired, cooking all those meals, doing all that laundry. A woman's work is never done, is it? Georges . . .'

I waited. I tried not to show any alarm. 'Georges?' I asked.

'Says that the war will turn you into a good housekeeper since nothing else could.'

'Georges and Tante Marie have always been critical of my efforts. It's only understandable.' But had they told him about Collin or said anything about Tommy and Nicki?

Schiller lit a cigarette, sat back, and took his time to study me, and I had to wonder, was he really asleep that time I went into his room?

'You're a strange one, Frau de St-Germain. Why the visits to Barbizon and that farm of your mother's?'

'To arrange for a farmer to take care of the place and share the harvest. There are three hectares. One I wish to have planted in alfalfa for my rabbits and his cows, one in wheat, the other in potatoes if we can get the seed. Good cash crops, Herr Obersturmführer. Is there anything wrong with that?'

'You must show me the place. Perhaps I can be of assistance. No . . . no, there's nothing wrong. It's just that the girl tells me she's never been there, to the house of your mother, but the boy says that before the war they both went there with your sister.'

Such a simple thing. Who would have thought he'd even ask?

'Well?' he insisted. 'What about it?'

Again, there could be no hesitation. 'That I really wouldn't know, Lieutenant. They're friends of my sister's as you've said. Neither of them have been there with me.'

'So why would the girl deny she'd been there?'

Merde, what the hell was I to say to this, since it was *me* who had really taken them there that first time to meet up with Nini? 'To save me trouble, perhaps. Michèle knows I've recently been to the farm a couple of times. She probably thought I'd not been given the necessary permission. For myself, Herr Obersturmführer, I wouldn't make too much of it. Oberst Neumann has asked her to give a little recital for him in Fontainebleau tonight. It would be a shame to make her so nervous she couldn't perform.'

'The *palais*, yes. The Feldkommandant and his staff will be there, but that doesn't mean she should lie to me. The matter will have to be gone into.'

How many times was I to hear him say that? 'And their "association" with my sister?'

Has he waited for me to ask it? 'Associates in a robbery, Frau de St-Germain. Apparently, some very valuable things have been stolen from one of the auctions at the Jeu de Paume. Your sister was reportedly seen there on several occasions, attempting to speak to your husband.'

'So why not ask her?'

'We are, and that is why I am interested in these "friends" of hers.'

A robbery.

'So now you will tell me about this violinist who calls herself Michèle Chevalier.'

As if it was a *nom de guerre*. He would have checked her identity card, would have gone through all her papers, even her handbag . . .

Marie came into the room to tug at my ear and whisper closely, 'There are noises, *maman.*'

'You must excuse me, Lieutenant. Marie has to go potty.'

'*Maman . . .*'

'*Ferme la, chérie!*' I gathered her up and headed for the door, and when he found us standing outside Collin's, he looked along the corridor past us but didn't say a thing, simply went downstairs, but let me hear him doing so.

Michèle was waiting for me in her room. 'Lily, I told him I *had* been there with you, that just before the defeat we went there to see Nini and your mother. Neither Henri-Philippe or myself would have *lied* to him about that. We had no reason to.'

But Schiller now knew it was me who had just lied to him!

Again, Marie tugged at me and whispered, '*Maman, monsieur le pilote,* he has cried for you.'

'And the robbery?' I asked Michèle.

'Four paintings. A Raphael, a Rubens, a Leonardo da Vinci, and an icon from the twelfth or thirteenth century. Something Byzantine.'

Nicki's treasures. For me, for us, Collin Parker was just a prelude to what was to come.

There's no sign of Dupuis and the others. Pink stucco, bullet holes, and broken shutters mar the château, but the sight of these hardly disturbs my remembering the call I made.

'André, it's Lily. Please, I'm sorry to telephone on the colonel's line, but my problem has come back and I'm bleeding quite badly. Could you come at once? I . . . I have also burned myself on the stove.' *Burns,* André. Please get the message.

The burn was on my left wrist. I had done it with the poker, had needed to have some way of telling him what was really up. I'd made myself a little bag of blood and had kept it in my pocket, and when I went in to ask the colonel if I could use his telephone, I broke that thing and let the blood run down the inside of my leg. Neumann had a green stomach when it came to women's things. He was your usual Prussian. Tall, big, blue-eyed, a little over sixty, grey and bristly haired, a monocle, the whole bit, but absolutely 'correct' with the locals because in those early days of the Occupation he'd been ordered to be 'correct' with the French and he considered me to be one of them.

André came with his little black bag and worried look. Because he was in the SP, the Service-Public, he had the use of his car and a small petrol ration. He appeared at dusk, and we went quickly upstairs. Michèle and Henri-Philippe were preparing supper. Schiller was in the library with Neumann, both taking their leisure with cognac before the fire, and we ducked in so that André could say hello to them. To her great credit, Michèle saw the need and immediately began to play her violin, for Neumann was particularly fond of Schubert and she'd been an outstanding success in Fontainebleau.

Letting André, still in hat and coat, into that room, I waited. He took one look at Collin, swore at me under his breath—a thing I'd never heard him do—called me stupid and selfish, and grimly said to Collin, 'You need to sleep. Let me give you some morphia.' Nothing else. Not, How have you stood the pain? Not, How have you hung on for so long?

We watched, the three of us, as the morphia went into that vein. I think Collin thanked him. I know he wished me well, but to see a young man die like that, to see his life simply slip away . . .

'Now you've got a problem of disposing of him,' said André. 'What you do is no concern of mine, Lily, so long as you do it well.'

We went into my room, and he made out a certificate for me, which said that I might possibly have a cancer of the womb. 'That ought to keep them from throwing you into the internment camp or getting too close.'

The Germans feared cancer, syphilis, and tuberculosis most of all. 'We'll just have to see,' he went on. 'They may, of course, simply shoot you.'

I longed to ask him about the robbery. He pulled two newspapers out of his bag and handed them to me. 'It was stupid, Lily. Stupid! What do those friends of yours think they're doing?'

'Just getting back what's rightfully theirs.'

No one had been shot in the robbery—nothing like that. The paintings had simply been carried out by two workmen wearing the usual *bleus de travail*. 'Cool-minded thieves,' the press said, not Bolsheviks, not yet—the war with Russia was still to come, so the Nazi-controlled press couldn't blame the Communists. Göring was, however, particularly upset, since he'd had his eye on the Raphael. Me, I had to wonder about the Vuittons, the Action française, and most particularly my husband, for he might have been blamed for having let the robbery happen.

But what do you do with a body in winter when you've only a wheelbarrow or children's wagon and the enemy are all around you?

'Rudi, could you to do a little favour for me?'

The breath steamed from him. He unslung a frozen Mauser and leaned it against the gatepost. 'Madame Lily, it would be the greatest of pleasures. Please, you have only to ask.'

All this was in broken French, interspersed with German, our lingua franca. His brown eyes were rimmed with red, the lashes half-frozen. Beneath the angular helmet, which all but hid his eyes and gave no possible warmth, there was the grey woollen cap I'd knitted.

This dumpling of a Gefreiter was my friend from the other side—*Ah, oui, oui*, I must confess it and pay homage to him. A figure out of Brueghel, a man who never wanted to go to war.

He saw how pale and shaken I was. The strain of everything had taken its toll, and he was troubled by this, for I was at once his benefactor and escape.

'Some of the meat the colonel very kindly bought for the Reichsmarschall's visit is bad, Rudi. He got taken, of course, but I don't want to embarrass him, you understand.'

'Bad in this weather? *Ach du liebe Zeit,* Madame Lily, how could this be?'

Remember, please, that he was a farmer, his family from generations ago. 'With this burn of mine, I can't do much.'

He looked at the bandage I showed him beneath the sleeve of my coat. There was the wariness of the peasant in his gaze. To burn oneself like that was questionable, other things as well.

'Help me to bury the meat, Rudi. Dig the hole for me.' I was firm with him. After all, he knew he was onto a good thing by being stationed with us, knew also that he had looked the other way often enough and that should I be forced to confess this to the Obersturmführer Schiller, I might.

'Where, madame? With this weather, the ground must be frozen.'

'In the cellars, beneath the stones.'

'The stench, madame. The hole would have to be deep and out of the way. If I were you, I would use some other place.'

'There's a small back room off the wine cellar. Rats have often got in there only to die from eating poisoned bait but, of course, they're awfully difficult to find.'

He thought about this, my Rudi. He knew there was an element of truth. Reluctantly, he reached for his rifle and followed me to the house. Neumann had gone to Paris to prepare for Göring's visit. Schiller, having sent Michèle and Henri-Philippe to Paris by car, was off somewhere, but I'd no idea when he'd return.

We buried the pieces I'd cut up and wrapped in canvas and butcher paper. Rudi never questioned me openly, he simply did what he'd been asked, and as a last stone was put back in place and the floor surveyed, said, 'Marie, has told me of this one, madame, but your secret is safe with me.'

I still have nightmares. All through the camps, I had them especially. Some are of the butchering, others of the burial, and in one Collin awakens to ask what I'm doing to him. In another, it's Schiller who asks and Rudi who answers.

I made five trips to the farm that winter in hopes of finding Tommy. I used the road, slogging it on foot or bike through snow, rain, or ice pellets with Marie. I would start out at five a.m. and arrive at about eight or nine, if lucky. There would then be a trip to Barbizon to check with the mayor and then the Feldkommandant because the house was empty and I was afraid they'd requisition it. Each time, I told them mother was returning in the spring and I was getting things ready for her.

Postcards, with preprinted messages in heavy black type,

were now being allowed through from the *zone libre* and I had heard from her at last, but as to her coming back, this I really didn't know. On the postcards, one crossed out the words one didn't want, and the rest allowed for so little after the censors had got at it with their black pens, that the result was often unintelligible.

The Nazis thought of everything, and if not them, their French friends in Vichy, especially the Maréchal Pétain, that old warrior who had given in, Pierre Laval, and others, too. Criminals all of them. Collaborators.

Nothing stirs but the occasional falling of the leaves. The sun has risen and it floods my courtyard to warm the bricks against which I stand and lean, and I feel their roughness, the indentations where the trowel has worked the mortar. All are like a map to my memory. As the Schmeisser makes its sound, the Sten has its own, the Bergmann MP-34, Mauser 98, Luger, Walther P38, and Lebel Modèles 1873 and 1896, too. So many different sounds the ear becomes tuned to them, as the ornithologist's is to each birdcall.

I've made a careful circuit through the forest and have come up behind my husband's house. Hidden in the forest, I can just see the faded, peeling white framework of my little potting shed. From there to the courtyard is about three hundred metres diagonally through the orchard. Sufficient brush about the shed still gives good cover and the washed-out orange-red brick of its half-walls form shoulders behind which one can hide, but will they come looking for me there? I desperately need to rest, still have things I must remember.

Tommy found me in the forest, standing here. I was watching the house just like now, was wondering what I should do as I tried to grab a moment's peace. 'Lily . . .' He had such a way of saying my name. Softly, urgently. My whole being simply rose to it. I turned. My back was to one of the trees. Suddenly, I had to tell him what I'd done to Collin and yet . . . and yet I couldn't.

'Göring,' I said. 'He's coming here.'

The loss of the Raphael had needed to be given the ointment of something else.

There were two very fine belle-époque chandeliers in our main dining room. Exquisite draperies of crystal and candlelight, but a lifetime to clean. The Luftwaffe did all that. The first of the lorries to arrive was Göring's mobile kitchen. Actually, there were two of them, with trailers and twenty or so cooks and cook's helpers. Stainless steel like I'd never seen.

They took over my kitchen, too, but backed those trailers right up into the courtyard. There were bushels of beets, onions, carrots, bunches of leeks, potatoes, cabbages, crocks of sauerkraut, pickled pork hocks, suckling piglets rammed on to skewers, sides of venison and beef, pickled beets, pickled cucumbers, enough mustard sauce for an army, Black Forest hams, et cetera, et cetera. Never had I seen so much food. Marie was quite intrigued; Jean-Guy absolutely mesmerized.

One huge man in white, with a cook's hat, sharpened a butcher knife that needed no sharpening. Orders flowed. The head cook, a Bavarian of sixty and of immense proportions, marshalled everything under his gaze and nose, the sweetbreads, the livers they would chop with onions, the pâté and the cheese, the wines—*Dieu merci*, they didn't seem to know of my husband's precious *cave*.

Magnums of champagne were offloaded: the Dom Pérignon, no less, the 1911. For the wine, there was such a selection: Château Lafite, Château Latour, both of early vintages, but German wines also; Bernkastel, Johannisberg, and Balbach Erben. Though I was terrified, depressed, so many things, I can still remember thinking, If only I could sink my teeth into some of this stuff, I could flog it off for the rest of the Occupation and never have to worry about money again.

They cleaned the house and laid the table, but never mind the china of the de St-Germains. Göring had his own: Augsburg silver from the eighteenth century, white porcelain dinnerware with fine gold rims and traceries of blue from the Royal Bayreuth factory in Bavaria, 1834, Venetian flute glasses, very old, very rare, 1732.

'Madame, my compliments. I'm Hauptmann Karl Janzen, the Reichsmarschall's adjutant and maître d' for your little dinner party. Please, the dress is for you, with the Reichsmarschall's compliments.'

Janzen clicked his heels smartly together and bowed. He was all grins and smiles, was of Tommy's age, tall, good-looking, your perfect Aryan who also spoke beautiful French. I was later to learn that he polished it on his mistress.

The strapless evening dress was of emerald-green silk, low cut and very finely made. Two of the *Blitzmädels* were with Janzen, hard-eyed, arrogant bitches but in smart blue Luftwaffe uniforms, not the field grey-green of the Wehrmacht that had earned most of them the epithet of the 'grey mice'. They were to take charge of the children and help me to get dressed, which meant a bath, a washing of the hair, a manicure, the whole bit, and *Ach du lieber Gott,* I'd better not object. You'd think I might have had lice or something.

But what do I remember most about that dinner party? The noise, of course, the gluttony and drunkenness, the women— good-looking, young *Parisiennes* who laughed a lot and played around a lot more: theatre people, singers, dancers, and models for some of the big fashion houses who were still all in business. My sister was there, too, and Michèle Chevalier. My husband had made certain of that, but there was one woman Jules hadn't known. An absolutely stunning redhead with lovely sea-green eyes: Nicki's wife, Katyana Lutoslawski. 'Giselle,' she said, extending a hand. 'What a charming little house you have.'

Neither Tommy nor Nicki had told me she'd be present, and had let her appearance come as a complete surprise. 'Just what do they intend on doing?' I asked when we had a private moment.

'Nothing. Don't worry. Let's just wait and see.'

The talk was most often in German and loud. There were perhaps seventy or eighty 'guests,' a real flowering of the Nazi and collaborationist elite, a party such as the de St-Germains might once have thrown in Napoléon's time. Beautiful women in absolutely stunning dresses, some caught with laughter in their eyes, their reflections imprinted in ornate, gilt-framed mirrors that were so old I can still remember them.

The Germans were mostly in uniform, those of the Luftwaffe and Wehrmacht, but there were others of the Gestapo and the SS, and those early dress uniforms of theirs were the colour of anthracite. Tall, short, thin, big, plump, fat, grey-haired, or not, some of the men were handsome, most quite ordinary, but all had varying degrees of the sinister, for these were the conquerors, and I still can't bring myself to think of them in any other way.

The buyers and dealers of art and antiques were among them, some from Switzerland, others from the Reich, and still others from each of the occupied countries and territories, but they were not in uniform. Instead, it was tuxedos or expensive business suits, and they appeared as sprinklings among the black, field-grey, or navy blue uniforms and all those lovely evening dresses. Yet it was business as usual for them and others, too, of the Paris elite. Everyone was overly polite, overly attentive, silly, or serious, and sometimes all in quick succession since few really knew one another and those who did were hard to find.

I circulated as I had to. I, the woman of the house who had recently butchered and buried the body of a young Canadian pilot, had to smile and welcome everyone because that's what a hostess does, and I saw that the Oberst Neumann, my star border, felt a little out of place. The Feldkommandant of Fontainebleau was flattered that the Reichsmarschall should pay his district a visit and stay, of course, in the *palais,* the hunting lodge of former kings.

The Vuittons were watchful. Always they kept that little bit of distance between them and whomever they were talking to. That bitch had her black hair piled high and pinned with spun gold skewers that were centuries old. She wore a low-cut gown of black velvet, a necklace of gold and turquoise, and I saw the gap between her breasts as a chasm.

Dupuis from the Sûreté smoked his pipe as he groused around

or stood alone, watching everyone in the mirrors. Clever, eh? He looked as if he'd still got his rubbers on, but don't let that fool you. He was far more sinister than most of the others.

And Göring? Göring was resplendent in the soft, dove grey-blue uniform he had made especially for himself and that the Führer had let be different from all the others. There were medals on his chest like I'd never seen before, but don't get the impression they weren't deserved. That one was a flying ace in the Great War and had a bullet from that, also splinters of paving stone and lead that were lodged in the thigh muscles and groin from something that came later, a Nazi thing. That's when he turned to drugs. He sat on one of the couches, all but filled it, his great hams spread. A glass of champagne was always in hand; the other often dunked into a cut-glass bowl with frosted nymphs that Lalique had wrought, a masterpiece that was filled with jewellery. Art Nouveau to please him, amethyst and aquamarine, rings, bracelets, little butterflies, the cheap and the gaudy hiding the good. Rubies and sapphires, my diamond earrings. Agates, malachites, and lapis lazuli, strands of pearls but most of all, emeralds to match my dress and remind me of the tiara of the Empress Eugénie. A little warning from my husband and his friends, but now there were other priceless pieces that were far more recently stolen in Paris from the Jeu de Paume auction.

Katyana was feeding the Reichsmarschall herring on toast, thin wedges of it. I was introduced again by my husband as the sculptress. Göring looked me up and down but didn't say a thing about the tiara. Did he even know what happened to the real one?

Jules said, 'She's the one who made that bronze of this one, her sister.'

He took Nini by the hand and brought us face-to-face with him. Nini had the shadow of a bruise under one eye, but with that Midi beauty it was perhaps hidden enough.

'Two sisters. Yes, I see the resemblance,' said the great one. 'The sculpture is very good, madame. You should do something more.'

Giving him a defensive shrug, I tried to find my voice. 'I haven't the energy, Herr Reichsmarschall.'

'Then your husband should see that you have all the help you need.'

Ah, merde alors, what an idiot I was. More Nazis in the house, more of their comings and goings!

It was Nini who took charge by sitting at his feet. 'Lily's really quite able to manage, Herr Reichsmarschall. Like all artists, she simply needs peace and quiet and the encouragement of an expert like yourself.'

'A bronze of the three of you, then. Yes . . . yes, that would be suitable. That one,' he points at Michèle. 'And yourself and that one.'

Katyana—'Giselle.' *'En costume d'Ève,* Herr Reichsmarschall?' she asked, for his French was excellent. Her eyes were saucy as she stroked his sleeve.

'Toutes nues?' he roared with laughter, his cheeks becoming bright red, the champagne sloshing out of his glass onto the Aubusson carpet. 'The Three Graces. Yes, that is exactly what I would like. ANDREAS!' he bellowed, the crowd quieting as glasses were deliberately lowered, but so slowly one would hardly notice. 'Andreas, another commission for you to negotiate.'

Walter Andreas Hofer was little, with thinning hair but sharp, shrewd eyes, a real dealer and the man who would play such a part in the evening to come. Göring's chief buyer could and did secure the release of wealthy Jewish art dealers and see them into Switzerland so as to use them there, a man with connections, lots of them, riding on the swift-winged horse of the times.

'Andreas, the Fräulein Sculptress will do a piece for me.'

Had he forgotten my name already? Remember, please, that he commanded the German air force and was responsible for what happened to Rotterdam, but failed to bring Britain to her knees.

'In wax,' I heard myself saying. 'Then you can take it to whichever foundry you wish.'

'Marcel could look after that,' said Jules. Was my husband so wrapped up in this crowd he has forgotten that he had kicked his former friend?

'Marcel, yes . . . yes. Marcel Clairmont, the artist, could see to the casting for you,' I managed to blurt.

'He's the one who handled that little piece we found in Carrington's hotel room,' said Jules.

'Yes,' said Hofer, who, like Göring, didn't know a thing about that room or the man who was killed instead of Tommy. Asking what the Reichsmarschall wished to pay, he suggested, 'Something modest?'

There was a curt nod, not only of dismissal but of censure. The pay-off. I was not really that good. Even so, Hofer and I began the negotiations. 'Three hundred thousand old francs,' I told him.

'We deal only in the new. It's the law.'

'Five hundred thousand, then.'

Göring overheard and spluttered, 'Five hundred . . . *Lieber Christus im Himmel*, get that bitch out of here!'

'Three hundred, then. New francs.'

'Two hundred thousand,' said Hofer, the Riechsmarschall now watching us closely.

'Two-fifty,' I told him.

'One-fifty,' says Göring. Was he trying to bait me? Had he sensed my hatred of him and what that air force of his also did during the Exodus?

'All right, for yourself, Herr Reichsmarschall,' I tell him, 'two hundred thousand francs.'

To him it had all been a great joke, but a deal had been struck and he knew I'd realized that, and anyway it was just chicken feed to what was to come, but I think it had excited him to see me barter. Quaffing champagne, he ate a slab of pâté Nicki's wife had offered, she laughingly asking, 'Are you sure you don't want yourself to be included in the piece as a Bacchus, Herr Reichsmarschall?'

To roars of laughter from him, the sounds of the room picked up, and I suddenly found myself alone with my husband and my sister. 'Behave,' said Jules. 'I'm warning you, Lily. Do exactly as he asks. This . . .' he indicated the crowd. 'Is very important.'

'For whom?' I asked.

Was there sadness in my husband's eyes? 'For you and the children.'

It was Nini who asked, 'What else could she possibly do?'

'You keep out of this.'

'I haven't done anything,' she said.

'It's enough that they've questioned you.'

Janine touched the bruise. 'This must show, Lily. Me, I'd better put something on it. I know I've forgotten to.'

Leaving him, we headed upstairs, but from the landing turned to look down the staircase past that chandelier to see the Vuittons looking up at us. Dupuis joined them like a grey moth to its candle, Nefertiti with her withered breasts and overly made-up eyes, that husband of hers like another moth, the gumshoe seemingly lost in thought, the moment trapped in my mind forever.

For all their former wealth, the de St-Germains had only one washroom and one toilet. Both of those rooms were impossible. The *Blitzmädels* were, of course, watching the children, but even so we checked on them and they were so happy to see Nini again, Marie was in her arms, all wet kisses and hands that explored the pendant, the earrings, the nose, the eyes, that bruise. Jean-Guy, I mothered, for I knew he was a little jealous of his baby sister. I was, too, once upon a time.

At last, we were alone. We'd stepped into the library past the two men in uniform who were on guard here. Crates had been broken open, and their contents set about. Surprises awaited the Reichsmarschall. There was a Gobelin tapestry, a masterpiece of royalty in a forest with hounds at the hunt and a ferocious boar being put to the spear. There was an icon, a *Madonna and Child*, a priceless thing that had the look of veneration, so many other pieces, it was like a private art gallery. 'Nini, what happened to you? How bad was it?'

My sister shrugged as we stood before an absolutely sumptuous painting by Luca Giordano: the fall of rebel angels, the winged knight stepping on them with upraised sword. Göring had a passion for the baroque painters of the seventeenth century. Nini was in awe of it, as was I. 'Did the Gestapo get rough with you?' I asked.

'A little, but the bruise isn't from them. It's from Jules. He's afraid, Lily. Terrified because of the robbery.'

'*Ah, bon.* How did Michèle and Henri-Philippe make out on their way into Paris from here?'

'Just routine. What about the pilot?'

I told her, and she took me by the hand to squeeze my fingers. It was such an immediate and intimate gesture of sympathy and understanding. 'We mustn't talk long,' she said. 'We've a network, Lily. It's spreading. Dmitry . . . Has he made contact with you yet?'

I shook my head. The Vuittons were now standing in the doorway, watching us. Nini pointed at the painting and said, loudly, 'He will. I'm certain he will.

'The Reichsmarschall,' she said to that bitch. 'He'll buy this one for sure.'

'Then everything will be forgiven,' said Nefertiti.

The Egyptian necklace had come from the loot of some tomb robber. The goddess Isis figured prominently in the centre of that thing, its wings outstretched towards the bony shoulders. There were hieroglyphs: snakes, birds, boats, crabs, beetles, too, and lions.

'Who is that redhead?' she asked, only to see us shrug.

'An acquaintance of the Riechsmarschall's, I think,' offered Nini. 'Doesn't Obersturmführer Schiller know?'

I waited. I remembered that Schiller paid Nicki a visit before the war, and asked myself, Was Katyana present? It was a horrible thought. Vuitton was too watchful; tense, like Jules: The whole business that night must come off well or else.

'Please excuse me, *madame et monsieur.* I must see to the other guests.'

'Not until I've finished with you,' she said. 'The Reichsmarschall is to have his pick and that includes anything on the walls of this house. Jules has agreed.'

'Then there's nothing to worry about. The things are his, not mine.'

It was she who did the talking for the couple. 'One word, one false step from either of you, and I'll personally see that you are held responsible should anything go wrong.'

They were really worried. 'Michèle not cooperating?' I taunted.
'That girl's a fool. She could have so much.'

'Maxim's suits her,' said Janine. 'To play in a French string quartet for the Germans every evening from five until ten thirty puts bread on the table, isn't that so?'

That Nefertiti couldn't resist saying, 'She gets many offers and refuses all. For her own good, you should warn her to accept some.'

'And those of my husband?' I asked. 'Or has he now forgotten all about her?'

The expression she gave was a mask out of antiquity. 'Jules is no longer interested in any of you. He has much better to occupy him.'

Yet he had suggested Marcel take care of my little sculpture in wax. 'Then I hope he's happy with them, madame, and that he doesn't get syphilis.'

I watch the house but none have dared to show themselves. Though the rooms and corridors are where my memory lies best, I must have strength for that. Always I would try to carry a little something in my pocket. A crust of mouldy bread, a piece of gristle from the filthy 'soup' they fed us in the camps, the leaf of a cabbage. I would try to save it to eat in secret, sharing only with myself, because only then does one come face-to-face with the friend and comrade that must be inside each of us lest we fail.

They'll wait for nightfall. They'll say to each other, She's coming then.

Like the leaves at autumn's end, they, too, must fall, but the sun streams through the branches as I move away to fade back into the forest and lie in secret, looking up at the sky.

Marie and Jean-Guy loved to make leaf people. Tommy would heap leaves on them or we would simply laugh and sit together while they played. Brief times . . . all too brief, but I mustn't cry. I must remember that night Göring first came to the house.

Schiller watched Katyana all through that dinner. Somehow I needed to warn her that he had made a telephone call to Paris and that the SS might have a photo of her.

She had a little handbag, a thing of beaded silk, very feminine, but heavy—bulkier than it should have been. This handbag was never out of her reach, Neumann being to one side of her, Göring to the other at the head of the table. Juices poured down his chin. Venison, pheasant, beets, borscht, mustard, wine, champagne, it all went in. *Ah, mon Dieu*, that man could eat! His eyes swam as if in water.

She pecked at her food. She'd noticed Schiller all right, and I felt him move suddenly. 'Mademoiselle,' he said from across the table and down it a little, 'your handbag, please.'

'My . . . ?' she blurted. 'But why?'

Her expression was one of utter dismay, but he snapped his fingers, and suddenly the table shut up. Cream fell from a spoon. Göring set his knife and fork down. '*Ach*, what is this?' he asked.

Again, Schiller snapped his fingers. The handbag was passed from guest to guest, Katyana seemingly shrinking from what could well happen. Her lovely red hair was so soft and light, but never had I seen such a look of dismay. It was as if she realized the game was up.

Schiller received the handbag. Does it hold a pistol? he wondered. Remember, please, that Göring started the Gestapo and that for us, they and the SS were one and the same, so Schiller could move himself up the ladder if he uncovered a little something.

'Be careful, Herr Obersturmführer,' said Katyana. 'There may be women's things.'

There was, *mes amis*, a slab of pâté wrapped in a napkin. '*Pour mon petit chat,*' she said, but this was greeted with suspicion by Schiller. He was certain she was going to poison the Reichsmarschall.

A small paper of white powder came to light. 'Icing sugar,' she said apologetically. 'From the kitchen, you understand, but please don't punish the cooks. It's simply very hard to get now and I . . .' She shrugged, and me I was willing to bet there were others round the table with the same idea.

Mustard fell on Göring's dove-grey lapel to join an avalanche of gravy. Lipstick, a compact—several other items came out of that bag. The key to her flat, her papers, all these were laid out. 'We shall see then,' said Schiller. He was very proper. The long fingers dusted the powder over the pâté. He used a dinner knife to spread it evenly.

Arsenic? I wondered, as did everyone else.

Some of the pâté was placed on a bit of bread. A little more of the white powder was added, and that thing, that monstrous thing, was passed from hand to hand to her.

'Eat it,' he said. Her eyes found mine. Was there apology in them? Nini began to stand up to stop her. Me, I wanted to cry out, Katyana, please don't!

Her gaze settled on each person around the table, then the 'Giselle' smiled wanly and said, 'Yes, of course, Herr Obersturmführer, but you must forgive me, all of you. No one else was involved. Only myself.'

The table waited. There wasn't a breath. Göring wet his lips. Had he ever watched a woman die like this?

She took a nibble, chewed, and swallowed most delicately, only to hear, 'All of it,' from Schiller, she hesitating as she touched the base of her lovely throat.

'You must excuse me then because I'm rather full.'

Ten seconds—is that how long it takes for the burning sensation in the mouth? I know it's a most painful death—I've read of this in detective stories. Who hasn't? The victim lies on the floor, cramped with stomach pains and vomiting hard, then the violent purging starts. But nothing happened. There was no poison. Just a sip of wine and then another. *'Salut!'* she said and grinned. 'Are you satisfied?'

The table erupted with laughter. The scar tightened. Schiller got to his feet and bowed as he handed the pâté in its napkin back and it was passed from hand to hand. 'For your cat, mademoiselle.'

As the handbag and its contents were returned, Dupuis didn't join in the fun, nor did Jules or the Vuittons. For them, as for Nini and myself, the agony had been too much.

'Seven hundred thousand francs.'

Göring sat like a potentate among the treasures in the library.

He never bid himself. That was always left to Hofer. He only smoked his cigar and watched.

The Gobelin tapestry went for something like a million; the Hellenistic terra-cotta sculptures, three beautifully done heads, and a small statue of a woman whose arms had been lost centuries ago, fetch a miserable one hundred fifty thousand francs.

The icon brought only five hundred thousand; the Giordano canvas one-and-a-half million. So many things. Göring had his pick. A set of Roman coins, some Etruscan glass, two of the Renoirs from the house—Jules hated to see them go, but they were the price he had to pay.

A Limoges enamel triptych, by Pierre Reymond, sixteenth century, was someone's loss. A Dürer *Madonna and Child*, in watercolours, caused the Reichsmarschall to hesitate, but he couldn't let it go and gave a nod before filling his mouth with champagne. As the treasures were carried out to a waiting lorry by men in Luftwaffe uniform, the rest were left to be fingered and exclaimed over, for the auction had been a bit of a sham since there was only the one bidder.

'From Avon, the train will make its way to Munich,' confided my little sister, 'and from there to Karinhall, his estate some ninety kilometres to the north of Berlin.'

She didn't tell me any more, simply because it would be safest, but I knew that some of Nicki's treasures must have been among those purchased, and that Katyana had apparently slipped away.

7

It's getting dark. Soon Jules and the others will be cold in that house of my husband's. Perhaps they'll light a fire and say, 'It will draw her in,' but I'm used to not having any heat. Have they forgotten this?

The Cherche-Midi was once a convent. Built in the reign of the Sun King, it had thick stone walls, airless corridors, iron-bound wooden doors, and moisture that ran down the walls to freeze. Each cell had a window—just a rectangle behind iron bars and of pearl-grey glass into which God had pressed chicken wire as if one might try to escape through such a thing.

Converted to a prison during the Revolution, it held us for a while, and maybe still my name is there, scratched on the wall among all the others. *Lily, taken 22 November 1943.*

From the Cherche-Midi, we were sent to Drancy in late January 1944, in the Black Marias the French called the 'iron salad shakers'. From there, in the dead of that winter we went by rail in cattle trucks to Birkenau and in the dead of the next winter to Bergen-Belsen, so me, I know a lot about cold. I know how the bones can ache, how the eyes glaze over and there are no thoughts because even that takes too much energy.

I know how Michèle Chevalier clung to life throughout all that cold because she believed in me and I had repeatedly told her she would survive. I know how they took us from our block at dawn and told us we were to die. *Cher Jésus*, the war was finished for them. They could have used a little humanity. Cold, I felt so cold. I tried to hold Michèle's hand. Her fingers were like ice. I said good-bye, said, 'I'm sorry I failed you.' And they made me watch! *Pour l'amour de Dieu*, those bastards, Schiller and Dupuis! Schiller had ordered the executions. Dupuis was still in Paris, I guess; Schiller, I don't know where. Just a voice on the telephone: 'Kill them.' Nothing else except, 'Yes, you are to use the axe.'

The axe!

My SS knife is really very sharp. I've taken the remaining bullets out of the Luger and its clip and have laid them on a stone while there's still light. Since there are only six of them, I'm cutting notches into each to make up the difference. They'll open up on impact. If caught with them, my death will be horrible as it was for others I knew who had done this, but I have to be sure of things. You see, Schiller and Dupuis used to interrogate me at the Cherche-Midi. The one would start, then the other would take over. They kept it up for nearly forty-eight hours, and when they were done, I laid on the floor of my cell for three days. I had so many secrets by then, one in particular that they wanted very badly, but I told them nothing.

Schiller . . . Is he still alive? Did he manage to get away, to hide some place? This I really don't know and wish I did.

Dupuis is still an inspector. Isn't that something. But since all of us had been killed, he could claim he'd only been doing his duty and that, in the final days, he had joined the uprising in Paris just like everyone else, a *résistant*!

He has a wife, a son, and two daughters, all grown by now, of course, and I won't hold it against them, only the father, and the others who were with him, but wait, please. To understand the Occupation, you have to consider that those times were often like a kind of ether. People drifted into and out of your consciousness. They came and went, and you wondered where they were.

By 1941, people had started coming out to the countryside from Paris to scrounge at the farms for eggs, meat and vegetables, or milk, and in the forest for mushrooms, acorns, even twigs for the stove. One still needed an *Ausweis*, the *laissez-passer*, and the *sauf-conduit* to do such a thing, and always there were the random searches on return and the danger of having everything confiscated and being accused of planning to sell it on the black market.

I think it was towards the end of April or perhaps into the first weeks of May when Dmitry Alexandrov finally showed up. It wasn't that long after Göring's visit. The war with Russia still hadn't started, but the Germans had gone into Yugoslavia and Greece. Malta was being pounded; Tobruk defended against Rommel.

I was working in wax. I'd blocked out the three figures and was beginning to concentrate on Katyana because I wanted to get her just right and I had this horrible feeling I'd forget what she looked like.

I'd decided to make the piece a little larger than the one I'd done of Nini. I worked in the kitchen and, as the days grew longer, threw myself into the sculpting and my vegetable gardens and the farm. My mother had returned, so that was good. Tommy would have a place to stay—at least a warning if things weren't right. We had worked out a system for this, but still there had been no word from them. It was as if they had disappeared forever.

Then Dmitry showed up. I remember that it was Jean-Guy who came to tell me he was in the forest and wished to speak with me. I set the pallet knife aside. Marie was working in wax, too, and had got it all over herself. As I cleaned her off, I said to my son, 'Take Marie and go and talk to Rudi. Keep him busy. Ask him to help you make a kite.'

'But we made one last autumn? It was lost in the trees.'

'Then get him to help you make another.'

Rudi . . . I was beginning to really worry about him. In his idle moments, our German guard would stray to the side door of the cellar and wonder about Collin. I knew that what I'd done plagued his conscience as it did mine. I didn't want him to suffer, nor did I want him to give things away. Please, you must understand the predicament I was in. Rudi was my friend, but at the same time he was of the enemy.

I think Oberst Neumann was in the library, for it was a Sunday. I know his car was in front of the house. Schiller had been recalled to Berlin on urgent business.

The fresh newness of the leaves gave to the woods that smell of things growing. There was the sound of the bees, that of distant birds. All these things came to me, then on looking back, the sight of my courtyard and kitchen door down through the long tunnel of blossoming fruit trees. That delicate pink-and-white gossamer of the apple was like no other, that pure, strong white of the pear, just as distinctive. Pastoral, the way life ought to have been.

Dmitry was sitting on a boulder behind some others. There were two suitcases, one a little larger than the other, both of brown leather, not new, not old, but scuffed. 'So you're back,' I said. 'Where have you been all this time?'

The clothes were old and rough, an open blue denim jacket, a black turtleneck sweater, brown corduroys, and boots that had seen much walking. 'Here, there, everywhere,' he said. 'Marseille, madame. I've brought you a little something you're to take over to your mother's for us.'

Why me? I wanted to ask, to say, Didn't they tell you the Germans are here nearly all the time?

'Your sister has asked this of me, madame. I'm only the courier.'

He indicated the suitcases. 'It's a British Mark II wireless transceiver, so you had better not let the *Boche* find you with it.'

'British? How did you come by it?'

Those washed-out, grey-blue eyes took me in. 'Felucca from Gibraltar to Marseille, the boyhood home of your artist friend Marcel.'

'Is he also involved?'

Dmitry couldn't help but see the worry I felt. 'He and others. We have to use whomever we can, it seems.'

'Just what do you mean by that?'

'Only that Marcel Clairmont finds himself in the unique position of being able to help us. He has friends, as you know, and they . . . Why they have other friends.'

Smugglers. 'Nini asked if you'd been in contact with me but she didn't say why.'

Dmitry dug a hand down through the neck of his sweater and fished out his cigarettes. 'Have we time?' he asked, indicating the packet. He was tired and probably hungry.

'A little,' I said, and quickly filled him in on my situation. 'I'll leave something for you to eat in the potting shed, but come after dark. About ten. If I can be there, I will.'

'The guns, madame. Janine has told me you uncovered my little cache. I need that Luger.'

For some reason, I shook my head—even now, after having thought about it so many times, I still can't think why I refused. 'They watch me all the time,' I said. 'I have to be so careful.'

He lit up, took a drag, passed the cigarette to me, and we shared that thing. I think I knew I had to, that it wasn't just an act of friendship but one of trust. Though I didn't inhale, it was the start of my using cigarettes, and very soon I found that they calmed my nerves and often gave me the opportunity to think things over.

'Janine says you burned the papers I stole.'

'It was for the best. Look, I couldn't take the chance.'

'Yet you kept the guns—still keep the Luger?' Our fingers touched as he took the cigarette from me. 'The transceiver is for the Polish one, madame. I gather among his other attributes, he insisted that he be trained in wireless work before the war.'

'I really wouldn't know. No one tells me anything.'

Dmitry set the cigarette aside on the edge of a boulder and stooped to spring the catches on one of the suitcases. 'There isn't room to hide these with clothing. This larger one is the transmitter, the smaller, the receiver.'

There was a varnished box of laminated wood in each suitcase. The larger one had a brown Bakelite panel with dials for coarse and fine-tuning, plug-ins for the earphones, and the Morse key, also switches and a six-volt battery.

'Remember that if you're caught with it, the *Boche* will know right away what it is, so you mustn't tell them anything.'

This last seemed so obvious and yet how many times was I to hear it? Our little prayer for silence.

'Get it over to the farmhouse as soon as you can. Be sure to let them know they mustn't be on the air for more than a couple of minutes and that they must use different times of transmission— preferably early in the morning. Between two and four hundred hours. That way, there's less chance of causing static in some villager's radio. There's also less chance of the Germans pinpointing the set.'

Dmitry closed the suitcases and handed them to me. I felt the weight—the larger was by far the heavier. 'A little more than twenty kilos in total,' he said of both, about forty-five pounds. 'They're too heavy to run with, so keep that in mind if you meet a patrol or have to go through a checkpoint. Don't panic. Just bluff it out.'

He scraped the leaves away and, with a stick, drew a circle in the earth. 'Paris,' he said with a stab of the stick. 'Nuremberg, Augsburg, and Brest. Wide scanners, madame. Cathode-ray tubes that sweep the air twenty-four hours a day to pick up clandestine transmissions. They get the larger fix on the set by a simple tri- angulation and notify the closer centres so that those can narrow down the location. Tell Alexis Nikolai Ivanovich that this thing is both friend and enemy. One can get lulled into thinking there's safety once a link with the home base has been established. Tell him that it would be safest to move the set about rather than to transmit from the farmhouse. For your mother's sake and for your own, as well as for the rest of us.'

'You seem to know a lot about it. How is that, please?'

The Russian remembered the forgotten cigarette and blew the ashes away from the stone before carefully wiping out all trace of his little sketch and replacing the leaves. 'I only know what I've been told.'

Had he used it himself? I remember thinking this at the time. If one could contact London with that thing, then Moscow was also possible. This thought worried me so much I reached for the cases. 'I'll leave something in the potting shed for you to eat. I won't forget.'

'There isn't time. If you could have got the Luger for me, I'd have stayed.'

'Then it's good-bye until the next time.'

His grip was strong. He had such powerful hands. 'When I get to Paris, I'll tell your sister you're okay.'

I think he was afraid I'd get caught with that thing. I'm almost certain he had thought it over and had decided to put as much distance between us as possible. I know he watched as I walked away, and when I'd hidden the suitcases in the shed, he was still there among the trees. I didn't wave. I just stood with hands in the pockets of my skirt. For perhaps a few more seconds, we looked at each other, then he was gone, and I had turned to head back through the orchard.

A transceiver. *Ah, merde!* How on earth was I to get it to the farm?

André de Verville is the last to arrive. As the others must, I see his car turn in. Getting out to stand before the gates, he's like an old, old man but someone shouts to bring the car up to the house. Was it Jules? I wonder.

No, not Jules, and not Dupuis, either. That voice . . . 'Have you had a chance to talk to her?' André shouts back.

Someone else says, 'No.' Dupuis, I think.

'We mustn't hurt her. I'm insisting. If you refuse, I'll turn around and take what's coming to me.'

Dupuis walks out to meet him halfway along the drive, but André nervously drops the cigarette that has been offered and stoops to pick it up and clean it off. They both look down the drive towards the gates, the road, and the forest beyond. 'Out there, my friend . . .' I can hear Dupuis saying. 'A note . . . She wants to speak to you first. Yes, you. Ah, don't worry so much. Just talk to her.'

All lies, of course, except for the note, but poor André who doesn't want to hurt me anymore is to be the negotiator, not Jules, and not the Vuittons, either.

He's much older, greyer, thinner, but is there really someone else, that voice I heard? Dupuis, Louis and Dominique Vuitton, Jules, André, and . . . Is it Schiller?

The back road to Barbizon was below me, down through the barren trees. In that spring of 1941, I was thinking of so many things as I rode my bicycle along it. Of Tommy and Nicki, of the robbery, the wireless set that was then behind me—everything, it seems. Marie was five, so she was in school all day, as was Jean-Guy, but would I ever see them again?

The big front carrier basket was full of things, old clothes, two bottles of wine, some cheese, bread, and eggs, for I'd good laying hens—cash for when I needed it—and the day was so beautiful I'd even undone the top buttons of my dress and was glad it had crept up to my knees. A gentle rise soon took me to another hill. I stood up to slug it until forced to hop off, only to hear what I simply didn't want: a Wehrmacht lorry.

As it passed, men leaned out to whistle and wave, so I smiled and waved back, but the thing stopped, and I didn't hesitate because if I did, it would be suicide. *'Schnell!'* one of them yelled. Two others hopped down. Hands pressed against my seat and touched my legs; others encircled my waist as I was lifted into that thing. There were perhaps twenty of them, sitting on benches that were on either side of the back: young men in their grey-green uniforms. I grinned, I smiled, I said, *'Merci, mes amis,'* and tried to act the silly young country girl, though of course I was not so young anymore.

One offered a cigarette, others looked at my bare legs, the sabots I'd been wearing lately, the undone buttons and heaving breasts. 'So, where are you off to today?' I asked.

In broken French, I learned that they were to do *un ratissage*, a raking of the forest. 'We can only take you to the edge of the woods.'

'A search for poachers?' I asked and raised my eyes in mock alarm.

The heavy one, a Gefreiter, let his gaze travel up my legs to linger on my chest. 'Poachers?' he asked. 'Are there such things?'

They all grinned and looked at me. It was illegal to hunt, trap rabbits or birds, yet lots did and I was just itching to buy myself a ferret. Three months in jail for a woman, if caught, forced labour in Germany for a man. This also applied to the illegal taking of firewood.

I shrugged and tried to look as if I'd been smoking cigarettes forever. 'So, if it's not poachers, what then?' I asked, flicking ash aside. I was really pretty good at it. Very saucy.

It was the Gefrieter who stripped me with his eyes and said, 'A man.' Nothing else. It could mean anything or everything, but was I sex-starved, they wondered, or was it that they already thought this, for it was crowded and we were all squeezed together. The bike had been taken to the front, where a couple of them steadied it between themselves. All had rifles and field kits, and *merde*, but that private first class thought he knew me. 'You're the one the Oberst Neumann stays with. The one with the big house and the kids.'

There was nothing for it but to agree. *'Oui, c'est moi,'* I said and flicked ash again, harder that time. 'Is it so bad? He seems okay to me.'

'Neumann,' one of them said, and the smiles began to fade.

'Schiller, too,' I told them.

The Gefreiter's's eyes found mine, and for a long time he looked at me in a different way until the lorry stopped suddenly and we all lurched forward and back. The bicycle went first and then myself. One leaped down to the road, another hung on to me while the Unterfeldwebel, who had been riding in the cab, gave the orders.

'Your papers, madame. It's just a formality.' This guy was even bigger, tougher than the Gefreiter.

They set up a roadblock. Three men were to be left while others worked the woods on either side. I handed over my papers. I didn't need an *Ausweis* to go to the farm, but the sergeant took his time. His thumbs were big and strong, the nails dirty, the skin cracked in places. 'What's the purpose of your visit?'

'To see my mother. To take her some things.'

He pawed through the carrier basket, found the wine and eggs, fingered the cheese. I hesitated. He looked at them and glanced at me. I shrugged, I started to say, 'Please don't break the eggs,' and then found the will to smile. 'Those are for my mother, but she has chickens of her own so you may have a few, if you like, but in payment for the lift, you understand.' It was but a guess, a gamble: Was I right about him? Dear God, I hoped so.

A swiftness came to the look he gave. One of the men produced a haversack and the stuff disappeared as if by magic, so I knew they'd done this lots of times. 'The rest is to trade,' I heard myself saying of the clothing, even though bartering was illegal and he damn well knew it. 'I need some potatoes to use as seed for my garden.'

It was a little late for planting them, but he let that one pass. 'What's in the suitcases?'

'More of the same.'

His arm brushed mine as he walked towards the carrier and I turned sideways to look at him. One of my hands was on the seat, the other on the handlebars, my sabots firmly planted but could I kick them off fast enough?

There was a rope that tied the suitcases down, and I'd wound it round and round and tied it tightly with several big knots.

We waited–all of us. The Unterfeldwebel favoured his chin in thought. He was from Mecklenburg, maybe, or Pommern. Thick-headed if he wanted, also swift and sly, but had he realized that the catches on those suitcases were British, not Continental? There was a difference, and this finally telegraphed its little message to me since even Dmitry hadn't noticed, or had he deliberately failed to mention it?

The men were as if rooted to the roadside, their guns at the ready. Bees hummed among the tall grasses and wild flowers. My dress was pulled tightly across my chest. It clung to my legs, and again I thought of making a run for the woods but knew what they'd do to me if I should—they'd all got that look about them.

My papers were handed back. 'Tell the Oberst Neumann that we were very thorough with you.'

I nodded, suppressed the quivering, folded the papers and tucked them away in a pocket, and finally had the presence of mind to say, 'Thanks for the lift. That was very kind of you.'

Sunlight streamed into the studio to find the pots, the shards on the floor, the dust that eddied in the air. When it touched the glazes, it brought out the colours, a royal blue, a deep jade green, the ochres and the browns, the earthy, rusty reds I have always liked best.

My mother sat at her potter's wheel. The kiln had been fired up. The place was very warm, and sweat trickled down her forehead. There was clay on the robust hands. Not for a moment did the wheel stop. The vase must be finished. After all, the Germans would buy it, and the money could be used for other things.

All the time she worked, we talked. Occasionally, the dark eyes flashed at me. Most times, they were swift and hard—worried. She was all French, that one, a Midi from the south, no longer the shapely young thing my father fell in love with but still . . . ah, there was that something. The liveliness of the eyes, the dark lashes and eyebrows, the hair that was pinned back. One could't define it. She exuded a kind of earthiness, had a ready laugh.

The face was broad. Wisps of hair shot from under the red polka-dot bandanna. The hair was jet black, no signs of grey. The lips were firm—Janine's lips and eyes. Yes.

Hairs sprouted from a mole on her neck, and she didn't give a damn about those anymore.

'You must bring the children with you, Lily. That way, the *Boche* will be less suspicious. Children always distract people. Bank robbers should use them.'

A little of the clay left her fingers, for she'd gestured—couldn't help but talk with her hands. 'Have they questioned you?' I asked anxiously.

'Them? *Bien sûr*, why not? They question everybody but the geese. I let them allocate me wood for the kiln.'

J. ROBERT JANES

'Don't try to be too tough, *maman*. I'm warning you.'

'Me?' A shrug. A slip of encircling hands up the vase, the fingers deftly shaping the lip. 'Oh, for sure, *chérie,* you know I'll be careful. So, you are still in love with this one, eh?'

Why is it that the potter's hands are often suggestive of something other than working the clay? 'Well?' she asked.

'Yes, and very much, and you know this.'

'Janine, she isn't interested in him?'

My mother always knew she could bait me. 'Janine had better leave him alone.'

The vase was cut off and placed on a board to dry. The wheel stopped. The hands were plunged into a bucket of cold water and rubbed together. The fleshy forearms were bare, the old plaid shirt and pink sweater rolled up above the elbows. 'Janine,' she said, and gave a nod. 'She regrets what happened with Jules. For her, the experience was painful.'

'She wanted to show me what he was like.'

'Now I hear he's got two others,' she said and clucked her tongue. 'One is eighteen, the other twenty-three. Janine says they have to report to the Gestapo, that they're really *mouchardes* placed in his bed by the Vuittons. Men *will* mumble things in their sleep.'

Informants. We looked at each other. It was an uncomfortable moment. 'Is Jules under suspicion?'

Again, there was that tartness. 'The *Boche* don't even trust their friends, especially those who work for them.'

'But there's something else, *maman*. Please, you must tell me.'

The hands were dried and warmed at the kiln. Sweat stained her front between the sagging breasts. A cigarette was needed. This she puffed at as if it was her last, then raised her eyebrows and held it out to me.

Three times then within a week, I'd shared cigarettes with people. 'Inhale, *idiote*! Don't waste it! You girls . . . Pah, what is the matter with you both?'

I handed the cigarette back to her. She said, 'The Vuittons suspect Jules of being too soft. They want you and Janine out of his life. It would be easy for them to arrange but for the moment, Jules still has Herr Göring's support.'

'But only for the moment?'

'*Ah, mon Dieu,* how many times must I tell you not to display your feelings like a billboard? Certainly, Jules is playing a very dangerous game, but the Vuittons need him and so does Göring, so the Lieutenant Schiller must bide his time.'

Nini had told her far too much, but I asked, 'Did Nini tell you where Tommy was?'

My mother went into the kitchen. From its window, the fields of the Barbizon Plain spread out for a couple of kilometres before rising a little into the forest.

'The Caves of the Brigands, but you mustn't go there.'

I remembered the *ratissage* and the roadblock, but asked, 'Why not?'

'Because the Germans are looking for him—for a tall man. Someone must have seen him crossing the fields.'

'Then Tommy stayed here last night, and it wasn't just Nini who told you things?'

She nodded. There was a quivering to her lips, and she turned away to hide this. It was all her fault. She was blaming herself for having let him leave, and now the Germans were searching for him. 'I was afraid to tell you,' she finally confessed.

I took her by the shoulders and said, 'I'd better go and find him later on. He'll need me, *maman*. His accent is terrible, and he's far too tall for most Frenchmen.'

'They don't know who the man is. I'm sure they don't.

'Then everything will be all right, and I can give him the things I've brought.'

'He'll be in one of the caves.'

There was a small, abandoned airfield nearby. During the Defeat, the men who operated this field wrecked what planes there were and hid ammunition in some of the caves, but the Germans quickly cleaned those out. Almost a year had passed, but this wasn't time enough for them to have forgotten the location.

'You'll only lead them to him, Lily.'

'Not if I'm careful. I'll wait until after dark. I'll go there then.'

Suddenly, I had to see him. Nothing else mattered, not our safety, our lives, not even my children.

The night is dark. There's no moon. The clods of earth break beneath my sabots. I stumble several times. When I reach the abandoned airstrip, I pause among the wreckage and hear the wind in the tattered canvas.

There were no lights on back then when I turned to look across the plain towards Barbizon and then towards the house of my mother. The blackout had seen to that. It had turned the French into a nation of nocturnal prowlers.

I'd left the wireless set with mother. It would be better that way because I might not have been able to find Tommy and, anyway, Nicki was the one who knew how to use it.

Crossing the little airstrip took only a few minutes. Surely, the Germans must have remembered this place, but they had far better airfields and their attention was now elsewhere. Perhaps we'd be safe after all. Perhaps this thing could be used some day to bring in planes from Britain. The wreckage was all down at one end where the hanger used to be.

Pretty soon, my stumbling got worse. At one place, I fell and cried out; at another, I feared I'd sprained my wrist and sat holding it, rocking back and forth.

In among the boulders and the rock walls, there was brush, the trickling of a spring. I was sure I'd got the right place. The Gorges d'Apremont were off to my right, the land rising into the forest.

The Grottes des Brigands . . . I needed to cross the road—the one that ran to the north, northeast, a T-junction, the leg of which led westward to Barbizon. I'd come along that road that day. The Germans had let me out not far from there.

The sound of the water returns, and with it, that of the wind in the poplar leaves and I'm right back there on that night. I can feel it all.

'Don't move. If you do, you're dead.'

'Tommy . . .'

'Sh!'

His hand slipped over mine. We waited. Perhaps ten minutes passed, maybe fifteen. Then someone not far from us lit a cigarette. Momentarily, we saw that moon face with its puffy pouches beneath the cow's eyes that were widely spaced, the bushy eyebrows, dark bristles of a beard that was seldom if ever closely shaven. The neck of the grubby shirt was open, the jacket unbuttoned.

He had the gut that one. It was Clateau, the butcher of Barbizon, lord of the meat cleaver and the damp-ended fag. He'd been out hunting rabbits with his ferret. The nets he used would be at his feet so, too, the sack in which there could well be six or seven furry little bundles, who knew? This guy was very good. Superb! And he knew it.

But had he seen or heard us? With Clateau, you'd never know. Pretty soon, he was gone and I was in Tommy's arms, but briefly.

The cave was found by first entering another, then squeezing through a narrow fissure into yet another cave, near the roof of which was a ledge that led to the final and bigger one.

I had the feeling that Nini had shown this to them, for she'd been there before, as I had, so long ago it seems. Me, I had to admit I was a little jealous of my sister, even though on his second visit, it was myself and the children who first brought Tommy there.

He shone his torch over things, and I can still remember drawing in a breath, still remember him saying, 'The Raphael, those two Renoirs of your husband's, the Dürer *Madonna and Child*, Lily. That Gobelin tapestry. Everything we stole from the Jeu de Paume as well.'

'The Giordano?' I asked. My fingers trembled on the rough boards of the crates that were stacked on a ledge against one wall. The place was good and dry, the roof of the cavern just above our heads.

'Everything Göring bought at your house.'

'Everything?' This I couldn't believe, but Tommy was so pleased with what they'd done, he was grinning from ear to ear.

'Katyana, Lily. When she left the party, she hitched a ride in the lorry. There were only two men to handle all that loot. Can you imagine it? She insisted on sitting between them, and when they reached the rendezvous, she jammed a pistol into the driver's ribs and told him to stop. Nicki and the others took care of things while I walked those two men down the road a piece. We switched the crates, substituted stuff we'd bought in flea markets. Bric-a-brac, chipped enamel, and plaster busts of Napoléon . . . Göring? Did the Reichsmarschall really buy this stuff? Just think of the look on their faces when they unpack those crates!'

Tommy thought it a huge joke. 'Explosives and guns, Lily. I told those two that's what we were after. They were so scared, they drove like mad to the station at Avon and loaded everything on to the railway truck and never said a thing about being held up. They both thought we were the ones who'd been fooled!'

'And when the switch is discovered?'

His grin vanishes. 'Look, I'm sorry, but we were strapped for a place to hide everything, and Nini suggested we use these.'

Nini . . . 'She's very pretty, has a gorgeous *cul, n'est-ce pas?*'

The torch was still in Tommy's hand. The crates all bore the Nazi eagle and numbers, and it was frightening to be standing among them, yet I was jealous of my sister and I wanted . . . My God how I wanted him.

'The Nazis are stealing everything they can get their hands on, Lily. What Hitler and Göring don't buy, others do. They're all competing with one another. Generals, high-ranking Nazi officials, art dealers—crooks. We can't let it happen.'

He was really serious. 'I've brought you a little something. It's at mother's, in the loft under the hay.'

Tommy nodded. He knew what it was, but said, 'Nicki's gone to Switzerland. He's really worried about Katyana, and so am I. After she left us, she took the train south. She was hoping to cross the Swiss frontier, but that's not easy anymore. One needs a guide. I . . .' There was much sadness in his look. 'If they do make it, they'll try to set things up so that we can get this stuff out of here before someone finds it.'

A fortune. 'You'd better seal the entrance. Some stones, bushes, old branches, and logs, anything to hide the cave that leads here.'

He hesitated, then said, 'That's why I came back but now . . . Lily, what were the Germans after today?'

'Someone saw you and reported it.'

He took a candle from a pocket and, lighting it, fixed it to a ledge and sat down to lean against that wall and look at me. 'Schiller?' he asked. 'Have they already opened those crates we substituted?'

I had unbuttoned my coat. 'Schiller was recalled to Berlin, so something important must have come up.'

'Then they know we made the switch, and the hunt's begun. I seem always to be bringing trouble down on you. I don't mean to, Lily. London made a deal with us. In return for helping them with information by wireless, they agreed to get Nicki and me back into France, Katyana convincing them of her usefulness. Janine's been a tremendous help. We simply couldn't have pulled it off without her. We needed Luftwaffe stamps and shipping labels for that stuff.'

'You once asked me about her. Now I have to answer: Nini's too daring, too impulsive.'

'Perhaps, but London also want us to organize an escape route. Who else could we have gotten to help us set one up?'

'Are you crazy? Robbery, downed airmen on the run, escaped prisoners of war . . .'

I still couldn't bring myself to tell him about Collin. Michèle and Henri-Philippe would already have done, and if not them, then André, but that one won't have told him how the pilot died. Not André. 'So, what will you do now?' I was trembling, couldn't understand why. It was a nervousness that completely overtook me.

'Seal up this cave and find my way back to Paris. It's easier for me there than in the countryside.'

Tommy said Michèle was very well fixed for information at Maxim's and was acting as a courier. 'Henri-Philippe is back in the Louvre at his job as a restorer. The Germans have insisted that the work must go on. A lot of paintings and sculptures have been returned, and the museum is now open again. He has access to when the auction sales are coming up and can tip us off.'

Those stamps and labels, were they but a warning of things to come? 'Is Dmitry working for the Russians?'

'Probably. Look, we really don't know. He's been very useful and can be a lot more now.'

But had the Soviets told him to make himself useful so as to find things out? 'And Marcel?' I asked. 'Me, I want to trust him, Tommy, but there's still that little something that isn't quite right.'

'Marcel's okay. Is there anything else?'

'Yes. Me, I'm sorry to have to say this, but you mustn't trust André.'

'But why?'

Since I couldn't tell him about Collin, I couldn't tell him all of it. 'Simone. He's totally devoted to her and to his work. If the Nazis should ever take her, he'll break.'

There, I'd said it, something I'd been afraid to admit even to myself, even after everything that had happened since. Back then, I knew, you see? I knew and I could have stopped him. Me!

As with Marcel, Tommy said André was okay and that I was not to worry so much. 'The firm in London will sure be happy when they hear we've got this stuff. They've a special interest in our work, Lily. Nicki's determined to get back what's his and whatever else we can grab, and so am I.'

They'd not take no for an answer. 'Then the robberies will continue and get bigger and bigger, is that it?'

He reached out, motioned that I was to come to him, but I remained standing with my back to those crates, 'What if the Germans find these? What if we're all taken?'

'Relax. Don't worry so much. Everything's going to be fine. Have you missed me?'

I felt my coat as it fell to the floor, still couldn't take my eyes from him. Candlelight flickered, throwing shadows across the wall, but was there time?

Quickly, I hiked up my dress and tucked it into my belt, kicked off those sabots, and heard them clatter away as my underpants followed and I knelt to one side of him. We kissed. I placed an exploratory hand behind his neck, felt the short curly hairs that were there as he fumbled with his belt, and I knew that his trousers would soon be down and that we'd make love that way, that for a brief moment we'd forget about everything else as we lost ourselves in each other.

Luck played such a part in things. It was luck that got me home that night and told me not to go to sleep, that the dawn would come too quickly.

It was luck that warned me I might soon have visitors and that they'd be asking a lot of questions.

Luck also brought the mayor of Fontainebleau to me first.

'Madame, we must speak freely. We both know that not everyone goes along with the Nazis, but if things should happen . . .'

Picard mopped his florid brow and ran a knuckle over the handlebar moustache. 'You'd better come in. The colonel and the lieutenant are both away. It's safe enough.'

The mouse-brown eyes looked at me. 'Nothing is safe, madame. Me, I have come out here with a warning for you. Last night, you returned from your mother's very late. Questions are being asked.'

'I had two flat tyres! Some idiot scattered broken glass all over the road!'

'The Résistance from Melun?' he asked, startled by what I'd said.

It was the first I'd heard of them. 'Résistance? How should I know?'

'The bicycle, Madame de St-Germain. Please, may I see it?'

'Do you doubt my word?'

'Not for a moment. I merely want to make certain. I don't want hostages to be taken.'

'For what, please?' It was my turn to be startled.

Picard blew his nose then mopped his brow again. 'For the robbery. The theft of several valuable works of art from the Reichsmarschall Göring's lorry.'

'Of this I know nothing, I assure you.'

He wasn't quite satisfied. I think, looking back on it, Picard and

I understood each other very well, but at the time he only nodded brusquely. 'The bicycle, madame. It might just help if the tyres were badly slashed by the broken glass of those people from Melun.'

'Then come and see for yourself.' I indicated the way, and he followed me round the house with his bicycle, which had those big, heavy balloon-type tyres.

I remember that it was very hot inside the shed. Picard sucked in a breath and ran his eyes over each of the tyres. 'Where? Madame de St-Germain, where, exactly, did you run into the glass?'

Had I learned well enough to lie even then? 'On the road about seven kilometres from here. There's a hill. It's an effort to climb when you're tired. It was a very long walk from there.'

He knew the hill. 'Will there still be some glass?' he asked, not of me, you understand, but more of us both. A simple man.

I took a chance. 'There will be. I'll see to it.'

Picard lifted his gaze to mine. I think then that he knew I was involved in things and that he had to make a choice, one way or the other.

Again, there was that brusque nod and a muttered, '*Ah, bon.*' I asked if he would care for a glass of wine. We sat, one on either side of the picnic table Jean-Guy and I had moved earlier. Picard's bicycle leaned against the nearest of our pear trees. 'It's a lovely garden, madame. You do well with it for someone who's not used to the soil. You use your head and plant for the future. For me, I should like a few moments in my garden now and then, but the Germans . . . Ah, they are such sticklers for the paperwork.'

'Let me get you some lettuce and green onions and . . . and some radishes. Yes, I have all those. And eggs . . . would you like ten?'

Ten! Such a thing was unheard of. 'Madame, you honour me, but it isn't necessary. With me . . . Ah, what can I say? Of course, we could use the eggs, a few, just a few, you understand. They'll give me an excuse to come back to see you now and then. Yes, that's what we'll do, but you must register the chickens and me, I must pay you for the eggs. Otherwise . . .' He gave a shrug, the universal gesture.

Our bargain settled, Picard rode off and I wondered then, how the Germans had known I'd come home so late?

It could only mean they were still having the house watched and that, in turn, most probably meant Georges and Tante Marie.

Luck made me think to cut the tyres, *bien sûr*, a terrible loss since replacements were next to impossible. Now luck would have to see me back on the road with several empty wine bottles to smash and kick about.

The things one had to do.

The sound of broken glass is like no other, and I heard it as he kicked it away again. I stood in the middle of the road waiting for Dupuis to say something, but he let the glass do the work. Fortunately, I chose the road from Barbizon to Fontainebleau, so for me there was the advantage that the Caves of the Brigands were just to the south of us and Chailly-en-Bière to the northwest. Barbizon was to the west some three, maybe four kilometres. Melun was between eight and ten almost due north.

It was quiet on the road, except for the sound of the broken glass. Even the birds had deserted us, and the two men who were with Dupuis when that black Citroën came to call, now leaned against the side of it, smoking cigarettes.

Both were *gestapistes français*. One I recognized as having been with that gang who attacked me, the Action française . . .

The glass was green, the sun warm, so that when Dupuis crushed a piece beneath the thick-soled shoes he wore, the sunlight broke as the sound of the glass came to me.

He wasn't satisfied. He waded into the tall grass at the verge and looked around. He examined the gravel right at the edge of the road. He was very thorough—painstakingly so, he always was.

I heard a piece as it tinkled, heard another and another. Dupuis wore a dark brown, lightweight business suit whose threadbare jacket was open, a white shirt, and a brown tie. He reminded me of a shoe salesman. How wrong can appearances be?

'Madame, you say this glass was here when you rode your bicycle back from your mother's after the curfew.'

'Not *after*, Inspector. I started out well before it, but the glass punctured both tyres and slowed me down so that, through no fault of my own, I arrived home well after it had started.'

'*Ah, bon,* but . . .' The small brown mole on this brown man's chin moved as he tossed his head. 'But the glass, madame. Surely, it should have been more flattened by now? A patrol passes by here several times a day. There are farm wagons loaded with manure, firewood, produce . . .'

'At this time of year? Forget about the manure, Inspector. It's very difficult to buy, and all of it has already been used on the fields. As for the firewood, the Germans don't get the French to cut logs at this time of year. They're too busy using up what they've already cut for charcoal and lumber. And the produce, you ask? What produce?'

'Pigs, cattle, horses, chickens. The patrols, madame.'

There were up to six a day sometimes, although their number varied as did their timing, but I didn't enlighten him. 'The tread of those lorry tyres is heavy and deep, is it not? On a hill like this, it would tend to scatter the glass rather than to push it in. Besides, I don't think you're right. You've not been walking back and forth along the road but wandering all over it. If you were to look closely, Inspector, you'd see there are tyre marks in the glass.'

There weren't, of course, but I wasn't going to go down easily. Dupuis walked up the hill to stand in the middle of the road and look back at me. We were perhaps one hundred metres apart. The forest was close on either side, but there wasn't as much underbrush as I would have liked, and those two by the car were just waiting for me to make a run for it.

'*Terroristen* from Melun. *Banditen, ja,*' Dupuis said using the Occupier's terms for such, but as if he was tasting something that's not quite right. 'Sabotage, madame. Is this what you think? If so, hostages will have to be taken and shot.'

He meant it, too. He waited. I waited. Those two waited—he couldn't be serious, but he was, and yet I asked myself, Are they really going to have someone shot for this? I couldn't believe it.

'Madame, *écoutez-moi, s'il vous plaît.* Oberst Neumann has no other choice. All acts of sabotage are to be severely punished so as to set an example to others.'

'But . . . but perhaps it wasn't sabotage? Perhaps a crate of bottles fell off a lorry or wagon and the men only cleaned up what they could?'

I was frantic and hoped my voice hadn't betrayed me. Dupuis took out his pipe, and I watched him slowly pack that thing. Then the pouch into the jacket pocket, then the pat to make sure it was safely there, then the match—would he strike it with the thumb-nail or on the cleat of one of those shoes?

It was the cleat this time. 'Glass,' he said, puffing away to get the furnace going. 'Madame, everyone who was at your house the night of the Reichsmarschall Göring's visit is under suspicion.'

'For what?' I managed.

The match was waved out and pocketed as always. 'For rob-bery, Madame de St-Germain. It is with regret that we must take you to Paris. There are some questions that need to be answered. The children you will leave in the care of your husband's gardener and housekeeper.'

Georges and Tante Marie. That bastard wanted them to pump my kids. He saw that I knew it, and all he did was smile. He'd got me right where he wanted me.

8

The mound of ashes is now almost totally grey. There are big chunks, little ones, powdery flakes—several shades, with lasting embers that only glow when the gusting wind decides to fan them.

I've built this bonfire in the forest knowing they'll see it from the house. As expected, they've sent André to reason with me, but I don't trust any of them. Why should I?

Having made a careful circuit of the area to be certain they've sent no one else, I let him wait. He doesn't yet know I'm close. I've walked in my bare feet—left those shoes they gave me by the fire, the stockings, too, so that he'll see them and think I've gone to relieve myself. He won't know that bare feet are so much better for hunting.

André has gained a good fifteen years, not the few that should have made him the fifty-seven he really is. The shoulders are slumped as if in defeat, there's no pride, it's all gone. The overcoat is the same grey tweed with the black velvet collar, but he has no hat and that just isn't right, not with him.

Even so, I step from behind the trees. Without the wind to fan the embers, there's barely light enough to see him on the other side of the ashes. '*Ah, bon*, André. It's been a long time.'

'Lily. . .' He's startled, casts a glance towards the house, wonders where the others are but somehow manages to ask, 'How did you . . . ? How are you?'

Searching the darkness for the others, I tell him it's not important how I came to be alive.

At once, he's irritable. 'The war's over, Lily. It's finished. Forget it.'

'Me? How could I?'

'Look, I know you must have suffered terribly, but . . .'

'What could you possibly know of my suffering?'

'Simone . . .'

'*Ah, oui,* Simone. I'm sorry she didn't make it.'

'She was the price I had to pay. Did she . . .'

'Say anything, this woman who loved you so much? Is that what you're wondering? Yes, she said lots of things. She asked us not to blame you for what you'd done, and when she died, I know her last wish was that others, not just myself, should show compassion towards you.'

This humbles him, and he stares at the ashes as a gust fans them to life. 'The Nazis left me no choice, Lily. They said they had arrested her, and that if I'd agree to give them certain information, they would look the other way.'

'The Vuittons told you that. Schiller was with them and . . . and Jules.'

'Yes. They all came to my surgery. Your sister was too involved, Lily. I couldn't . . .'

'My sister, yes. And Michèle Chevalier, André, and Henri-Philippe Beauclair. You told those bastards where they could be found, but Janine, she managed to get away.'

'They ought to have known better! I warned them many times. Janine was too impetuous. She took far too many chances. Michèle was far too innocent. She didn't know how to lie, for God's sake. She . . .'

I wait. He knows it's no good trying to tell me Michèle was the first to break. At last, he says, 'How did Simone die?'

He really wants to know, and I can see that he must have dwelt on this matter day and night.

'Bergen-Belsen, André. Can you believe it? We'd been in

Birkenau, the death camp at Auschwitz. Finally, they sent us to Bergen-Belsen, a so-called convalescent camp. Typhus, dysentery like you wouldn't believe, mass starvation, no water at the end. Sixty . . . eighty thousand of us, the men in one part, the women in another, the soup so rotten and thin, everywhere people were dying so fast their last breaths made a constant whisper. A hush as the squeaking, lime-encrusted wheels of the carts hauled the heaps of bodies to the pits for burning and burial by those who were left and could still wield a shovel, myself among them.'

He says nothing. He can't lift his eyes, but I feel no elation, only an emptiness that is hard to describe because he was once my friend. 'Bergen-Belsen, André. Do you know what that must have meant for a woman like Simone? She was so thin. She needed rest, warmth, love—medical attention. You're a doctor. Surely, you can appreciate that?'

Doubtless my voice shows traces of madness, but I have to get it off my chest. 'That camp is in a kind of fir forest, low and swampy. Mud is everywhere. Always there is the mud, but on the morning she died it was all churned up and frozen solid. The spring of last year. March the 20th, so near the end and yet so far. They always woke us at four thirty in the morning for the roll call. The *blockova* would bash her truncheon against the wall of the hut, then scream at us in German, *'Raus! Raus! Schnell, Huren!'* Out! Out! Hurry, whores! *'Herunter!'* Down!—that means down from our so-called beds, André. The din is horrible, the panic indescribable. Sleeping, half-dead, exhausted women tumble from the *Kojen* where, tier upon tier, crammed head to foot, we've spent our nights. Arms, legs—sticks of bone; ribs showing—we fight to reach the floor and get outside. We have to get outside. It's an order. AN ORDER!

'Fog blankets the camp. Frost rims the ground, the barbed wire, and the trees in the distance. Huddled in our filthy rags, we wait under the blinding glare of the searchlights. Always it's, *'Achtung! Achtung!'* from the loudspeakers. *'Zum Appell! Fünf Seite an Seite!'* Line up, five (by five), side by side. Sixty thousand of us . . . One hundred thousand. I really don't know how many. Lots and lots of men and women, but segregated, of course. Oh, yes.

'The frozen mud hurts our feet. Some have shoes; some have none. Socks are mismatched, rags bound around their feet. Shit and blood and pus. Simone? I ask. Where's Simone?

'Frantically, I began to look for her. I ran back to our hut, but Pani Nalzinski, our *blockova*, wouldn't let me get her. 'Please,' I begged. 'She's okay. She's just a little tired. I guarantee you, she'll be on her feet all day.'

'It began to snow, but it wasn't snow, André. It was ashes from the cremation fires that burned in the open. The *blockova* gave me one across the seat and another across the shoulders, shrieking at me to get back in line, me begging her to let me get my friend. 'All right. Both die. If one no good, other no good.'

'At eleven, the roll call was completed. Eleven, André. Nearly seven hours in the freezing cold and God help you if you had to relieve yourself. Eleven was the time for our block to go. There was a mad rush as the doors to the latrine were thrown open. Screams and yells accompanied the pandemonium, laughter, too, wild and shrill and broken by the insane. Blows rained on us from everywhere. Some vented themselves and fell under the blows to be trampled. Some tried to pick them up and were hit for so doing. Others just wept.

'The hole received us. It was huge. You couldn't have asked for bigger. A funnel that was fifteen metres deep, brimful and surrounded by a low wooden rail and the milling throng of fighting, pushing, shoving, anxious women.

'There were no spaces—all were taken. There was no shame, how could there have been? The slippery earth was puddled with half-frozen excrement, the stench of ammonia so unbearable it made one weep.'

I pause. I let this information sink in, giving him time to lift his gaze from the ashes, but he can't bring himself to face me.

Again, I wonder why he's forgotten his hat. Is he still the Judas he was? 'That rail, André, it was stained and greasy. Neither Michèle nor I could touch the ground with our feet when we sat on it, so for us it was a special ordeal to grip the rail, relieve oneself, and cling to your wife.

'Simone was dizzy. She'd had constant dysentery. Months on end of it, poor thing, but she didn't slip, André. We didn't let her fall. Please, you must understand this. The three of us had stuck together through so much.

'There was a shriek from one of the guards. We had to let go of her. She simply fell back into that cesspool, but if you ask me, I think she wanted to. The alternative for her was to be injected with phenol.'

His mouth gapes. A breath is caught and held. There are tears. He wants to hear the last of it and begs me to tell him.

'She drowned. She threw up her arms in panic but never cried out, simply tried to swim to the edge, to claw at the mud and drag herself out, but they pushed her away, André. They laughed. Everyone watched her die like that—all of us, the women in their rags, the guards who'd pushed her back, the *blockovas*. A great circle of people, the fog of the ammonia rising all around her.'

He breaks at last and blurts, 'I didn't want them to take her away. I tried to kill myself, but they threatened to kill her if I did.'

He's weeping now, but I won't go near him. 'They beat me terribly, André, for having tried to help her, but they let me live. Why I don't know and I never will, for I wanted only to die.'

The wind fans the embers. There's a spurt of flame that lets him see the Luger in my hand. That last plea of Simone's comes back to me, and I know that before she went under, she begged me to forgive him. 'Go and tell the others to come out one at a time. I want to talk to each of them alone.'

'They'll never agree to that. This was your only chance. Come and settle things now.'

'I'm setting the terms, not them, and definitely not you.'

Again, he's irritable. Again, he says, 'Let it go, Lily. Forget it. You need psychiatric help. You're suicidal.'

'Simone was my friend long before she ever met you. When she died, a part of me went with her.'

There's no response. He thinks I'm going to kill him, but again I remember that final look of hers and ask, 'Who else is in there with Dupuis?'

'The Vuittons.'

'And Jules?'

'Yes, Jules. Lily . . .'

'Who else? There's someone else.'

Something moves off to my right, another to my left. It's Schiller. I know it is and hear it on André's lips even as I fire.

The sound of the shot is all around us, flat and hard and echoing in the night. I run, slip, and fall, scream at them to leave me alone and fire blankly, once, twice, three times before sense returns and I hear Dupuis calling, 'Madame . . . madame, come back. There's something you should know.'

Schiller's with them. Schiller! What am I to do? There are only two bullets left, and my chest aches so much I think I'm going to die.

Still they search for me, and I wait for it all to end, but finally they give up and go back to the house.

The slug has taken the back off André's head. The hole in his forehead is really very small, just an entry—an excellent shot. Putting on those socks and shoes, I kick ashes over him as we did in the camps, then look for the lime but finally realize there just isn't any.

Schiller . . . so Schiller has come back to join forces with them. Thinking of him puts me right back in Paris, just after that little episode of the broken glass, 3 June 1941. Me, I remember the date because it was Simone's birthday and I hadn't expected to find her hauled in with the rest of us.

The small hotel Dupuis took me to was on the avenue Matignon. A swastika hung above the entrance, but there were no guards standing in the rain, so I knew it wasn't one of their major centres of interrogation. Indeed, except for the flag, you wouldn't have known it was anything other than a delightful little hotel. Very upper class, very posh and convenient, and once an *hôtel particulier*, a private mansion.

Would we have to take the lift? I wondered. So many crazy

things ran through my mind. The rue du Faubourg St-Honoré was at the corner, and just around it was the shop of Monsieur Langlois, where I had first met Tommy.

'Madame,' said Dupuis, tugging at my sleeve.

Tommy caught up with me there. It was there, in front of that very hotel, that I threw the ten thousand francs into his face and slugged him. Dear God, how our lives had changed since then.

Dupuis shoved me ahead, but suddenly I wanted to throw up, though knew I mustn't. That place was only one of several the Gestapo used. Their real headquarters were at 11 rue des Saussaies, in the offices of the Sûreté Nationale, so I knew they'd take me there afterwards. Then it was prison. The children . . . what was I to do about them?

Michèle Chevalier was sitting at the near end of a long wooden bench. She was the first I saw, but there were benches on either side of the marble corridor with its fake Roman friezes and columns. All the places had been taken. On one side were my friends and people I thought I might be able to trust or simply didn't know. On the other were a few of the dealers they'd managed to drag in, a few of the girls, and even some of the women of substance—all of them were guests at Jules's dinner party for Göring, all were French, too, and therefore under suspicion.

Michèle was terrified. Looking the thin, bespectacled student of philosophy and politics he never was, Henri-Philippe was guarding her violin in its case and holding her by the arm. His glasses winked in the unnatural light.

We were forbidden to speak but, when I walked past my sister, she smiled and jerked a thumb-up and made all kinds of signals to say, It's okay. They know nothing. Dupuis took it all in and let me wonder how long they'd all been cooped up and what they'd told them.

Simone and André were next. He was angry with me, but Simone, she had a calmness I can see even now. Remember, please, that she'd hidden Tommy and Nicki and that Tommy was probably again back with her, hence André's anger.

'Lily, it's so good to see you.'

'*Chérie*, it's your birthday. *Ah, mon Dieu*, I've forgotten to bring your present. Dinner . . . can we have dinner together? I think I have enough coupons. Yes . . . yes . . .' I fumbled in my handbag. I didn't know whether to laugh or to cry. Her long black hair was all frizzed out. She'd been drying it much to André's dismay.

'You can't be serious,' he said, knowing we were breaking the rule of silence.

'Oh, but we are,' said his wife and laughs.

We kissed, we hugged. Dupuis was embarrassed. 'Madame, it is forbidden. Please, Obersturmführer Schiller is waiting.'

Simone touched my cheek and gripped me by the hand to reassuringly squeeze the fingers. 'Don't worry, darling. Everything is okay. It's only routine. Someone stole the Reichsmarschall's things but us, ah'—she shrugged her slender shoulders and threw out open hands, palms up,—'how could we be involved in such a thing? You'll stay with us tonight, of course?'

Dupuis hustled me along to an office as I looked back at her and said, 'We'll have a little party for you.'

I had with me an overnight bag, which I'd been allowed to pack. A change of underwear, a nightgown, and toothbrush, my cosmetic case, a few other things, all quite civilized. Dupuis demanded that I hand it over before entering the office, and it was taken by an orderly in jackboots and the black uniform of the SS, but he was not armed, and I had to wonder if the guards had been hidden and if they wanted us all to make a run for it?

Yes, that was exactly what they'd done, for once again that corridor was like a cage of frightened mice. No one knew whether he or she would be the first to bolt, but several knew for sure they'd follow if given but half a chance.

Schiller was in uniform, smoking a cigarette, lost in thought, perhaps, and standing over by one of the windows down whose sides heavy blackout curtains hung. He was looking out at the street, was immaculate—tall, slender, well built, the flaxen hair catching the light.

There was a desk, big, wide, a hectare or two of misplaced Georgian antiquity. Miscellaneous chairs, a carpet, et cetera, because none of it really mattered except for this: the desk, his chair behind it, the one that was directly in front, and the one that was behind that one.

Dupuis cleared his throat and said something subservient but was embarrassed to let me see him like this.

'Frau de St-Germain,' said Schiller. 'A seat.'

'Which one?'

It was that shabby, collaborationist gumshoe's turn now, and he said, 'Madame, you're in grave trouble. Behave accordingly.'

I sat where I was supposed to. Dupuis pulled off his coat and hat, and sat directly behind me while Schiller built church steeples with his fingers, and that duelling scar had a paleness that emphasized the narrowness of his face, the lips especially. 'Katyana Lutoslawski,' he said. 'Perhaps you had better tell us about her.'

'Me? Perhaps first, Lieutenant, you had better tell me who this person is.'

'But surely you remember,' said Dupuis. 'How could you forget?'

The dinner table, the supposed white arsenic. '*Ah, mon Dieu,* Lieutenant, I honestly don't know who you mean.'

'The redhead,' said Schiller, still with church-steeple fingers tapping themselves impatiently.

'The one who called herself Giselle,' said Dupuis, causing me to turn to look at him, something I should never have done, for the shriek that lifted from Schiller made me jump.

'The wife of Alexis Nikolai Ivanovich Lutoslawski!' he shouted, was suddenly red in the face and on his feet with a threatening fist, and I knew for sure for me it had begun. The tiara and all that ancient history was soon pouring from him, everything the Action française thugs pried out of me in the forest. 'Thomas Carrington, your lover!' he shrieked.

'My ex-lover. That business was over before it began, and if you can prove otherwise, Lieutenant, then you will only prove yourself wrong. And as for this . . . this woman, I never met her.'

'And Lutoslawski?'

'The robberies are linked to him, to objects he once possessed,' said Dupuis.

'Stolen from the Russians, our ally,' said Schiller. 'They want them back.'

'You two are crazy. I've nothing to do with this. Why not ask my husband? Ask the Vuittons, eh? They'll tell you all you need to know, and as for Russia being an ally, if you Germans keep saying the things you do, I think you can forget it soon.'

'You were seen talking to that woman,' said Schiller.

'By your sister,' added Dupuis.

'Why not? I was the hostess, wasn't I? Should I have ignored her?'

'When did you notice she had left the party?'

'I didn't. I was in the library with everyone else, but personally, after what happened to her, I'd have left a lot sooner.'

'The loot, madame. Where did you people hide it?' asked Dupuis.

'You'd better tell us,' said Schiller. 'It'll go a lot easier on you.'

'Listen, you two, I know nothing of this.'

'Your papers . . . papers,' snapped the lieutenant. 'You're English.'

I handed them over, but he knew all about them. 'I have a cancer,' I told him of the letter he was opening.

'De Verville . . . yes, yes, I can see that he's signed it. A German specialist will have to be consulted. I'll see that we find one to examine you.'

Me, I was done for—finished—and I knew it, but realized then that he'd led me to this little point, the cancer of my womb. 'Your sister, Frau de St-Germain, why is it that she has French citizenship and you don't?'

My shrug was automatic, and I don't think I could have stopped it had I wanted to. 'Janine has always considered herself to be one hundred percent French. For myself, I'm fifty- fifty.'

'A lover of the British. We can prove that Janine Marteau was involved in the robberies,' said Schiller, still caressing my papers.

He let me think about it, then said, 'Marteau is the last name of a former lover of that mother of yours. He's the father of that illegitimate bastard you call a sister.'

There had been one slip-up, Nini the result, but our father had never held it against *maman*. Janine he loved as if his own, as did *maman*.

'The paintings,' said Schiller, 'and the other things that were stolen. Where are they?'

He'd a short, black leather strap folded over once, its two ends clutched in the right hand. Maybe it was five centimetres wide, maybe six, but it was thick enough to do lots of damage, and I had to wonder if Dupuis was the one who would have to hold me.

But there was a knock at the door. It was the orderly who took my suitcase. He crossed the room to confide something to Schiller who looked at me and smiled. 'Your children, Frau de St-Germain. Apparently, they have more to say about this than yourself.'

'A coffee, please, and some soup—thin soup, you understand. Put lots of water in it. And . . . and I'd like some bread. White, if you have it. Not black.'

The little restaurant is on a side street in Fontainebleau. If you want the truth, the thought of Schiller being with Dupuis and the others has really unsettled me. I also couldn't take the cold and the loneliness after what happened with André. I had to come in for a while.

'Madame, is it really you?'

Matthieu Fayelle is just the same, complete with thumbprints on his apron, the stomach of his wife's good cooking, the moustache, and thick brown hair that's still a little too long.

'It's me. I have to get warm. I need a bit of rest.'

'Are you on the way out to the house? Madame, there's nothing left. The Germans . . .'

'Have taken everything. Yes . . . yes, I'm on my way for a last little visit. Matthieu, I need to be quiet. Look, Tommy was your friend, isn't that right? He helped you, so now you must help me.'

'A table in the sun. I'll make sure no one sits nearby, but the soup, madame? Surely . . .'

'Just the thin soup and a half-and-half coffee and water, no milk, no sugar. I'm still not used to things.'

He wipes his eyes, this great big guy who once drove a *gazogène* lorry for us. 'We thought you dead,' he says. '*Finie!*'

'And me, I thought you also,' I say, looking up at him in warning.

He ducks his moist brown eyes and mutters, 'It's over, madame. They've all gone. We can begin to live again, eh? A little place . . . If you need a bed, a room, you have only to ask.'

'I may need help. Please don't forget this.'

'For me, for us that are left, you have only to ask.'

'Good.'

I sit in the sun and warm myself. Just a corner of the town hall can be seen, the *hôtel de ville et Feldkommandantur,* and I remember Matthieu and the others, but they came later. First there were the two robberies, then the interrogations, then my children and what they had inadvertently revealed to Georges and Tante Marie.

The soup is thin, as I've requested. Just a few slivers of onion, a little grated pepper, cheese baked on top, with butter, real butter. This I can't believe. It hurts to look at it, to smell the aroma. Such simple things we all took for granted.

The bread is crusty. When broken, it soaks up the soup. The coffee is real. Matthieu flutters around. His wife has come out of the kitchen but is afraid to approach.

I tell him the soup is excellent, exactly what I need.

'Was it hard for you?' he asks. He's all upset and twisting his hands in that apron of his.

'It doesn't matter. Look, I need some quiet, eh? I must think things through. I have a job to do and must be careful.'

He nods. *Ah!* he understands and says, 'I've heard that Monsieur Jules and his friends are back.'

'Then you know it will be wise for you and your wife to say nothing of me. Not until I make contact with you again. Hey, listen, my friend, can you get me some nine millimetres?'

He understands and leaves the restaurant. I finish the soup by running the bread slowly around the plate so as to catch the last droplets. Memory comes.

I drain the coffee cup.

Dupuis waited. He was very grave. He knew and I knew that somehow my children had betrayed me and that Georges and Tante Marie had much to say.

I'm right back there: 3 June 1941. In a gesture of sympathy or whatever—me, I don't know—Dupuis had taken this opportunity to show a little compassion.

Before witnesses, of course, he fed me a bowl of soup and a coffee. A last supper.

'Madame, please, it's time to go.'

I got up and walked out to his car and we drove to the house. Marie . . . I remember that she was wearing her pink dress, with the white socks and glossy black saddle shoes. She was getting tall—growing like a weed. Her hair had been severely brushed, and it glistened as it fell below her shoulders.

She was so pale and frightened she didn't say a thing. Jean-Guy eyed me suspiciously. No doubt Georges had been filling him full of things—adultery, the de St-Germain name, et cetera.

'Monsieur Tommy,' said Tante Marie. That old hen was bristling by the stove, just waiting to spill it all.

'What about him?' I asked.

'He was here,' she said. 'Isn't that correct, my husband?'

Georges nodded. 'The boy has told us, madame.'

'Of course, Monsieur Carrington was here, but that was ages ago, and the inspector remembers this.'

It was a gamble, but it worked. Luck was with me again. Jean-Guy had told them of Tommy's earlier visit, when Dupuis had first come here looking for him on a charge of murder, February 1940.

'But he's been back since?' hazarded Dupuis.

Both of my children shook their heads. 'Ah, no, monsieur, he couldn't have. He would've gone to prison, *n'est-ce pas?*' said my daughter, widening her lovely eyes.

'Prison,' said my son. 'He's a bad one, Inspector. A number. I hope you catch him.'

Dupuis was exasperated with that old couple and gave them the blazes for being so stupid, but at the door he said, 'We both know it won't be so easy the next time.'

Matthieu Fayelle returns to take the dishes away. As he reaches for the soup plate, a spill of cartridges leaves his hand. 'There are more if you should need them.'

As my hand closes about them, I say, 'Get me a Schmeisser, two fully loaded magazines, and a grenade. Have them ready for me.'

'But surely the police . . .'

'You leave the *flics* out of this! Dupuis is with them at the house. It's a private matter, Matthieu. I want no interference.'

Down through the beeches, I can see the millpond before the small, quaint farmhouse of the Poulins, whose white stucco and green shutters form a tidy place where geese are force-fed while the husband basks in the sun. It's a scene out of Sisley. Good people, those two. Before the war, I used to bring the children here in my little car to buy eggs and goose livers. While they were with Madame Poulin, I would bathe at the far end of the pond behind a screen of reeds. Henri Poulin would stand in his flat-bottomed punt, pretending to fish, and I didn't mind if he saw me. I rather liked the idea. It was, in a way, a chance for me to repay him.

Janine and Michèle came for a visit early in July of that summer of 1941, and the three of us rode out here on our bicycles. The pond is southwest of Fontainebleau, on the road to the village of Ury, so you pass through the forest and, for us, it was to be a little holiday.

They had both obtained an *Ausweis* for the weekend. Michèle had asked the general who was interested in her to help, so we had two days and the weather was perfect. Marcel was at the house and when that Saturday's school was out, the children would be with him.

It was a chance to talk. Our bicycles lay in the grass behind us, we on the blanket Janine had brought. A wicker picnic basket provided everything, along with two bottles of Château Latour-Blanche, the 1927, my having plundered my husband's cellar. Bees hummed among the daisies, buttercups, and sky-blue chicory. Nini lay on her back, Michèle on her tummy. Me, I sat right where I'm sitting now. 'We have to leave it for a while,' I told them. 'Lie low. Let Schiller and Dupuis plug away, but don't do anything to stir things.'

It's Michèle who said, 'Henri-Philppe told me there's to be a big auction this autumn, that it looks like Göring's Luftwaffe will finish off the Russians and the Wehrmacht will be in Moscow by then.' The Germans had invaded Russia on 22 June.

'And you . . . what do you think about it?' Janine asked her.

'Me, I don't even want to talk about it!'

'*Idiote!*' said my sister. 'The *Boche* are going to lose.'

'But Göring will still be there for the auction. Henri-Philippe's certain a notice has been sent to Hofer. They always send notices to him when something's coming up. Jules is in on it, too. He and the Vuittons have been over the lists of works that are to be sold. Now leave me be!'

She was so near to tears, we let her rest. I even lowered my voice. 'Nini, I meant what I said. That trip to Paris with Dupuis finished me. I've the children to think of.'

'And Tommy?' she asked.

'I'm going to ask him to take the children and me to Switzerland or out through Spain. It's worth the risk. I can't stay here.'

She flung her straw away. 'Neither are possible! If they were, Tommy would have done it. Besides, we have to move people. Those places are reserved for them.'

This was my little sister. The Midi beauty was still there, the black gloss of her short hair, the flounce of it as she tossed her pretty head or settled those dark eyes on me. 'Nini, Georges and Tante Marie have become a problem. They watch the house constantly and report everything.'

'So what are you going to do about it?'

'Me? Are you crazy? If anything should happen to them, Schiller and Dupuis would immediately suspect me and you know it!'

'Not if you were to do it the right way.'

Ah, merde, I couldn't be hearing this, but her words were to haunt me for months. 'You try to be so hard, Nini, but underneath it all I know who you really are.'

'Then you have failed to realize that the *Boche* are going to be driven out of France. Russia will be the end of them. More and more, the Reich will have to move its forces to the east. Dmitry says it's only a matter of time before the tide turns, that Stalin's going to suck the Wehrmacht in and crush them. One hard winter is all it's going to take. Their supply lines are far too long as it is, and they must know it, too.'

'And how is Dmitry these days?'

'Busy,' she said and shook her head to indicate I mustn't say anything more in front of Michèle.

'Go for a walk, you two,' said our violinist. 'I don't want to listen!'

We moved away to sit in the shade. 'She's terrified, Lily. I wish we could get her out of Paris and into the Free Zone. Schiller knows she's the weaker of us. He's taken her to dinner twice—she couldn't refuse—so he sits there at Maxim's every night he can and watches her play her violin. To counter this, I've asked her to take the general as a lover, that this would be by far the safest thing for all of us. She's promised to think about it. I've given her the weekend.'

Nini would do that, too. 'And yourself, *chérie*? What about you?'

There was a grin I recognized, a lifting of the breasts with cupped hands. 'The Folies Bergère. One of their bare-assed nudes. The feathers tickle my nose, and it's cold up there on that big staircase with all of them ogling me, but it's a living, so one must do it, I think.'

'How's Tommy?'

'Fine—at least he was the last time we met at Marcel's. He's gone into the Free Zone with Nicki and Dmitry. They've taken the wireless set with them and two packages for Spain. Switzerland is impossible. We can't even get the artwork out that way, so they're hoping to set up something else.'

And sending information back to London, the 'packages' being downed aircrew or others on the run. 'Did Katyana make it?'

Nini gave a nod. 'She's with friends, but Nicki's afraid she'll try to come back. With that red hair she refuses to dye, and those green eyes, they'd pick her up at once. We never knew exactly when Göring and his entourage would pay you a visit, so she had to infiltrate them. She's got guts, Lily. I think she'd kill for Nicki, and if she does come back, you take good care of her because we may need her again.'

'I wish we could get those things out of that cave. It's far too dangerous having them there. Someone's bound to find out, and if they do, it's the end for us.'

'You worry too much. You always were such a worrier.'

Janine kissed me on the cheek, and I can still feel the softness of her breath. 'I'm scared, Nini. Scared all the time.'

'Who isn't? Hey, listen, you, we moved eighteen packages last month. Eighteen! Who would have thought it possible a year ago? Seven were escaped POWs. Now that Russia has come into the war, we'll be getting drops by parachute from England. Weapons, Lily. Things with which to fight back!'

She was so eager, she asked me for the names of people I thought we could trust, and I nodded towards the house that was across the pond. 'Matthieu Fayelle as well.'

'Him?' she asked.

'*Oui*. I'm sure of it, but honestly can't tell you why. Clateau also. His butcher shop in Barbizon has been used for meetings. Mother's certain of it. He also has the use of his *gazogène* van.'

'Then there's hope. Where one is found, there will be others.' She was like some sort of missionary.

'What about Marcel? How's he been shaping up?'

'Jules has been to see him twice with offers of peace.'

'Then we're in trouble.'

'Perhaps, but for myself, I'm more worried right now about Dmitry. I'm certain he's really working for the Soviets, but we don't know what they want of him. Whenever we need false papers, he gets them, but still won't reveal his sources. The Communists are good, Lily. I'm sure they have a powerful transmitter in Paris and that the Germans, though able to detect it, can't precisely pin it down because the security is so tight. But when I ask Dmitry, he simply shrugs and says he doesn't know, that so far he's been unable to make contact with them, so he tags along with us and he watches. He's useful, yes—very, but he also worries me, and I'm the one who brought him in.'

'Will you be sending escapees to the house?'

'It's too risky. The committee has decided you're to be left out of things as much as possible.'

This was such a relief, I'm ashamed to admit that I knew nothing of such a committee. 'Let's go back. Michèle will be wondering where we are.'

Nini shook her head. 'She understands it's safest this way. Our visit's not just for pleasure or to talk things over. Henri-Philippe really is certain about that the auction and that there's a good chance of our stealing quite a lot. Tommy wants us to, and so does Nicki.'

'Then take it someplace else! Don't involve me. *Bon Dieu, de bon Dieu de merde,* are you people crazy? Schiller will be down on me like a flash!'

'Look, it has to be done, so that's all there is to it. You, me, Tommy, and Nicki are the only ones who know where that stuff is hidden. There's lots more room. If we have to, we can use it again. In the meantime, help us organize. Find those we can trust. Build a network for us here so that we'll have that help when needed.'

'No self-respecting Frenchman, *résistant* or not, would ever work for a woman or even include her in any such meeting.'

'Not unless she was British, and not unless she had access to a wireless and could call on London for arms drops, so there, my little friend, you have your reason and permission to tell them if necessary. About the wireless, that is. Nothing else.'

'Thanks. Thanks a lot!'

Michèle lay in the sun, lost to the embrace of sleep and exquisitely so. 'Telling her that she should have an affair with that general isn't fair of you, Nini. She and Henri-Philippe should be having children and building a life for themselves.'

The sky became more hazy as the afternoon grew. We had our picnic, had our time. Lots of laughs, lots of talk about little things, too, not just about the Occupation and what we might have to do about it.

A last memory is of Michèle and Janine standing timidly knee-deep in the water just beyond the reeds. Both were naked. Both faced the opposite shore where the sun still shone and Poulin was mending a bit of fence.

They had gorgeous figures, really superb bottoms. Poulin squinted into the sun and shielded his eyes as his wife called sharply to him and my sister waved and cried out, 'Oo-oo, Monsieur Poulin, we're over here. *C'est moi,* Janine. Lily's too modest to come in.'

We were still there at dusk, three heads bobbing in the water upon whose surface were mirrored the threads of sunset and the wings of dragonflies.

The noise of someone digging comes to me through the forest behind the orchard. I pause. I listen hard. I ask myself again, as I have so often since I killed André, is Schiller really with them, was that voice I heard his?

Everything comes at me: the shrieks, the blows, the threats. He has the power of life or death over me, and I want so much to die, but he won't let me. Not yet. Never yet. The sound of digging stops. There are no voices, no muted curses or arguments.

Through a gap in the trees, down from me a little, Jules is burying André's body. He stands in a shallow pit. A Browning automatic is close to hand, a 9 mm and one of those the British dropped to us later on in the war, but don't ask me how he came by it.

There's no one else around. Just the two of us. It's such an opportunity, but I haven't seen him in so long I find my emotions torn. On the one hand, there is a loathing I can't stop; on the other, pity. He's older, but still very handsome—distinguished. Unused to digging graves. Already there are blisters.

As he stoops, the jet-black hair falls over that brow. He never tried to intercede when we were in the Cherche-Midi, not that it would have done any good. For myself, I understand this, but how is it that he's still around, that he wasn't at least sent into forced labour?

I can only say that he was far too useful to Göring and all the others. For him, we had simply ceased to exist—finished, just like that. *Puff!* And up the stack. Perhaps he even had an apéritif with some new woman.

He's married again. Her voice over the telephone sounded young and excited, only to become distraught at a strange woman asking for her husband. Jealousy is so instant in the young, especially when one is in love. Me, I pity her. He must be running around with someone else, and already she's beginning to notice his absences.

They have a flat in Auteuil, on the rue Boileau. Very posh, very handy to everything, the quays along the Seine, the Bois de Boulogne, et cetera, and a baby girl who is three months old. Is he any better as a father?

From time to time, he pauses to tidy his hair and brush off the jacket's sleeves. When it's back to digging again, I have to wonder where the others are.

Making a wide circuit through the forest, I see that André's car is gone. They've split up, but it's a trap. It has to be. That's the way Schiller and Dupuis would work, but have they left the car down the road a piece? Are they now walking back, the one well ahead of the other?

In spite of this, I take a chance. It's only a short distance from the coach house diagonally across the drive and into what was once the ground-floor study of my husband's father. Voices come to me as I step inside—Vuitton and then that sharp-tongued wife of his. They're in the kitchen.

'The lieutenant is right, Louis. We can't stay bottled up here waiting for that *salope* to come to us. He and Dupuis were right to go out and hunt her down before she kills us.'

'And what then, my dear Dominique?'

He's so dry about it all.

'We'll have to deal with him first and then Dupuis. You know that as well as I.'

'Perhaps that Sûreté can be persuaded to help us. With Schiller out of the way, we can . . .'

'Jules shouldn't be out there alone like that. She'll . . .'

'My dear Dominique, is it that you're still worried about the life of our protégé? Of what earthly use is he to us now?'

'The three of us must stick together, Louis. The lieutenant . . . I've seen the way he looks at Jules and ourselves.'

'As does Dupuis. Her killing de Verville can only have helped them, but perhaps we'll be lucky, perhaps she'll finish off the two of them and we can negotiate with her ourselves. She can't be entirely unreasonable when she finds out about all of those who are still with us.'

'Fool! She's insane. She'll strike when we least expect!'

Their voices rise and fall. From where I'm standing in the corridor, I can just see a sleeve of Vuitton's coat through the splintered boards of the doorjamb but does he have a gun in that hand?

'Let's go together to Jules, Louis,' says that Nefertiti. 'Don't leave me alone in this house.'

'Jules will be all right. Lily won't kill him.'

'*Ah, mon Dieu*, me, I'm not hearing this! How can you say such a thing?'

Vuitton gives a snort of derision. 'Because he knows what happened to their children, and she'll have to hear it from his lips alone. Now please try to calm yourself while I have a look around.'

'I'll go and stay with Jules. Someone should.'

'You'll stay here where I can find you.'

'I'll go up to the library then. From up there, I can watch the road.'

Vuitton is tired of her nervousness and exhales a, 'Very well, do as you like. You always have.'

The sleeve moves, and I hear him step out into the courtyard.

Fastidiously, Nefertiti picks her way through the house and up the stairs, and I watch as she reaches the landing but doesn't look back.

When I come to the library, I find her crouched among the books that are littered everywhere, but what does she search for? Answers to what must happen? Portents of the future, wisdom from the past?

Very quickly, she tires of it and stands to one side of an empty window, gazing out over the drive to the road beyond. She has a little pistol clutched tightly in her right hand. The high coat collar frames the piled up, jet-black hair where pins and skewers of beaten gold and carnelian hold it in place.

This one had my children killed—I know she did. There was fighting, that tragic, terrible sound of guns. I heard Jean-Guy cry out to someone, 'There's my mother! Yes, there!'

I heard Marie screaming, 'Jean-Guy, please don't! *Maman . . . Maman*, they are going to kill you!'

Marie could think only of me, even at such a time. 'Madame Vuitton, I've come to execute you in the name of the Résistance. Please do not attempt to turn around or cry out.'

Not a muscle moves as I place the Luger's muzzle against the back of her neck. 'Now drop the gun, madame, and I'll give you a moment to ask God for forgiveness.'

The seconds pass, and it's really far too quiet. Just the two of us, eh, and the musty smell of books.

'Fool, my husband is right behind you.'

In an instant, I see him grinning at me, he having used his wife as bait, but one slug tears off his lower jaw and the other slams into his chest and throws him back into the corridor.

And her little gun has jammed, or so she thinks. She can't believe it hasn't fired. Finally, I hear myself saying, 'So, madame, luck is with me yet again, eh? Now please allow me. It's simply the safety catch. This one, that's right next to your thumb, you have to push it up.'

She begs, pleads, cries at me, and backs away until she gives a startled scream, and I hear the sound as she hits the steps below.

Exhaustion comes. It's always swift after a killing. One feels totally drained, but I know Jules is out there and will have heard the shots, as may Schiller and Dupuis yet, for a moment, I can only stand and listen to the house, to its silence and the fragments of memory.

Her body lies sprawled on the steps. Blood drains from her broken head. Vuitton is very dead, but I can't take the chance. One slug for him and two for her. I'm just like Schiller. I've crawled right back down into the cesspool with him and all the others, and this I don't like about myself. For this, as for so many other things, I am ashamed.

Making my way carefully downstairs, I step over her body and leave the house to my husband. I know I must remember how it was back then, that only in my doing so is there salvation, and that before I die I must confess everything.

Now, where did I leave off remembering? *Ah* bon, that autumn of 1941 and my sister's request that I recruit men to help us. Yes . . . yes, that's where I was but did I tell you we were to rob a German train? Can you imagine such a thing? A mother with two kids? A woman in love, warm, sensitive still, one even willing to forget and to forgive so long as she could escape with her children.

What an idiot I was.

There are some rocks, a place to hide, and I'm near the tower, but won't go up there yet. Too many memories, too much feeling.

Clateau . . . Yes, yes, I'll start with Clateau, the butcher, and the loft above his slaughterhouse in Barbizon. It was full of tobacco smoke. I was the only woman present, and it was very late. Well after curfew. I'd ridden my bicycle all the way there through the pouring rain and was still freezing.

There were seven of us sitting around the table on which a single lantern burned among half-empty bottles of Armagnac. Four of the men were from Melun—distrustful guys who'd just as soon cut our throats. Two worked for the railways, a third was with the police, and the last a pious schoolteacher. Two Communists, one Socialist, and one Radical Socialist. *Ah, mon Dieu,* it was quite a combination. All were over the age of fifty, and all of them knew that, if caught, they'd be shot and their families and closest relatives taken, the women sent into forced labour, the men, from the age of eighteen on, held hostage until needed to atone for the actions of other *résistants*, the children sent to reform schools in the Reich or to the camps.

Clateau and I formed numbers five and six, but it was to the seventh that we needed to turn: He of the *gueules cassées*, the broken mugs from the 1914–1918 war, those poor unfortunates whose facial features have been disfigured by shrapnel, machine-gun fire, or other such things. Paul Tessier lived in the little town of Bois-le-Roi on the Seine and about eight kilometres to the south of Melun. The main railway line to Paris went right through there. Tessier was a wood-carver whose services were not much in demand those days, but his fingers were of a surgeon. Later I was to discover that he knew all about explosives but, more than this, that he enjoyed them.

'This railway train?' he asked.

He was of about sixty, I suppose. 'One railway truck. Only one,' I told him. 'The paintings and other works of art will be sealed inside it by welding the doors shut.'

'It's too risky,' said the schoolteacher, reaching for the cigarettes I'd brought along with the Armagnac from my husband's cellar. 'Who's to say the things will stay in France, should we get them?'

He was emaciated, possibly tubercular, and wore glasses that served only to hide his blue eyes and then, suddenly, to expose their nervousness.

'Right now, my friend, the stuff's slated for Germany, so why argue?' I asked. 'Something has to be done to stop it. Isn't that right?'

It was the *gueule cassée* who said, 'What interest have you in this? The way I see it, your husband's in bed with the *Boche*, and we shouldn't trust you.'

'He's my husband only in name. Look, I haven't slept with him in over two years. We stay together because . . .'

'Because she's British,' interceded Clateau, 'and her husband needs her to watch over his family's house. In turn, she needs him to keep her from the internment camp.'*

'A fine match!' said the smaller of the two railwaymen, one whom you wouldn't trust with his mother's handbag. He'd sunk half a bottle already and was brave, but not on the drink, had the innate courage of a cornered rat. 'Your railway truck, madame. Why, please, will it depart from the Gare de Lyon?' He was smart, too.

'Because Göring is afraid the RAF might bomb the train, so he's taking no chances. The train will be routed south to Dijon and from there to Mulhouse on the Rhine and finally to Munich.'

---

* Curfew times were often changed at will, though generally settled down to the above.

He was impressed. 'How is it that you know all this?'

'I . . . I can't say. Look, it would be foolish of me to reveal my sources. The less others know, the better.'

'How many men have you?' snapped the *flic*. He was not in uniform, but one can always tell a cop.

'That I also can't reveal. When the time comes, you'll know by the armbands they'll wear.'

'Our funeral?' the schoolteacher said with a snort.

There was only one way to handle this. I got up and said 'I'm leaving. Forget you ever saw me. Forget I asked for your help. France is being plundered of her art treasures, and all you can do is drink my brandy!'

'Sit down, madame. Please, it's all right. Don't be put off by our little questions,' said Tessier, but was the broken mug their leader? He had a way with him I liked. He dragged out a map of the district and began to spread it on the table. 'The bottles . . . come now, boys,' he said. 'Don't knock them over. The lady's been generous.'

A forefinger traced out the line from the Gare de Lyon through to Villeneuve-Saint-Georges and on southward to Melun and Bois-le-Roi.

'We must discuss the repercussions first,' he said, lifting those small, hard eyes to look fully at me, and I knew I couldn't shrink from this initial defiance, for he had the twisted face of a deformed potato, the wired jaws that must have hurt terribly in the damp and the cold. 'Since hostages will be taken and shot, madame, from where, please, would you like this to happen? In my town, or theirs?' He indicated the four from Melun. 'Or yours?' His voice had the flutter of dry wind over paper.

'Fontainebleau,' I heard myself saying, 'is far too close to my house. We need to stop the train somewhere . . .'

'We need to switch it on to a siding,' said the smaller of the two railwaymen. 'Villeneuve-St-Georges would be suitable and far enough from all of us, but the closer one gets to Paris, the more Germans one has to put up with.'

'How many other railway trucks will there be?' asked his pal. 'Is it to be a goods train, madame, or one that also carries passengers?'

'I . . . I don't know yet. Look, as soon as I find out, I'll get word to you.'

'How?' demanded the schoolteacher.

I was getting to like him less and less. 'Through a friend of a friend.'

Tessier clucked his tongue and waved an impatient finger. 'Arnold, be quiet, eh? Let the lady tell us if she'll have a cutting torch to open that can of beans and the lorries with which to move the stuff once we have it.'

There were so many details to work out, it all seemed hopeless.

'You really do need help, madame,' he said, 'but where are you going to hide everything if we should manage to steal it?'

'I have a place but can't tell you where it is.'

'Then it's no deal,' said the schoolteacher.

'Arnold, *pour l'amour de Dieu*, be quiet,' snapped Tessier.

'Surely the *Boche* will have a guard on this train?' asked Clateau. 'We haven't any guns, madame. There's bound to be a fight. Some of us will get . . .'

He left it unsaid, but butchers the world over tend to be practical. Tessier ran his finger down the railway line, and I knew he was still worrying over the problem of hostages. 'Nemours,' he said, 'where the line curves into the Bois de la Commanderie. The woods will help us. I'll go to Paris and make the complete run. I've a cousin who lives in Nemours. He's a real shit, and in bed with the Nazis, so it'll be good to get in touch with him. That way the *Boche* won't be suspicious of me.'

'I could meet you in Avon on your way back, if that would suit. My children go to school in Fontainebleau so I have the excuse of being there when they get out.'

'At five' he said, lifting those puckered eyes of his. 'Well, what about it, Gaston?' he asked the taller of the two railwaymen.

'Five . . . no, the five thirty, I think,' said that one. 'It'll pass through there on the way into Paris, but you'll only have a few minutes and the platform will be guarded.'

Those schedules could have been off as well, but I nodded. It was too good an opportunity to miss and I had to do something.

Tessier squinted at me. I think, then, that he finally said, Okay, to himself, for he smiled and shook his head. 'A woman with two children should limit her risks, madame. Let me get off the train and have my supper someplace. A little café, a bistro—surely Fontainebleau has such, or have the *Boche* turned it back into the luxury of the kings?'

I mentioned the restaurant of Matthieu Fayelle, and all of them understood.

'Then I'll see you there at four thirty, madame, should the train not be delayed. We'll have an acorn coffee or perhaps even an apéritif. It will be my pleasure.'

'What day?' Already I was thinking I could really trust him and it was such a relief.

'Which day would suit you best?' he asked. 'For me, my time is more or less my own, since the wife runs our little *tabac* without too much assistance, especially now that there's so little tobacco and what there is of it, leaves much to question.'

'Friday.'

'*Ah, bon,* and not a no-alcohol day.'

As were Tuesdays, Thursdays, and Saturdays, but could I get cigarettes from him? I wondered. Oh, for sure, the rations were being cut and cut and women still weren't allowed a card and tickets, but there were ways, weren't there? Always. 'Yes, Friday would be best. It'll give me time to talk to some of the others.'

'No names,' said the schoolteacher. 'From now on, please.'

'It goes without saying, eh?' I told him. 'Of course, we'll be careful. You also.'

'I have a van,' said Clateau. 'I can help you with that.'

His grizzled moon face was deadly serious, and it was then that I realized he must have known Tommy and I were near the caves the night we saw him.

I nodded. I said, 'I knew I could count on you.' But could I really? One never knows. Even butchers can be tempted.

The glasses were filled, the cigarettes gathered. We drank a toast to our little venture and one by one left that place.

Those guys from Melun had come by bicycle as had Tessier, so

I was glad I was not any of them. For me, there was probably only one patrol, for them perhaps as many as three and, of course, for me the distance was much shorter.

It seemed strange, listening for the departing squeaks of their bicycles. A dog barked. Clateau gave a muted curse as he slipped a parcel of sausages into my hands. Good ones, too. The night was full of rain, but that would make the patrols less likely. I passed the farmhouse of my mother, rode across the plain, and up into the forest. When I had to, I walked, and when, finally, I got near the house, I headed through the orchard to the potting shed and left my bicycle there.

Then I made a careful circuit and when I found Georges standing under an overhang, smoking his pipe, I knew I was going to have to do something about him.

I had only a brief memory of that next meeting with Paul Tessier. I knew that I had brought him something very dear to the hearts of all true Frenchmen. A bottle of absinthe, the real stuff—illegal, of course, since before the 1914–1918 war when the government banned it for fear of its causing a decline in the birthrate.

I didn't know about that, but did know its happy combination of alcohol and aromatic herbs or whatever, would help him. He understood my unspoken reasons for the gift but said only an embarrassed thanks as he tucked the bottle out of sight in his haversack.

Matthieu Fayelle brought our 'coffee.' There were several Germans, and he was understandably nervous and quickly went back into the kitchen.

'Madame . . .' began Tessier.

'Please call me Lily. It's easier, and for what we have to do, less formal.'

'*Ah, bon, merci.* So, Lily, listen carefully. What we need is a dummy railway truck. This must be the same in every way as to the one the *Boche* will use.'

'Rolling stock is too hard to come by. Even I know they've taken far too much of it.'

'Yes, but the impossible must be done. Somehow the switch must be made, then later we can cut open the other one and remove everything in relative comfort.'

I know I must have said something, but it's lost to me. He spoke of welds and cold chisels, of the noise, the terrible delay the work of opening the railway truck would cause.

I was to organize the taking of the train only if all else should fail. 'We have to trust them, Lily. Those two railwaymen will come through. Don't worry so much. Just look after the emptying and hiding of all that artwork. You'll have enough to do with those.'

'And the schoolteacher?' I asked. 'What will he do?'

'He has no more problems since he met with an accident on the road home. It was necessary. I'm sorry I couldn't have tipped you off, but there was no possible way.'

The streets of Fontainebleau are almost deserted, the restaurant is half-empty. No one pays much attention to me. The bar, *le zinc*, is polished.

'Matthieu, I think I'll take you up on that offer of a bed for the night. I find I'm really quite tired.'

'A little supper, madame? An omelette perhaps?'

'Yes, but in the room. Let me eat it alone.'

Fayelle has his reasons for not having pointed the finger at my husband at the end of the war. Some of these reasons are bound up in his dealings on the *marché noir*, some in the actions of his wife's father and brother, some, too, in what we had to do. The carpet of the past is a useful thing and it often hides so much.

Alone, like me, we are the only two who are left, though he obviously has his friends and I obviously know that he has them. The Schmeisser I've requested is lying on the bed beneath a folded comforter. There are two box magazines of ammunition, a British Mills Mark I grenade, and something else, a spool of piano wire and pair of cutters.

He's thought of everything and swears he'll help me if I need him.

The bed is like most others, not flat and of bone-hard, rough boards and so tightly cramped one can hardly move. It's soft, a real bed like I had at the clinic. Clean and smelling of newly washed sheets, but I'm still far too used to the other. I doze, drift off fitfully. At twelve, I awaken with a start to hear the lonely whistle of a train. One, two, three short blasts and then it's gone, straight through Avon without stopping. How is this, please? What has happened? Get up! GET UP! Something's gone wrong.

A cold sweat has broken out all over me. Instinctively, I've slipped a finger through the loop of the grenade.

The door . . . Those steps out there . . . Are Schiller and Dupuis waiting for me?

The Schmeisser lies on the carpet. The Luger is hidden under my pillow, and I'm remembering. I can't help but do so. It was late in the autumn of 1941, and I'd just been to Nemours to meet Paul Tessier. Paul had some questions, has raised an issue I can't answer.

Word had filtered through to him that it could be a trap, that there would be no railway truck of paintings and other pieces, but one full of German soldiers, that Obersturmführer Johann Schiller had been to the Gare de Lyon to inspect the train and had given that empty railway truck more than a passing scrutiny.

In the morning, I find Matthieu and tell him I must borrow a bicycle with a carrier basket, and will need a lift to the railway junction that is just to the south of Bourron-Marlotte. 'I must closely examine the line again so as to remember exactly how it was.'

'You're ill, madame. Why not leave all this to the work of others?'

'Because they have their lives to live and mine is nearly over, so what about that bicycle, eh?'

His eyes dodge away and for a moment he tries to find a suitable answer, but finally confesses, 'Certainly, madame. We have a very good one. A German soldier sold it to my wife at the Sunday flea market, just after they . . . they took you away.'

It can't be my bicycle but it is. I'm so struck by this, I burst into tears, and for a few moments can only manage to stand in the yard holding on to it.

'Madame . . . madame, you must try to forget, not to remember.'

I shake my head. 'We must never forget, Matthieu. Never! Not in a thousand, thousand years.'

'But what about those that are waiting at the house for you? Surely Dupuis and the others will begin to understand that you're trying to remember things? They'll start remembering, too, madame. They won't just sit around and wait for you to settle on something.'

'But that is what I want, Matthieu. They are *also* to remember how it was.'

Vineyards are on either side of the road, the air cool, the light so incredibly sharp. The last of the harvest is in, and I'm again remembering as I should.

The twin villages of Bourron-Marlotte are six or so kilometres to the south of Fontainebleau. Below the road, the land falls gently into the valley of the Loing, but here it is primarily on the north shoulder, next to the forest, that the climate and soil are suitable for grapes. Everyone who can has some. The enclosures are many, and from where I'm now standing, the rows of vines, unpruned as yet, are wine-red and ancient under the autumnal sun.

It is at once the most beautiful thing I have ever seen and yet the most frightening, for it's here, a little to the south of Bourron-Marlotte, that the main line from Paris through to Nemours and on connects with a branch line that runs off to the southwest to eventually meet the one from Paris to Pithiviers.

This branch line is a crazy one. After meeting the line to Pithiviers, it swings abruptly to the southeast and then south. Throughout virtually all its length, it passes through fields and farms. It's what Tommy once called a 'milk run' and therefore was ideally suited to our purposes.

I start out. I know that for me this is going to be particularly hard. The trees are bare as they were back then.

The land sloped steeply up into the forest. Icy water covered the ditches on either side of tracks, down which a German patrol had stopped.

I pushed the bicycle towards them. In my coat pocket, I clutched one of the leftover grenades from Dunkerque that Paul Tessier had given me to deliver to the others. Once the pin was out, I would need count to three but me, I wouldn't throw it. I'd not let them take me.

'Ihre Papiere. Papiere, bitte, Fräulein.'

They'd come down out of the forest to cross the railway line. There were eight of them: two with Schmeissers, the rest with Mauser rifles, their sergeant in the lead.

I leaned the bike against me and handed my papers over. In broken French with bits of *Deutsch,* I told them I was on my way to the village of Ury.

'But you live near Fontainebleau?' he managed. He was really suspicious, this *Feldwebel.*

I was still clutching the grenade, but found the will to say, *'Ja, Herr Oberst, ja,* but this route it is shorter, and I must visit some old people to see how they're getting along.'

Curtly, he nodded at the bike. 'What's in the carrier basket?'

'Food for them and for *meine Kinder, ja?'*

Five other grenades, three pistols, and a small quantity of ammunition, again from Dunkerque in 1940 and via the *marché noir* since. Also one stripped-down, stolen Schmeisser and the regulation two magazines that were with it.

'Und Apfelmost,' he said.

The cider I'd left out, plain as day, nestled in cloth, a favourite of *les Allemands.* 'It's so hard to get these days.'

He held up one of the bottles, put it to the sun. I waited. I heard myself saying, *'Bitte, Herr Oberst,* please put that back. It's my daughter's birthday, and I want it to be a surprise.'

He did. He betrayed that he knew a little more French than I'd given him credit for and slid that bottle into its nest and wished me a good day. Until I was almost out of sight, I knew they were watching me, but I didn't turn to look back at them and wave.

Then I reached the clearing and pushed the bike up into the forest to meet the road that came by there. It was the first of many patrols, and I knew they must be on the lookout for someone.

The millpond is dark, the geese timid. One slips and goes down on its bum. The others raise a racket and stretch their necks.

At last, a few succeed in reaching open water and the gander ushers the rest of them in. Henri Poulin is talking to Schiller and Dupuis, only Schiller's not in uniform—he was that day I came up here from Ury in the late autumn of 1941. A staff car was parked on the road, it's driver polishing the chrome.

But Schiller acts as though he's still in uniform and, of course, Dupuis is still subservient, deferring always to the other, some habits being simply too hard to break.

Tommy . . . I knew they were after Tommy, and there wasn't a thing I could do about it except to go home.

They've used André de Verville's car, have taken it from in front of the house, but as if in the present, though well in the past, I hear, 'Lily, wait! Don't turn around. We're right behind you.'

Nicki said that I must lead a charmed life and that I had the most interesting friends. 'Those two in particular,' he said. 'Schiller and Dupuis.'

I turn. I have to, and, of course, Tommy and Nicki aren't here. How could they be? It's not the autumn of 1941; it's four years later, but I must remember the robbery because for us, everything changed after that.

9

Below me, down a tumbled slope through trees whose autumn leaves have fallen, Schiller and Dupuis are picking their way among some boulders. Schiller's older. *Mon Dieu*, he's iron grey and looks unhealthy, but is he also afraid because I'm the only thing that stands between him and the hangman? Is he remembering how it was?

Dupuis, though just as shabby as before, has obviously been eating as he did during the Occupation, ration tickets or no tickets, simply shopkeepers and maître d's who wanted to please, cash, too, of course, and the never spoken, always present threat of Sûreté muscle.

Both have drawn their guns and I could perhaps kill them, but that would be too easy. They chased me on the road in that car of theirs back in the autumn of 1941, and I took a little detour. The Fontainebleau Forest is full of such things—side roads, woodcutter's trails, hiking paths, those of the kings themselves. Les Monts des Chèvres, the Mountains of the Goats, that's what this place is called.

They've remembered what I've remembered. Schiller found it then, and as I look down on them, it's the lieutenant who looks questioningly up towards where I'm still hidden. Perhaps two hundred metres separate us, not just the years, the camps, and everything else. He's thin, stooped and pale, so gaunt lines crease that narrow face, the scar glistening even more, but the right eye is also all but closed. Shrapnel, I wonder? The Russian front, but well after the robbery, after the interrogations, the beatings, and the torture, right at the end in 1945 and in or near a Berlin that was being mercilessly destroyed.

'She's not here,' says Dupuis. How I remember that voice.

'I'm sure I saw something. What about that woodcutter's hut? It was up there, back of that ridge.'

That's also a voice that brings instant apprehension, but it's Dupuis who says, 'She's got a bicycle just like in the late autumn of 1941. Is it that you're forgetting this?'

'You sound as if you don't want us to go up there after her.'

Dupuis shakes his head and stuffs his pistol away. 'I'm merely stating the obvious. That one knows the woods, and we're still together. If she can draw us out and separate us, she will because she wants to have a word alone with each of us first.'

'We've nothing to say to her; she nothing to us.'

'You're forgetting her French side. De Verville got his little lecture. For myself, I think she might not even have wanted to kill him. Far better a very public humiliation and Résistance trial.'

He's only partially right about André, but it's Schiller who snorts and says, 'You French were always so weak. Follow if you like. I'm going up to the hut.'

'Perhaps that's what she really wants.'

They begin to climb. It's not difficult, a few boulders and gullies, and certainly I could let them have the grenade, but a stone will do just as well since they must be made to feel it as we did: hunted and in absolute terror for their lives.

That bouncing stone whistles past Dupuis who cries out and buries his head in his arms as Schiller laughs and says, '*Dummkopf,* a loose rock! Where would she have got a grenade? Plucked it from the trees?'

'*Sacré nom de nom,* she may still have friends and could have made contact!'

In spite of this, they continue, but take the main gully that leads away from me. Just as they have thought, I do have my bicycle, but it's hidden in a hollow beneath a covering leaves. It's beside the trail that leads to the hut and when they reach the top, they walk right past it, just as they did back then.

Dupuis, however, stands back as much as possible and lets Schiller nudge the door open, but both must stoop to enter and it'll be dark in there, for there are no windows, not even a stovepipe hole, and if I had the Schmeisser assembled, I could give them a couple of bursts and terrify the hell out of them, but the bicycle will be as safe as it was before and I can come back for it later.

Sacrificing one bullet from the Luger, I place it in the middle of the trail where they're sure to find it notched.

Due north of the Mountains of the Goats, there's the Rock of the Salamander—quaint, isn't it, to have such names? Now I'm perhaps a kilometre to the north of the woodcutter's hut and among tall oaks, and from here, I'll walk across a tableland to find the copse of cedars with its moss-covered boulders that's still so clear in memory.

Even the lean-to Tommy and Nicki used is where they left it, the roof now a webbing of dry and seasoned sticks. There's evidence of a last campfire whose ashes are damp as I bring a pinch to my nose and shut my eyes. Immediately, as in the camps with all those dead and dying people around me, I'm right back here in time with Tommy, who fed his tiny fire with such love and care, and sat to one side of it, Nicki to the other. The map Paul Tessier had given me that day in Nemours had been spread on the ground. 'The train is to leave Paris at four thirty in the afternoon, 10 November,' I told them. 'It's to be a mixed one of goods and passengers.'

'How many of each?' asked Tommy.

'Eight of passengers, twenty-two of goods. The passenger carriages will come first.'

'And the shipment?' asked Nicki.

'Somewhere among the others. This our railwaymen won't know until the train is finally made up. Right now the truck is sitting on a siding at the Gare de Lyon.'

So it was anyone's guess where it would be located in the train. 'What about machine-guns and extra guards?' asked Tommy.

'Probably, but none that we know of as yet, just the usual anti-aircraft gun on its flatbed, but this, I think the *Boche* will want to keep as far from the art treasures as possible.'

'What about the dummy railway truck?' asked Nicki. 'Will our railwaymen be able to make the switch?'

It was to wait on a siding near Bourron-Marlotte. 'That's out. There are no spares.'

'And the cutting torch?' asked Tommy.

'Clateau has promised one from the garage in Barbizon, but must have it back well before dawn.'

'And if he doesn't manage to get it?' asked Nicki.

'Cold chisels, hammers, and explosives if necessary. Once the truck is located, the rest of the train ahead can be released and sent on down the line. Only two trains a day regularly use that route, so there should be lots time between them for ours.'

It was Nicki who said, 'What's to prevent the engineer from stopping near La Chapelle-la-Reine and getting a warning out?'

This little village is about four kilometres to the south-southwest of Ury. 'Dmitry will have cut the wires by then,' said Tommy. 'We have to trust him, Nicki. It's all been arranged.'

'That Bolshevik?' said Nicki. 'There's far too much at stake for us to trust him.'

'Listen, you two, it's crazy anyway for us to attempt this. You've got to call it off. Paul's certain it could be a trap.'

'Tessier and those railway boys are just nervous, Lily,' said another whose voice I knew well enough. 'There are crates and crates of artwork waiting to be shipped to the Reich from the Jeu de Paume and the Einsatzstab Reichsleiter Rosenberg. It's too good an opportunity. Dmitry's one of us, Nicki. Me, I can guarantee him.'

I turned and my sister was there behind me, having watched my back without my knowing. There was a Walther P38 in her right hand, and I had to ask myself, Has she slept with Dmitry, and I had to answer, Probably. 'Why does it have to be done, Nini?'

Unfortunately, those lovely dark eyes flashed a fierceness I'd never seen before. 'Because for us, it's to be the catalyst. A whole train, Lily. *Pour l'amour de Dieu*, think of it, will you? No one has ever done such a thing. When word gets out, other *réseaux* will be sure to form and we'll be stopping trains everywhere!'

'What she means, Lily, is that London wants us to pull this off,' said Tommy dryly.

Anxiously, I looked at Nicki who said, 'To go forward, though, we'll absolutely need you to help us.'

'Me? Hey, monsieur, aren't I too well known?'

'Lily, that train has to be made to stop just before it's switched on to the other line. That way it will be starting up and we can jump aboard just a little later, so you must get on at Avon. You can purchase a ticket for Saint-Léger, the crossing that is just to the south of Bourron-Marlotte. That doesn't require an *Ausweis* for you, so no one will question it.'

'Except the one who sells the tickets and the ones who punch them. You're all crazy. There are German railway police on all of our trains; French ones, too.'

Again, it was Janine who insisted 'We *can't* chance its not stopping, can we?'

'Tommy . . . Tommy, it's impossible for me. I'd need a very good excuse to get off at that little place. The Germans are bound to question it. Schiller . . .'

'She's right,' said Nicki. 'We'll have to think of something else.'

'No we won't,' said Janine. 'She needs wax to finish Göring's sculpture and can easily visit the beekeeper in Saint-Léger.'

She had thought it all out beforehand. 'Wax . . . *Ah, merde*, I . . .' Why must she do that to me? 'All right, I'll do it. I can take my bike with me and still be home in time for curfew if I hurry.'

'Lorries?' asked Nicki. 'What about them?'

'We'll "borrow" them from the Wehrmacht,' said Nini. 'There's a driver I know who can be bought. I'll tell him to bring a friend and make him an offer he can't refuse.' Herself.

'We have lorries enough of our own. Would you insult their owners?'

Clateau and Matthieu Fayelle. 'Of course not. We'll use theirs as well, but the German ones will offer perfect cover. Now you'd better get home. Say hello to the children and give them each a big hug for me.'

Jules has moved the body of Madame Vuitton, though Schiller and Dupuis haven't yet returned with André's car, but the past still tugs and I can't let go. It was the morning after I left Tommy and the others. Jean-Guy had given me a message and it took me down the road.

'Georges, what is it you want of me?'

He gave a whack with the axe, and the head of another rabbit fell. 'Madame, I must speak with you.' *Whack,* and it was the front paws that time, then the hind ones.

'So speak.' *Merde*, had he an endless supply of rabbits?

'The wife saw that sister of yours in the forest today. Janine, she was with two men.'

'Since when has my sister not been with men? They were hikers probably.'

The skin was slipped off. Blood dripped from his hands. 'They didn't look like those to me.'

So he'd seen them too, had he? 'Perhaps they were friends from Paris, but Nini hasn't said anything of them.'

'The one came here before the war, madame. I'm sure of it.'

I shrugged. I didn't turn away nor avert my gaze from him, but had to wonder why Georges hadn't let Dupuis know, and concluded he wanted something else.

It was not long in coming. 'These times, they're not easy, madame. Monsieur Jules . . . Sometimes he forgets to pay us.'

Ah, bon, but had he really given me a possible hold over him? 'Perhaps I could help. The Germans give me an allowance for their rooms and meals.' It was an opener and he saw this, but I'd have to offer something else to pry the rest out of him.

'One hundred thousand francs?' he asked.

I wanted to fiercely object but couldn't look in the least surprised. 'That much, if necessary. Yes, I could manage that. I would have to go to Oberst Neumann, but there shouldn't be too much of a problem.'

This caused him to grind his false teeth. 'Not the Oberst, madame, nor Obersturmführer Schiller.'

To show a little surprise was then best. 'Georges, are you asking me to pay for your silence, and that of Tante Marie?'

Again, he lifted that axe. Again, another rabbit lost its head and then its paws. Again, blood drained on to the chopping block as he paused to study me and I had to ask myself, Does he think the *Boche* might now lose the war, and if so, is this the only chance he'll get to ask me because I'll soon be taken away and Jules will never know about the money he's demanded?

Salaud, I wanted to cry at him but reason intruded. Capitulating, I told him, 'Okay. You'll have it in a few days.'

'Tonight, madame.'

Cher Jésus, what the hell was this? He was in far too much of a hurry and that could only mean he knew far more than he was letting on. 'Georges, I can't possibly get it that fast and you know it.'

'Then take some of the silver. There's so much of it, a little won't be missed.'

'One hundred thousand francs' worth?'

'A little more, I think, since it isn't cash and time will be necessary to dispose of it properly.'

'On the *marché noir*, is this what you mean?'

There was no answer, just the ruthless emptying of the rabbits, the kidneys, the livers, and the hearts being picked out. 'All right, there's some jewellery from the old monsieur's mistress—I'm sure you and Tante Marie must have seen some of it in days gone by. Perhaps if I were to . . .'

'That would be fine, but the silver also.'

November's nights were damp and cold. It was the fifth, and in a few days I'd help to rob a train, but Georges and Tante Marie only made my worries greater. Long ago, it seems, I'd taken them some silver—a gorgeous tureen we never used, a sauceboat with cherubs and angels, salt and pepper cellars, some of the jewellery, also. A diamond pin, a brooch with studded seed pearls, some cufflinks of old Monsieur de St-Germain's that Jules was saving for Jean-Guy, a small handful of rings, a topaz, an opal—those may well have been fake, but I knew I couldn't leave it another day. Something had to be done, you understand? Please, you must. You see I had the lives of everyone to consider, not just those of my children, or of Tommy even. Nini had gone back to Paris; Tommy and Nicki were at mother's. Paul Tessier and the others would be counting the hours.

Schiller and Neumann were away, Rudi Swartz fast asleep, and even from my kitchen I could hear his snoring.

Jean-Guy and Marie would sleep through anything, but would Georges be out trapping rabbits or watching the house again?

Dressing in dark clothing and bare feet, I took from the cellars the six bottles of petrol I had carefully hoarded before the war and its subsequent Occupation. I found some rags.

Clouds closed over the moon. It was perhaps two a.m., and there was a heavy frost that hung along the road and over the adjacent meadow, and as the moon crept out, an ethereal light made the frost ghostly. I was alone, and dear God, would I be able to bring myself to do it?

Georges and Tante Marie kept a dog. It had no name but that. I fed it the cheese I'd brought and some pâté—things I knew it loved.

The front door was bolted, the back, too. I set the bottles down and tried the windows. There was only one whose catch Georges had forgotten to repair, making me glad I wouldn't have to find a rock and quietly break in, but could I really do it? Me, the mother of two children?

Opening it, I climbed in to hear that old clock of theirs. Close and warm, the air was ripe with all such smells. In the kitchen, the fire had been banked, but I knew I couldn't chance it and told myself I had to start up the stairs. It was the only way.

There were two little rooms, just enough space on the landing to turn around. The one was for the son they never had; from the other came the sound of disturbed breathing, for Tante Marie had asthma. Mucus gurgles; Georges simply snored, yet I waited. Again, I told myself, I couldn't do it. I really couldn't.

May God forgive me, I had to.

Those cutters made such a tiny sound, my mind magnified it out of all proportion. The wire was stiffer than I'd have liked, and as I looped it around the doorknob and then one of the railings to tie their bedroom shut, I told myself it must be done.

The smell of petrol was like no other and, suddenly, it was everywhere downstairs and over the front door, the inside and the out. The dog whined and fussed—it couldn't understand, or could it? I nudged him away from my hands, hissed at him, 'Bad dog. Don't you dare bark at me!' only to remember that he was always hungry and that he knew I knew this. 'All right,' I told him, and he took off like a rocket.

Then the match was in my fingers, its flame bright and brighter still as a corner of the rag caught fire. Even then, I could turn back, I told myself, but how could I, given what I'd already done?

I dragged that rag after me. I was moving fast, then to the front door I'd closed and wired, then to the windows and round the house to the back to drop it at last and run into the meadow as the place went up like a tinderbox, and I plugged my ears until the sky was filled with light and the air with their screams.

'Madame, what has happened?'

It was Rudi, and he'd heard that dog at my kitchen door and come out to find me standing in the road.

'The stove,' I told him. 'It must have been that. Georges was always going to clean the pipes but would never take the time.'

Rudi knew I was not wearing a nightgown. He could see this clearly for the moon had betrayed me. *'Benzin,'* he said, giving the *Deutsch* for petrol. 'I can smell it even from here.'

The little station at Avon is much the same. I lean the bike against the wall and walk towards the wicket. Few people are about. There are no guards, no swastikas or eagles, no signs in German, and I find this puzzling.

November's greying light is impoverished. A flock of pigeons makes a circle, racing high above the empty tracks. Homing pigeons? I wonder. They're against the law and anyway should all have been eaten by now.

This, too, I can't understand.

'A one-way to Saint-Léger, please. I don't have an *Ausweis*. At the *Felkommandantur* in Fontainebleau, they have said . . .'

He looks at me and I wonder who he's going to report it to, but he says, '*Pardonnez-moi*, madame, but there is no longer any need for such things.' Begrudgingly he takes my money. He's young and new. Me, I've never seen him before.

'I've a bicycle,' I tell him.

'They'll look after it for you.'

The return trip must be done by bicycle or else I must stay over. That's all there is to it. But no one ever gets out at Saint-Léger. Thinking they won't stop the train just for me, I drag another cigarette from the crumpled packet.

'Madame, allow me, please.'

It's the one from the house and I know he must be Gestapo! '*Merci*, monsieur. The train, it's always late.'

He smiles that plainclothes smile. Very nice-looking, you'd think. A salesman perhaps. 'It's the war,' he says. 'It'll take years to get things going properly again.'

I turn away, can't look at him anymore—listen for the sound of the wheels—but he asks, 'Were you in the camps, madame? Please forgive me, but I'm looking for someone.'

It's all lies! I know that his accent is British, but that like others of the *Boche,* he'll have learned that English first before the Parisian *français*. 'Which camps?' I hear myself asking, but with hand on the Luger in my pocket. I'll shoot him if I have to.

'Auschwitz and then Bergen-Belsen.'

He's watching me too closely, and I know I'll have to kill him but say, 'I couldn't possibly know anything about those places. I'm simply going to see my sister.'

He touches the brim of that fedora of his. 'Sorry. Didn't mean to intrude.'

That's so British, I'm taken aback, but you can never tell with these guys. The lack of guards could mean they're just waiting to pounce.

It's an anxious time, and when the train finally does come in, there's only an engine and several passenger carriages, and this, too, I simply can't understand.

Taking a last drag, I grind the butt out under one of those shoes they've given me as my bike is taken by this man who offered me a light and earlier came to the house. He's sticking close, so okay, he'll soon know he shouldn't.

As I hand my ticket over to be punched, the *chef de train,* is startled. 'Saint-Léger?' he says. *'Ah, non,* madame, a moment, please. I will have to consult with the engineer.'

It could take ages. 'Saint-Léger,' says the one with my bike. 'Would you happen to know a beekeeper there?'

'Merde, what would I want with beekeepers?'

The *chef de train* comes back. I've caused a great fuss, but they'll stop the train only this once. Climbing aboard, it's like a century ago for me. The coaches are crowded, the uniforms different— American, British, and French, but I see only German ones, hear only their loud laughter and boisterous talk, know only that Gestapo is still watching me and that I'm going to have to kill him and a few of the others.

There were six coaches ahead and one behind, then the goods trucks, all twenty-two of them, among which would have been placed the Luftwaffe's antiaircraft gun. With such a heavy load, the engine labours, and I told myself, no wonder there was a fuss about their stopping. I'd such a small part to play in what was to come, but since I had to ride my bike over that way, should I not at least see how it all went? After I got the wax, of course, but maybe Monsieur Raymond wouldn't be there. Wax was so hard to come by those days—practically impossible.

Wax and petrol. The Gestapo were investigating the fire. The day before, a team came to take a look at the ashes. Jean-Guy was the one to tell me this, but I already knew of it because they'd come to the door.

'Two old people, madame.'

'Yes, I know. It's very sad. My children are particularly upset, myself also. The Morissettes had been with my husband's family for years.'

The train crossed the ring road that encircled the Fontainbleau Forest. There were barriers then—new ones with lights. A car was patiently waiting, the beam of its headlamps catching me in the face, causing me to wonder about the blackout and think of Schiller and Dupuis as I heard their shrieks, felt the blows, saw that brimming bathtub and knew they were going to shove me under again!

Dupuis would come to take a look at the ruins of the farmhouse. He and Schiller wouldn't let a thing like that lie, not with me around. They'd search for evidence, and I'd be charged with murder, and I wondered if I'd ever see the children again, only to hear the sound of those wheels. We'd gathered momentum. The Wehrmacht's boys were singing loudly and laughing. Some French girls had joined them. Cigarettes had been offered, and the image of those girls was etched in mind by their wavy, shoulder-length hair, ersatz lipstick, rouge and bright, toothy smiles, their skirt lengths shortened then to all but above the knees.

Saint-Léger . . . It seemed to take an eternity and then, beyond the windows, everything outside was pitch-dark as the squeal of the brakes finally came and I heard the railway trucks banging their couplings one against another. 'Saint-Léger, madame.'

'*Merci. Ah, mon vélo, s'il vous plaît.*'

He tipped his hat again, that *salaud* of a Gestapo, and as the *chef de train* saw that the bike was handed down, I glanced back a last time.

The train would now be secretly switched on to the other tracks. A coach passed by me, then the first of the railway trucks, and I counted them off, all twenty-two of them, the last trailing away into the darkness.

The long barrel of the antiaircraft gun was clear enough, an 88 mm and perfect against Spitfires and others, but also an exceptional antitank gun, as was discovered in the desert war.

'Wax? How could I have any? Those *salauds* take everything.'

'Liar, I know very well you set some aside!'

'You . . . Why you . . . Who the hell do you think you are coming here after dark to say a thing like that to me?'

Sacré nom de nom, he was a son-of-a-bitch himself, that beekeeper! 'I'm Madame de St-Germain, damn you!'

'That rich bitch, eh?' He hit his forehead with the heel of his hand, kissed his fingertips, shoved two of them up in front of me, and said, 'Well, suck on someone else, my fine one. There'll be no wax for you.'

'But . . . but I have to do a commission for the Reichsmarschall Göring. I'm a sculptress. They'll arrest me if it isn't finished. I have two kids.'

'The de St-Germains, isn't it? Two kids, eh? Hey, me, Yves Raymond of Saint-Léger, now has you pegged, madame. My father, your father-in-law, and beeswax for his candles!'

His vulture's eyes narrowed, the thin lips puckering in anger. He had a goiter, I was certain, and needed a shave.

'Seven thousand francs, madame, plus the interest. You pay me what that family of your husband's owes mine, and I will gladly sell you the necessary wax.'

'My father-in-law's been dead for years.'

'But not your husband, madame. If I understand things correctly, he's in the pay of the Germans.'

'Look, all I want is ten kilos.'

'Ten!' He was electrified. 'For that, you'd need to pay me ten thousand francs.'

'And the seven your family's been owed all these years?'

'Of course. Twenty it is.'

The French never forget the interest. Me, I was so agitated I wanted to sit down to calm myself, but he said, 'You'll have to hurry if you're to make it home before curfew.'

It had again been extended to midnight, which would give me a little more than five hours to ride the twenty or so kilometres, if I headed straight for home.

We went out to the shed where he kept the clarifier, the smoke pots, nets, and other things. He'd been making more hives, and the place smelled of pine sawdust, wax, and honey.

Patiently, he counted the money twice, to be certain. 'As it happens, madame, the *Boche* and the cooperative allow me to sell ten percent, so you're in luck.'

The block of wax he set in the carrier basket and said, 'Happy sculpting or whatever else you do. Hey, wait a minute. De St-Germain . . . ? Yes, now I remember.'

'More debts? I haven't a franc left.'

'Wasn't there a bad fire up your way? Two old people . . .'

He knew damned well who they were, but I told him anyway, and that their stovepipes must have needed a good cleaning. 'I was always telling Georges this, as was my husband.'

'But did you see it happen? The flames?' he asked. 'The corpses?' Like the French everywhere, he really wanted the details.

I shook my head and heard myself saying, 'We were asleep, otherwise I wouldn't be here. My hands and face would have been badly burned trying to rescue them.'

'*Peut-être,*' he said, giving me a knowing smile before pinching his windpipe and adding, 'Some are saying things aren't right with that fire.'

Stung by this, I pushed my bike into the darkness, but the lane seemed to take forever and only when I reached the road did I look back to see him still standing in the doorway of his house, ignoring the blackout.

I was some three kilometres almost due east of the robbery, but long before I got there, I heard the sharp bursts of a Spandau and knew the worst had happened. There was the crump of an explosion, the broken, agitated, and far-too-rapid sounds of inexperienced rifle and pistol fire, but the Spandau stopped, just like that! I hurried, came to a rise, and looked down on a scene of utter chaos. Two of the railway trucks were burning.

Men were racing about. The antiaircraft gun was being readied. They were aiming it at our lorries! Clateau was racing for his van. Tommy had leaped up on to the flatbed. A German soldier turned. There was a burst from Tommy's Schmeisser, and the man fell back to lay half on and half off the flatbed as others swarmed in on the antiaircraft gun, with more bursts of firing and ragged shots all along the train. One of our men fell, and then another, and I called out to Tommy, 'ON THE ROOF!' only to realize he'd never hear me.

Men ducked and ran, yelling, 'Over there! No, underneath, behind the wheels! In the woods. Stop them!'

There was more and more firing, the constant racket of it and the crackling of flames, the sight of those burning cattle trucks as a great wall of sound began to rise. It was the terrified screams of those that were being deported and were inside. Fifty, a hundred— two hundred, four hundred? I wanted to scream at Schiller for he'd done it on purpose, but I was unable to run to their assistance.

Nicki raced through the flames. There was a burst of firing from the gun in his hands. Hot iron was flung away, and people poured from the truck, gasping for air. In ones, twos, and threes they were helped away, but I heard someone urgently shouting, 'Leave it! There's no time. We can't just let the artwork burn!'

A ladder was brought. It was run through the milling throng by two men and leaned against the side of a truck. Clateau returned to fetch the cutting torch. Matthieu Fayelle was still helping people away from the fire.

Tommy climbed the ladder. There were flames on either side of him. He pulled a set of goggles down over his eyes and yelled something to Nicki, who stood at the base of the ladder. 'Tessier . . . *Vite, vite!*'

Dynamite. They were going to have to blow the door. That *gueule cassée* appeared and went to work right in the heat of the flames. Two sticks, three, four, I don't know how many, but something was needed to contain the explosion, a sheet of metal—anything so as to direct the force if possible.

With a bang, the door lifted off, and the men rushed in to

fling out the corpses of the four German soldiers who had been sealed inside.

Not realizing that I would be outlined by the fire, I stupidly waited, though I knew I had to get home and that my job had been done, and when the muzzle of a pistol touched the back of my head, I wanted to cry out in alarm but couldn't.

Paintings—large canvases not in crates or anything—were being hustled out of that railway truck and raced towards the waiting lorries and Clateau's van.

'Let go of the bicycle, Fräulein, and raise your hands.'

'As you wish, but please, you must understand I've nothing to do with this.'

'Save it for later. The hands!'

It was a German officer who had lost his cap and was burned about the face. Sweat clung to the scorched brow. Pain registered in his eyes.

'Yes, I've been hit,' he said in perfect French.

'Where?' I asked.

'In the guts.'

'Then let me help you. Look, I don't know who those people are. Honestly, I don't. I've been to buy some beeswax for our church and am on my way home.'

Not for a moment did that gun of his waver, and I can see him still, even after all that's happened to me. He wasn't young or old, was a man with a family perhaps. 'Have you children of your own?' I asked. 'I've two that are waiting for me.'

As I tore open his tunic and picked my way through the blood-soaked clothing, he kept that pistol at my head. Part of his intestines was showing in the light from the fire. 'It's bad, isn't it?' he said.

How had he managed to get this far? 'Not too bad. Yes, it'll be okay, I think. Let me cover the wound with something. I've a shawl in my carrier basket.'

Why should he trust me? he wondered but said, 'All right,' and I ran for it, headed straight for the woods and dove into them to roll about and hit my head against a tree!

Dazed, bleeding—scared, damned scared—I waited for him to end it all, but saw him teetering in the middle of the road with the fire and the confusion behind him. That gun had fallen from his hand. My bike was to one side, the block of wax having tumbled away.

Slowly, with difficulty, I crept forward and when I was at the edge of the woods, stood up. Our eyes met, and he began to drop for the gun as I raced for it, grabbed it, and pulled the trigger. I can still hear the sound it made and smell the cordite.

He was lying there, sprawled on his back, his face torn away, and the gun was still in my hand—it would always be there because I couldn't comprehend what I'd done. In four days, I'd killed three people.

'*Maman*, will Georges and Tante Marie go to heaven?'

'I don't know, *chérie*. Does it matter so much?'

She nodded, this daughter of mine. Those great big hazel eyes had such sensitivity. Her hair was then a light brownish, that soft shade of amber, and long. She was incredibly beautiful.

'Rudi says it matters. That only if people are good to one another will they enter the kingdom.'

The kitchen was full of warmth and the aroma of baking bread, for I'd a full house: Schiller and two others, also Neumann and his adjutant, and Rudi, of course. Poor Rudi.

The *Boche* were conducting another sweep of the forest and surrounding district. Hostages had been taken. Eleven German soldiers and one captain were killed during the robbery, five of ours, all of whom had far too many relatives.

'Me, I think God should punish the *Boche*!'

'DON'T YOU DARE CALL THEM THAT IN THIS HOUSE OR ANYWHERE ELSE! ARE YOU CRAZY?'

She burst into tears and ran away to her room as I bowed my head and tried to get a hold of myself, but knew that for us, the agony had just begun.

'Jean-Guy, go and see if there are any more eggs.'

'I've just been.'

'Then look, damn you! Wait . . . wait, please. I'm upset. Scared.'

'You should be!' he yelled and ran out the back, leaving the door for me to close as again I plunged my hands into the flour the Germans had begrudgingly provided. Kneading the dough, working it, I finally shaped a loaf. Would I make a dragon for Marie, one with big, woeful eyes and a long tail with spikes?

It was Jean-Guy who caused me a problem. It was always guns and tanks and aeroplanes with him in those days. ME-109s, Heinkels, and Stukas. Rudi and he had been talking constantly about the war, especially in the east. Our little German was very worried. The fire down the road was one thing; that corpse I cut up and he buried in the cellar, another, and then the robbery. Schiller had given him hell and had again threatened to bring in SS guards, having accused Rudi of being slovenly, and I knew in my heart of hearts that it was only a matter of time until he talked.

The aeroplane I made was a Spitfire, but I daren't put British insignia on it and substituted that Maltese cross the Prussians had liked for far too many years.

'Rudi, your lunch is ready.'

He'd been out by our gate for more than five hours, marching steadily back and forth across the drive and seldom, if ever, standing still, and the dampness and freezing wind had been heartless. 'Madame Lily, it's not safe for you to stay here. Obersturmführer Schiller has asked me about that old couple and their house. I've not told him the truth, have said we were all asleep, but that one, he didn't believe me.'

The woollen cap I knitted protruded from below that helmet of his. There was also a scarf I'd knitted out of an unravelled sweater, a vest, too, and mittens, but there was no sense in my denying I was responsible for that fire. 'Is it to be Poland again?' I asked.

We both looked along the road in the direction of Georges and Tante Marie's house whose ashes lay just beyond a last gentle rise. 'Poland,' he said. 'They've taken thirty-six hostages from the surrounding villages and towns, Madame Lily. One is to be shot tomorrow, then two on the following day, then three, and so on until all are gone unless someone comes forward to tell them who the robbers were and where they've hidden what they stole.'

Eight days, then.

'This war, Madame Lily, it's never going to end.'

I had my children to think of, he his family and little farm, so the lie came readily and I gave it to him with the gentle touch of a caring hand. 'They're sending you to Russia.'

'Me?' he managed, stricken.

I nodded grimly, even gave him a quick hug, for he'd been a friend. 'Please, I'm sorry you should hear this from me, but I thought you should know ahead of time. Obersturmführer Schiller is insisting that Oberst Neumann get rid of you.'

There were tears. He was devastated but would he run, be shot in an attempt to desert, or simply wait for what he believed would be his orders?

It was all a gamble. Everything. 'You've been such a good friend, Rudi. We'll all miss you terribly but when this war is over, you're to come and see us. Please, I must insist. Your wife as well.'

Liar, cheat, fraud, coward, I silently cursed myself, for he was the one good thing in all the slime.

'I knew this could never last,' he said, indicating the woods, the pasture, the house, and the cushiest job he could ever have asked for had he had any choice in the matter. 'Russia. I won't come back from there, Madame Lily. This I know.'

'Come in and get warm by the stove and have some soup. Perhaps if you eat a little, things won't seem so bad. I'll try to speak to Neumann. I know it's not to be for a few days, well one or two. I can't be sure.'

Ashes . . . there were ashes all around me, the remains of Georges and Tante Marie's house. Bundled in overcoat, scarf, fedora, and gloves, Dupuis was standing where the front door used to be, while Schiller's jackboots waded in the rest.

It was the inspector who picked up the twisted remains of a wine bottle, but the lieutenant who said, 'What have we here?'

He was behind me and I didn't yet turn, for beyond the farmyard, along the edge of the forest, German soldiers with rifles had formed a line, each three metres from the other, and the lightly falling snow had made their grey-green uniforms greyer still. It was freezing.

'Well?' shrilled the lieutenant.

'Well, what, please?' I asked.

The scar tugged at his chin. 'Silver. Where did they get it?'

The thing in that black-gloved hand had bubbled with the heat and was the size of a small pancake and about as thick, and as our eyes met, I told him as calmly as I could, 'How on earth should I know? They didn't exactly *like* my living in my husband's family home.'

'You were afraid they'd talk.'

'Me? Why?'

'Madame, this fire was deliberately set,' said Dupuis. He was still holding that wine bottle.

'Deliberately set? You're crazy, Inspector. Who would wish to do such a terrible thing, especially since they had no enemies? Not that I knew of.'

'Is any silver missing from your husband's house?' asked Schiller. They'd got me right between them.

'Silver? I'll have to check, but with so many visitors . . .'

'A list of the contents, I think, Herr Obersturmführer,' said Dupuis. 'Have her prepare one. We can get the husband to check it over.'

He thought of everything. 'Just why are you so certain the fire was not an accident?'

'Because, madame, there are melted bottles where the front and back doors were, and also at one side of the house. That one.'

Where I had found a window I could easily open. 'Georges loved his wine, Inspector. He made it, borrowed it, and stole it from time to time. If you look closely, you'll find bottles all over the place. That shed is full of those he had been gathering for sale.'

On the *marché noir*, but Dupuis didn't say this, because it was then Schiller's turn to go at me.

'And these?' said that one. He was very pleased with what he'd found, and as the wind teased the ashes from that black-gloved hand, he took on the air of a triumphant archaeologist confronting a competitive colleague with the remains of a pair of gold cufflinks.

Instinctively, I shrugged. His hand lashed out. Knocked almost off my feet, I found my lip was bleeding and my jaw hurt like hell, but it was Dupuis who fetched the dog. Grousing up to me, that poor creature with the beaten eyes found the will to wag its tail and lick my fingers, and I heard the inspector saying, 'So, madame, perhaps you would be kind enough to tell us what has happened here.'

In panic, I fought for composure and stiffly said, 'I'll make the lists as you have requested and my husband will, I'm sure, thoroughly check them, but should anything be missing, I can't vouch for any of the guests he's had, nor for these two old people who knew that house and its contents far better than myself. They were always taking things, even in the time of my husband's father, or so I'm sure my husband will inform you he told me when he first brought me here to meet them.'

'And this dog?' asks Dupuis. 'It knows you and wouldn't have barked.'

'That dog has always been fed by me and my children. If you will release it, I'll tell it to go to my kitchen.'

They watched as that creature made a beeline for its supper, and I realized suddenly that I'd just condemned myself, for it was Dupuis who says, *'Ah, bon.'*

The noise from the dining room was almost more than I could bear—laughter, hooting, jeering. They'd rounded up most of those who escaped from the cattle trucks, had shot a few and had a bit of fun, were still breaking dishes and glasses when the moment struck them. Jackboots graced the dining room table. Brandy, cognac, and wine had been looted from my husband's *cave,* and I'd had to do the cooking and feed them all.

The sculpture was in the storeroom. Schiller rested his fingers on the head I'd done of Michèle Chevalier. She had such a fine young body, and I'd been true to it in every detail, but a general in Paris seemed likely to caress the real one, not himself. 'Herr Obersturmführer, I've told you before and I'll tell you again, I had nothing to do with that robbery or that fire.'

He fingered Michèle's buttocks and thighs, didn't care for the feel of the wax and turned the piece to gaze at her front again, for she was leaning back and the three figures were holding hands in a circle.

'Yet you take the train on the evening of that outrage and end up but a few kilometres from it?'

'Chance, that's all. *Ah, mon Dieu,* Lieutenant, I've a commission to do, an *order,* damn it, from the Reichsmarschall Göring. It's not easy for me to find the time. It's taking a lot longer than I had thought.'

Now it was Katyana's body that he fingered, and I knew he was going to tell me that I had earlier denied knowing anything of her, but instead, he said, 'The piece looks finished enough.'

'Not if you keep pawing it! Besides, there is still the base to make. Something very French and of the Fontainebleau Forest. Leaves, vines, rocks, birds . . .'

'We'll have a little surprise for you tomorrow.'

I stood before one of the dining room windows, looking out through the icy rain across the emptiness to where Rudi was again on guard and marching back and forth with that Mauser appropriately over his shoulder.

I waited. Cigarettes wouldn't help, but those bastards from the *ratissage* had left packages and butts all over the house, and there were plenty for me to pick up. It was now nearly noon of the following day, and they hadn't yet come for me. Has Schiller forgotten his little surprise, or is the delay simply more torture?

The children would be in school. I lit another cigarette and took a few quick drags. Tommy and the others hadn't been caught yet, not in so far as I knew, but Schiller's surprise could well be that they had, and when I saw Rudi turn suddenly to look along the road, I felt the cigarette leave my lips to pause as the smoke trailed up into my eyes.

A breathless Alphonse Picard appeared on his balloon-tyred bicycle, obviously struggling desperately against a clock whose hands would not stop, and when Rudi challenged him, the mayor simply shouted, 'Emergency! Out of my way.'

The wind and the rain beat against my face when I stepped outside. 'Madame, hurry! Hurry! They're about to shoot your son.'

'Rudi . . . RUDI, IT'S JEAN-GUY. HE'S HOSTAGE. I MUST GO TO HIM!'

Continually, Picard called out to me, 'Madame, please wait! It's best to arrive at the same time!'

They were all in the street before that school—the children, their teachers, everyone in town. Most were without their coats and hats in the pouring rain.

Two sad-looking men had been tied to posts in front of a wall. One was younger, the other older, my son a third. I pushed my way into the crowd. A gap opened for me, but no one said a thing, and when I was at the edge of that semicircle, it was Jean-Guy who cried out, *'MAMAN!'* nothing else. Not, please tell them what you know. Not even, Please, *maman,* they're going to shoot me!

The Wehrmacht kept the crowd back. There were forty or fifty of them: lorries, cars, machine guns, helmets in the deluge. Schiller and the Oberst Neumann were near, the latter grim-faced, the former all business as a priest begged them to release my son, but he was not our regular priest. Father Damien was away in the south for the duration.

The lieutenant nodded to one of the officers. I started to cry out in anger, but bit my tongue as Jean-Guy glared at me from across that distance. He couldn't believe I wouldn't come to him, nor could any of the others. To them I was to be damned, and I knew this was what Schiller also wanted.

Someone tried to take the bicycle from me, but I yanked it back, had to stand firm. There was the metallic sound of the rifle bolts being slammed home, but if I offered myself in Jean-Guy's place, I'd be made to tell them everything.

The younger of the two men found a last shred of bravery and cried out, *'Vive la France!'*

I tried to tell myself to run to my son, that nothing else mattered, but turned aside to sob, 'No . . . please, no,' and as the sound of the shots came to me, I felt Jean-Guy in my arms. They'd cut the ropes and let him go, and I was smothering him with kisses as Schiller stood over us saying nothing.

Only then did I realize that I had been pleading with them in English, and that I must have said a lot more than I could ever remember.

In my orchard, there were old apple trees much revered for their gnarled, outreaching branches and their bountiful harvests. Rudi would help us pick the apples. When he first came to us, those trees at the back of the orchard formed a bond between us.

His helmet lay on the ground catching the rain. Beside it were his rifle and, neatly folded, the greatcoat they'd issued him. 'Rudi, forgive me.'

He made no sound. He'd bitten through his tongue and lifted his eyes to a heaven I was not sure he even believed in. The rain had plastered the dark brown hair over his brow, and as he slowly turned, I begged him again and again to forgive me. A dear, dear friend.

Jean-Guy tugged at my hand. Marie, in her white dress, hesitantly stood in the kitchen doorway, down through the tunnel of barren bows, afraid to join us, horrified by what had happened. It had been a morning of utter agony.

'Maman, why didn't you try to stop them from shooting me?' He had to know—had every right to be told.

I looked into the eyes of my son. 'Because I couldn't. Because for all of us, there are more important things than one single life.'

I couldn't tell him that they would all have been killed had I given up and told the lieutenant where they were, but he knew, and I knew, too, that at the moment of that execution I was thinking of Tommy more than of anyone else. 'Don't hate me, *chéri*. Just try to understand.'

Schiller was so clever. He knew that by exposing the truth to my son, he could turn Jean-Guy against me. This wasn't to be a sudden process, but something so gradual I didn't notice until it was too late.

10

Out over the Barbizon plain, there are distant lights in some of the farmhouses, the night at its darkest just before dawn. Instinctively, I search for the ashes of my mother's house and find, on the near horizon, the deeper darkness of her willow.

Dupuis and Schiller kept the pressure up all through that winter of 1942. There were repeated searches, the executions of all the hostages, the endless days of waiting, never knowing if someone would talk.

I was sent to Paris for a medical examination by a German specialist, but fortunately André saw me first and gave me an anticoagulant so that I bled like a stuck pig, became weaker by the day, and was finally allowed to go home. They gave me six months to live. Actually, it was nearer to three years.

As soon as I could, I came out here to the caves to see if everything was all right. Then, as now, the gurgling of the spring caused me to feel for a foothold. Though I'm now wearing those shoes they gave me, as before, I still hear a whispered, 'She's not coming.' It's Dupuis, and it's so like it was in that winter of 1942.

'The loot must still be here,' says Schiller as Dupuis lights a cigarette.

The silhouette of that gumshoe's fedora, scarf, and threadbare overcoat are clear enough. Schiller's behind him and taller, but even as Dupuis says, 'It's impossible. These caves are far too small. Rodents would have got at everything,' the lieutenant vanishes.

'Not necessarily,' comes that other voice from above me and now much closer. 'The Chevalier girl told us Lutoslawski and the American would have been very careful.'

Michèle had screamed that at them in the cellars of the Cherche-Midi but had also cried out, 'They would never have told me where those things are hidden!'

They beat her anyway. They very nearly drowned her. 'Cement,' says Schiller, 'into which stones have been pressed so as to make them look as if fallen.'

Tommy didn't use cement, how could he have, but I manage to move a little away as Dupuis says, 'There will definitely have been dampness.' He's now much closer to me.

'Who gives a damn anyway? It's the collections of rare coins, smaller pieces of sculpture, and icons that we want,' says Schiller. 'Enough to buy our way out of France and set us up in Argentina or Chile.'

'You shouldn't have come back. Even the Americans are looking for you. Those so-called war crimes, eh? Poland and all the rest. Without you, we could have . . .'

'Dealt with her, you and the Vuittons and that former husband of hers? Admit it, you need me.'

Irritably, Dupuis pinches out his cigarette but doesn't throw it away, not him. It's thrust into a pocket. 'So, what are we to do? Wait here until someone finds that you killed those two old people and left them to their geese?'

Ah, non, Henri Poulin and his wife. It's all my fault!

The leaves make a sound that terrifies even though I've the Luger in hand. Wire cutters, knife, and a grenade are still in my pockets . . .

It's Dupuis who says, 'She'll have figured us out and will have gone after the others.'

Schiller doesn't answer, and again it's Dupuis, 'Vuitton simply wants out, but that wife of his is demanding a share of everything. If you ask me, our Dominique sees it as a way to buy them back into favour should anything be said, which it will be if we're not careful. She'll simply hand everything over and turn us in.'

Clearly, they don't yet know that I've already dealt with them, but again it's Schiller who makes no sound, and as Dupuis continues to whisper, the other hunts for me just as they did that night I came back here. Using his silhouette, I see that the lieutenant is now standing on the path above and not three metres from me, his head cocked to one side. He moves away just like he did on that night, me to follow because I have to cut him off from Dupuis, taking out the one and then the other, no 'lectures' now because there simply won't be time.

Yet they've anticipated things, for Dupuis has now come up behind me, and so it goes, the one ahead, the other behind, the path running from the caves through the forest to the little clearing where I left my bicycle.

Schiller must have traced it out that other time. Me, I thought I was so clever then, but when he discovers the bike this time, he can't resist giving a snort of triumph, even though I'm almost upon him.

He turns and I feel him grabbing for me, hear Dupuis breaking through, but the Luger's jammed! Schiller's now got a hold of me! Rolling over and over, I try to get at the knife in my pocket, try to hit him with the butt of the Luger, but it's of no use. A forearm is pressed hard against my throat, and he's straddling me. I can't black out. I mustn't! I've got to get that knife. The blade leaps, and I stab him hard at least twice, maybe more, and he screams, 'Dupuis!' and rolls off. 'Dupuis, the bitch has cut the hell out of my leg!'

Leaves, branches, trees—everything is in my way, and I know I must roll away from him and get up, but now it's Dupuis. 'Madame,' he shouts. 'Madame, your children . . .'

Hitting the side of the Luger with the heel of my hand to clear the mechanism, I fire at him twice, but he's darted aside, and I can hear him crawling through the bushes. 'Madame,' he gasps. 'Madame . . .' Is he wounded, afraid, terrified and wanting to beg, or has he simply lost that gun of his?

Breaking through the woods, I reach the road and pause to catch a breath, hearing them still as they shout to one another, but they mustn't find the Schmeisser in that carrier basket of mine. They'll kill Matthieu if they do, so there's no other choice. Me, I have to go back, must circle round.

As the dawn breaks, I see them on the road below me. The right leg of Schiller's trousers is soaked with blood and he's limping badly, has made a tourniquet that might not be working as well as it should since it's high up on that thigh. One arm is draped over Dupuis's shoulders and when they get to that little car of André's, it's Dupuis who reaches for the handle only to have Schiller shout, 'Don't! Look first.'

They're both badly shaken by the sight of the grenade I've wired to that door handle, and they search the line of the forest for me. There's fear in those looks but also the thought that I must be insane and that they'll never really be able to figure out exactly what I'll do next.

Finally, it's Dupuis who cries out, 'Madame, your children are alive!'

My children. Those faces haunt me. They're all so little, so gaunt-eyed. One asks for water, another for bread, and I have to tell them I have none.

This they accepted. The oldest, a boy of seven or eight, sagely nodded and said, 'Water tastes so good, isn't that right, madame, but bread is much better.'

'Have you seen two children from the Fontainebleau area? One is a girl of nearly nine, the other a boy of twelve. She has lovely soft brown hair and hazel eyes; his hair is black and the eyes are very dark.'

'Their names, madame?'

I told them, but they shook their heads, and I heard the shrieks and felt the blows from one of the guards. It was not the first time for me. *'Sprechen verboten, ja? Verboten!'* the guard shrieked. Always so many simple things were forbidden and always I had to search if I could.

Michèle tugged at my arm. For this, she was punched, kicked, and hit with the butt of a rifle. Somehow I dragged her to one side. 'Your ribs?' I asked only to see her shake her head and try to swallow.

The children were marched away. It was a long line of them that day. They were going for a picnic, eh? Down to the pretty little house with its garden gate of fir bows and its smoking chimneys. There'd be soup, bread, and maybe some cheese. Yes, cheese, real cheese, and warm milk.

My hands clasped Michèle's head. The fuzz of her hair was still so soft I found it hard to resist stroking. It was so like Marie's.

'They're dead, Lily. You know this. They died at the house. You do remember, don't you?'

Simone de Verville found us, and we three went off to report for duty. We'd be sorting shoes that day, maybe handbags, who knew. They'd be baling them for shipment once we'd got them sorted.

There were mountains of clothes in the shed they called Canada. No one else seemed to be around, but it was warm in there and perhaps as safe as any place could be in that little corner of hell.

'You . . . yes, you,' said another guard.

Michèle stepped forward and he said, 'Behind the bales.' That was all, but in *Deutsch*.

The knife lays in the mud- and rag-strewn black earth that is constant to us. There's blood on its blade. The SS possessed such beautiful knives but it's cold and suddenly I'm freezing for I know I can't escape.

I've done such a terrible thing. Me, I've killed the guard who attempted to rape Michèle in the shed they call Canada. The bastard lies beside his knife, only he's not here, not now, and I'm in the woods, have come for my bicycle, yet can still hear Michèle sobbing her heart out.

With difficulty, I stoop to pick up my knife and wipe its blade on the leaves before closing it up and slipping it into a pocket. I wish I could have killed Schiller like I did that guard. They shot one hundred women and beat countless others senseless because of it, but they never thought to ask us. For a long time afterward, Simone and I kept a close watch on Michèle.

My bicycle is where I had left it. Schiller hasn't touched the carrier basket. The Schmeisser is safe.

'Some soup, a little bread, and ham, please, and half a glass of wine to which water will be added. Just a taste, you understand. The red, I think. Yes, yes, that will do and then a coffee with lots of milk, but later you understand.'

The proprietor of Barbizon's Coq Royal looks at me as if I've just demanded the world, but I couldn't care less. This place still reeks, and he doesn't know me, not really. There were always too many Germans here. In the autumn of 1942, the Résistance from Melun asked me to deliver to the proprietor one of their little black pasteboard coffins: Its lid had a cross at the top, then the name, and finally the cross of Lorraine with a V for Victory on either side, and all in white chalk. The man had ignored repeated warnings. An example had needed to be made.

His wife's brother came from Chailly-en-Bière to take over the business, but if you ask me, he was no better, yet I must have something to eat and a place to rest, and daren't go back to Matthieu's for fear Schiller and Dupuis will find out about him. So I sit here by the window where I can watch my bicycle and the street, and I have a cigarette and try to think.

That whole business at the caves was far too close for me. I can't be dropping from the present into the past and back again like that. They're bound to catch me out. And I've hurt my left hand. The middle finger is stiff, the others only a little less. Have I sprained it?

Schiller was only partly right about the cave. Tommy did seal it up, but there was far too much to hide. Some was simply left with the German lorries we had borrowed. Some went to the loft above Clateau's slaughterhouse and then, piece by piece, to other places.

Luck . . . we had such luck. The Germans did find the warehouse where Matthieu Fayelle and others had emptied a lorry, but they never once connected it to Matthieu. This I still can't understand.

The soup comes. This pig of a proprietor has spilled it and his thumb is wet, but such things shouldn't bother me, not after what I've been through. I set the cigarette aside, but its smoke trails up, and suddenly I'm reminded of things and can't stand the sight of it. Too many memories. Every one of those SS and Gestapo or *gestapistes français* knew how terrifying the upward curling of cigarette smoke could be. Never mind touching the burning end of it to my breast or using the leather belt or holding me underwater for what seemed like hours. Just sit me naked and helpless before them and let that smoke curl upwards in silence. Me, a mother whose two children they had killed!

Through the window, the main street of Barbizon seems strange—hauntingly so. It's odd to see it like this after knowing for so long that I'd never see it again. The *pâtisserie* is over there under its flaking gold letters and doing a reasonable business. Two middle-aged women have just come out: brown coats, hats pulled down, no stockings yet, and nothing new. Their woollen socks have lost their elastic. It was always so hard to replace. The wind even tugs at their hats and tries to open their coats, as laughing, they turn away, and I watch them pass the milliner's without a look, and finally the burned-out, boarded-up skeleton of Clateau's butcher shop.

That fire must have come late in 1943 after he'd been killed. The family would have been sent to the camps, not even into forced labour, and my guess is that none of them survived, for by then the Germans were being very thorough.

Reminded of my hunger, I eat my soup. I'm really very good at this, but the ham I must cut into tiny pieces. And the bread . . . what can I say, but that it's like my own. So good, I must extract every morsel of flavour and keep a crust for my pocket.

Tommy came back in the spring of 1942. I remember it was Jean-Guy who first discovered we weren't alone. We'd gone into the forest and were heading for the stone tower, but Marie wanted to check the bathing pool, so we went first to the stream that was a little to the west of our usual route, perhaps a kilometre. The leaves were very green, and I remember thinking

there would be a good crop of wild raspberries along the road-
sides that year, but we'd have to be careful that others didn't get
them first. I was settling back into the routine of being my old
self and trying hard to forget the war and its Occupation that
might never end.

I had the gardens to think about, the fields, rabbits, chickens—
the geese at mother's farm. So many things. The hope, I confess,
that the Germans would leave me alone and that the Résistance
wouldn't call on me.

'*Maman*, there are ships,' said my son. I know Marie was intrigued. Both timidly advanced to the edge of the pool we had
made with stones and mud.

The sails were of one-hundred-franc notes skewered on masts
of sharpened sticks, the hulls patiently whittled out of bits of
driftwood. '*Bonjour*, Lily. *Bonjour*, Jean-Guy and Marie.'

Automatically, I turned away in a flood of tears to search the
woods for the enemy while he tousled Jean-Guy's hair, only to
have my son yank his head away as Tommy reached for Marie's,
his grin the same.

He was armed, of course. There was a rucksack and a Schmeisser.
'How have you been?' he asked. 'Missing me a little?'

Setting the knife and fork down, I swallow hard and have to
shut my eyes, but the memory keeps coming back, and I can't stop
it though I try, for in the camps they forbade us to even remember
and tried their best to wipe it all out, but Tommy's so close, I can
feel his kisses still, the very breath and warmth of him, and I don't
ever want to let those go.

It was Marie who tugged at his sweater and said, 'We have two
SS guards, monsieur, and the colonel. The Lieutenant Schiller has
been sent to Russia.'

'And the inspector?' he asked of my daughter.

She was very firm with him. 'Still asking his questions.
Only yesterday I have seen him go into the Tabac Ribault. Me,
I waited fifteen minutes, you understand, but he didn't come
out, so we know he's working with Monsieur Ribault who is a
dirty *collabo*.'

Only then, did I notice how Jean-Guy was looking at Tommy, and when the sails were taken off the little ships and bankrolled to me because children didn't have money like that, and he knows his friends and the shopkeepers would only notice and start talking, the thanks he gave were empty.

'I don't know what's come over him,' I said later that night when I went to Tommy by myself. 'Ever since the robbery, he's become increasingly distant. Jules and the Vuittons were here when I was in Paris and maybe they put pressure on him.'

'The son of an important family. You have to remember the boy's growing up. Jules can't have been all that bad or you would never have married him.'

'Women make all kinds of mistakes this Occupation only reinforces.'

He added another dry stick to the tiny fire he'd built among some screening boulders. There was no possible warmth except for the mind and soul. 'What will you do?' he asked.

'Lie low for a while. My SS guards watch me all the time. Neumann has been repeatedly eyeing the contents of the house and has made another list of his own: the small things that can be easily taken. He's edgy, Tommy. It can't have been easy for him having that train robbed. He'll be worrying about the Russian front just like the rest of them.'

'Was Schiller really sent there?'

There were so many things we didn't know. One guessed simply because that was all one could do. 'Maybe yes, maybe no, but deep inside me, I have to feel he's near.'

'And Dupuis?'

'Just like Schiller, he believes I was involved in the robberies, but more than this perhaps, that I'm the key to the rest of you, so they both tolerate a modicum of freedom for me as they wait to see what I'll do. I can't become involved again, Tommy. I mustn't. I don't want to be the one who leads them to you and Nicki and the others.'

'Marie seems very reliable.'

'She and Jean-Guy argue vehemently. For days on end, she

won't speak to him, but when I ask, it's always some stupid thing, never the real reason.'

'Could she take a message into Fontainebleau?'

'No! I absolutely forbid such a thing.'

'I have to contact Matthieu and through him, Paul Tessier. We're moving over to the offensive. Now that America's in the war, it's only a matter of time until the Allies invade the Continent.'

Pearl Harbour—yes, I've forgotten to mention it—7 December 1941. But you do see how small our war here really was? We learned of this tragic event both from the BBC French broadcast and the German-controlled Radio-Paris. We also knew that as Tommy had said, it would only be a matter of time.

'We've a parachute drop in ten days, Lily, near that abandoned airfield.'

The caves and my mother's farm.

'Just hang on for a little longer. As soon as the drop's done, we'll clear off and leave you out of it. Some of the arms are to be smuggled into Paris. Marcel is working for us.'

'You'll all be arrested!'

'Somehow I've got to contact Tessier. He's the only one who can teach the others how to handle the explosives that will be dropped.'

'I'm not hearing this. I'm really not! And where, please, do you intend to hide stuff like that?'

'As far from the caves as possible. The loft of Clateau's slaughterhouse probably.'

'Ah, nom de Dieu, why? Barbizon is a little place that's crowded with Germans and collaborators!'

Not only had he a place in mind, he let me say it: 'My coach house, among the crates.' Aghast that he should even think of such a thing, I offered an alternative: 'The Poulins, Tommy. Yes, we must take it to their farm. Henri and Viviane will help us. It's far enough from the drop zone and won't arouse suspicion.'

Me, I knew he had planned it all along, for he finally said, 'We'll have to check the location out.'

I remember nodding with dread at this while gazing into the fire, remember saying, 'You want me to go there tomorrow to ask them, and if I do, Marie must take a message to Matthieu? That restaurant of his is so full of the enemy, Tommy, the French ones especially will know who the hell my daughter is!'

'But she runs errands for you? The post office, the shops, eggs even to the mayor.'

And he'd done it again. Led me straight to where he wanted. 'All right, I'll ask her to take Matthieu some eggs first thing in the morning. Jean-Guy can take five to the mayor, so as to divide the responsibility and silence the argument.'

'Nicki will go to the Poulins with you.'

'And yourself?'

'Will be watching your backs.'

The surface of the millpond is dark and still, the geese tightly flocked before the door where Viviane used to feed them. They question, they wait, they crane their necks in expectation and complain to one another as I lean the bike against a tree and walk towards them. Me, I know what I'm about to find. Even so, I don't take chances. The Luger is in my hand, the Schmeisser Matthieu got for me in the carrier basket beneath a blanket that hides it.

The geese see me and crane their necks my way. They fidget— the whole flock moves in unison, eddying in uncertainty only to flow right back to the doorstep as a burst of autumn sunlight makes their feathers a starker white against the russet hues of the fallen leaves and the chalk-white of the stucco.

Rubbing the glass of a windowpane, I peer inside. Grey-haired and tied to a chair, Viviane sits before a cold stove, and I know Schiller's cut her throat.

The geese move towards me only to ebb, then wait. They're in a constant state of flux, the poor things. Finding the pail of feed in the barn, I toss them handful after handful, throwing it towards the pond until the racket of them is more than I can bear and they've parted enough for me to see Henri.

Mired in their puddled excrement and feathers, he lies face-down. Though I've seen far too much of this, I bite my knuckles to stop the tears, for it's not just that they're gone. It's all my fault and I know this. Am I softening, or is it simply my memories of this place and the pond that once held so much for me and the others?

The water's cold, and I know I can't go bathing, but on that spring day in 1942, it was deliciously warm in the shallows, and through the spray I could see and hear Tommy laughing at me. He had such a good laugh, strong and full, such a wonderful body. We came together—splashed—chased one another until we fell into each other's arms among the tall grass and wild flowers, me touching his hair and his brow, and thinking of Henri Poulin who might be watching, though the pond seemed empty of his punt when I sat up to look.

'Tommy, I'm worried about Marie. I must get back. It's crazy for me to stay here like this,' but he lay on top of me, and it felt so good to have him there.

'Nicki and Dmitry are on the lookout. We'll be okay.'

A wren flitted nervously among the flowering dogwood, and in the distance I could hear the geese. Viviane would be feeding them again; Henri would be . . .

'It's been ages, Lily.'

Halfway between the millpond and the village of Milly-la-Fôret there's a place of much beauty called the Trois Pignons, the Three Gables. It's a plateau of uplifted little escarpments that have been cut by gullies and strewn with scattered boulders.

Always when I come here, I feel wild and free, able to climb to the highest parts, breathless while looking out over the surrounding terrain. It's windswept up here in the late autumn, open to all weathers, and I can't resist the temptation to stand out and let Dupuis and Schiller see me holding that Schmeisser if they're nearby.

Me, I wish I was wearing the brown beret, rucksack, Norwegian trousers, and boots that I used to have hidden with the Poulins, you understand. *Ah, oui, oui,* I always took precautions—everyone did. When things got tough, I had places to go to, but please don't misunderstand. The Forest of Fontainebleau was far from wild and empty. During the Occupation, there were times when the Germans would come like tourists to hike or simply wander about, and times, too, when Parisians and others had to get out of the city, if allowed, to scrounge for mushrooms, acorns, and berries, or attempt to buy things from the surrounding farms.

There were, and still are, lots of little restaurants and cafés on the fringes, some even in secluded bits of woods. We never used any of them, but with the worsening of the Russian campaign, that feeling of emptiness grew because men and materiel were steadily being withdrawn to the east. The Nazis had also increased their demands for forced labour. Though the Service du Travail Obligatoire, the much-hated STO, didn't officially come into being until February 1943, any man between the ages of eighteen and fifty-five could find life precarious. As a result, some took to the woods, and when we could, we helped those who wished to join the *maquis*, who were beginning to form in the mountains of the Auvergne and other places.

Tommy and Nicki were constantly on the move. I don't think they ever stayed anywhere for long. A night, a few hours, no more.

Using the potting shed, Dmitry did, however, end up with me, and I came to like him less and less, for he tried hard to pump the location of the artwork out of me. I knew he must be working for Moscow, yet I couldn't get word of this to Tommy and the others.

Of Dupuis, I saw little, of Schiller, nothing. It was as if the lieutenant had vanished. Occasionally, Nini brought word of Jules and the Vuittons, as did Simone and André, so it was, for me, mainly a time of summer, of working in my gardens and fields. That first arms drop was, however, a total bust since the aircraft never even showed up, but then it happened, right out there on that plain among the farms and fields. Clateau had given me a lift in his van with three others. The Feldkommandant in Barbizon had a taste for horsemeat, and Clateau had talked him into providing the necessary papers for being out after curfew. Tobacco smoke filled the cab, but I was hooked on cigarettes anyway and had brought some I'd filched from my boarders, cognac, too, and of course I was just as excited as everyone else. Scared, too, who wouldn't have been, but I liked the company of these simple men. It felt good to be with them. And when we got to the drop site, everyone listened intently and craned their necks to search the darkened skies until, finally, the engines of a Whitley were heard and that drone increased with a slowness that was agonizing, for we all knew the *Boche* could also be listening.

Clateau flashed his torch on and off in sequences of three but no one could have seen it from up there, yet when the chutes started coming down, everyone started running after them. Step-ins, slips, a chemise, and a blouse were on my mind, for they were of such beautiful silk, those first chutes, and we had such luck that night. There were six canisters, but it wasn't until we got them to the Poulins' that they were opened. Mills grenades, blasting caps, sticks of Nobel 808, fuse, wires, and pistols, too: Webley .45s with fifty rounds each.

Tucked in amongst everything else were chocolate bars, ciga-rettes, even tea and a fifth of brandy. Every space had been used, and we knew that the British didn't have much themselves.

A fortnight later, we met in the forester's hut that nestles among the boulders on a rocky ledge not far below me. Even with the Germans insisting on the French constantly logging the forest, this hut had remained empty for years, just like the other one.

There's still no sign of Dupuis and Schiller nearby, but far out on that plain, a small dark car is parked at the side of the road and the glint from a pair of binoculars is clear enough, for even as I have remembered the location of this hut, so have they.

Satisfied, I begin to pick my way down. The boards are weath-ered grey and someone has left the door slightly ajar, but are there trip wires?

Feeling around it, I search. The latch is but a simple hook and eye. My fingers move up some more, reaching out a little now, for the roof's low, but there's still nothing. Have I been wrong about their having anticipated me and having been here recently? Have they not remembered that we also used this hut?

Below me, the gully opens in ledges of rock, spills of boulders, and clumps of brush. Sparrows and finches are after seeds. I walk away, find a boulder, heft it as a cricketer might, and toss it at that door, knowing there won't be time to duck, but nothing happens.

With the muzzle of the Schmeisser, I ease it open since I need to get in there, to remember how it was. The table's still here—there's a ruin of splintered chairs. Bullet holes are everywhere, the one little window completely obliterated, but as if God had willed it, the soot-clouded glass of the lantern is perfect even though glass was really what it was all about on that first night we met here. Broken glass, and Schiller will know this.

Paul Tessier lovingly held one of the time pencils. That badly disfigured face paused to search out each of us. 'You crush the right colour, eh? It releases the measured amount of fulminate of mercury, which begins to eat its way through the wire. Thin for a fast delay; thick for a slow one, and very thick for much longer.'

About one-third of the time pencil was colour-coded. Tiny phials of fulminate—the acid—encircled the wire whose thickness varied with the colour and its length. 'Red means a delay of four-and-a-half hours. Violet . . .' He traced the length of the stem. 'Violet, *mes amis*, gives one of five-and-a-half days. Orange, yellow, green, and blue provide delays that are in between, so you squeeze the woman of your choice, break the cherry, let the acid flood out to contact the wire, and *voilà!* it eats its way through. The striker pin is then released and the detonator struck.'

I ignored the chauvinistic inference. No one stirred. There was not a murmur. All eyes were riveted to those hands until a finger was held up. 'But beware,' he said. 'These things are sensitive to heat and sudden shock. The glass is so thin you could easily kill yourselves, so I'm recommending you carry them like this.'

He took off his beret and shoved the time pencil between the Croix de Guerre and the material beneath it. 'Mind you don't become too hotheaded, though. Heat speeds up the rate of reaction.'

'Aren't there shorter delays?' asked one of the railwaymen from Melun.

Paul was all gestures. 'We'll get them next time perhaps.'*

'And the "plastic,"' asked another.

Tessier was firm with us. 'For now, it's the Nobel 808 and a much stronger stench of bitter almond, so don't breathe in the fumes too long or your head will split.'

The map was unrolled. Roads, towns, villages became clear in miniature. The Forest of Fontainebleau was like a green stain. Railways were simple lines of black with tiny crossing lines spaced at regular intervals. Two for a single; four for a double.

'The line from Paris,' said Nicki. 'London wants us to hit it close to the city where it will hurt the most.' He was now totally committed to the offensive. What fools we were. Every person who was in this hut that night is dead except for myself.

London would only have shrugged at the loss, or shaken their heads and said, 'What a pity.'

More likely, still, they would have blamed our lack of security, not realizing that we took what precautions we could.

'Villeneuve-Saint-Georges,' said the taller of the two railwaymen. 'The Port Courcel and the bridge, the roundhouse and the marshalling yards along the river.'

These were just downstream of the town, but it was the little guy who objected. 'That bridge is so heavily guarded they open up if you fart ten kilometres from it.'

'So fart then. We simply shoot them,' said the bigger one.

It was Tommy who reminded them, 'The whole idea is to do the job in secret and get away, that's why the time pencils. We let the sabotage happen when they least expect it.'

'We want to make them afraid of us,' said Nicki. 'Certainly, the damage is important, but so, too, is the psychological effect. Kill only if you must, and then quietly.'

There were nods of agreement. 'With a knife,' said someone,

---

* Improved time-pencil fuses came later: one-half, two, five-and-a-half, twelve, and twenty-four hours in colour codes of red, white, green, yellow, and blue, respectively.

and I realized it was Dmitry and that it might be to Moscow's advantage if all but he were killed.

The gully is still empty. There's only the sound of the birds and the wind as it sweeps under the eaves to lift a tattered piece of roofing paper. Out over the plain, some of the fields lie fallow, others before the plow, while behind me the escarpments climb and I know I should get out of here before Schiller and Dupuis come, yet I can't seem to leave, can't stop wanting to remember the past.

Tommy handed me his cigarette. Hurriedly, I took a drag and handed it back, but he was not there anymore, though I *wanted* to warn him of Dmitry.

That supplier of false papers was waiting for me when I got to my bicycle. 'Dmitry, I don't think it's wise for you to use the potting shed anymore. I'm sorry, but I must ask you not to come back with me. Tommy feels Schiller must be up to something.'

'And what does Lutoslawski have to say about it?'

'Nicki? The same, I think, but perhaps you should catch up with them and ask. If they okay it, then fine.'

'Trust is basic to everything we do, madame. I've risked my life time and again.'

'As have others, myself included. Look, it's not safe, that's all there is to it.'

'Then I'll come with you and pick up my Luger.'

'That's not possible. I've already passed it on to one of the others.'

He knew I was lying. I could hear him following and yet I kept on pushing that bike of mine through the darkness until his voice came at me again. 'Moscow wishes me to inform them of the hiding place, madame. They would rather the Germans didn't recover the stolen works of art since some of them belong to Russia.'

Nicki's things . . . He had grabbed my bike! Suddenly, I couldn't breathe. In panic, I tried to fight back but he was too strong. With a final yank, he threw me to the ground, and as I lay under him, I heard the sound he gave as his throat was cut.

'Tommy had to be convinced,' said Nicki as he helped me up, 'but for myself, I'm sorry I had to use you the way I did.'

Where once there had been a mound over the hasty grave, there's now a shallow depression. I'm not sorry Dmitry's dead, only saddened that it had to happen. There's still no further sign of Schiller and Dupuis. The forest is as it was back then, and soon, all too soon, there's the sound of train wheels in my head, and I feel myself rushing inevitably towards the abyss. My children were beside me, and we were on our way into Paris, me with two large hampers, hidden in each of which were a kilo of Nobel 808 wrapped in much decorated bread dough, two Webley service revolvers, and a packet of cartridges, and I knew it was suicidal to attempt that. Having flour, even the grey of the 'National' was one thing. I'd added onions and had sliced some of them and bulbs of garlic, too. Though it was always chancy bringing food into the city, it was the smell of the Nobel that terrified me.

'*Ihre Papiere, bitte. Ausweis und der Passierschein, ja? Schnell!*'

This Scharführer couldn't seem to let go of my papers but I'd raise his rank anyways. 'I must have a medical checkup, Herr General. I'm pregnant.'

He didn't give a bloody damn. 'What's in the baskets?'

'Food, a few spare clothes, a little bedding for my children. Things I'll need so that the people with whom we're staying overnight won't have to provide everything.'

He still didn't give a damn. 'Their names?'

'Dr. André de Verville and his wife, Simone.' He got the address, too. This he carefully wrote down in a small notebook before closing up my papers and handing them back. He knew I'd said 'people' instead of 'friends.' He thought Jean-Guy might be Jewish—sometimes it was hard to tell. Marie was far more Aryan, and he lay the tip of a forefinger under her chin and asked, '*Mein Kind,* what's really in those baskets?'

'*Bitte,* Herr General, my daughter only knows a few words of *Deutsch.*'

'Guns and bombs,' said Marie *en français.* 'That's why I've brought my paints and paper.'

I stammered something and tried to pass it off with a grin, but he slapped her face and shrieked: 'I could have you shot for that!'

The Gare de Lyon was crowded. *Flics* in blue capes with their leaded hems seemed everywhere, so, too, those in plain clothes, but somehow we got through, and soon the station was behind us.

'Will we see Papa?' asked Jean-Guy.

'Of course. As soon as we get to Simone's I'll call him to tell him we're here.'

'Are you really pregnant, *maman*?'

It was Marie who asked and I couldn't lie to her. '*Oui*. Is it such a bad thing, Jean-Guy?'

'Only if you don't know who the father is.'

'Hey listen you, it's Tommy's, and you'd better not say anything about it for all our sakes.'

Marie looked up at me. There was such innocence in her eyes. 'Will Dr. André help you to get rid of it?'

I shook my head, and she heaved a contented sigh and locked her arms more firmly about the handle of the basket. 'Then I will help you and we'll have a baby brother for Jean-Guy and me to play with.'

Paris in the late autumn of 1942 was, if anything, shabbier than before. Oh, for sure, everything was wide open for the Nazis and those that were with them, but there were the beginnings of doubt even amongst the most ardent of collaborators. On 8 November, the Allies had landed en masse in Algeria and Morocco, on the 11th, the Wehrmacht, in retaliation, had ended the existence of the *zone libre* by taking over the whole of France, but were being held up at Stalingrad. If the winter should be particularly harsh, they might be stopped, even turned back, and the Allies were determined. Everyone knew there would be an invasion, but when?

Sometimes we'd hear the RAF going over to bomb targets deep in the Reich, or they'd come closer to home to hit the Renault Works in Boulogne-Billancourt, a suburb of Paris. I remember being with André and Simone in that flat of theirs and watching. I remember so many things but what was it about the rue Mouffetard that made me so edgy? I'd left the children and the things I'd brought with Simone. Marcel was to pick up the Nobel 808 and the guns later when he came for me. Normally, there was a street market every Sunday morning, and there was one that day, but it didn't seem right. Lots of people milling about, not a lot for sale, but it was as if everyone in that street sensed that something terrible was going to happen.

The street climbed steeply. It was narrow, paved with blocks of stone, and you got that lovely closed-in feeling of a village and its market. The grey and pale-green of slate and copper roofs were often four or five storeys up to attic garrets and but a jumble, since some of the houses were very old. Innumerable chimney pots reached for the sky, the windows shuttered or open, but no balconies. Shops lined the street. Basically, it was a nation of small shopkeepers, but many were down on their luck.

I hurried along but kept asking myself what could be wrong? Me, I felt it, you understand, and at a point, one hundred metres from the courtyard that led to my sister's flat, I foolishly broke into a run, someone immediately yelling, '*Halt, verfluchte Französin!*' as another shouts, '*Hände hoch!*'

I tripped, fell, banged my knees, and tore my only pair of stockings, but found that the courtyard door was locked. I shouted at it, nearly breaking my fists while down the street, people turned to watch. 'JANINE, LET ME IN!'

Throwing a shoulder against that door, I yelled for her again. Suddenly, it was flung open, and as some boys leaped aside, I ran the length of that courtyard and darted into the open doorway. The concierge looked out from her *loge* and started to object, but the Himalayas of those stairs were almost more than I can manage. One flight, two flights, round and round, me knowing they were after me now, that they wouldn't stop until they had me, and never mind the child that was inside me. I had to get to Nini before they did, but there was no one in her room, and my heart was hammering so hard it was going to burst.

The washroom was at the far end of the corridor, and I made a bolt for it, had to hide, but knew it was of no use, for the mirror was still there on that wall in its cheap frame, cracked like all such mirrors, and I saw myself breathlessly saying, 'Nini . . . *chérie*, it's finished for us!'

That door opened. 'Lily, what's the matter?'

'The street. The *Boche*. There were none of them until I began to run.'

There, I've confessed that, too. I broke. I panicked.

She grabbed me by the hand, and we raced back to that room of hers. Parting the cheap lace curtains, she glanced down at the street and said only, 'We'll have to go over the top.'

'I can't, Nini! I'm five-and-a-half months.'

'*Idiote!*'

A whistle shrilled, the first of several, but all too soon there was the sound of motorcycles and the squeal of brakes, the cries of *'Raus! Raus!,'* the hammering of hobnailed boots and bashing of rifle butts.

Dragging a small suitcase from under the bed, she flung a few things into it, and as we reached the head of the stairs and I looked down, that spiral came rushing up at me. 'Go down,' she said.

'Nini, I can't!'

'Carry your coat and hide that hat. Act naturally. Bluff it!'

Give her time to get away.

Two German corporals were going from door to door, bashing them in and yelling for everyone to get out, but they were still on the first floor, and some of the tenants were leaning over the railing like I was, wondering what to do. But the child gave a lurch, a tear that caused me to grip my middle and wonder if the baby had dropped. 'Nini . . . Nini, I love you. *Bonne chance.*'

'The Jardin du Luxembourg, but watch your back,' she said as we briefly embraced. 'I'll see you later.'

I started down. For me, it was the most difficult thing I'd ever had to do. Schiller and Dupuis would be waiting for me, one at each end of the street. My coat was over an arm, my hat hidden. When I reached a woman with two small children hurrying out of a fourth-floor flat, I heard one of them asking where they were going, and I took that little girl's hand in mine, smiled at the mother and said,

'To see the puppets, *n'est-ce pas?*' It was a last desperate gamble, a prayer.

The street had been cordoned off, and there was a wall of German soldiers at either end of the sector they'd chosen for the house-to-house, and as we walked towards the nearest, we did so uphill, until a Feldwebel's unfeeling eyes searched mine and I heard myself asking, as if of the weather, 'What's the trouble, Officer?' and I couldn't understand the person who had said that. I couldn't! It was like I was two entirely different people.

He shook his head, tore the papers from my hand, looked at the two children, at their mother, and thrust my papers back at me.

I thought I was going to have the baby right there, but they were looking for someone else.

It took me a good hour or more to shake those who were tailing me and get to the Jardin du Luxembourg. I remember that the ribbon of the Légion d'honneur was pinned to the old man's blazer and that he rented toy sailing boats with a defiance that was admirable, for he refused all German requests. Instead, children vied with their parents for them as the statues of the queens of France looked down from their terraced heights.

Among the plane trees around the Fontaine Médicis, lovers sat on stiff-backed benches holding hands and doing other things, though kissing in public was still illegal, as was dancing, and considered an offence to all our boys who were locked up as POWs in the Reich.

Lots of people were about, even though the afternoon, now late, was grey and cold. The puppets fought, as they always did. Out on the rue de Médicis, a calliope played while roasted chestnuts were sold near that gate and the trade was brisk. Around me, there were German officers and other ranks, most of them with their *Parisiennes*. Strolling *flics* were about, Gestapo gumshoes also, French ones too, and *collabos*, maybe even a few black-market dealers, but I saw no sign of my sister. Perhaps she'd not been able to make it. This I couldn't bear to think, and with hands in the pockets of my coat, I started for the *palais*, only to remember that the Luftwaffe had taken it over and that it was not permitted to go near it.

But suddenly, I felt her slip an arm through mine, and she gave it a squeeze, was breathless, and said, 'So you got through it, eh, but me . . . Ah, I didn't think you would, but am sorry to have kept you waiting. Were you apprehensive about me?'

'How long have you been living like this?'

'Long enough. Look, it doesn't matter. One lives the way one has to.'

It was an old argument. 'Is everything set for tonight?' I asked.

'Yes, of course, but we have to talk, just you and me. With that thing inside you, it's impossible. You do understand?'

We were near the greenhouses and the school of mines at the back of the gardens. 'What, exactly, is it that you want to say?'

'Schiller and Dupuis will guess who the father is, so what's the sense of your hanging on to it? You'll only have the child in prison. It'll die anyways.'

'But . . .'

'Look, I'm sorry, but you'll just have to live with the lie of your illness. A tumour, Lily. Cancer of the womb. André has agreed, under duress of course, since he's holier than the holy, but has finally seen the sense of what I've told him at that office of his.'

Me, I couldn't believe what was happening and finally blurted, 'But what am I to do about the children, the house, my rabbits, the chickens, and the potatoes I still have to lift?'

Anything but what I really wanted to say, but it was Nini who insists. 'Go and see Jules at the Jeu de Paume. Tell him you haven't been feeling well and that you're afraid it might be bad news.'

'He won't care, why should he? Besides, the children already know I'm expecting and that it's Tommy's child.'

'Must you confide everything in them?'

'One has to trust if one is to gain their loyalty.'

'Schiller must see you talking to Jules. He must be made to think . . .'

I pulled her round to face me. 'What?' I demanded.

Nini never backed off when cornered. 'Why do you think Schiller and Dupuis have left you at the house? They hope you'll lead them to us. We were just lucky that the *rafle* in my street happened at the same time and that they didn't know about it.'

'But they know where you live. They can pick you up at any time. And Michèle and Henri-Philippe.'

Again, there was a look in her dark eyes that I'd never seen before, and I wondered if that was what the Occupation had done to her.

'All right,' she said. 'I'll tell you because I must. There's to be another big auction next Wednesday. Göring's flying in for it. Schiller must think we're going to try to knock it off, so we keep him thinking that. You go to see Jules, and Schiller sees you with him, and it all makes sense—you're sizing things up for us, and he thinks he can use that stuff to bait the trap while we go off to blow up some other trains. It's neat, Lily. Only, you absolutely have to have that tumour removed. You'll be away from it all. He can't connect you with any of it, and we're safe as well.'

Bien sûr, I had thought of the dilemma. A child without a father is one thing, but a lot of women had those now, and I didn't want to lose this one. Suddenly, it meant more to me than anything, and I said, 'I want to talk to Tommy first. It's as much his as mine.'

Gripping my hands, she told me that he mustn't know, that we could always make another, that the war wouldn't last forever, that the Russians had surrounded the Sixth Army on the outskirts of Stalingrad. 'It's happening, Lily. The end's in sight.'

'Dmitry . . .'

She turned away from me. 'Yes, I know. Tommy's told me. He was very useful, and I don't honestly know what we're going to do without him. I really don't. Organize something, I guess. Always it's me who has to cover things up and organize something to replace them.'

Turning back, she kissed me on both cheeks and said, 'Now cheer up and I'll take you to see that husband of yours who's in bed with the Occupier. Perhaps if we're seen together with him it will help the cause. Two sisters, yes. The nearness of the death of one of them, the anxiety, and a few tears, of course.'

There are only fragments of memory, glimpses of that business. Simone was so upset. For her, to lose a child like that was to commit murder. André and she argued, but I said so little. In the end, I think it was done at about two thirty a.m. I hadn't even made out a will, had so little of my own, but what I did have, I wanted to see properly disposed of. When I came out of the anaesthetic, who should be sitting there but Dupuis, holding a large glass bottle in which a tumour was submerged in formalin.

Promptly, I threw up and passed out, but he was still there when I came round. 'You're full of surprises,' he said.

I could hardly speak. 'Have I been out for long?'

'In and out for three days. It's Wednesday.'

I shut my eyes and tried to slip back into unconsciousness, but his words, when they came, were of no help. 'It's not the length of time, madame. That's only understandable. It's the things you inadvertently said.'

'What things?'

'Rudi Swartz, madame? Orders for the Russian front?'

Me, I had to turn away, couldn't bring myself to face him, though I had to say, 'Poor Rudi, he was so terrified of being sent there.'

'But there were no such orders.'

I had to face him, I needed to. 'Weren't there? Rudi thought so. Please don't tell me he was mistaken.'

'A cave, madame? "The cave," you said and repeated it several times. Also, "the farm." By that, I presume you meant your mother's.'

'I really wouldn't know, Inspector. I've always wanted a farm of my own. It's been a lifelong dream.'

'And an emerald-and-diamond tiara? That of the Empress Eugénie? Has that also been a lifelong dream of yours?'

To this I could say nothing. Hunched in that chair of his, sucking on a cigarette, he took a moment before adding, '"Flames," Madame? "Screams in the night. Must get away. Mustn't let them find me here."'

'I was delirious, in shock, and in a great deal of pain.'

'*Bien sûr,* but you kept asking God to forgive you for something. God and Thomas Carrington. "Tommy," I believe it was.' He consulted his little black notebook. 'Yes, here it is,' and he showed it to me. *Tommy . . . Tommy, forgive me.*

I think it was on the 18th or 19th of January 1943 that they took me to the farm. The Russians, I know, had lifted the nine-hundred-day siege of Leningrad. The German Sixth Army at Stalingrad had all but been destroyed. No one in the car said much. I think they were all wondering what it must mean for them.

I remember that there had been the usually insufferable cold and damp, even a thin layer of newfallen snow, but that the ashes of my mother's farmhouse still smouldered and there was the stench of burning cloth and rubber.

Blood matted the jet-black hair where the bullet had entered. Schiller stood looking at her. The wind tugged at the collar of his greatcoat and made the tops of his ears red beneath the cap with its death's-head.

'There was a wireless set and you knew of it,' he finally said.

'I didn't! How could I have?'

He hit me then. Still weak and dizzy, I fell to the ground, where he kicked me. Doubled up in pain, I tried to think what was best to do. They'd use Jean-Guy and Marie to make me talk. They wouldn't hesitate.

A shot rang out, and I saw the gun in his hand leap. Another spurted up the earth beside me, and as I lay waiting for the final one, Dupuis stepped between us. 'Of course, she'll talk, Herr Obersturmführer, but only if her mother receives a decent burial.'

'I've nothing to say. I don't know anything.'

In anger, Schiller fired at me again, Dupuis losing all colour. 'Obersturmführer . . .' he began.

'Answers! I will have answers!' shrilled that SS. Four others of those stood around with machine pistols. Dupuis let go of me and stepped back as Schiller pressed the muzzle of that gun of his to my forehead and said, 'The cowards smashed their wireless and left her to face the consequences. You will tell me where they are and the names of all of their contacts, and you will tell me the locations of the artwork.'

Me, I didn't know how long mother had been lying here, a day or two at most. Tommy and the others could be anywhere, but I'd have to tell him something, otherwise he'd have the children brought before me. 'There's a hut in the forest, at a place we call the Three Gables. I'll show it to you.'

They stopped off at the barracks in Fontainebleau to get more men. I think then that the feeling of being very much the hunted now, rather than the hunters, had begun to come over them. I do know that they moved through the forest stealthily and that I was forced to wait under guard in one of the cars. Dupuis even lit a cigarette and passed it to me but said, 'You know that wasn't a tumour de Verville removed. It was a child.'

Two of the others had been left to guard us. There were some cars behind, and then a couple of lorries. 'You can think what you will, Inspector, but I know what it was and so does the German doctor who examined me before the operation.'

That one had been perfunctory, a taking of my pulse, a signing of the necessary papers. Me, I think he must have been on his way to Maxim's when André caught up with him in the corridors.

'The lieutenant will pry everything out of you, madame.'

Me, I kept listening for the sound of gunfire and hoping Tommy and Nicki and the others were nowhere near. The shackles hurt, and every time I lifted the cigarette to my lips, that length of chain made a rattle. 'Listen, you, I have to pee and would prefer not to in the car.'

He unlocked the handcuffs and the door. 'Try to make a run for it, and you won't get far.'

The cigarette pauses and I blink. I know it's Dupuis and that he's finally caught up with me, the past having become the present, for he has just said exactly the same thing, though now he adds, 'Lift your hands slowly.'

'Where's Schiller?'

'In the house.'

'Is Jules with him?'

'If still alive.'

Crouching, he teases the Schmeisser from me. 'Now the Luger, eh? Easy . . . Yes, yes, that's it.'

Having committed the unpardonable of living in the past so intensely, I had forgotten the present. 'There's a knife in my left coat pocket.'

With the gun pressing against the nape of my neck, he frisks me, and finds the wire cutters. 'Where's the knife?' he asks.

My hands are well above me and it's so like it was back then, I have to say, 'I don't know. It must have fallen out.'

Again, I'm frisked, but now his breath comes quickly, and I ask myself, How many times have I smelled those peppermint-flavoured anise bonbons on that breath of his, that face pressed close to mine?

'So we'll take a little detour,' he says, 'and you'll tell me what we would like very much to know.'

Snatching up the Schmeisser, he tells me to head for that old stone tower, but me, I haven't told you how it came to be that I spent more than nine months with Tommy and the *maquis* of the Auvergne. We blew up a lot of things, caused trouble in widespread places, even infiltrated back into Paris to link up with Michèle and the others.

As at my final capture in the late autumn of 1943, there's still so much to say yet no time now to say it, for the Forest of Fontainebleau, that hunting ground of kings, opens out below us and I'm reminded of my daughter and son, of the fighter planes we once saw, of Jules and me, and then of Tommy and me.

For me, the tower and the edge of this cliff are to be both the beginning and end, yet I'm not unhappy. To fail in life is nothing; to learn to live with it everything, and I've felt again the loves I once knew, have heard again the voices of my children and my friends.

Dupuis mentions the clinic and asks how I managed to get there.

'The British liberated Bergen-Belsen on the 15th of April. From there, I went first into a military hospital near Bremen, but there was trouble with my chest, so when I asked to be sent to Switzerland, to a clinic, they took it upon themselves to do all they could for me.'

'The Médaille de la Résistance was awarded posthumously.'

'Was it? *Ah, bon*, but you see, I had no wish to let people know I was alive. I wanted to be dead, Inspector.'

'But they had the numbers that are tattooed on your arm? Surely, those would have given them your name?'

'Quite obviously they couldn't have had it on their lists. So many people died at Bergen-Belsen, sixteen thousand in one month. Me, I should have died, too, and probably that was all the Free French really knew. In any case, it was no gift to have been spared. On the contrary, it was and is to my everlasting shame. They killed my friends. Michèle . . . I saw them chop off her head.'

'So, the cave, madame. Where is it?'

'Not far, but you'll need me to point it out.'

Dupuis shakes his head but doesn't smile. 'I'll give you a few minutes while the sun is still with us, then I'll kill you simply because I must.'

'And Schiller, what of him?'

'After I'm done with you, I'll kill him and the others.'

What others, I wonder, except for my husband? 'Could I have another cigarette?'

He tosses me the packet, but it sails over the edge of the cliff as if by accident, so I feel for my blouse pockets and tell him, 'Maybe I have some others.'

That knife . . . it was in my sleeve, and when I raised my hands, it slid down under the blouse to end up next to the scar, trapped against skirt and belt. '*Ah, bon*, Inspector, there's a packet in the left pocket of my blouse.'

'Give me one.'

'I must unbutton my coat first. Is that okay?'

'Hurry then, the sun is almost gone.'

As I slip my hand under the sweater, I pluck open the blouse. 'The entrance to the cave, Inspector, it's not easy to find. We tumbled a lot of rocks down in front of it. Sixty million francs worth of stuff are hidden there. Old francs, you understand. Probably a lot more. Dürer, Rubens, Rembrandt, and Cranach . . . lots of those. Some lovely paintings by Gauguin and Renoir, boxes and boxes of collectors' gold coins. Other ones, too.'

He reaches out with the match to light my cigarette, and I lean towards it, knowing that he's forgotten what the sun on the horizon can do to the vision. Drawing in, I feint suddenly to the left, ramming that knife into him with a quick upthrust to the guts while seizing the gun in his hand.

Shock registers. He gasps and tries to grab me as blood rushes into his mouth and he coughs, then blurts, 'Your children . . .'

Nothing else.

The sun is gone, but through the open gates to the château I see the dark silhouette of a car I haven't seen in years. It's parked behind the little Renault André had used, and I know at once its colour is a dark forest green, see at once Tommy sitting on my steps, eating an apple. There's a cake beside him, a splendid cake. '*Maman,* please! He will eat it all.' Marie . . . can my children really be in there?

Jean-Guy has long since been forgiven, but if they are, I must somehow let him know that what he did doesn't matter anymore, that I love him just as much as Marie.

The driveway curves through the tall, sear grasses. There are cedars of Lebanon. From their cover, I watch the house and try to figure out what to do, but the images keep coming at me. Dupuis and I on that road to the Three Gables. Those two guards, me asking to have a pee, his, 'Try to make a run for it and you won't get far.'

I did, and Tommy and Nicki and Janine were right there to help. Gunfire all around us. A hail of bullets, Dupuis cowering behind the car with pistol in hand. An explosion as the first of the lorries went up, then another and another as I ran.

Trees, dawn in the forest—almost a year was to pass. We had come back to raid the house and try to kill the Reichsmarschall. There were thirty of us. Jean-Guy had been my contact in the house, but it was Marie who cried out, '*Maman*, they are going to kill you!' and I knew Jean-Guy had betrayed us.

Suddenly, again, there was gunfire all around me, but this time I'd been smashed to the ground, hit with the butt of a rifle. Broken teeth, broken lips, as hands dragged me up for more of it, and I was flung against the courtyard wall to hug those bricks. Ragged firing still came, short bursts of it, and every time I heard it, I cringed because I knew what was happening to those who'd been caught and that my son had done this thing because his father had told him he must and he felt betrayed by the mother who ran away to be with the terrorists.

Blame me, if you must, not him. Never him.

The side door to the cellar opens, and I step into the darkness and over the place where Rudi and I buried Collin. Then it's the *cave* and broken glass—glass everywhere. A rat scurries away. I know that must have been Tommy's car. Only someone like Tommy or Nicki would have gone after what was rightfully theirs no matter what, but where is he now and where does Schiller have my children? And will Jean-Guy betray me again?

I remember that man I encountered who first came to the house and then to the station at Avon, that offer of a light and his, 'Were you in the camps, madame? Please, I ask only because I'm looking for someone.'

Tommy must have got him to do that because of the telegram I'd asked Dr. Laurier to send to Fairfax, Gordon, and Scharpe in London.

The storeroom is pitch-dark and full of rubbish. The shelves have been toppled over, the cupboards smashed. There are splintered boards, broken bottles, tin cans, even some of what must be dried beans or peas that have escaped the foraging rodents. Automatically, I gather up some of these last and stuff them into the pockets of this coat they gave me. Food must never be wasted.

Ah, merde, stop living in the past, I tell myself.

The kitchen is next, me seeing it as it once was and now must be, for moonlight breaks briefly over the orchard and even the Schmeisser in my hands casts a shadow. Cautiously, I step into the corridor, but there's so much debris it's hard to pick my way through without making a sound. Instead, it's an agony of delays.

Listening hard, I find I *do* smell tobacco smoke, but it's thin, just a trace. Even so, I lift my eyes to the ceiling above, but there's not a sound, and when, halfway along the corridor I encounter Jules, I immediately know it's him by the feel of his face and hair. Schiller has shot him in the chest, but where is Tommy? Has he also been killed? He would have called out my name and hurried up those front steps, not known, not suspected Schiller or any of the others would be here.

Or would he have?

Stepping over the body, I finally come to the foot of the main staircase and feel the pile of papers I had earlier gathered, but all thought of my torching the house must now be set aside. Everything in me wants to call out to my children and to Tommy, yet I know if I do, Schiller will only use them against me.

Climbing the stairs at a crouch takes forever, and when I feel another body, I know it's Tommy. Silently leaning the Schmeisser against the wall, I run my hands over him, feel his neck, try to find his pulse, duck my head down, and try to listen to his chest.

He's alive, but just, and I must somehow get him to a doctor. The front of his shirt and jacket are soaked with blood. Though I want to help him, I can't. I must continue.

Schiller I find in the bedroom my husband and I once shared. He's over by what remains of one of the French windows I used to look out of even when naked, knowing always then that my reflection would be caught in the mirrors, and that if Jules was present, he'd be looking at me in them as well as directly at my-self.

Flattened against the floor, I wait as the moon comes free of cloud. Schiller stirs but has he seen me, and where, please, are my children? Has he also killed them?

The moon goes in, and I start to move towards him, and when, finally, I feel a shoe, I discover that its lace has been tied in the double knot I taught my Jean-Guy to use.

His ankles have been tightly tied with what must be the arm

of one of my blouses. He's lying flat on his back and will be much taller, but I mustn't touch him anymore, for if he's alive, he might try to tell me what's happened and that will give Schiller a warning.

Instead, the lieutenant has tied a length of cord to the boy's wrists, which are also tightly bound and stretched out, flat to the floor, but now I know my son is alive, for I can hear him breathing.

Everything in me wants to tell him he's been forgiven, that I understand why he betrayed us, but I can't even do that.

A match is struck, and I know all is lost and flatten myself against the floor, but the flame goes out. Now there's only the glow from the end of that cigarette, but the memories rush in, and I'm naked before the lieutenant. My left breast is held, and as he smiles, the *salaud* teases the nipple to a hardness I can no longer bear.

Again, the moon comes out from behind the clouds, and I realize that I haven't screamed as I did then and many times more, but where is Marie?

She's sitting upright between his outspread legs, he holding her against him, and her wrists will be tightly tied by the other end of that cord. If Jean-Guy makes a move, she'll telegraph this to the lieutenant and he'll simply start shooting.

Though he and Marie are still maybe four metres ahead, and Jean-Guy is now two behind, I know I haven't a chance, but that food I picked up in the storeroom is definitely dried peas. I always kept seeds for the garden in a can. Flicking one well to the side, I hear it hit the far wall.

Nothing else happens. The moon takes its time, the clouds closing over as I flick another and another towards the opposite side of the room knowing I absolutely must do something or Tommy will die without help.

But again nothing happens. Schiller's far too clever.

Moving forward, avoiding that cord, I work my way towards him and Marie and finally find that her ankles haven't been tied, but her breathing can hardly be heard, and I wonder if she's wounded and try to still the rising panic.

'That's far enough,' he says. 'Now you'll tell me where that stuff is and help me, or I'll kill the three of you.'

He's not asked for the Luger yet, but must have that Walther P38 of his against the back of Marie's neck. 'You'll kill us anyways, so why should I tell you anything?'

'Because I'll let the children go.'

I touch Marie's hands, feel her fingers anxiously grasp those of my left hand, and know if I yank, she'll come towards me, and I can fire at him without hitting her.

'You're never going to go anywhere,' says Tommy from behind us. He'll have that Schmeisser I left.

Schiller fires two shots towards that far doorway, me I just give him all I have and grab my daughter.

There's snow on the ground, and from the window of the kitchen in my father's house, I can see Tommy and the children going for a walk with our dog.

That time of the hunting ground has passed, and I'm now much better. Really I am. Me, I'm happy to say Dr. Laurier took my advice and stayed out of sight until it was all over. I call her less and less now, and she keeps saying there's no need unless I feel I must.

It's only once in a while that I wake up in the night, crying out in terror. Tommy's there, and if not him, then the children. It'll take time—years, I suppose. Perhaps never. But me, I'm okay. Kneading bread dough and making such lovely sculptures, catching up on life and doing so many things. Come spring, I'll be back in my garden.

Apart from some damage, we found the paintings and other things generally in excellent shape. Most were returned to their rightful owners or placed in trust for their descendants if found alive. Those pieces that were Nicki's went to his remaining children, since both he and Katyana didn't survive.

My sister died with them, as well as Clateau and the others. Besides Matthieu Fayelle, only Marcel survived—he hadn't been with us, hadn't been involved in that last effort at the house. He remains the Marcel I once knew, painting in poverty, cadging money whenever he can, and talking big as always. Me, I've sent him a little money. Not too much, you understand, but enough.

And Tommy? you ask. Tommy was taken during the attempt on Göring's life, but managed to escape in Paris and to remain free in spite of that accent of his. When he could, he came back to the house on his own and took the children with him to Spain and looked after them as if they were his own. For him, the last days of the war were spent in Britain working for the S.O.E., the Special Operations Executive, who refused, for his sake, to let him return to France until after the Liberation.

He searched for me. Of course, he did. That's partly why he left the artwork in that cave, although there were also questions of ownership that the firm had first wanted to settle.

And why didn't he point the finger at Dupuis, the Vuittons, Jules, André de Verville, and Schiller? Why, when he knew so much? Me, I think he was waiting until I came home.

Copyright © 2013 by J. Robert Janes

cover design by Mauricio Diaz

ISBN 978-1-4804-0073-3

Published in 2013 by MysteriousPress.com/Open Road Integrated Media
345 Hudson Street
New York, NY 10014
www.mysteriouspress.com
www.openroadmedia.com

THE ST-CYR AND KOHLER MYSTERIES

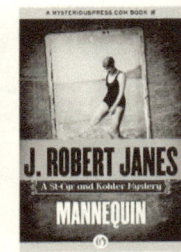

MYSTERIOUSPRESS.COM

Otto Penzler, owner of the Mysterious Bookshop in Manhattan, founded the Mysterious Press in 1975. Penzler quickly became known for his outstanding selection of mystery, crime, and suspense books, both from his imprint and in his store. The imprint was devoted to printing the best books in these genres, using fine paper and top dust-jacket artists, as well as offering many limited, signed editions.

Now the Mysterious Press has gone digital, publishing ebooks through **MysteriousPress.com**.

MysteriousPress.com offers readers essential noir and suspense fiction, hard-boiled crime novels, and the latest thrillers from both debut authors and mystery masters. Discover classics and new voices, all from one legendary source.

FIND OUT MORE AT

WWW.MYSTERIOUSPRESS.COM

FOLLOW US:

@emysteries and Facebook.com/MysteriousPressCom

MysteriousPress.com is one of a select group of publishing partners of Open Road Integrated Media, Inc.